PRAISE FOR ROSS ARMSTRONG

'Addictive and eerie, you'll finish the book wanting
to chat about it' – *Closer Magazine*, Must Read

'A twisted homage to Hitchcock set in a recognisably
post-Brexit broken Britain. Tense, fast-moving and
with an increasingly unreliable narrator, *The Watcher*
has all the hallmarks of a winner.' – Martyn Waites

'Ross Armstrong will feed your appetite
for suspense' – *Evening Standard*

'Unreliable narrator + *Rear Window*-esque
plot = sure-fire hit' – *The Sun*

'Brilliantly written… this psychological thriller is
definitely one that will keep you up to the early
hours. Five Stars.' – *Heat*, Book of the Week

'A dark, unsettling page turner' – Claire
Douglas, author of *Local Girl Missing*.

'Creepy and compelling' – Debbie Howells
author of *The Bones of You*

'*The Watcher* is an intense, unsettling read… one that had
me feeling like I needed to keep checking over my shoulder
as I read.; – Lisa Hall, author of *Between You and Me*

Ross Armstrong is an actor and writer based in North London. He studied English Literature at Warwick University and acting at RADA. As a stage and screen actor he has performed in the West End, Broadway and in theatres across the UK, where he has worked opposite actors such as Jude Law, Joseph Fiennes, Kim Cattrall and Maxine Peake. Ross' debut title *The Watcher* was a top twenty bestseller and has been longlisted for the CWA John Creasey New Blood Dagger.

Head Case

Ross Armstrong

ONE PLACE. MANY STORIES

HQ
An imprint of HarperCollinsPublishers Ltd
1 London Bridge Street
London SE1 9GF

This edition 2018

1

First published in Great Britain by
HQ, an imprint of HarperCollinsPublishers Ltd 2018

HB ISBN: 978-0-00-818223-6
PB ISBN: 978-0-00-825765-1

MIX
Paper from
responsible sources
FSC
www.fsc.org   FSC™ C007454

This book is produced from independently certified FSC™ paper

to ensure responsible forest management.

For more information visit: www.harpercollins.co.uk/green

Printed and bound in Great Britain by
CPI Group, Croydon CR0 4YY

*For all those who
think differently*

'Hush little baby
Hush quite a lot
Bad babies get rabies
And have to be shot'

1

'Dee. Dah dah dah dee dah, dah dah, dee dah…'

It was a year of miracles. The year I learned how to walk and talk again, the year I met Emre Bartu and the year the girls went missing.

But first came December.

The weekend before my first week as a Police Community Support Officer began. The last week in which my brain's valleys, ridges, streets and avenues remained in perfect working order.

Back when I thought a lot differently. Before I became 'Better Than Normal' as Ryans says. He says that because in some ways I definitely am. Better than you, I mean. No offence.

It's a Christmas gift that will lie under my brain stem, wrapped in the folds of my cerebellum, romantically lit by my angular and supramarginal gyrus, for the rest of my grateful life.

So let's go back to the last week when the inside of my skull was anatomically 'correct' and aesthetically as it had been since the day I was born.

When my brain functioned as it does for the 'normals'. The others. The ones devoid of irregularity or uniqueness. No offence.

Before the fractures. Before the accident.

If it was an accident.

2

The truth about Gary Canning is revealed to me by Anita herself. Like most things, I don't see it coming.

I imagine Gary as a P.E. teacher, displaying his sporting prowess and gym-earned physique to the kids of Tower Hamlets as he coaxes the unwilling into exertions like rugby, basketball or maybe even worse. But in actuality, Gary is a Geography teacher with a fair to middling beard. It has pretty good coverage but is patchy in a way that suggests inconstancy of character, a fatal lack of conviction in his genes, or a rather flawed grooming technique. I know this because I find his picture on social media. That's when I first see the face of Gary Canning.

Gary Canning blogs about food and travel and seems to have ambition beyond the school system. Photos find him caught candidly by the camera lens in clearly orchestrated scenarios, curated to paint him as a soulful character; playing a banjo with his eyes closed, or blowing bubbles with some sort of child, or larking in a European villa while holding a float to his head like it's an antenna, in a move that will soon be lauded by his fawning friends as 'classic Gary bants'.

He lists his favourite world cities as Tangier, Iquitos and Bobo-Dioulasso. Only half of one of which I've ever heard of. But I guess it isn't surprising Gary Canning has been to places I've never even heard spoken aloud. Given that I've never even been to Paris. I thought about taking Anita once but then I forgot to book the tickets and my life moved on. But I'm sure Gary Canning's been to Paris. Paris is child's play for Gary Canning. Gary Canning probably went to Paris without even realising it. Because that's just Gary Canning. Good old Gary Canning.

Anita's hours have always seemed wildly inconsistent for a job I'd always thought was fairly strict in terms of time frame. Which I've never wanted to bring up for fear that it will seem like I'm misunderstanding her life, or being sexist, or teacherist, or some kind of combination of everything that shows me for the true chauvinist idiot I didn't know I was.

When her late-homes stretched to late nights, I stopped asking questions, as I disappeared into my world. One dominated by online gaming and films I'd seen when I was younger but wanted to watch again to check if they're still good. Or the lure of sports results on my phone, or direr still, merely staring blankly at the screen glow waiting for that appetising hit of something. Not even current affairs; I can't handle that, everything is a killing or a manhunt and it gets me down. No, I prefer the safer land of sports news. Where the only tragedies are poor tactics. Where the only manhunt is inane 'gossip' about a Portuguese manager 'tracking' some sixteen-year-old French-African midfield wunderkind.

The Thursday night before the Monday I'm due to start my latest career experiment begins typically. Anita arrives home and I detach myself from the smart phone umbilical cord to greet her with my best conversation and the second half of a bottle of wine that I've started before her arrival. Already one in, having apparently 'decompressed' with a single glass on the way home 'with her colleagues', she tells me about her day and I listen loyally, retroactively defending her where appropriate from the passive-aggressive comments made by the head of the History department, my mind only occasionally drifting to how much a truly world class defender costs these days and what exactly I'm going to do with the rest of my life.

I'm always a good listener because it's easier when the other person talks. After all, I know all my stories and listening is more relaxing than talking.

She suggests we go into the bedroom so she can tell me something. This is nothing particularly new as we both like lying down and the light is more relaxing in there. She's never loved the feel of my parents' old house but it suits our situation and I like it just fine. But then, I'm easy going, genial to a fault perhaps. I've always wanted a simple life, which is the subject our conversation turns to as we both stare at the childish glow-in-the-dark stars we'd put up on 'the night of the moving in', which had somehow stuck around to bother the ceiling with their pretty and naive shimmer.

It feels like we're on the cusp of so many new things tonight. I don't know why I've chosen tonight, in particular. But I have. Call it instinct.

I go to kiss her but she instinctively lifts a limb to flick me away like a holiday fly. It's a feeling I've become used to of late. Her eyes flicker with uncertainty before she speaks.

'What do you do in your training anyway? Is it all rolling over cars and firing at moving targets?'

'Yes, it's a bit like that but without the guns. Or the car, or the excitement,' I reply, adjusting my head on the pillow.

'Ha. I think you're going to be really good,' she says, turning her head to me, her cheek gaining a green sheen from the plastic stars that barely light the room at all.

'I did do a personality test the other day though,' I say.

'Did they find anything?'

'Ho ho. Yes actually. They said I was very empathetic.'

'Good,' she says, pushing her hair behind her ear.

'Compassionate.'

'Good. Well. You are.'

'And they thought compassion might be my main strength, as they said I'd scored very badly on observation.'

This does make her laugh, like hot tea, warming and over-stimulating me. But she soon cools. She seems to pull away, sensing a renewed push for intimacy in the air. Not that she fears my close proximity; we've remained very intimate, in all ways but one. And I'm told that's a bit of a thing with relationships after a while.

'They said that if I'd scored any lower they'd have had to declare me legally blind.'

She laughs, somewhat nervously, I think.

'Although he said that some blind people have scored very well on these tests, so that's probably unfair on them.'

As she laughs, I realise I don't have to tell her anything about my personality. She's the person who knows me better than any other. Who has been witness to my best and worst emotions. This is the being that I had picked above any other to eat with and sleep next to, the one person whose hair it is vaguely permissible to randomly stroke and smell, who has looked at my face over the past six years a good deal more than I've had to myself. She knows me from the tiniest colour in my eyes to the softest things I've ever said. I reach down into my pocket.

'You're just... I'd say your personality is... doughy.'

'Sorry what?' I say.

'Doughy. Just a lovely, happy, doughy man.'

'Kind of sounds like you're saying my personality is fat.'

'No, you're not fat,' she says.

'No, I know I'm not,' I say, vocally straining.

'I mean, soft. Lovely. Like bread.'

Our eyes lock and she withdraws her hands, as if thinking four moves ahead and wanting no part of what comes next.

We turn and look up at the fake stars in a silence that turns over many times. It has endless pockets where it feels like one of us may speak. It runs on and on until at one point it has a little hate in it and at another a delicacy so fragile that it would shatter if you were to reach out and touch it.

Then I feel something. One of the tiny stars has fallen and is resting on my thigh. Then Anita looks down at it and finds a look somewhere between care worker and executioner. As she tells me that she's been doing it with Gary Canning in the staff room after school for a term and a half. Her back against the pigeonholes. Her pencil skirt hitched up.

She doesn't say all of that of course, but that's what I hear. I want to be angry and after she leaves I do a lot of pacing and fist clenching as I examine Gary Canning's social media output. I'm not really the sort of guy who raises his voice. I'm naturally better with compassion than passion, I suppose, and it's not good to force these things. And she's my best friend. It's hard to be angry with your best friend with tears in her eyes.

The fact that she's already arranged to stay with a friend leaves me logistically as well as emotionally lonely. But I'm always good with my own company and nothing if not resilient. Although resilient isn't the word she used in the only moments of our conversation that bordered on unkind. Something about 'ambition', I don't know. I log onto a gaming community as my heart pounds away further back in the mix.

The last time my heart pumped so hard, was during a training session with a self-defence specialist. I made myself a dead-weight to prove the demonstrator couldn't lift me and the next thing I knew we were both on the matted ground, him with his knee poised over my chest, having dug it into me as we fell together. I gasped for breath as I looked up at the crowd of faces who leant over me. I hadn't been so vulnerable since I was a child. And here I am again.

I met Anita at the party of a university friend I was already making plans to see less. I was pretending to be a smoker, and doing it pretty badly, as an excuse to not be inside with some awful people. Passable on their own, the flat was small and the men in particular were drunk and brash, which was a potion that ensured we were both having a terrible time. She spotted me coughing on a light cigarette, like a child taking it as a punishment, and we quickly decided that as we both hated smoking we should persevere together, mostly to stay away from the noise and fury of fellow twenty-two year olds newly arrived in London and convincing themselves they were 'cool bro', and having a 'wicked time'. Batting away my cynicism on a cluster of topics, she made me laugh more than anyone had in my three years as an undergraduate and when it rained we sheltered under a tree and stayed until the last drops from the fern tumbled into the mud below our huddled bodies.

I want the days after she leaves to be the kind of textbook break up weekend I've always heard about, comprised of time spent in my pants and regular doses of alcohol, but that's a little too close to the norm for comfort. So instead, I run, racking up 15k the day after she leaves and double that on the day after. Getting fit again has been one of the pleasures of the training process, but today I am running just to run. A picture show clicks on through my head with every thud that my feet beat on the tarmac. Each sting observed and recognised. I look out on the streets and streets that pass and see little of interest, which is at least in perfect keeping with the training officer's perception of my observation skills, and Anita's of my consistency. Somewhere in the distance, Gary Canning rests his back against the pigeonholes and doesn't even laugh. He breathes deep and leans, blissfully unaware of me, and thinks of India.

I reflect on this as I reach into the pocket of the jeans I was wearing the night she left. I may never be praised for my instinct, I think to myself, as I look at the tiny box in front of me. The one my father had pulled out in front of my mother in far more romantic surroundings many years earlier, under real stars, under the lights of Paris.

I think about my sense of timing, as I examine the little diamond before me. And as I wipe my eyes with my index finger and thumb, I laugh.

3

'You're my little one
Say I didn't love in vain
Please quit crying honey
Cos it sounds like a hurricane'

It's one degree below freezing on Seven Sisters Road but I'm not complaining. The first thing officers have to combat is the weather. Christmas is three weeks away and snow has settled, shrouding Tottenham in a crisp white blanket. Towelling it up like a baby after a bath. Hugging it close and singing it a lullaby.

I breathe into my gloved hands and watch the cloud stream onto them and then up into the slate coloured sky. If you don't like being out on the street, then try another profession. It's our job to know our neighbourhood, which means mostly being out on foot or on your bike. Fortunately for me I've got one advantage. I know these roads like the back of my arse. I've lived here most of my life.

I've watched corner-shop keepers get older and kids I went to school with become upstanding members of the community or, more frequently, go the other way. I've seen their little brothers, once new born babies who held on tightly to my finger in their mother's arms, grow up to get their very own ASBOs. I've given them out myself.

Or rather ABCs, the ASBO is the last resort before criminal charges are brought. An ABC comes before that.

That's my first act on my first day, Monday at 10.10 a.m. Drawing up an Acceptable Behaviour Contract for my schoolmate Dom Minton's half-brother, Eli. He'll probably be the last kid around here to get one, as they're soon to become defunct, so I suppose you could say this is a bit of a Kodak moment.

Eli has a birthmark that wine-stains the top left hand side of his face and I feel sorry for the kid. School is hard enough without the kind of stares it must bring.

I take advice from my sergeant on it all. I look at Eli's case notes and write down a few of his greatest hits. Then I ask if he would agree to the reasonable suggestion that he should've thought better of them.

The severity of his list of misdemeanours escalates sharply. Something dark in me struggles not to laugh when I glance at them over his shoulder as he reads:

CONTRACT

I will get to school on time.
I will not graffiti my school toilet wall.
I will not climb into any lift shafts.
I will not throw rocks and debris at passers-by.
I will not attempt to set fire to people.

'Does that sound fair, Eli?' I say.

He looks up and recognises me. It helps that I know his brother. But he's saying nothing.

'Think you can manage not to set fire to anyone? For a while?

Maybe try not to ignite anyone just for this week and see how it feels. Sound like a plan?'

I'll probably learn not to take the piss at some point but I'm new at this. He looks at me, stone-faced, then signs.

'And you understand the consequences of not sticking to the contract, don't you? Eli?'

All I hear is the sound of engines and tyres on the road.

'Eli? I need to hear you say it, mate.'

He looks up again, having been fascinated by the pavement for a few seconds.

'Yes I do, PCSO Mondrian.'

He leans quite heavily on the 'SO' and not so much the 'PC' as if to make a point, but I still pat him on the shoulder and attempt a smile that aims for reassuring, while steering clear of any local-bobby-earnestness that might engage his gag reflex.

He barely looks half of his fourteen years to me. But then he did throw a brick at a pram and try to set fire to an old man so perhaps I shouldn't feel too sorry for him.

I wish I didn't feel this way. But living around here, experience tends to toughen your opinions.

His dad grabs him by the shoulder I patted and leads him back to their car, clearly not delighted at having to take an hour off work for that. I hope he isn't too hard on him, I hope he isn't one of those dads, but then it's difficult to tell. Eli pulls away as if the shoulder already holds a fresh bruise that's more than a little tender.

On Tuesday I see my first dead body. I'm early on the scene at a gruesome traffic accident, a head-on collision that's killed the driver of Vehicle 1 instantly. His chest and the steering wheel are an item. His jaw is locked wide open. His passenger and the driver of Vehicle 2 are taken away and are in critical condition. I meditate on the nature of suffering, the end of things and déjà vu. Then I sack it all off, take an early lunch and have a steak and kidney pie.

On Wednesday I check out a break-in where the intruder has done nothing but broken a window, nicked one laptop and shat on the bed. People are very strange. Some watch videos of executions. Some change names on gravestones so they become rude words. Some are purely vindictive with their poo.

On Thursday the highlight is standing out in the cold for five hours, making sure the peaceful demo about closing the local library doesn't erupt into a volcano of bloodshed. There's no chance of that. It was more the sort of event where someone erects a cake stall, but on this occasion no one even did that.

Thursday's lowlight is getting a call telling me that Eli has neglected to turn up for school. His dad, out of town for a few days, was contacted immediately and ominously asked in a mutter over the phone if he could 'deal with it' himself. None of this seems very good for Eli, so seeking some other option I trudge over to his brother Dom's house.

'What can I say, the kid's an evil little fucker at times,' Dom says, hands tucked into his jogging bottoms. 'But he's my brother.' This much I have already gleaned.

'Do you think your dad's... a little hard on him?' I say, searching for the most delicate way to put it.

'Dad's no soft touch. Never thumped me. But then Eli is... Eli.'

'Eli? Eli!' I call, seeing his face peeking out unsubtly behind the kitchen door.

Before Eli drags his bones towards me, Dom hangs his head and then whispers to me, 'Sorry, Tom. He's having trouble at school, they're pulling him into some gang. It's nasty. He asked if he could hide out here.'

As he enters, I see the picture of a kid stuck between the devil and the deep blue sea. Shitty dad at home. Shittier kids at school.

Eli clearly isn't ill and I have a choice to make. He's breached his contract and I've stumbled in on him doing it. Let him have it and dad will come down hard on him. But at least a full blown ASBO would give him a legitimate reason to stay away from his new friends in the evening.

One thing's for sure, Eli is getting fucked from every side whatever I do. He's contributed pretty amply himself, yet I know I could save him some hassle if I just look the other way on this occasion.

But this is my first week, so I keep it simple and I call it in.

Later, he'll say I was 'victimising him'.

And what's true is, I could've been kinder. I think they call it tough love. I hope, in that tiny moment of decision, that everyone else isn't too tough on him as a result.

*

It's been a week. I can't quite tell what sort yet. But it's certainly been a week. Friday has come shaped like mercy.

*

'Dee. Dah dah dah dee dah, dah dah, dah dee…'

I get these tunes in my head sometimes, I think everyone does it.

Earworms. People say you choose the tune because the lyrics associated hold the key to something you're mulling over in your subconscious.

But I don't know about that.

I barely even remember the words. I try to keep it down as I zone out, muttering under my breath as I walk.

'Dee. Dah dah da, dee dah, dah dah, dah dee…'

I get a call on my radio about a minor accident at the other end of the main road. I need to go and direct traffic. I'm not sure this is what I was birthed for.

At least you can pick your hours, within reason. You have to cover thirty-seven in a week and they like you to take one evening. So I went for a five-hour evening shift on Thursdays, seven till midnight. Then took eight hours on all the other weekdays, leaving my weekend free. I consider the merits of this time format. Even my thoughts start to bore me.

I count them as they as they plod through me. Dry and empty.

This is a thought.

This is a thought.

This is a thought.

Then one comes along covered in this morning's regrets:

I was called to a house after a neighbour had complained about frequent raised voices and commotion, as well as the sound of skin on skin contact and not the friendly kind. I didn't bother the neighbour on the right side of the house before calling on the home in question. They had been brave enough to make the call and I didn't want to give them away by paying them a needless visit first.

As I approached, the neighbour on the left side came out, and when she saw me she hustled back inside quickly. She had a look of intense fear about her. I wondered if that came from the build-up of what she was probably also hearing through the walls, night after night. A man, taking out his stresses on his wife. Or whoever else.

The neighbour looked spooked so I didn't say a word. She didn't want any trouble, and to her maybe I meant trouble, so she shot back inside to avoid whatever was about to happen. She gave me a funny feeling, her presence sparking a strange sensation close to déjà vu.

When he answered the door, the man, bald, moustached and

laying on the innocent look as thick as it comes, led me inside, where a woman, presumably his wife, sat in the kitchen giving little away.

An extraordinary sense of creeping unease came over me, a tingling on my skin, which had started when I saw that neighbour's face.

I asked the woman if she was okay. I asked him the same. They both replied with a nod. It felt like something hung in the air between us that I wasn't allowed to touch. There seemed to be a palpable prompt the scene itself was giving me, other than the possible violence between them. Another cue that I wasn't picking up on.

The silent couple... The noises through the wall... That neighbour's face.

'There've been reports of a disturbance coming from this residence. I'm duty bound to follow that up. So... anything I need to know?'

Nothing but the shaking of heads.

'Anything at all?'

In the next deafening silence, I tried to communicate to her wordlessly that she didn't have to take any shit. And to him that if he was doing something to her then I'd be back with uniformed friends and trouble. But all I said was:

'Well, we're a phone call away.'

I shook off the tingle and reluctantly got out of there, resolving to do the only things I could: make peace with my limitations, and with the sour fact that she would probably never make that call, and record the encounter in my pocket notebook.

I can feel my mind listlessly erasing the encounter, as I make my trudge through grey reality towards traffic duty.

But then, they've recently found you can't erase memories. They're physical things. They make visible changes to the brain. Some are hard to access if you haven't exercised them recently, but they never disappear. If you took my brain out of its case, you could see it all.

- There's the crease that holds my parents' smiles at my fifth birthday party.
- There's the blot that is my first crush's face.
- There's that neighbour's face, just next to it.
- There's the dot of possible heroism. Watch me be disheartened, watch it degrade and fade.

This is not the electrode up my arse my life needed. This isn't even a power trip. Perhaps I should have stuck with charity fundraising on the phones, say my thoughts. But I guess mum and dad would be prouder of me doing this.

The radio kicks in.

'PCSO Mondrian? This is Duty Officer Levine, over.'

'Yeah. Yes, this is me.'

'... You're supposed to say over.'

'Over,' I monotone.

'So when someone calls for you, say *go ahead, over*. Over.'

'Go ahead, over.'

'Understood? Over.'

'Yep.'

A pause. I wait.

'Don't say yes, say *affirmative*. *And* you didn't say *over*. Over.'

I sigh, away from the walkie-talkie. Then steel myself.

'This is PCSO Tom Mondrian. Affirmative. Go ahead. Over.'

'Understood. Hearing you loud and clear. I'm over by the loos, over.'

'Understood... over.'

'What a wanker,' I mutter to myself.

Cccchhhhhh...

'And after you've finished speaking, take your finger off the PTT button. We all heard that.'

Crackles of laughter from someone else on the line.

'You forgot to say over, over,' I say.

I remember to take my finger off the button this time as I walk along.

'Not funny, over,' he says.

But it was a bit.

Levine is clearly the pedant of the bunch. I keep walking, my feet crunching in the snow.

Here we are. Broken glass on the tarmac. Red faced fella at the side of the road. A light blue Astra with one door open, diagonally up the kerb. Levine sees me and holds up a hand. His posture says, 'I've got this thing locked down, you just stand way over there.'

La-di-dah. The beat goes on.

The ABC. The body. The beat. All firsts.

I wonder if anyone has ever fallen asleep while directing traffic. Could be another first for me this week.

I check my watch and see there's an hour until my week ends. Nearly time to head back to the station locker room, change, clock off. Maybe a drink with the team if I'm unlucky.

Levine signals me to allow traffic around the car from my side, while he holds vehicles at a stand at his end for a while.

I signal. I smile courteously at the drivers as I do so. La-di-da.

I see many faces I recognise.

Amit from the paper shop down the road. Zoe Hughes from Maths drives past, averting her eyes to ignore my existence. She didn't always.

I glance to the cluster of shifty kids on the other side of the road to make sure they see traffic is being held and let through at intervals. I'm only looking out for them, but they take one covert glance at me, put up their hoods and scarper off, one holding something weighty in a black plastic bag that's got them pretty excited.

I probably should be curious about what it is, but that's not really very me.

'*Dee. Dah dah dah dee dah, dah dah, dah dee…*'

I stop the flow. I can barely see the driver in front of me through his tinted windscreen. But I squint to get a look at him in there and see his outline change. He taps the wheel, jittery, maybe coked up, which would account for the nerves. But I'm not going to create any extra trouble for myself. He glares at me, stiller now, as I hold my ground, letting him know I know there's something up.

Then I wave him through. He shoots away hastily, as I snigger, enjoying my power to intimidate. Then I move to the side of the road, making sure I'm still visible to passing traffic.

Blue car. Red car. White car. Mini. Bus… Bus…

Oh!

I feel tired. Not just tired, faint. I shake my head. Somewhere I hear the bus stop but I don't see anything. It's darker now, all around me. I feel sick. I'm fighting to keep my eyes open. I try to go to ground, layer by layer, as a tower block might be detonated or dismantled.

I feel like I'm going to vomit but I don't want to in front of all these people. It's a shame-based reflex. I try to hold it in. I try to hold it together. There are shouts behind me.

The sound of footsteps. Running. I just need to reach the floor and everything will be okay. But my ears are going crazy horse. A high-pitched squeamish noise. A fresh white blah blah blah. Like TV failure.

Nearly at the ground now. It all flashes. I swallow ocean breaths. I wonder whether I'm causing scenes. My hands reach for the tarmac black. That high pitched squeal blazes on.

The world looks like it's under a slow strobe.

Then my back is against the kerb. Clouds forming, crowd forming. I know something is wrong for sure.

I pull out my phone and try and call the... or should I use my... what's the number for the 999...

I stare at the phone. Not fainting yet. Holding on.

Its numbers are strange. Just lines. Like Greek, or Latin. Symbols I don't understand. I comprehend nothing.

My head is wet with something. But I don't know what. I see Levine running up to me. I'm not sure whose blood this is.

I shout to him to check everything is all right.

'Take the hard road up.'

I don't know why that comes out. It's not what I intended.

I try again. As I crawl towards him, off the pavement and onto the road.

'Perhaps the hard road's impossible!' I shout as I crawl and my hand drags past more wet.

'Take the hard road up. Anything is possible!' I shout.

It doesn't feel like my voice. He's nearly with me. I see the bus has emptied and its passengers are looking at it. And me.

It's slow motion. It's hard tarmac broken glass music video inner city incident news commercial heartache.

That high-pitched squeal sings on and on.

A song from a passing car radio strikes up.

'We lived in this crooked old house
some cops came over to check it out
left on the step was a little baby boy
In a soft red quilt, with a rattle and a toy.'

My hands shake beneath me like an engine does before it stalls. A guy with a busted tooth shouts something.

Before my head falls, I notice the bus has two broken windows. One on each side.

They're all on their phones. It's a picture that blurs.
My ears still work though. Listening to the radio song.

'You're my little one
Say I didn't love in vain
Please quit crying honey
Cos it sounds like a hurricane'

I wonder how those windows got broken.
That's my last thought for now. Before I go.
It's just one of those things.

Some days you meet the person you were always meant to be with.

Some days you get shot in the head.

4

"Can't get that, dah dee dah, dah dah, my head..."

'Good. You're awake. Looking good,' says the voice.

Male. Warm. My thoughts run slowly like traffic jammed cars. His face comes into view.

I'm cold. I guess I should do something. Say something maybe. Missed it. The chance has come and gone.

We sit in silence for a while. Everything has changed.

'Cold,' I say, trying to get things moving, in my head.

'Oh yes. It is a little chilly.' He turns and nods to someone. He smiles. I lift my head to see who he's looking at, but by the time I do they're gone.

Where am I? A hospital. I guess.

'How's it all feeling?' says the man.

'Unsure,' I say.

'You're unsure how you feel? Or you feel unsure?'

'The second one.'

'That's understandable. Any pain?'

'A little in the head.'

'Also understandable, that's just swelling in the cranium.'

'What's the... chrysanthemum?'

'It's a flower that blooms in Autumn, but that's not important right now. Your mental lexicon is still recovering, which I'd expect. Say after me, cranium.'

'Cramiun.'

'Good. Your skull. Your head. We had to get in there a little.'

'In there?'

'Yes, we had to remove the bone flap. But we replaced it. Everything went reasonably well.'

'Re... Re... Re... Re... Reasonably?'

'Well... your sort of accident isn't the sort of thing one always recovers from. But things are looking up.'

I'm putting it all together again. The bus. The shattered glass. The man running towards me. A man I know?

... Doreen? ... Liam … Loreen?

'I assume you haven't been told what's happened to you then?'

I assume I haven't as well.

I drifted in and out. Of the light and the grey. I don't know what was a dream and what was... whatever this is. I've seen many faces hover over me. I remember being moved, I think. One second I would be one place. The next, the ceiling would tell me something else.

I realise I have no concept of how long I've been here. It could be weeks. Months. Longer.

'How long?' I say.

'How long what?'

I struggle with the structure of the question. I feel my eyes rolling around in my head. With each tiny movement, there's a crack of pain somewhere deep inside my thinking organ.

My eyes begin to water as I strain to process the question, to hold onto my thoughts. I make some sounds from deep within me. I breathe deep, trying to speak, but I can't. Instead. I cry.

My nose runs. Hot tears roll down my cheeks. Big old-fashioned sobs, despite myself. I don't feel like crying. And yet, I am crying. Every breath shudders with effort between my lungs and my mouth. I feel like a puppet controlled by an inebriate puppeteer.

My hands scramble around for a tissue. There is one next to me but it takes me an age to drag it out from its cell.

He waits, watching. Patient.

'Tom? You asked me... how long?'

'How long... from then... till now?'

'Today is Sunday, you sustained the injury on Friday.'

It seems impossible. If he'd said I'd been here a year, or two, I'd have believed him. My muscles feel brown and dappled. I grapple with the controls like a madman, a blind pilot. I must be older. Two days? They have to be lying. But to what end?

It's then that I notice there is someone else in the room, to my left. My neck turns so my head can look at him. He looks back. His face is difficult to read. He looks apprehensive. I look away and he does the same. Then I look back at him and he looks me in the eye. He says nothing. Just analyses me. He must be some underling. He's younger than the other man. Although I couldn't say how old the man in front of me is. My brain isn't giving me all the answers I need yet. His voice interrupts us as I go to look at the silent man for a third time.

'Yes, it may seem longer. That can happen. Would you say it seems longer?'

'Yes. Yes.'

'That's interesting.'

He writes that down. Out of my periphery I analyse the silent man. He faces the doctor, too, not moving a muscle.

'Do you know what happened to you, Tom?'

The question lingers in the air...

The bus. The shattered glass. The blood. The shouts. People with their phones out. I crawl across the road. I feel sick. No pain. But I feel faint. I hear a song from a nearby car radio. The man runs towards me.

'I... I... had... a stroke?'

'Hmm. Interesting.'

He writes that down. Then scratches his nose. He turns as a nurse comes into the room and hands me a glass of water and a pill.

I take it off her. Steadily. I look at my hand and try to will it to do my bidding. I put the pill in my mouth and force the water down the dry passage of my throat. I stare back at my hand and order it to give the nurse back the glass. When I turn back to the doctor he is checking his watch. His eyes meet mine and he smiles, sunnily, full beam.

'Now, how long would you say that took? That little sequence of taking your pill and drinking your water.'

Is this a trick question? What is their game?

'Ten... twenty... ten... seconds?'

He glances to the nurse.

'That took six and half minutes. But don't worry. I'm confident things will get easier.'

He comes a bit closer now. The man next to me does, too. It's become intimate.

'Tom. You were shot. In your head. Do you understand?'

I want to laugh. So I do. *Ha ha ha ha ha.*

There's no gap between think and do. *Ha ha ha ha ha.*

The tears roll down my face again. The others stay stock still. As I laugh and cry. I don't know why I do either of these things. My feelings fire off in all directions like stray sparks. I laugh, I wail.

Then I stop. I look at the nurse. Then at him.

'No. I wasn't shot. I can't have been. It didn't hurt. I'm alive.'

He breathes in, cautious, unsure how to put this.

'The brain has no pain receptors. The nerves in your skin can't

react fast enough to register impact. A little bullet, at that speed...
It just went in.'

'And out...'

'Err... no. It just went in.'

'And you got it out?'

'No. My God, no. Much too dangerous to move it, I'm afraid.
It's still in there, in three pieces. But don't worry, it doesn't pose
you any danger. Think of it as a souvenir.'

He pops out a one-breath laugh and turns to the nurse for
support but she doesn't join in. When I straighten up, so does
the silent man. Copying my body language is supposed to make
me feel comfortable, I suppose. But he is eerie.

'So,' says the doctor, 'all your vital signs are remarkably good.
Another twenty-four hours of monitoring and tests, then, all
being well, you'll move from intensive care to a general ward
for recovery. Then you'll spend some time in the rehab unit, and
that'll give us an idea of what outpatient care you'll need after
we discharge you. Sound good?'

My breath rattles. I want to say things but thoughts rush at me.
I grasp at consonants. I try a 'p', an 'm', an 'n'. Then back to a 'p'.
He comes closer and puts a hand on me. I am calmed.

'But I was shot... in the head?' I murmur. I hear myself. I sound
like a malnourished tracing.

'Yes. But I'm confident you won't be here too long. I think
you'll walk with a limp for a good long while and certainly a lot
slower than before, for now. And so will your speech be. Slower,
I mean. But you should be... next to normal, in no time. Better
than normal perhaps. I look forward to seeing how it all pans out.'

He looks at me, smiling indulgently. I take a note of his
features. Ogling them for what is probably five or so minutes.

He has a beard. He has small brown eyes. He is half bald. He
is lightly tanned. He has soft grey hair. He has a striped blue
shirt. It has a purple ink stain on it.

'Somebody... shot me?'

'It would appear so, yes. Now, all I'd ask of you is to take it slow. I will be with you throughout this process. You certainly don't have to go back to work for a good long while yet. And they'll absolutely look after you well, financially speaking, so you don't need to worry about any of that. You were injured on duty, you're getting the best treatment money can buy. In my opinion, ha! You shouldn't want for anything while you recuperate. If there are abnormalities – and considering the places the bullet debris has come to rest in, there may be abnormalities – I'll be with you every step of the way. We're going to handle those... differences... together.'

'Sorry. Sorry. Sorry. Why am I not dead again? Why is my head still on my shoulders? What was I shot with?'

'Well. A gun. A sub machine gun, I'd say. But just once, so that's good.'

'In... in... war... in films... in war... the head means... dead.'

He's excited by this, standing and taking his pen in his hand to gesticulate with.

'Good question. Good cognitive reasoning. Now, I can only tell you that when you've seen people shot in World War whatever, or Kill whoever, or The Murder of Whichshit, the science is somewhat... bollocks. Sorry! Poppy cock, I mean to say. You do often die with a shot to the head. Very, very often. But a bullet wouldn't really have the momentum to knock your head much to the side let alone blow it off its shoulders. Think of it this way, if a gunshot were powerful enough to throw your head back significantly, the momentum of firing it would throw the gunman back violently, too. And that's not the sort of device that would be very viable on the mass market. What a gun is, is a compact handheld product made to eject sleek aerodynamic discharges that glide smoothly into flesh. So along with the shock and speed of the event and the way the device is engineered, of course you wouldn't feel a thing. Which is a bit of a result in a way, isn't it?'

I'm not sure how to feel about this statement at this point.

'Ask us one more question for today, please. It's very good for you to ask questions. It's a useful process. You're doing very well, Mr Mondrian.'

'Will... I... get... back to normal? Normal normal? Absolute normal?'

The nurse averts her gaze. The cold room seems to get colder. He clicks his pen a couple of times and then comes further towards me, his face so calming. His rich voice echoing as if it falls all around me. He has me. I am his captive audience.

'The brain is an incredible thing. It has helped us to achieve amazing feats. Like building aeroplanes. Performing complicated long division in our heads. Constructing the internet. So on, so forth. But do we really know how it works? Not really. I certainly don't and I'm one of Britain's top neurologists. Ha.'

He looks at the nurse. No laughs again. But I like him. I'm usually good for a pity laugh, but humour is difficult to muster at the moment. The cues are difficult to pick up.

I laugh, a good minute too late. The room nods patronisingly. Then the Doctor steps in again to save me.

'So, in short, to say "I don't know what's going to happen" is an understatement. I mean it's an understatement to say it's an understatement. I mean I don't have a single clue. I don't even know if I don't know! But I'll tell you what. Whatever your brain throws at us, we'll just work it out. Sound like a plan? It's fair to say it's already making adjustments.'

'Adjustments?'

'Yes. Adjustments. It's an incredible machine. It will adapt. It has *plasticity*. It will learn to work in a different way. That's what it does. That's the one thing we do know. So... will you get back to normal?... No, I shouldn't think so, no. Is normal something to be desired? To some people, yes. Is normal changing monthly and are you going to think in a completely, wonderfully, excitingly, unique way? Yes. I think so, yes. And. Whatever. Happens. We're going to tackle it together.'

He claps his hands lightly.

'Does that sound good, Tom?'

'Yes. You are. You are. You are?'

'Jeffrey Ryans. We have met before but don't worry. You've been in and out of consciousness. No need to feel gauche. Any more questions?'

'One.'

'Fire away.'

I collect myself. Trying not to turn to the man. But I have to ask.

'Who... who... who is... this man sitting next to me?'

'Sorry, who?' Jeffrey says.

'Him,' I say, pointing to the reserved gentleman on my left.

'Ah. Now that is interesting.'

'What?' I say.

'You don't recognise him?'

My eyebrows furrow. I squint. I try to conjure something.

'No. Should I?'

Dead air. The nurse's face has collapsed.

Ryans smiles, a mixture of amusement and compassion.

'Well. Tom. That's you.'

I don't understand this concept. I look at him pleadingly. He speaks again.

'That's a mirror, Tom. You see its edges? There?'

I look back at the face in the frame. No memories of this man. Nothing. Not a flicker. I shake my head. The silent man shakes his head, too. I don't trust him. I turn away, then back quickly, trying to catch him out.

I turn back to the Doctor. I shake my head again.

He folds his arms. He understands.

I open my mouth.

'Blossom,' I say. 'Fruits. Fucking fuck! Blossom. Bollocks. I mean... blossom. Argh!'

5

'Because it's bigger than you,
But you're lighting a fuse
And you're playing to lose
Because it's bigger than you'

'Tom? Tom? Sorry. Tom? Tom?'

'Yes,' I respond straight away.

'You'll be stationed with PCSO Bartu?' says the man dressed as a policeman.

I turn to him and nod. He smiles back. Nicely. Nice guy.

'Great. That's great. Do I... Do I...'

The room waits for me to find my thought. Giving me supportive eyes.

'Do I... have to have... a partner? I'll... be okay. On my own, you know.'

The others look to the main man. He sucks in his bottom lip and wets it. His eyes flicker to the left. Then to the right. To the other six people seated either side of us in the locker room. Some men. Some women.

'We're going to put you with Bartu. Just for now. It's standard procedure for anyone who's had extended time off. Even if it's only three months.'

No, it's not. I've had time on my hands. I've been filling in any gaps of knowledge on all sorts of areas but particularly police procedure and neurology. I want to understand what's happening to me and what I'm getting myself into. Above all, I want to be aware of those two things. So I've been researching. Voraciously. Every day, with a fire and will I've never had before. I use a program that reads to me. But I always read the first three words myself, I'm rigorous about that, even if it takes an hour. Then I let the voice take over and we learn together.

'You don't need to go on your bike either, until you're ready. So Bartu will be keeping fit with you on foot or if you need it you also have access to a vehicle.'

'I'll drive. Let me drive!' I shout.

They recoil a bit. No sudden movements. I remind myself. It makes the 'normals' tense.

'I can drive,' I say. Softly. Watering myself down for the room.

I'm now what's called Preternaturally Sensitive. It means my inhibitions have receded due to injury to my frontal lobe. So if I want to say or do something, I usually do it.

You won't find me shouting out swear words as with Verbal Tourette's, which is a turning off of inhibitions as well as an enlarged tic-like propensity to say what shouldn't be said. It's just a new facet of my character. Not that I am psychiatrically different, as such. No, like Tourette's, it's not a psychiatric issue, but rather a neurobiological one of a hyperphysiological sort. Which is quite different. With me? Good.

This replacement of inhibition with drive arrived as if by magic. Soon after my first couple of meetings with Dr Ryans, I wanted out of there. Away from the hospital's warm arms and succour. Not in a fearful way, I just had things to do. I felt charged. Like someone had put a new kind of battery in me.

After I eventually made it out, when they were satisfied that I could do things like document distinct memories and walk (not perfectly, I tend to drag my left foot more than I pick it up and good lord I'm not ready to ride a bike yet) I started devouring knowledge in a way I'd never even considered before the bullet. Doctor Ryans says I merely wanted to make up for lost time, to test my consciousness and attention span to see how much more it could do for me. To see whether, if I tried hard enough each day, if I laboured then slept and then woke and then laboured again, each sleep could take me closer to home. To the mind I used to have. That's how Ryans put it, but I wouldn't say it was that. I didn't want to be the same as I was before. I wanted to be better. I felt somehow I already was.

'Pre-bullet' I was directionless. 'Post-bullet' I had a lust for the world. I started to feel sorry for the 'pre-bullet' me. Listless. An apathetic approach to the possibilities of the day. I was motivationally shambolic. 'Post-bullet' me could have him for breakfast.

The physio would come each morning. We would work. Then I would sit in front of my computer and use the programme to find gaps in my knowledge. Once my shopping was delivered I would make myself a new recipe I had found online that'd intrigued me.

I would learn more.

I would do my exercises.

I would defecate perfectly.

I would write a poem, or lullaby, or do a pencil drawing.

I would get headaches and cramps and fears.

I would ignore them.

I would learn more. Then I'd sleep.

I sleep less. I found I didn't need as many revitalising hours as I had previously indulged in. Getting up before sunrise was now a regular thing. I like waking in the dark. It meant I could engender a routine. I could warm up before physio and make myself something with perfect nutritional value for breakfast.

I learnt about health and the body obsessively.

Did you know that a stitch when you run is caused by your diaphragm? It gets pulled around when you jog, so if it hurts take a slower, more even pace and longer smoother breaths.

Did you know that if your food wasn't mixed with your saliva then you wouldn't be able to taste it?

Did you know the average person falls asleep in 7 minutes?

Did you know that stewardesses is the longest word you can type using only your left hand when utilising a standard keyboard in the correct manner?

Did you know 8% of people have an extra rib?

I used to be an eight hours a night man or I was useless. I need only five and half now and they serve me better than my sleep ever did before. In my waking hours I feel more awake than I ever have.

I couldn't read, my brain wasn't letting me yet. But I could focus on the little things and block out the distracting thoughts. In short, I could listen like a motherfucker. Pardon my French. Lack of inhibitive reflex plus mild aphasia there: 'impaired ability to speak the appropriate word for the scenario, or the one your brain is searching for.' In other words, I send for a good formal noun, in this case 'genius', but by the time it comes down the chute some joker has switched it for 'motherfucker.' Apologies again.

I longed for things passionately, like I never had before.

I wanted to run.

I wanted to watch movies and fully understand them.

I wanted to climb remote exotic mountains.

I wanted mystery and love and mysterious love.

I wanted to be able to drive.

'For the moment, it's best if you don't drive. Order from on high. Probably an insurance thing, something like that.'

41

I know he's lying but I appreciate his tact. He has an upright stance. He has initiative. Gumption. I like him. I give him a thumbs-up.

A crease in his face tells me he's not sure whether this gesture is an ironic manoeuvre. Little does he know I don't have anywhere near the outward mental processing speed required for irony yet.

He moves on and says some more things with his mouth. I take my cheat pad out of my pocket and write. You see, I can still write, as the part of my brain that turns thoughts into symbols works fine, but curiously the bit that interprets those symbols back into words? Different matter. Pun intended.

So I know I won't be able to read this back but the act of writing it down helps me commit it to memory. I observe. The others peer at me but I block them out with ease, with my genius focus. I write:

Upright stance. Gumption. Fair and balding. Wire frame circular glasses. Highly Caucasian.

On the upper left of his jacket, where his breast would be, are some symbols. A word I think. It starts with an L.

L. E. Then one I can't make out, then an I, and it ends with another E. The process takes a while and my straining to establish the word at this point has become a spectacle, which everyone is pretending manfully not to notice.

LE_I_E. Lee? Can I call him Lee? Leon. Lean? Levine? Levine! I've heard that somewhere before. Ah. Of course. Levine. So that's Levine. I remember him. I think he's recently been promoted.

Levine. Or Upright-Gumption-Bald-Glasses-White-Face. As I will call him. In my mind.

I turn and see another man to my right, close to my head.

He holds out his hand, luckily, because that means he might whisper his name. I may have seen him before, it's quite possible. I'll probably remember him. Because, you see, it's not the remembering exactly I struggle with. No, it's not that, it's another thing.

'Hey. I'm Emre Bartu. Good to meet you,' he says with a wink.

Yes. He'll do. I keep out my cheat sheet and start to write.

Bouncy. Kind. Black hair. Deep voice. Brown face.

I realise I haven't said anything back to him. As is certainly customary. I think I just locked eyes with him and started writing.

Multi-tasking is hard so I have to stop for a second to mutter something pleasant-sounding to him.

'I'm Tom Mondrian. Can you stay still please? I'm looking at your head.'

He smiles and does so. He nods, his eyes flicker to the side, which indicates he's a bit confused by all this. Then he holds his pose like he's having his school photo taken.

A thought hits me from nowhere that someone once said he was Turkish. I don't know where I got that from but my mind has offered it to me as useful information so it's best to follow it up.

'You're a Turkey,' I say.

'What mate?' he says.

'Sorry. I mean. You're a Turkey.'

'What?'

'Sorry. Shit. I mean. You're a Turkey. Ahhh,' I shout, frustrated. Damn aphasia.

The room looks up for a second and I hold up my hand to apologise. They go back to talking about their beat, what they have to do that day, that kind of thing.

43

'Sorry. You're a Turkey. Shit! You're... Turkish?' I bend my voice at the last minute, it had taken so long to splutter it into the world I'd forgotten that it was supposed to be a question.

'Yes, mate. That's right.' We nod. Agreeing with each other. I'm pleased with this. I run the words over in my head.

This word pattern forms what is called a Feature by Feature Recognition Strategy. I slip the note back in my pocket.

*

The physio came to me every day but I had to go and see Dr Ryans twice a week. The journey itself was a good test and I'm sure he was aware of that. We went through a series of facial recognition exercises as that was his biggest area of interest. It was discovered I had prosopagnosia – an inability to recognise faces. Which is a particularly cruel word if you also have trouble reading.

We talked through strategies and the face cheat sheet was certainly the best. By far the most disquieting side effect of my accident is the inability to recognise my own face. Typically, Ryans also had a few methods to deal with this frightening daily occurrence – the part where I wake and scream because I don't know who the man in my mirror is.

'It's suggested that success can be achieved by making your own image as distinct and memorable as possible. Prosopagnosiacs often choose to grow characteristic facial hair. But what works best, in fact, is when this is coupled with headwear, perhaps a bandanna or...' He pauses, catching me mulling this over.

'No offence, Jeff, but as well as having all my brain disorders I'd rather not dress like Hulk Hogan.'

Amazing that despite not being able to pick out my parents faces from a line up in Dr Ryans' tests, I can picture Hulk Hogan clear as day. But then, he does have that characteristic beard and bandanna combo we prosopagnosiacs seem to really respond to.

'Get a cat,' he says as I leave.

'Sorry?'

'I'd advise you to get a cat. For a few reasons.'

'I don't like cats.'

'It will like you. But you won't come to rely on it. Soft companionship. That's reason one. Understood?'

'Er...'

'You really hate them?'

'I'm indifferent to them.'

'Oh, that's different. That's fine. Here's reason two: It'll anchor you, by which I mean you'll judge time better by its presence, it will remind you how you're progressing in relation to it and therefore will stop you getting depressed.'

'I don't feel depressed.'

'Well, you could well get depressed. Reason three: The stroking is nice. You'll just fucking like it. Trust me. Get a cat!'

I sometimes think the sudden outbursts of swearing are in my imagination, but I think he's just like that. He's come direct from the wayward 1960s. His hair is kind of shaggy, his formal jacket sits awkwardly on his shoulders above his loose fitting slacks, like he was dressed by his mother this morning, but even the jacket itself is finding its place on his torso pretty inappropriate and is mounting a slow escape.

I've often seen him hurriedly extinguishing something in a drawer as I enter the room, his desk gently smoking as our conversation begins. His pupils a little dilated and the room smelling leaf green.

'Okay. I'll get a cat,' I say.

'And you can have it as what people call an emotional support animal. There are perks of this. For example, if you go on a fucking plane you can take it with you and have it on your lap. You're allowed almost anything if it's for emotional support. Big dogs for instance. One chap even got a small horse on a long haul.'

'What? In the cabin?'

'Yes. A tiny one, but it was still a horse. Listen, trust me, in my line of work I've seen far fucking stranger things than that.'

I leave. I get a cat. Now I have a cat.

*

Draw a line between the middle of your forehead and the top of your left ear. Make a mark directly in the middle of that line. Then make another mark one centimetre above it. That's where the bullet went in.

Right there.

6

'Dee. Dah dah girl dee dah, dah dah, my head...'

'So... Stevens and Anderson are to follow up with the girl's family. Bartu and Mondrian, you're giving a talk at the school.'

'What? I want to follow up the missing girl,' I exclaim.

A hush. 'I want' isn't a word combination that often gets an outing in the debrief room.

It's been a big deal, me coming back so early. They wanted it for me. And for my part, I needed it; I couldn't stay at home any longer.

Brains need other brains to develop. If I'm kept out in the cold, in exile, mine will start to recede before it's even rehabilitated. People go mad when left in rooms with nothing but their own thoughts to haunt them. Inmates in solitary confinement, deprived of sensory stimulation, have been known to forge their own deluded realities, even see things that aren't there and hear voices. Try not speaking to anyone for a full day when home alone on sick leave, and you'll feel the chill the icy hand of madness leaves on your shoulder.

That's a microcosm of where I am. That's the narrow end of it, a fleeting taste of the mouthful.

But they need to know I can be trusted. They've shown a lot

of faith in a man still trying to get a grip on the newly coloured world spread out in front of him, because in truth, I'm not sure whether I can be trusted or not. Sure, I'll give it a crack, but I'm certainly not making any promises.

'Me and Bartu will check up on the missing girl. Sounds interesting. Anderson and Stevens, you do the talk at the school. That okay?' I blurt out.

If you don't ask, you don't get.

'Err... sorry, Tom. That's not really part of your remit. You get to do... other things. Community work, which in some ways... is the most... important work of all.'

My face seems to tell Levine everything he needs to know about the validity of that statement.

'Look, a couple of months on the straight and narrow and they want to bust you up a bit. Get you on the force maybe. Fast track. You've been told this, right?' Levine says.

'Yes.'

'There's so much... good feeling around you, Tom. Good press. Good public err... you know. You're well thought of, Tom. You. And your story. It's... uplifting. So, you know...'

I'm not sure I do. I mean, I think he's telling me to behave or I won't get what I want. It's been a long time since someone's had to tell me to behave. I used to stay out of trouble, stay in the corners, under the radar. Not anymore it seems.

'So the school for you today please, Tom. The school,' Levine says.

'Yep. Course. Yep, yep,' I say, folding my arms and smiling at the rest of the team. Faces and faces staring back at me. Stubbly ones. Pink ones. Pale ones. Happy ones. Sad ones. I've no chance of keeping them all in my head. So I just smile.

We get up to go. I think about the missing girl. It interests me.

*

Emre is somewhere between twenty and thirty. I can't do any better than that for you, perception is difficult.

But his physical energy, his spirit, if you can imagine such a thing, is by turns fifteen and forty-five.

He's springy but with a coolness that belies his youth. He could have a high IQ. Or perhaps it's a centred temperament that's learnt. Maybe it's a religion thing, but I don't know what religion he is so it's difficult for me to comment on that, but he's definitely smarter than he looks. I decide to tell him that as we walk toward the school.

'Hey, I think you're definitely smarter than you look.'

'Thanks. You're pretty blunt. Do you know that?' he says, observationally, no side to it at all.

'Yes, I know that. Thanks,' I say, politely.

'Is that you? Or your brain?'

'Is there a difference?'

'Were you like this before the accident?'

'Does it matter?'

'No. But I'm interested.'

'What was the question again?'

'Were you like this before the accident?'

'Ah yes.'

'Well... ? Were you?'

'Do you know what, Emre Bartu? I have absolutely no idea.'

I don't like it when people call it an accident. We don't know if it was an accident. Not yet anyway.

I prefer The Incident. Or The Happening. Or The Bullet.

I listen to our footsteps and think about people. People like to think their personality is separate from their brain, as if their personality is in the mind.

The mind, that thing that is the actual self, is presumably located somewhere above the skull, floating free of the brain's complicated mush of blood, cells, flesh, neuroglia and wires.

49

This 'mind' is unbound, simpler, and yet capable of far more complexity than the biology and flaws that pervade within the strait-jacket restraints of the human brain.

The brain holds people back: from finding the perfect words over dinner that will make our friends revere us as debonair and articulate. If only the brain could take some lessons from the mind, that reliable thing that is uniquely us and always right. The centre of our genius that no one understands.

All that is utter cocking fantasy, of course. But we can easily fall back into the idiotic grasp of these thoughts if not careful. If we don't remind ourselves that we have nothing else to think with, but this miraculous lump that contains who we are completely and is all our best idiosyncratic parts.

When patients wake from strokes, and sometimes during them, they often describe not being able to distinguish themselves from the world that surrounds them.

Their arm is the wall.

Their head, a computer.

Their genitals are the trees and landscape outside the window.

This is reportedly often a euphoric feeling rather than a scary one. It appears to me that this is getting closer to a truthful condition than the general way of thinking. Not misled by the structures we have learnt to see, that define us as the protagonists and everything else as the scenery, these patients accept their place in the world in those moments, on a par with everyone and everything, comfortable with the fact that they are no more than their anatomy.

'Normals' think of themselves as beautiful hand-crafted originals that always know best, who will prevail even as their bodies fail them. They think their brain contains only facile learnt sequences that make it easier to put your trousers on or cut a cucumber. If only they knew better.

One day I'll fill Bartu in on all this. But for the moment I keep this enlightenment as an advantage over them all. Everyone is on a need to know basis, and I'm the only one who really needs to know.

My inner thoughts work so much faster than my mouth. I can think it all exactly as I want it. But it doesn't come out quite that way yet. I speak in imperatives, everything slow, but with exclamation marks. I can virtually see them hang in the air after every sentence.

'This is the school here, right? Really doing this are we?' I say.

These words pierce the silence we've been in for a good five minutes. Bartu would probably have preferred this trip to be filled with witty repartee, rather than the dead air of one man thinking and the other waiting. He'll have to forgive me. I don't do patter easily yet. I don't do off the cuff. Sometimes I forget to get out of my head.

A car with blacked out windows passes and my eyes follow it away.

He considers my question. Luckily, I'm pretty comfortable with silence as it's the condition in which I've lived the majority of my life up until this point. Even pre-bullet.

'Look, don't worry. You don't have to speak, if it's uncomfortable or difficult. To the kids I mean,' he says in an almost whisper.

'It's not uncomfortable. It's just boring.'

'Fair enough. I'll do the talking.'

'We're not teachers. We're officers of the law.'

'We're not really officers of the law.'

'We're community support officers of the law.'

'We're part of the uniformed civilian support staff.'

'Same diff.'

He laughs. A genuine one, I think, not for show. People are sometimes afraid to laugh at me, or with me, but not Emre Bartu.

We look at the school, it's a tidy set of red bricks with a pair of pointy roofs. It also contains a playing field full of my past sporting failures and the scene of many rejections and one good kiss.

Her name, Sarah, flashes into my head and I pat my brain on the basal ganglia for the remembrance. Without the ability to show me Sarah's face, it merely reminds me that she was pretty, freckled and mysterious, and that I hung around to wear her down. And that sometimes people told stories of the strange things she did. But I can't recall any of them.

Old sights, sounds and smells allow you to go down neural pathways you don't frequently use. The resultant sudden rush of seemingly lost memories is what causes strong emotions in such places.

I observe this feeling and let it pass through me. None of my teachers will be here, the turnover is pretty fast. Things change swiftly in cities. They change double swift around here. This is a foreign land.

I won't announce that I am alumni. I'm not sure they'd care anyway. Some bloke whose biggest claim to fame is getting shot in the skull. I'll wait till I've done something more auspicious with my broken head before I bring it back here and try to hold it high around the corridors.

He brings out 'the bag'. I've had to handle 'the bag' once before, in a training session, but today he has 'the bag'.

'I'm going to do the talking. You be a presence,' he says.

'I can do that.'

'Good. Any questions? Anything you need?'

'Yes.'

'Go on.'

'Right. The girl that went missing, did she go to this school?'

'Forget about that,' he says, scolding me just enough.

'Okay. But did she?'

'Err... yes. I think so,' he says in a sigh.

'You think so? Or know so?'

'I know so,' says Emre Bartu.

He wants us to go but I can't walk and think smoothly yet. My stillness means he can't move. It'd be rude.

He waits. I pause. I think. Then speak.

'Okay. I'm going to ask about her.'

'Who?'

'The missing girl.'

'No. Please don't.'

'Why is that?'

'It's being handled elsewhere. It'd seem... odd.'

'I don't mind that.'

'Yes. But others would. Others are assigned to it.'

I shrug and nod at the same time, committal and non-committal all at once. We both stare at the school, he grips the bag, I blink hard.

'It would be interesting. Quite interesting. I'm interested,' I say.

'Please, don't. Just trust me, no one wants you to do that.'

'Okay. I won't,' I say.

He touches me on the shoulder.

'Good man.'

He turns as he bites his bottom lip, a tense mannerism that intrigues me already. It's always the little things that intrigue me.

'Ready?'

'Yes,' I say, my movements getting smoother all the time. I can feel myself growing already, spreading out to encompass the space the world outside my room has provided for me.

'Good. Come on then,' he says as he walks.

You just have to say you won't do something. That's what they want. Little compromises. Promises. Words.

It's as easy as that.

We sign our names and put on those badges with the safety

pins attached that ruin jumpers and would do unfathomable things to a face.

Then we're in.

7

'Dreams, keep rolling, through me
Dreams of you and I,
Dreams that drift far out to sea
Why does my baby lie?'

Being back here is sinister. The hallways hum with spectres. Dr
Ryans said he didn't think I'd suffer any amnesia or losses, as
the bullet didn't seem to rupture anything where my memories
lie, but then the brain is unpredictable. I hear the song of distant
thoughts as we walk under halogen strip-lights to the school
hall. Traces of said things in half remembered classrooms pass by.

It's like a dream and not the good kind. Forced into your old
school hall, dressed as a policeman, with a bullet in your brain.
I look down and expect to see my penis but only my trouser
crotch stares back at me.

Bartu sees me staring at my own crotch and when I raise my
head again our eyes meet and I smile. He does, too, trying not
to let on how much I concern him.

He makes conversation with the head of year. She is called
Miss Nixon. She is all brown and grey hair and clothes she's had
a while. I write down a brief description on my face cheat sheet.

She is Caucasian. Has church-going hair. Wears dangly earrings.

The last one is her most distinguishing feature, in fact. If she took them off, she'd disappear.

I start to hum a song I made up called 'Dreams'. When my senses were kicking back in and my brain was repairing itself I found I had the overwhelming urge to make up little lullabies. Conjuring a tune and putting words to it was one of many exercises I set myself. I didn't write them down but I won't forget them, there must have been hundreds.

'Dreams are rolling through me…'

The cleaning fluid smells the same. Even the cold crisp door handle's touch against my skin sings deep-held memories back to me. Along with fears that I might stumble through the wrong door and end up in a classroom some miles away, where Gary Canning pushes my would-be fiancé up against the blackboard and her back slowly rubs off what was once written on it.

A group of kids pass us on our left, keeping their heads low, as if the sight of everything above shin level depresses the hell out of them. One of them has an unmistakeable birthmark, so distinctive that even I can't forget it. He pretends he doesn't see us, but he can't fool me. Eli cold shoulders us like we've never met. That's life in your home town. These instances that come and go. As fate blows us into each other's paths like debris in the updraught.

That childhood kiss with Sarah drifts into my mind, then blows away, escaping through my ear.

When we get to the hall, its unmistakeable chafed parquet flooring under my feet, the kids are waiting and Emre Bartu wastes no time.

He claps his hands, a surprisingly effective attention drawing tactic that turns their chattering heads towards him.

'Hello Year Eleven! My name is PCSO Emre Bartu and it's a real pleasure to speak to you today. We're usually out on the street, you may have seen us about, so at this time of year it's just nice to come in and get warm.'

It's not the kind of gag I would open with but he's certainly come in with confidence. He reaches centre stage, the exact spot the headmaster stands to give out end of term awards, where Martin Humball gave his Fagin, and precisely where people were invited to stand and play clarinet or present some kind of talent if their ultimate wish was to be punched by their peers at lunch break. Bartu's not a natural public speaker, his thumbs tucked tightly under his police vest tell me that. He needs something to hold on to for comfort. But I like Emre Bartu, and they are warming to him, too. Although I'm sure I hear someone mutter the word 'Tosser' as he pauses to collect his thoughts.

'So why am I here? I hear you all ask. Well, myself and my friend and colleague PCSO Tom Mondrian at the back there...' he says pointing to me.

They turn to look. 'Friend and colleague.' Very kind. We've only just met. I'm not sure what I'm supposed to do at this point. So I put my index and middle fingers to my forehead and salute. I'm not sure why.

No one smiles. A morass of shaggy haircuts turn back to the stage. I see a grimace somewhere inside Emre Bartu. He falters.

'We... me and Mondrian... PCSO Mondrian... (a cough)... wanted to talk to you about a few things you should be aware of as you lot start to taking your drivey theoring tests. Driving theory tests.'

He reaches for the bag. He picks up the bag. He unzips the bag and puts his hand inside. I whisper to Miss Nixon, 'Have you heard this talk before?'

'Six times,' she says.

'That's a lot,' I say.

'Mmm,' she says. Small talk over.

He pulls out some goggles from the bag.

'Now, who would like to come and "road test", these special goggles?'

No hands shoot up. No enthusiasm reaches fever pitch.

'Come on. Anyone? Or I'll pick on you.'

One hand at the front lifts with the energy of something pained and waiting to die.

'There we go. Round of applause please!'

The sad sound of twelve people clapping in a room of over a hundred. The echoing acoustic is a cruel partner to their dwindling will to live.

'These are my beer goggles,' he says. Some merciful vocal response occurs. We are underway. Bartu gets the boy to put them on.

I think about the missing girl.

Bartu asks the boy to tell us what he can see.

I wonder whether she's playing truant; most likely.

The boy says the words 'wobbly bodies' and the kids whisper and laugh.

I look to Miss Nixon and she looks away.

Bartu says, 'The problem is... drink driving is actually no joke.'

I think about asking her about the girl. My body shifts towards her.

Bartu looks at me from the stage and doesn't like what he sees.

I think about openers: 'We wondered... I'm interested...'

'Drink driving isn't a petty offence, it's life threatening...'

I settle on 'Incidentally, is...' and slot it into the firing chamber.

'... both your lives and the lives of others are at stake...'

She turns to me. She stares at the scar on my head.

He speaks while still staring at me. He knows what I'm up to.

She recognises me from the paper, I think. Unwanted celebrity.

He speeds up, rushing through the script as we lock eyes.

'This is my old school,' I whisper to her. She softens.

'... all for the sake of being too lazy to walk home...'

Her face makes an 'Oh, right' expression.

'So next time you think about drinking and driving...'

'Yes. That was a few years ago now, ha. Incidentally...' I say.

'Remember the beer goggles and think about if you...'

'Incidentally, is the girl that went...'

'...really want to put lives at stake for the price of a taxi home, thank you!'

Applause. The noise of which ruins our moment. I ask her the question again but the decibel level rises further.

'The girl that went missing, was she...' I say.

She can't hear me. The suddenly exuberant boys and girls seem to be letting off some boredom steam through sarcastic cheering, rather than earnestly thanking Emre Bartu for his performance. But whatever the reason, they're making too much noise for me to proceed. Advantage Bartu.

'Great! Thank you for listening. Thank you for having myself and PCSO Mondrian.'

He looks to me to try and cue a simple thank you. This is his tactical error. I step forward and speak at full volume.

I knew something was going to happen. This is it.

'Right, before we go we'd just like to ask if anyone has any information about the missing girl?'

Silence.

A shuffle of feet.

I sense Miss Nixon's stony visage in my periphery.

More silence.

I scan their stunned faces. Maybe Bartu's right, maybe I am pretty blunt these days. I make a judgement. I think they had no idea that one of their number was missing, until now. That's what it looks like. I check just to make sure.

'Anyone at all? Know anything?'

Emre Bartu's open mouth comes into focus, making a small dark 'o'. His eyes are like snooker balls, bare and marmoreal.

I wait a few seconds. One, two, three. Then someone speaks. But unfortunately it's only Emre Bartu.

'No? That's fine. Thank you. Dismissed!'

They detonate into a flurry of chatter, standing and jostling each other as they start to flow out. Nixon comes towards me and speaks out of the corner of her mouth.

'PC Stevens agreed we shouldn't tell them about this yet,' she says.

'Sorry, miscommunication. It's standard practice to... throw it out there early, you know.'

Emre is at the back. Trapped as he sees me talking to Miss Nixon.

'I wish you would have told me you were going to do that.'

'Apologies again. He shouldn't have told you it was possible to keep it under wraps. I can only apologise... on his behalf.'

'So what do we do now?' She says.

Emre hears none of this. He can only see our mouths move as he swims through the crowd, smiling, trying to seem in control. He turns for a second and mouths a few words to a couple of them. This allows me to do what I do next.

'Here you are,' I say, palming her my number.

I decided to make a few cards and keep them in my right pocket. You have to be prepared.

If you want to dive in face first.

If you want to crawl against the current.

If you want to make your own tide.

'Let's see what happens. You might get a knock on your office door. If you do, let me know about it.'

I'm pleased with the clarity of my sentiment.

'Putting an idea in the water always tends to dig up something,' I say, mixing metaphors like a real pro.

I do all this while scratching my head as if talking about the weather, keeping it casual for the eyes of Bartu, the mirage of small talk when it scarcely gets much larger.

But he suspects by now. He's not smiling anymore, no matter how hard he tries.

I beat him.

I won.

I got to ask my questions.

He puts his hand up, drowning in a sea of boys and girls. He's too far away.

He's paralysed to stop what comes next.

8

'Can't, Dah dah dah dee dah, out of, my head…'

The girl's home smells of orange. Not of oranges. Not citrus. It smells of the colour orange. I'd learnt to associate smells with colours, a new trick, and not one of my willing. Another brain adaptation, an aroma-based synaesthesia. You can, in effect, see scents.

It's got stronger every day since the bullet. A purple fog appearing in the school as I smelt the cleaning fluid, a waterfall of light green trickling from the ceiling of Dr Ryans' office made by his herbaceous smoke remnants.

But orange grips me hard here as her mother lets us into the house. If it were a musical note it would be an 'A'. I picture an orange letter 'A'. It's my mind's automatic reflex.

Then a pink smell intrudes. I can't hear it's note yet, but I see it snakes through the orange mist.

As I watch the colours move, I decide to wow them with a deduction I've made.

'It was good of you to get Tanya that cat she wanted so much, what with your allergy,' I say.

'I'm sorry, what?' Ms Fraser says.

Our stilted conversation hadn't turned to cats or allergies on the way here, so Bartu is left pondering how we move on from this non-sequitur.

'It's just that there are two single hairs from a Siberian on the settee, just enough to suggest that someone who's usually here, probably Tanya, grooms her meticulously and that on the odd occasion the cat does make it into this room she's quickly removed, leaving little behind her. People get Siberians because they're supposed to be better for allergies, but I question the science on that. Your eyes aren't reddened and you're not wheezing, which tells me the air filter on the floor is doing its job. I'd also advise you to keep the window open but I imagine you did until it turned too cold for that. And then there's the pink smell of Neem Oil, found in cat but not human shampoo. Smells like Tanya promised to wash her, twice a week I'd say, as another way of persuading you it'd help manage the dander that causes allergies.'

Bartu shakes his head and gives Ms Fraser an apologetic look. 'I can't smell anything.'

'You wouldn't. My sense of smell is… a little keener than most, and you can't sense habitual smells in your own home, due to what's called olfactory adaptation, giving you no chance at all, Ms Fraser. Also, your cat has diabetes.'

She stares at me. 'I'm sorry, I don't have a diabetic cat.'

'Well, the kitchen roll Tanya seems to have stashed in various places about the house, just in case of emergencies, suggests otherwise. I'm guessing her toilet habits have recently become more unpredictable, plus there's a subtle scent of sweetness in the air, the odour of which would be consistent with diabetic cat urine. Not that your home smells of cat urine. You've hidden it well and you're a kind mother. Again, I just have a keener sense than most.'

She gives me a look that suggests two things. Either this

woman is dumbfounded by the diagnosis. Or she doesn't have a cat. Either way, it's probably best to move on from this.

'Could you show us her room?' I ask.

I also picture numbers as distinctly coloured.

The number one is purple.

Two yellow.

Three blue.

And I picture them circling my head whenever they come to mind.

1 is at a ten-degree angle to my forehead.

2 is at about twenty-five.

Then the rest disperse themselves in fifteen-degree intervals around me. This side effect doesn't seem of much practical use but the brain isn't always trying to help, sometimes it's merely trying to exist the only way it can.

The walls appear to me vaguely orange, the carpet on the stairs is orange, the pictures in the hallway are all various shades of orange, the scent of cinnamon and pine, I imagine, subtle notes of a recent Christmas that only I can smell. The girl's bedroom door is the same colour.

Bartu looks at me, barely disguising his discomfort at being here. Exactly where he didn't want us to end up. But when Miss Nixon revealed that the missing girl's mother was coming in to speak to her, I couldn't resist asking if I could have a word, too. Nixon had agreed to do the introductions by the time Bartu caught up with us heading to her office.

When I suggested to Ms Fraser that we come over to check a couple of things, it was difficult for him to protest. He had to silently pretend this was all standard procedure, so as not to scold the semi-famous local hero with a bullet scar on his temple.

Ms Fraser said two officers had only just come to her house. I'd expected her to say this. But I hadn't come up with an answer to it yet. I was still for a second before simply saying:

64

'Nowadays we're lucky enough to be able to double up...'

It's curious how far a uniform and the simplest jargon gets you.

'... in case anything gets missed. Due diligence and that.'

This is nonsense of course. Stevens and Anderson are the officers with the day-to-day relationship with the school. They liaise with social services about everything from gang violence to sexual abuse, and when their enquiries unearth the necessary dirt, they hand it to CID. So where do we come in? Absolutely nowhere at all. But I'm a curious man.

Bartu's body tightened as all this unfolded. He didn't back me up but he didn't stop me either. He let things play out, aware that I'd made my moves and there was little he could do to stop me now the wheels were in motion.

She gave us a lift back to her place. Emre didn't look at me the whole way. But he's going to need more tenacity if he's going to stop me doing exactly what I want. I'm a hard act to follow. A hard book to match. A hard book of matches. One of those.

The inside of her car smelt yellow. Cheapish air freshener and hot change in her coin draw.

But the house definitely smelt orange.

Emre Bartu glares at me intermittently as we peer into Tanya Fraser's bedroom.

- A mess of bed sheets, crinkled like storm clouds
- An abundance of small ornate mirrors scattered around.
- A childhood bear peeping out from her half-open ward-robe.

Both of us stand on the precipice, not wanting to break the barrier between us and this sacred space.

'Was she part of any after school clubs?' I say.

'Tennis club. Badminton. Running club. I told the others this.'

Bartu lightly sniggers. But everything helps.

I don't find anything about my day humorous anymore. Her room has altered me somehow, taking away any thrill of the puzzle, focusing me in on the dark import of all this.

'Is she a messy girl? Or do you think she left in a hurry?' I say.

'No, she's not messy. She'd have tidied up if she knew... she'd be mortified if she knew... she'd have guests... that there'd be people in here.'

Ms Fraser darts into the room on impulse, her voice cracking. She makes a grab for the duvet to cover up the shame of the unmade bed.

'No. Don't touch anything,' I say. She stops and looks to me.

I follow her in smoothly.

'Best not to touch anything. Just in case,' Emre says, stepping inside tentatively, his hand brushing the clean white doorframe.

'In case of what?' she says.

'In case there's anything here that might give us a clue as to her whereabouts,' Emre Bartu says, the word *clue* sticking in his throat like a bone, as if the necessary drama of his job occasionally embarrasses him.

'The others weren't like this. The others just asked a few basic questions,' she says.

'That's why it's best to double up,' I say.

I scan the room. Her bed is pushed into the corner, under the window, which I imagine her opening in the summer to let the air flow in. She has a chest of drawers facing the end of the bed, up against the wall. The bottom drawer is not fully closed and instinctively I want to push it shut it to make it level with the others. To the right of her bed as we look is her wardrobe, one panel of it dusty white, the other a mirror.

I take a few steps towards it, its jaws ajar, the bear looking at me from inside.

'When did you say she was turning seventeen?' Emre says, behind me.

It occurs to me I hadn't even asked her age. I hardly know a thing about her.

'Not until September. She's still a baby,' she says. But she's not. She's old enough to go out on her own, old enough to get into trouble. Old enough to do a lot of things her mother doesn't know about. It's her prerogative. It's a must. For boys and girls. Rites of passage.

'She have a boyfriend at all?' says Emre Bartu.

I put my hand out to open the wardrobe and feel their eyes on me.

'No. Nothing like that.'

I stop. My hand goes back to my side.

'Not one you know about anyway,' I say over my shoulder.

'No. I'd know. We tell each other everything. We're mates.'

I draw breath, wondering how to put this, then I just say the first thing that comes into my head.

'She may still be a little girl to you, you know, but –'

'She lost it to a boy called Asif Akhtar in the form above about a year ago. He's the only boyfriend she's ever had. He cheated on her at the bowling alley. They don't see each other anymore.'

She fires it all out with absolute conviction and a hint of triumph.

'We'll need to speak to him,' I say.

Somewhere behind me Emre Bartu is rolling his eyes. He thought I just wanted to have a play around and then I'd leave it alone. He's wondering how we ended up here and how he'll tell Levine, if he'll tell Levine. I open the wardrobe.

'Hi, I'm Teddy, let's play! Let's play!' The bear shouts as it hits the ground.

I stumble back, almost crashing into Emre behind me.

I walk back towards the wardrobe and see her childish

things crammed hastily into the bottom below her carefully ironed dresses and tops. A soft yellow pony with long pink hair. An etch-a-sketch. Annuals and books about wizards and vampires.

The woman above. The girl just below the surface.

If you close the cupboard and tidy the bed, then only a woman remains. I place the bear back inside and close the cupboard.

Something smells blue. If it were a musical note it would be an 'F'. If it were a texture it would be mahogany. It arrives all at once. A blue mahogany 'F'.

'We should go. We do try to leave everything as untouched as possible. Both to maintain evidence in the last place we know her to have been... and "cos we don't like to intrude..." Emre says, breaking off as he sees me climbing onto her bed.

I lie face down. They say nothing. Emre is forced to nod and give the impression that all this is pretty normal stuff.

I breathe in. It's a man's smell but I don't think he's been in this bed. I admit this must look unorthodox.

I reach down into the gap between bed and wall and pluck out a piece of paper. I act like that's all I needed. I pull it out. Cream A5, full of colour on one side. Purples, greens, blues, reds. The picture started as a useful subterfuge, but now I look at it, it could be more than that.

My eyes scan it and see patterns. Triangles here. A grid. I map it in an instant. I understand the components, the smallest minutiae of shades within shades, but my mind can't quite make out what it's supposed to be.

'What is this?' I say.

'It's a picture,' she says.

'It's a house next to a playground,' Emre says.

'Does she like drawing?' I say, taking a slow step toward her.

'Probably. I don't –'

'Know everything about her, do you?' I say.

68

'She's a girl. She takes art. I'd say she likes drawing,' she says. I've riled her a little.

'Why draw this?' I say. I have to focus to see what they see so easily. The house and playground coming into shape like a constellation.

'Why draw anything?' she says.

'Exactly!' I say.

Emre Bartu shuffles from side to side.

'I don't know, I don't recognise it, it's just a picture,' she says.

'It's quite childish,' I say.

'She's a child,' she says.

'Not really,' I say.

'She's sixteen...' says Bartu, taking no side.

'Would you say she's childish? Young for her age?'

'Not really. She's mature. We have adult conversations.'

'Then why does she draw like this?'

'It's just a picture,' she says.

'Have you seen it before?' I say.

'No...' she says.

'No "definitely not", or no "maybe"?' I say.

'It's just a picture,' Bartu says, as much of a reproach as he can muster without it seeming like a professional dressing down.

I toss the paper away and head for the chest at the foot of the bed. I open the uneven bottom drawer. I run my hand along the materials inside.

I smell blue again.

Winter garments. My hand rummages further, I feel something underneath a patterned scarf, I lift it up and underneath I feel cool, smooth, synthetic material. Then I take a look and step back again, vocalising my surprise with a level of drama I didn't intend.

'What is it?' she says, as she goes over to look.

Emre looks at me. I was rooting around too much. I don't

want to intrude or offend, I only want to help, but my new brain makes delicacy difficult. And it's too late for regrets, I've found something.

She pulls them out from under the scarf. She looks at me tersely, then back at them.

Did you know that photo paper is mostly made from gelatine? Our images are preserved forever, burned onto crushed animal matter. You need the thickening agent of the gelatine from cow's bones to hold the glossy silver halide crystals together.

She holds them for Emre Bartu to see and then quickly draws them away. I don't like surprises. I didn't want to see a young girl's naked body. There are twenty or thirty pictures.

'Do you think she took these herself, Ms Fraser?' Emre Bartu says.

'I don't know. I don't think she has a Polaroid.'

'Maybe a friend has one,' Bartu says.

'I wouldn't know, I'm sorry.'

I could say, 'I think there's an awful lot you don't know' at this point, but I manage not to. She's looking at me differently now. Grudgingly pleased we've shown a bit more fervour than the last two did. I don't want to spoil this emerging good will.

'Should I be worried about this?' she says.

'Depends what sort of friend took them,' Emre says. Careful, Bartu.

'Yeah, it does,' she says, staring at them. She offers them back to me, unsure what the protocol dictates. Her hand shakes a little as she pushes them it towards me.

'No! No. Put them back where we found them, I think,' I say, glancing at Emre.

We can't bring evidence back with us. We'll have to do this without analysing anything, officially anyway. We need to leave everything as we found it, like night thieves covering their tracks. That way it will be longer until we're found out.

'Thanks for your time. We should go,' he says again.

'Please, take my number, in case you need anything,' I say, handing her one of my pre-prepared cards. Emre tenses up again as I do so.

'Thank you,' she says. She's grateful. A profound sensation of joy comes over me. We head downstairs, I think about the blue smell as we reach her door, the smell that would feel like mahogany, and sound like an 'F' note.

'Who wears the aftershave?' I say.

'No one, we haven't had a man in this house for five years.'

My olfactory sense is good but not that good.

'Tanya's dad?'

'Is in Canada. They've never met. And they don't need to.'

'And five years ago?' Emre says.

'A boyfriend I was seeing, but I'm through with all that.'

We nod and I work through the possibilities. A man has been there and not so long ago. That's what it smells like to me.

'It's probably my perfume you can smell. Is it important?'

I take in the oddness of the structure of this sentence. They both take in the oddness of me.

'No, not important. Yes, it's probably the perfume,' I lie.

Then I notice a Siberian cat with canary-coloured eyes creep up to the front door and pry in. It looks up at me, I return the favour and we understand each other somehow.

'Monkey,' she says. 'Come on in.' She picks him up and gives me a look. Bartu is as amazed as he should be by this partial confirmation of my previous deduction. But I don't even smile, I just revel in it. Then ponder…

Monkey? What sort of name is that for a cat? You can call it any stupid name you want, but don't call it the name of another existing animal. Language is tough enough without that kind of nonsense. That really annoys me for a second. I resolve to

71

remember to name my cat, but be a lot more careful than she's been about it.

I nod to her and turn to leave abruptly. Emre follows, saying 'Bye then'. By the time she says it in return I'm ten feet away and walking back to the station.

I notice it's getting dark as Emre appears alongside me. I think about what sort of man would've worn that aftershave. I think about the colour blue. I think about why she's lying to me.

9

'My body is tired, tired, tired
But my brain is wired, wired, in the night
My liver is fired, like a fire alight in the cold
Think we'll keep the thing alive before we get too old'

'We're not done in there,' I warn him in the locker room.

'Tom. We're extremely done in there. We're not going any-where near her or this ever again,' he says, *sotto voce*.

'Come on. You know that's not true. We're just getting started,' I bark back.

There's no one around. The others told us on the radio that they were back on time and were heading home. Emre is extra annoyed because he had to tell Levine that we're late in because 'someone thought there might have been a break in at the library, but it turned out to be nothing'.

Liar. That was his first lie. I try not to tell lies. He probably does, too, but he got backed into a corner and didn't want to get into trouble.

In reality, the only other thing we had to do on our shift was to go and get a description of some shoplifters from John's Food and Wine. Shoplifters always get me down for some reason. That and the school visit wouldn't have taken up our whole time, even it was a half shift. So he needed to create another event to explain us coming back twenty minutes late.

He could've said we lost track of time.

He could have told the truth and put it all on me.

But he didn't.

He told a lie, a white one but a lie all the same. Now he's with me, we're bound together, because I know about the lie and I know he's the sort of person who isn't averse to deception. It'll be tough for him to get away from me and my plans, but he doesn't know that yet. I can only wait for his reticence to wither and then drop off.

'We can't do this anymore,' Bartu says as we step outside in our civvies.

'It sounds like you're breaking up with me. It's only our first date.'

'I'll lose my job. I need it. I've got aspirations.'

'Yes, me too, I've got aspirations, Emre Bartu.'

'I don't think they're the same aspirations.'

He lights a cigarette. Emre smokes.

'What's the matter?'

'You smoke.'

'Yes. What's wrong with that? Don't say the obvious.'

'I have to say I see this as very weak.'

'Really?'

'But then I'm very judgemental.'

'Everyone's got their thing to get them through the day.'

'I don't like to be dependent. On anything, never have.'

'They don't smoke me. I smoke them.'

'I'm not so sure.'

'What's your thing?'

'Words.'

'But you can't read properly, right?'

'I'm working on it. Why don't you try quitting?'

74

'Because I'm dedicated.'

'You're not that dedicated. You're giving up on this case.'

'It's not my case to give up on. Give me a break will you?'

This all happens quite slowly but it's the fastest bit of conversation I've been able to take part in for a while and I'm pleased with myself.

I batted it back and forth, it was a decent rally. My mind is getting sharper. I break into a broad smile, pleased with myself for everything that has happened today. He clocks this as we arrive at his car. I go to get in on the passenger side.

'What are you doing?'

'I need a lift.'

'Ok, fine. Where do you live?'

'By Seven Sisters station.'

'That's not on my way.'

'Are you going to make me walk? I got shot in the head.'

Emre just sighs and cracks; he likes me, he's trying to pretend he doesn't, but he likes me.

He backs the car out as I find an open packet of bonbons in his glove compartment.

'Headlights,' I say, popping one into my mouth.

'I was just about to. You're Mr Rules all of a sudden, huh?'

'Can't see without headlights,' I say, shrugging. He's flustered.

Our lights crawl along the road in front of us as we cut through the biting evening air. The misted breath of the passers-by rises and drifts up to join the milky clouds above. The temperature has dropped and it's going to start snowing again soon apparently. It hasn't snowed since the day of my accident. This is supposed to be one of the coldest winters in London on record, something about a cold front from the Atlantic. 68 days of snow were scheduled so that gives us a few more by the end of a freezing February, by my reckoning.

I'm not interested in the photos. Teenagers are mostly into that stuff. Once you hit fifteen it's all warm cider and dick pics these days. *Look at me! I've got one of these! Observe me!*

I'm more interested in the picture she drew.

The scent of aftershave in the house.

'Hey Emre, remind me to remember that Ms Fraser had a rosewood coloured afro that nicely complemented her skin tone, will you?'

'Okay. Why?'

'So I remember who she is.'

'We're not going back there.'

'Well, just in case.'

'You spent an hour with her, are you that forgetful?'

'I'm not forgetful at all. I'm just not so good with faces.'

'Is anyone that bad with faces?'

'Yes, I am. Since the accident. Tomorrow I won't recognise you either unless I write it down. No offence. Everyone's face is like a plain black suitcase. I see the shapes and they means nothing to me, it's like a foreign language. You know that phrase, I don't remember names but I never forget a face? That's the opposite of me. Don't tell anyone though, they won't like it.'

'Hmm. No shit. That's not typically how you'd want a member of the police force to be.'

'Nothing about me is typically how you'd want a member of the police force to be. But then I'm not a typical person. And I'm not really a member of the police force.'

'Okay. I think I understand that.'

'Good. Then we're on the same page.'

'I wouldn't go that far.'

He's right, I'm not on the same page as anyone, not anymore. We're not even in the same library.

We drive past low price trainer stores and a football ground.

'Listen, Tom, I can't come with you on this trip you're on.

So I'm just going to tell Levine he should find you someone else.'

'What will you say?'

'I'll say we don't get on.'

'Why lie?'

'How do you know I'm lying?'

'Because you can't fool me, you like me.'

'Is that right?'

'Yep. Also, you've already told a lie and I know about it and if I tell them about it, it won't look good for you. I could make trouble for you, Emre Bartu. And I don't want to do that.'

'Is that a threat? Are you threatening me now?'

'Yes, but it's only 'cos I like you. Pull over.'

'What?'

'Pull over!'

I grab the wheel and that forces Emre to slam on the brakes. We both fly forward but our belts do their jobs and we don't even suffer a minor whiplash, so I don't know what he's so angry about.

'Are you crazy!?' he shouts

'I'm not crazy,' I mutter as I get out and approach the black car at the side of the road that had drifted into my vision.

Ever since I heard the words 'missing girl' I've been looking for a blacked out car. You don't see many cars with blacked out windows and you certainly don't see many halfway up the kerb without number plates front or back.

I stalk around it and Emre follows.

No broken windows. Tickets all over it. Possibly dumped. Hubcaps missing, which tells me it's been there long enough for people to start stripping it for parts but not long enough for it to be towed.

'Tom? Can we do this tomorrow? We can check it out then if you're interested, but I wanna get home to my girlfriend.'

Most support officers don't carry batons due to the 'non-confrontational' nature of our work, but we are authorised to do so. I told Levine it would make me feel more comfortable.

'You've got a girlfriend? Nice, good for you,' I say, smashing into the passenger window with my baton.

'Shit! Tom? Don't do that. Let's do this when we're on the clock tomorrow, okay? We'll do it together. We'll stick together, I promise, but not now.'

It takes a few hits to get through. Then I clear off the loose shards and take a look inside.

It smells chartreuse. It would taste of ink and sound like an E flat. Owing to the blacked out windows it's dark. But it's the smell I'm interested in. He joins me, poking his head inside.

'What would you say that smell is, Emre?'

'Er, I don't know. I can't smell anything.'

Chartreuse, refined yellowing pear-like green, a colour named after a French liqueur.

'I can't see anything either,' he says, interest growing. But I spy the outline of a patterned glove, that I'd say is part of a set. But the other glove, and the possible matching hat and scarf, are nowhere to be seen. Leaving the single glove there, alone, lying limply on the back seat.

Girl missing: Blacked out windows.

It's like word association. It's just how my brain works now. That's not to say I'm right, but if a girl goes missing there are only so many options.

1. She's gone of her own free will.
2. She's walked into a trap.
3. She's been picked up and taken somewhere against her will.

And if she's been taken somewhere you're going to have to do that with a degree of care. You're going to have to pacify her, or make sure no one sees her struggle, hence the blacked out car.

Robbery: blood on broken window.

Arson: check the insurance.

GBH: check romantic history.

Missing girl: car with blacked out windows.

It's just something I do. 'Be open to the fact that the simplest answer is sometimes the best one.' Even the training officer said that. In other words, clichés become clichés for a reason. They're neither to be worshipped or ignored.

I should've been watching Bartu instead of wandering through these thoughts though, because when I turn to him he's in the process of doing something uncharacteristically stupid.

'My phone's got a torch app, but it's dead. Here,' he says, flicking his Zippo alight and leaning it into the car just as something tells me that the chartreuse might be something to be concerned about.

'No!' I shout, grabbing him. He drops the thing and I throw both of us back as the car goes up in flames. We hit the ground, hard.

The next thing I notice is the white smell of our burnt hair.

I close my eyes, half expecting the whole thing to go up – boom! But it doesn't. It's not quite how you'd want it to be. But it's still a spectacle the upholstery definitely isn't going to survive.

'Fuck!' he shouts. He'd definitely be worse off if he'd leaned further in, and ended up half the man he used to be facially.

The car blazes beautifully against the night sky, as snow begins to fall. Embers rise, passing white flakes, kissing them hello and goodbye as they rise towards the abyss above.

'Fire Alight' starts playing on a loop in my head. It's another lullaby I wrote in the ward; you won't know it. My subconscious has a dark sense of humour.

Missing girl. Blacked out car that sets alight. If all this doesn't pique Emre's interest, then it damn well should do.

The chartreuse and blue are linked. I think the scents have shades of each other within them, now I picture them together.

'Fuck,' he repeats, more from anger than pain.

I face the flames. I'm resolved. It's my time to shine.

I pick him up and dust us both down. Then I pull him back again, as something goes *bang*!

We fall down onto our arses. And watch the car shake. Muffled cracks and bangs rumble away in there.

Bang. Crack. Bang.

I picture the shadow of a jittery guy in a blacked out car on the day I was shot. This car, I'm guessing. I sniggered as he sped away. I'm not sniggering now.

Cars don't explode if you shoot into the petrol tank like in the movies. It wouldn't happen that way, trust me. Cars don't tend to do anything that dramatic, unless they happen to be, for instance, filled with fireworks.

Boom!

The boot lifts clean off and rolls a few metres away from us. Lights pulsate from the back of the car, then are flung out onto the ground causing three-second long lakes of green and red sparks, as high-pitched whistles join the other noises and we hold our ears.

But still, it's the fireworks not the tank that has exploded. Because petrol tanks don't tend to explode.

Unless, for example, those fireworks spark an even bigger fire, that heats the petrol in the tank below to combustion point.

Whoomph! A noise that puts the gunpowder *bangs* into context. I'm closer than I want to be, as the tank explodes.

Grey smoke and debris shoot into the night air.

Then a single rocket escapes and shoots over the London

skyline. It's a hell of a show. You can't help but just sit, watch and shake your head at the spectacle of it all.

Fire. Gunpowder. You slam some things together and the world reacts accordingly.

Me. Bartu.

Girls and boys.

Bullets. Brains.

The smooth neck of the London city sky and everything else, that glints blade-like underneath.

We watch it in wonder.

'Fuck' indeed.

The sky lights up. A millisecond of day in our evening time. Like sheet lightning.

Documented Telephone Conversation #1

It rings.

'Hello?' she says.

'Hello.'

'Hello. Who is this?'

'Err...'

The silence drags.

'Oh,' she says.

'Hmm,' comes the non-committal noise across the line.

'You hid your number,' she says.

'Did I?'

'You know you did,' she says.

'Yeah…'

The caller starts to tap their knee nervously. The receiver of the call shifts her seating position, but she doesn't feel the need to talk. Then she gets up and moves into another room, perhaps so she can speak more freely, it is the evening after all and she may not be alone. She settles down in her new position, wherever that may be. She hasn't been wherever she currently is for very long. Then she breathes a sigh across the line.

'Are you alone?'

'How've you been?' she says, not taking the bait.

'I've been worse. I've been better.'

'Do you need to talk?' she says.

'Yes, I do, I need to talk. I don't want to, but I need to.'

'What do you need to talk about?' she says.

'I just need to talk, and hearing your voice isn't bad either. Not too bad I suppose.'

'How's your new job going?'

'It's going,' I murmur.

I know that she senses the tension of it. Anger or the unsaid can so easily sound like flirtation but that's not what she wants. She doesn't want any of it. She wants to get on with her life and to not feel bad for wanting that. She feels that as it was me who called, the onus is on me to drive beginnings, otherwise it's like someone insisting on coming to your house in the afternoon only to lie dormant on your sofa. We both feel the silences take on different forms, which is one of the miracles that everyone has felt since the advent of the telephone call and has been repeated thousands of times all over the world since. It's a kind of telepathy. We've picked up where we left off.

'So what's happened since we last spoke? Anything big?'

'You could say that,' I say.

'You sound different,' Anita says.

'I am,' I say.

'What happened?'

Amongst the many fragments of advice that Ryans has given me, talking to someone I knew well before the accident stood out. He would even like to meet with somebody who can attest to certain changes in me. 'It's difficult to know where you're headed if we don't know where you've been', he says. But there is only really one who knew me before and I don't want her talking to him about me.

I should talk because I'm told that it will help. But it stings.

'The fundamental requirements for my work. Do you remember I read them to you?' I say.

'Yes. I think so.'

'Inspire confidence with your presence. Don't jump to conclusions about what you see and hear. Win co-operation through good-humoured persuasion. Display good stamina for working on foot.'

'So... how are you doing?' Anita says

'Well... my stamina for working on foot is good.'

'Ha.' She laughs her laugh.

'Don't laugh.'

'I wasn't laughing at you. Have you lost your sense of humour?'

'Yes,' I say. 'Can't find it anywhere. Also, I've become impulsive. Also, you're subtly slurring, which indicates you might soon get a migraine. I read a new study. You should take magnesium tablets.'

'Seriously, none of this sounds at all like you,' she says.

'So you've said. I should tell you, a thing happened. There was an accident, a bad one. It happened to me. Don't you read the paper?'

'No. What accident?' she says.

I breathe. Quick ones. Three in and three out.

'I won't bother you with it. I needed to talk. Now I have.'

'Are you okay? You seem so different.'

'People change. Goodbye,' I say.

'No, I want to see you. Please. I'm worried. I still... I do love... '

'I don't want to hear that. And no, I won't want to see you.'

'I'm going to come round. Stay there. I'm coming round now.'

'Please don't. That might make me very angry. People change. Good luck.'

10

'Can't. Dah dah dah dee door, dah dah, dee dah…'

I see a girl, when I say a girl this time I mean a woman, mid to late twenties. My age. She wears a green dress. There is a song playing. She is walking away from me towards a car near a forest. I follow her. She knows I'm there. She looks behind her to check. When she sees me she doesn't smile and nor do I. Smoke rises from the forest. But it doesn't seem to be on fire. It smokes majestically, like a cigarette. She has blonde hair.

'Can't. Dah dah dah dee door, dah dah, my head…'

She slides into the car and waits for me there. I lift my pace. I take a look behind me. Around the corner comes a man. He also has blond hair. He has something in his pocket. I turn forward again and speed up but don't want him to know I'm scared. I don't want him to know I'm up to something. I get faster, incrementally, but I'm getting no nearer the car she lingers in, her seat pulled back so she can lean into it languorously.

The car seems further away with every step I take, and I can see she's waiting, not dreamily now, somehow agitated. She pulls her seat forward and starts the engine. I'm so far away.

I turn. He's right behind me. He's so close. It ends.

It feels like a dream. And this time, it is one.

*

When I wake it's 2pm, I stayed up most of the night 'reading' and thinking. We're on the night shift this evening. I do a couple of half-shift nights in the week to mix things up. Then I take Saturday off and do only five hours on Sunday.

I rearranged the spread of my week when I came back as my priorities had changed. I want to work pretty much as many days as possible now to keep up my routine. Bartu wanted a different rota but I said I 'like my way', and he's stuck with me for now, so we left it at that.

I lock eyes with the cat. He's probably pretty miffed that I haven't spent much quality time with him thus far. I've fed and watered him well though and we already had a cat flap from a brief stint with a feline named Muffin when I was young, so he can't deny all the facilities are there.

'You okay, cat?' I say, solemnly, unsure of my method of approach.

He gives me a certain kind of fuck you look and takes a seat on my ankle. The naming issue is becoming a significant one for him, I infer, so I set off on a trial run.

'You okay... Dean?' I say. Nothing.

'You okay... Chris?' Nonplussed.

'You fine, Mr... Chair,' I say, having looked around for inspiration.

'You okay, Mark?' A meow. This confirms a suspicion I had earlier. I knew he was a Mark.

I thought of the name as soon as I saw him and considered how interesting it could be to try to dictate a story about his life if it were so. 'Can I ask you a question, Mark? Question-mark.' One section would go. I wonder whether technology has developed enough for an app to decipher this sentence. I realise it's an odd thought but I have copious alone time and the mind does wander. An excess of which is exactly what Mark is supposed to combat.

I stare at him and urge myself to connect. It would be good for me, Ryans had promised.

'Can I ask you a question, Mark?'

I take his quiet as compliance.

'What sort of person has that many fireworks in the boot of their car?'

He breathes out and deflates almost entirely. I jettison the possibility of conversation and do my exercises. He watches disapprovingly, silently judging me with his smart arse eyes, waving at me mockingly every so often with his smart arse tail, tasting every bit of himself with his smart arse tongue.

The buzz of seeing the car go up took a while to fade. To our surprise, when we reported it, what came out was the truth: 'We saw a car on our way home and thought it seemed suspicious. I was a bit overzealous, Bartu made an error, but no one got hurt.

'He wasn't to know it was filled with carbon monoxide, or that the boot contained enough fireworks to mount a decent church display. Anyway, it made for a hell of a back to work celebration, sir,' I said.

'At first, we thought it was a car bomb, chief,' said Bartu.

It wasn't, but that doesn't mean it wasn't a trap. All options are open.

The chief is supposed to be in charge of this place but he seems to me to be a rather nervy and unimpressive man. He was more concerned about me on the whole. How I was 'feeling', if I was 'safe'. We were told to be a lot more careful around cars in the future. We nodded like children, then the chief placed a reassuring hand on my shoulder, which was anything but. Then he went back to his paperwork before I knew that the conversation was over, like an errant stepfather doing just enough to make his lover's kids feel like he actually cares.

But that was it. No further reprimand. Workers in Argos

break TVs when they come down the chute. Milkmen smash glass bottles. Cats piss on the carpet. PCSOs blow up cars filled with Catherine Wheels. It's nothing to worry about. Consider our wrists gently slapped. Our one point of contention came when the chief sent us to file a report with the duty officer, who seemed to take umbrage with my claim to have smelt a leak.

'That's not possible,' said the duty officer.

'Really?' I said, concealing the fact that really I saw it rather than smelt it. And that it tasted of ink. And sounded like an E flat.

'It's odourless. Humans can't smell it.'

'Oh. Well I can, it seems.'

'It's odourless,' he said, perplexed.

'Oh, well. Just lucky I guess.'

I discovered in my home research that it's not entirely true that carbon monoxide is undetectable or odourless. Some people have been known to sense it but up to now all of those people have been dogs. I'm not entirely sure how dogs have made that clear, or why my sense of smell is more akin to a dog's, but there we are.

In the debrief room myself and Emre Bartu say little. We're playing a game I think, which is tough for me, I'm better focusing on the literal than anything that involves subterfuge. It makes me seem a touch autistic, I suppose, but that's not it. People with autism often don't like the nature of ruses themselves, whereas I'd love to partake in one, I just find it mentally difficult to squeeze out anything but the truth.

So, I'm attempting to pretend to be concentrating on various things. Our notes. Thinking through our work plan for today. When, in fact, we're both listening. Pretending to take no notice in an update Anderson and Stevens are giving about Tanya Fraser.

They say they checked her home and there's nothing to

suggest any foul play there. Which I suppose there wasn't if you weren't looking effectively.

They say that they're 'not ruling anything out' but are 'interested in her truancy record'.

They say they know she's gone missing overnight before, and it turned out that she and a school friend were staying with her cousin in Essex, where they roamed around parks and shopping centres, smoking.

Having taken advice from the missing persons bureau, who use data compiled from 3,000 previous cases, they leaned heavily on the belief that she would, in all probability, come back of her own accord.

You see, two hundred and twenty thousand children go missing in Britain every year. Thirty percent of fifteen to seventeen-year-olds come home without police intervention. Eighty percent of missing teenagers turn out to be less than 40km from their homes. Just over ninety-nine percent are back home within three days. I know the maths is on their side, I did the numbers myself, but what if Tanya's story lives in the minorities?

At least an inspector named Jarwar has also been asked to give it the once over. And let's hope she shares our curiosity, because to me there were a hundred unfinished sentences in the bedroom alone.

*

We head out into the night on foot to collect CCTV footage from the supermarket. They have a confirmed sighting of a convicted shoplifter returning to his old stomping ground. We'll bring the footage back at the end of the shift and by tomorrow morning he'll be back in a cell. Need for stimulation, impulsivity, poor behaviour controls, shoplifters always get me down. Now I remember why…

A spark goes off in my mind that ignites a memory of a story told about that girl I once kissed. A gossipy girl went over to her house and my kissing girl showed her a collection she had in her room. A cupboard full of carefully arranged items: bubble gum balls, fizzy drink cans, eggs with toys inside, all of them unopened. She had stolen one item a week from the off-license for the past year. Soon the girls started to wrestle, lively girls they were, and only twelve. Then the door flung open. My kissing girl was taken off into another room. The other girl heard her being thumped, but no tears. Then dad, or whoever he was, drove the other girl home in silence.

We walk the beat saying nothing, as the local characters pass.

A woman with short dark hair waves from over the road.

A guy in a tracksuit nods discreetly as he passes on a bike.

I smile excessively at them all, safe in the knowledge that I surely know them, despite their faces meaning precisely nothing to me. I construct an indiscriminately friendly edifice, brick by brick.

'I think there's a man in the house,' I say.

'What house?' Emre says.

'The Fraser house.'

'What? Because of your aftershave theory?'

'Yes, because of my aftershave theory.'

'Why would she be hiding them?'

'I don't know. A) Ms Fraser has a perfectly innocent boyfriend but doesn't want the finger pointed at him. B) She has a not so sweet one she fears could have done something with her daughter, or C) She has one who her daughter simply wanted to get away from.'

'Going along with this... for a moment. If there is some guy of hers she's protecting, he could live somewhere else. How do you know he's in the house?'

'Because I can smell him.'

Emre Bartu stops in the street. Puts his top teeth against his bottom lip. His habit.

'Of course you can smell him. Obviously you can smell him. Dunno why I asked. You can smell scentless gases so obviously you can smell a man hiding in a house. Obviously.'

'I'll bet you a tenner he's in there.'

Bartu looks around, wondering whether he's indulged me too much.

'We're not going back there.'

'Not for a tenner? Or are you afraid of losing? Tenner?'

Amit waves from over the road. He was two years below me at school. I know it's Amit as he has a particular way of waving, as if he thinks it's necessary to make himself taller and lean towards you slightly for you to see him. He works most of the hours whoever sends in a corner shop, which is excellently named 'The Corner Shop'. He seems to be beckoning us over. Emre Bartu uses the opportunity to cross the road and escape our conversation.

I see a girl with blonde hair. Not a green dress, but similar enough to the girl in my dream from behind. Emre starts to come with me as I follow her, but soon gives up. His voice fades away behind me as I hurry after her.

'Tom? Tom!' he says, his timbre disappearing into cold wind.

I can tell by her walk that it's her. Yet I've never seen her face in my dream, a dream I've had many times since the bullet. Not that I'm even sure I can see faces in dreams. She knows I'm a few feet away, I think, as I fight my way through a litany of smokers braving the chill who've spilled out onto the street from the pub. She weaves in and out of them. If I shouted I could make her stop but I don't know what I'd say if I caught her. If we want to make an arrest, we have to call in the 'real police'. If they run, you can hold onto them, that's about the extent of our powers. Many PCSOs have got black eyes and fractured cheekbones that way. Anyway, I don't want to arrest her, I just want to see her.

'Stop!'

She speeds up as she hears this and ducks down an alley.

I'm running, a kind of run anyway, my left foot dragging behind me. I'm causing a scene. I slip slightly. It's icy underfoot, the snow has turned to slush. I want to shout 'Stop that woman!' but that would be too much. I could claim mistaken identity as soon as I saw her, and still get my good look and make my assumptions. I follow her down the alley. It's dark. I see her silhouette emerge from the other side. I'm panting hard.

'Lady with the blonde hair. Stop!' I shout as I get to the other end of the passage, but all I see is my breath in the clearing, nothing else around but a few trees and some residential streets. She could live in any of those houses, or none at all.

I feel suddenly unsafe. I turn and head back through the alley, almost holding my breath, a fear gripping me hard. Paranoia means 'baseless and excessive suspicions'. However, what I have is different. I'm dressed as a target and I've already caught a bulls-eye in the head once. Somehow I've never felt vulnerable until this moment, but now I do and I don't think it's baseless. Paranoia comes from the Greek so really should be pronounced *paraneea*. Maybe I'll claim that as my own. I'm rightfully afraid: I have paraneea.

I see something come out at me.

'Argh!' I let out a yell, the biting air filling my lungs afterwards, my body hurting like I've just hit the line after an ultra-marathon.

A couple pass me on the other side laughing quietly to themselves. A man in uniform, filled with dread and shouting all on his own. I get it, it's funny, I suppose. My hands go to my knees and I work hard to regain my cool and catch my breath. I guess I don't look like the ideal person to be looking after the streets. But looks can be deceiving.

Back at The Corner Shop, Amit and Emre are deep in conversation about nothing in particular.

'Hey, where d'you go? Try not to walk off like that, okay?'

'Thought I saw someone I knew,' I say, mostly composed.

He gives me a look that suggests, understandably, that he finds that pretty hard to believe.

I hear barking, perhaps in the flat above or next door.

'Hey, Amit, you got a dog?' I say.

'Nah man. It's been barking on an' off all day. Someone left it in a car. Cruel, if you arks me.'

'Which one?' says Emre as we step outside.

'Over der I reckon,' says Amit, pointing to a rusty Metro on the corner. Emre and I are drawn to it. We approach, Bartu with his torch-app on this time and his lighter firmly in his pocket.

Bark. Bark. Bark.

The first thing we notice is that there'll be no need for my baton. The dashboard is partially lit up in there. So I'd guess the key is inside and we could open the door if we wished to.

Bark. Bark. Bark.

'Looks like they didn't think they'd be gone long,' he says, running the possibilities through his mind.

Bark. Bark. Bark.

I press my hand onto the chilled car window, then push my head against it, peering in to see through the steamed up glass.

'Shit!' I say, leaping back as the dog jumps up. Emre comes around, wipes the window and sniggers. A Chihuahua puppy sits there. Its tongue lolls out and its dark wet eyes stare up at us desperately.

Bark. Bark. Bark.

'What d'you think of this?' Emre says, his torch skimming over the windshield. I take a look. A kind of jagged heart-shape symbol and three exclamation marks drawn on it in lipstick from the inside. I make a mental note of it to save for later.

'I dunno,' I say, my eyes wandering to his.

He knows that at this point I'd rather open the door and take a look inside, but as there are people around and Emre respects a bit of restraint, I choose to stay circumspect.

'Registration check?' I say.

He calls it in as we head back into the warmth of the shop. I don't want to have to take the dog to the pound. It'll break my heart. Mostly I'm made of stone now, whereas before the bullet I'd cry at mid-afternoon soap operas, but when emotion creeps up on me it does so with ferocity. Someone else will have to take the thing; I'll crumble and break before I get there.

I wonder about the lipstick marks. I consider the heart-shape.

'This is Emre Bartu, over.'

'Mona speaking, over.'

'Hi Mona, can we get a registration check? Over.'

'Yes, go ahead. Over.'

He does so as Amit and I shoot the breeze behind him.

'Got it. Okay, Emre? That's registered to 42 Park Drive. Oh wow. Okay. That's...'

'Mona. You there? Go ahead. Over.'

'That's registered to a... a missing person. A girl.'

I hear it and take a step closer.

'Mona. Are you saying that's registered to Tanya Fraser?... Over. She's only sixteen... over.'

'No. Err... No, it's a seventeen-year-old girl called Jade Bridges. She was reported missing earlier today. Over.'

Bark. Bark. Bark.

We stare into space. The noise of Amit clearing up the place is the only sound.

'Okay, thank you, Mona. We're heading back. Over.'

Two missing girls. Two abandoned cars. One explosion. One dog. And a lipstick heart on a windscreen.

From nowhere, a man in a black hoodie charges into the store.

Amit shouts, Emre is a few steps away and can't get to the guy, he's over six foot and his intentions are clear. He comes for me, pulling a six-inch blade out from his pocket. Without thinking, not consciously, I reach for Amit's coat, which was resting on the door handle next to me. I grab it as the man ghosts in and by the time he is thrusting his weapon towards my chest I manage to step to the side and force him to stab into the coat, which allows me to wrap the thing around his arm up to the elbow and pacify the weapon.

I see it in small moments.

Like a graph.

It seems so obvious.

I needed something to protect myself and that was all there was around. I thought he'd be faster than me, which he should've been, but I saw it coming. My paraneea was calling me. I grab his hand through the coat and turn the knife away from me. I do all this with my right hand as it just seems to make sense logistically. Then with my left hand I grab the back of his head and drive it into the glass of the door. Not excessively, but enough to let him know I'm there. His head shatters it, and he bleeds instantly through his balaclava.

He loses his grip on the knife altogether as this happens and Emre is there to grab it when it hits the floor.

'Hold him! Hold him! I'll call it in,' I say, getting my radio out.

We're not allowed cuffs. I consider beating him unconscious with my baton but I doubt that would go down well. We certainly don't have a Taser. Or a gun. We just have our hands.

'This is Mondrian requesting police support, over.'

But as I look around, he pulls far enough away from Emre to be able to gain some room to elbow him brutally in the sternum, and dash away as Emre hits the ground. He breathes hard and so do I, my hand to my head. Almost exactly where the bullet hit.

I want to give chase but instead I slowly sink to the ground. For a moment I think I'm going to faint but manage not to. This first few days back have provided me with more stimulation than I've had in the entirety of the rest of my life. I've certainly hit the ground running, and I set the pace, but now I'm struggling to keep up.

We both sit with our arses against the freezing floor, our lungs working overtime. Amit rushes around, giving us a bottle of water each. I saw the man's face, briefly, his balaclava riding up in his struggle with Bartu. But then faces mean nothing to me. They're just bags of skin stretched over bone.

Emre composes his respiratory system, rises and kicks the door with frustration. I can't seem to catch my breath at all, it seems to dart around and keep slipping through my fingers.

I've been targeted. Do we add this to the lipstick, the dog, the cars, the missing girls and the explosion? Or is this something else? I turn it over in my mind. I breathe deep. We all do. A symphony of breath.

'Amit. I'm sorry about your door,' I say, as I push my spine against the wood panel behind me and let my head fall back to meet it. Struggling against the onrushing thoughts and events that arrest me. Swooning as the world drifts in and out of focus.

Bark. Bark. Bark.

11

'Are you okay?
Doing it your own way.
You've got to listen to the sounds,
And turn your life around.'

Can't move.

If I do it'll blur the image and we don't want that, but I'm not good at lying still, it makes me uneasy. I'm gripped by the same thought I had the last time I was in here. I've heard that MRIs have been known to drag and shoot large pieces of equipment around the room, such is the force of the magnetism it creates. It happens. People have died from the blows caused by such projectiles so I'm not being dramatic. Look it up.

Thankfully, I can't have an MRI, as the bullet fragments in my head could heat up and cook my brain from the inside or even tear their way out of my skull and fly into the machine. The CT is supposed to be the softer option but I still feel horribly hemmed in as the 'O' runs its rule all over me.

I've always been claustrophobic, haunted by buried alive dreams, and having stillness enforced on me triggers the dose. The only way I can stop thinking about how stuck I am is by drifting away, listening to the music in my headphones, from an iPod Ryans handed me before stepping out of the room and leaving me stranded here. He's created a playlist called 'Soothe and Distract', and I try my best to let it do that to me.

'It's a shame, in the rain, here it comes again... .'

I try to ignore the whirrs. The clicks. And the nurse's words that 'It's just like being pushed through a large doughnut, people don't tend to feel claustrophobic at all, so don't worry', which only served to make me feel even worse; I was already feeling the tingle as she proceeded to stick me with the needle and push the contrast medium through my body, a liquid that heightens the definition of the scan, that I imagine as a tiny purple poison worming its way through the minuscule canals of my arteries.

The final insult as my chest tightens is that when Ryans' voice says 'we're going for one', I have to hold my breath for a full twenty seconds. Which I do as I close my eyes, and it moves.

Breath locked in, I consider the change that has come over me. Not just because of the attack with the six-inch blade, although that will certainly do it. I felt it before that. Like my body was telling me something was coming, had sensed it like the vibration along train lines. From the atmosphere to my bones. I try to control my moods through diet, mental stimulation and as much exercise as I can muster. But the darkness comes over me from time to time.

My breath shoots out as the conveyer belt stops and I chance a look up, and Ryans signals that he needs 'one more'. I take another deep draw, keeping my eyes open this time as it moves, and I try not to quake so we can get it over with.

The music plays.

'The sound of the river as it floats on by. And by and by...'

I stare down at my hand in this soft rock coffin. It quivers when I tell it to sleep. My face twitches and a thought takes hold. All the things I saw don't mean a thing.

The picture.

The dog.

The blacked out car.

The girl.

The lipstick on the window.

I listened to a book last night by an economic theorist. The amazing thing about humans, he says, is that we look at clouds and see faces. Everything a pattern, every mess a picture. Dot to dot to dot. But what we don't think is that sometimes the pattern goes: 3, 6, harpoon, hash tag. You're probably trying to work that one out now but don't bother. It's just the world throwing things around in a whirlwind. Shit doing what it does: happening. Like my brain in between coherent dreams whacking things together and seeing what comes loose. It signifies nothing. There is no meaning. It's all just random things.

I see them circled around my head and coloured. I can almost touch them. But I will never connect them. We are not connected. Us. People. We are separate and always will be, distant and misunderstood. They are scattered images that signify nothing. And I, in the middle of them, am alone and trapped and always will be. Forever.

Held at arm's length. From any truth. From any warmth. Trapped in this body. Trapped in this head. In this cell.

Forever.

Forever.

Forever.

My legs kick. I hear Ryans talking to me from outside. My headphones fall away from my ears. I can't hold on to the purpling air inside me anymore. I shout. He says something back over the sonic wash in my ears, my terrorised head conjuring harsh white noise from the deafening cacophony of medical silence.

'Aaah!' I hear myself call.

His soothing call comes back.

'One more please. Stay as still as you can!' he says.

But it does me no good as the belt moves me, and I picture being pushed towards cremation fires. My hands ball into fists and I punch and kick the ring as it comes past. The bullet feels hot in my head, and my body shudders like it's being pumped with thousands upon thousands of litres and chemicals and volts.

'Stop. Tom? Stop! We're done. It's done. It's finished. Tom?'

He leans over and puts his body on mine. I feel him. He holds my wrists calmly. He breathes into my shirt. I feel its warmth. I feel his forehead against my cheek.

'It's okay to be scared.'

'I'm not scared.'

'It's okay anyway.'

We stay there for a while, a strange sight, as my breathing returns to normal. Then he straightens himself out and beckons me to sit, as if nothing happened. Like all of that was of no more significance than a handshake. He stays close. Studying me without giving that impression. Putting his hand in between his legs to grab his chair and drag it further towards me.

'That's expensive equipment, you know,' he says, deadpan.

'I know. I'm... I mean I am... I mean, I'm... sorry.'

'You may feel like this. We all feel like this from time to time. But you may feel like this when you least expect it. Things are still settling. You're still figuring out how to be.'

I nod. His words hold me up and scold me all at once. They're a reminder that I'm still in rehabilitation. I expect too much of myself. He speaks with utter realism.

'Do you feel... different? You seem... different.'

'It will pass. At night. I've felt it before. In the night. It will pass.'

'Everyone wants the best for you, Tom. But I do worry this is all too much too soon.'

'It's not. I'm fine. It's been good for me.'

I steel myself against his kindness.

'No one wants to stop you living a normal life.'

'Good, I'd hope so.'

'But this attack. Is someone... after you? Did you... do something?'

Not that I can remember. I don't think it's anything like that.

'No. It's nothing like that,' I say, still rejecting the offer of his gaze.

'Look at it this way, I wouldn't let you play a fucking contact sport, why on earth shouldn't I do everything I can to prevent you playing tag with some bastard with a machete? I thought you said that PCSOs just walk down the high street saying hello to shop keepers?'

'Sometimes it goes a bit further than that.'

'Yes, I can see.'

'The way I do it anyway.'

'Yes, I can see!' he says, his voice strained with concern.

'But I'm going to live my life the way I want to live it. No matter what,' I say, quietly, mostly breath.

'You can't take another blow to the head, Tom!'

It goes quiet. The nurse, somewhere behind me, leaves the room.

We look at each other for the first time today. I've been told this before of course. Maybe that's why this time he's shouting it, to make sure it goes in. He goes on.

'You can't. Most of the time you probably feel okay, better than okay, but never forget that the contents of your head are extremely delicate. It's held together with science and chance, some luck and a lot of goodwill. It can't take being shaken around like a snow globe. It won't survive it. It will fall apart. I'm sorry, but it will. Look, Tom, I'm not going to sugar coat anything. All it will take is one firm blow.'

I'm calmer now. I don't know why. It doesn't suit what I've just been told.

'I see smells in colours, have I told you that?'

'Yes, that's not impossible. It's a type of...'

'Synaesthesia, I know. I looked it up.'

'Of course you did. I'll add it to the list. Mild aphasia. Prosopagnosia. Synaesthesia. Anything else?'

'Yes actually. I see patterns, in things. Like the other day I saw a picture, a child's drawing, I could see the individual strokes that made it with absolute clarity, the psychology behind it even. But I couldn't tell you what the picture was of, at all.'

'Silly question but do you find this hinders your work?'

'Possibly, but it helps me, too. I found the picture in a girl's bedroom. I think it's the key to finding her.'

'Right. What makes you think that?'

While I think, he writes scruffily on his pad.

I look down at the squiggles, but they mean nothing to me. He sees I'm looking but doesn't flinch or get self-conscious for a second. He looks up, waiting for an answer.

'It makes sense to me. It stood out. It didn't fit the pattern.'

'Of what?'

'Of the rest of her room. We were surrounded by attempts at adulthood, and there was this childish affectation. Then the picture told me the artist wasn't just young, but also had an incredibly low IQ.'

'I wouldn't rush to judgement on something like that –'

'I can tell –'

'We've been trying to discover what's going on inside the mind using external exercises for years. It's indistinct –'

'Not for me –'

'Look, we can tell little things from this work, but to profile a person purely from something they drew? Even for someone with significant problems, it'd be difficult to tell the difference between someone who's had an accident like yours, or a syndrome from birth, or had their mind warped by a cult or –'

'No, no, that's not it –'

'Or it's just a child's drawing.'

He smiles, takes a sip of water, adjusts the way he is sitting.

'Trouble is, Tom… it's possible that you see patterns that others don't see. But it's also possible that you may see patterns that aren't really there. Not in any usable sense. Your brain is working on another level entirely. Another level that perhaps has nothing to do with the realities of the flesh and bone world.'

I place my palms on my knees and centre myself. He's reciting my well-worn fears. But I push them away

'But –'

'Now, I don't work in law enforcement. You know, I've no experience of that. But knowing what I know I can only advise you that the stimulation of the thrill of discovery, will be setting off all sorts of things in your brain. You see things others don't, but maybe those things aren't always… things. It's only right that I tell you this. But I'm not… doubting you.'

'Well, you are a bit.'

'I'm saying know your limits.'

He takes out a torch and starts examining my face. Looking into my pupils from about ten centimetres away. Then holding open my left eye with his thumb and index finger and glaring the light source right into it.

'Do you think I could be dangerous to a police investigation?'

'I think you think very differently. I like difference. But I think it could go either way. If I were standing next to you? I have to be honest, I'd be wary of you. Always remember the importance of where you are and what's at stake. Above all else, remember that. I say that as a professional and as your friend, I hope.'

'So, then. Following the natural direction of… all that. Do you think it's possible I'd be better off without this job? And that it would be better off without me?'

'I didn't say that.'

'But you know it can be dangerous. And so can I.'

'I know those things now, yes.'

The light runs over to my right eye then he withdraws the torch and places it mechanically into his inside pocket.

I in turn push my hands into my pockets. I peruse the room for a second. It spits and cracks at me. The inside of my retina firing colours against the plain white medical equipment that has me surrounded.

'So, do you think I should quit?' I say. Honestly, without a challenge. I'm willing to take advice for once.

'I'm saying be careful, Tom. Be very careful.'

12

'Those pretty eyes that scream for more
Can drop you screaming through the floor.'

I hadn't formally met Inspectors Turan and Jarwar before. It's possible they were in some unnamed room earlier in the week but I was still getting my head together.

Jarwar is a cool-mannered, self-possessed woman who had been here before Christmas but our paths had crossed only briefly, I think. There are a lot of faces in the world, I can only catch the smallest few in my outstretched net as they gush past. Even those I wrestle into my clutches are a struggle to keep hold of, like trying to keep a butterfly between two cupped hands. But I'd heard the name and it stuck in my head.

Turan transferred from another borough this January. It's customary for PCSOs in the Safer Neighbourhoods team to have some contact with the inspectors from nearby wards, even if it's Levine that we report to, but this hadn't been the case so far for reasons Bartu couldn't explain to me. They were overworked, he guessed, had a relatively large area to cover, that had seen a lot of action recently, and both had kudos that made them sought after.

Jarwar for her part seemed pretty personable as she sandwiched an introduction in between talking to Levine about checking in with Jade's parents at 42 Park Drive. The second girl. The girl with the dog and the car. I sat frozen next to Jarwar, and an increasingly softly spoken Levine, prying with my outsider's ears, but could only glean that she was going over there later in her shift. Levine's wary of me and doesn't tend to speak so freely when I'm around. This doesn't seem to me to be highly professional, but I don't mind, I don't tell him everything I'm up to either.

Turan seems like an altogether rawer character. He's not plain-clothes, that's the privilege of the swaggering CID, but he uses his personality and connections to diminish the effect of his badge, integrating himself within the community, trying to limit drug crimes and gang violence. If Jarwar is a classic 'toe-the-line' insider, then Turan barely feels like he works for the force at all, and Bartu for one is wary of that. We share these moments now. These honesties that signify our growing trust. You wouldn't think upon shaking his firm hand he'd have a bad word to say about anyone, but he seems to be implying something about Turan that I'm just not catching. It's odd, because Turan's Turkish, too. Not that that means anything. It's a multicultural world, we're all free to dislike whoever we please. He's similar in build to Bartu, maybe a fraction more imposing, but I noted a warmth that he projects with his whole body. He disarms people. It's a skill he's mastered. You can feel him meeting you on your level and adapting himself, and I for one appreciate it. It's certainly a technique that's way out of my wheelhouse.

They definitely seemed to know who I was, so maybe I just enjoy the notoriety, but I liked them both a lot. I'm certainly planning to stay on their good sides. We might need them later.

*

We wait, my knuckles fresh from rapping on the door of 42 Park Drive, not knowing if anyone will be home. We didn't call ahead. We just want to get there before Jarwar does, make as little fuss as possible and even less of an impression. I like the look of Jarwar, she's long-limbed and steely, which tells me she'd be useful in a scuffle and that she probably used to run for her county. She also seems appealingly sexless, possessing elements of both genders in a manner I find quite absorbing. I have friend ambitions towards her but resolve to keep those designs for a later date. We're in much deeper than we should be and don't want to bump into her at the deep end.

The door flings fully open and smacks against the wall. In a towelling dressing gown stands a short, pear-shaped man holding a mug of tea. He is red faced. He looks like he's been up for days. He says nothing but stands aside for us to come in.

'I thought you weren't coming until later?' he mumbles, inside.

I'm not sure whether this is a reprimand or an apology for his appearance, but I decide to ignore it and let Bartu field that one.

'Inspector Jarwar will be along in a while but we wanted to check one thing first.'

'And who the fuck are you then?' he says.

It's not as hostile as it sounds, but it's not far off. And it's a question we were hoping in vain might not come up, the idea having been to get in and get out without too much explanation. The mother of the family enters and I decide to take over.

'We're community support officers. Come to offer our support.'

'You're what?' he says. I'm not sure if he's being slow on the uptake or if it's meant to be not-so-passive aggressive. I decide it's the former and repeat myself much louder and with utter clarity.

'Sir. We. Are. Community. Support. Officers,' I say. There's nothing stealth-like about this exchange.

'Is he all right?' Mr Bridges says, specifically to Bartu, pointing at me and then tapping his own head.

'Yes. He... he is. We want to check one thing,' says Emre Bartu.

'Nah, we don't want your lot. The bloody part-timers,' he says.

'And why's that, sir?' says Bartu. Indulging with intent to defuse with good humour, just as our training officer taught us to.

'I don't even agree with your jobs existing. I'm paying for your fancy dress costumes with my bloody taxes,' he says. Shooting a look to his wife who says nothing. He's throwing his weight around but I get the feeling she's the one who's in charge.

'Be that as it may, sir, we're here, and we're here to help find your daughter,' says Bartu.

'With what? Your whistle and the little badge you got off the weekend course?' he shouts.

'The training course is a full eight weeks long, sir. The whole process is quite a hassle if you really want to know,' I say, articulating clearly for him, so he understands.

'Who the fuck is he? Is he all right? What's his malfunction?' he says, deciding to aim everything at Bartu, as if he's my carer.

As I'm being left out of the conversation my attention wanders. Clothes lie lazily shambled against skirting boards. The wallpaper has the occasional unexpected dark mark that makes its pattern more unpredictable, which I soon identify as cigarette burns. There is the odd carpet tile missing with only glue left in its place, causing a kind of ripping sound from my shoe whenever I happen to stand in it for too long.

'We do understand you're upset, but –' Bartu says.

108

'But fucking what?' he says.

'We. Just. Want. To. Check. One. Thing,' I say.

'I tell you what, I'm going to fucking lamp him in a minute!'

'What do you need?' says Mrs Bridges.

Mr Bridges is at last subdued.

'We need to see Jade's bedroom.'

Mrs Bridges leads the way and luckily her husband stays below. I'd say that's what grief and worry does to people, but maybe he's just like that. A bit of an arsehole I mean.

I don't waste any time. Forcefully, but with some cursory care for the lady of the house, we shake down the room. She stays leaning on the doorframe, scared to enter as if we are working with chemicals and hi-tech equipment rather than our ham fists.

Upstairs is tidier than what lay beneath. It looks like Jade enforced more order in her quarters.

The options fill my mind. I picture the three possible Jades. They surround my head at fifteen-degree intervals.

The good girl. Keen to obey.

The meticulous one. Tidy by her own volition.

The planner, intent on her parents suspecting nothing before her getaway.

Then these possible girls stare out at me from a cork board photo collage she seems to have made. Printouts from phone photos, I'd imagine, but it's nice to see hard copy all the same. She stares wanly, like a ghost of herself, captured, cut out and framed. A picture of her at twelve-years old, wearing make up for the first time, I'd say, smiles proudly as I consider what sort of girl she grew up into.

The versions haunt me as I search through her cupboards.

Rock band T-shirts, board games and spare bed sheets.

I rise to fumble behind duvet covers, looking for the holy grail.

Emre does the same on his side of the room. In the most likely place, the chest of drawers, the place where girls keep secret things.

'What is it you're looking for?' she says.

I look back to Bartu and then continue. We shouldn't release that kind of information. But then we're not doing anything how it should be done.

'A diary? Anything like that, which might help us with her whereabouts,' Bartu says with a bit of savvy.

He rifles through jumpers and tops, skirts and winter tights, hoping to feel cool Polaroid. This time, we won't make the same mistake. This time, we will take one or two for ourselves so we have something of our own. Bartu has a link at the lab so, despite my protestations that they're not the most interesting thing we've found, we can check in with them and see what secrets the photos hold, if any. If we can even find another set, that is. If we're right about the nature of the link.

Anderson and Stevens. Jarwar and Turan. They're all fine, but we need to make sure things are done properly. What Mr Bridges and us have in common is a slight mistrust of local police. So we're going to do an audit, then make some assumptions of our own.

Then, beneath the bed, under the valance, I see a drawer ajar.

'You done yet?' she says.

'Very soon,' I say, eyeing Bartu and dropping to the floor.

Bartu comes to join me as I struggle with the other drawer next to it. It's stuck but we pull hard and it comes open.

Pillows, a chemistry set, clay model-making materials.

The woman above. The child below.

But there are no photos to be seen. As Bartu gets up wearily to make his apologies, I grab something from the drawer, stuff it into my pocket and follow him.

Downstairs Mr Bridges has continued to wind himself up.

He stands in his living room, barring our way, now apparently keen to stop us from leaving rather than get us out.

'You cracked the case have you? Cagney and Lacey?' he says.

We have to get out of here. We've stayed too long.

'Mr Bridges, thank you for your time today, please know that this was useful for us in light of the details surrounding the other missing girl in the area,' Bartu says. Almost catching himself as he sees Mrs Bridges' face fall into shock.

'What other girl? No one's mentioned another girl?' she says.

Bartu makes a move to try and get past Mr Bridges as she speaks, but he moves to the side, too, pinning us in the hallway.

'No one's told us this. What the fuck is going on?' he says.

It's then I see Jarwar through the front window. I tug gently at Bartu, drawing him away from Mr Bridges and out of the light, while taking over the talking duties.

'Mr Bridges, that was what we came here to tell you. While no one wanted to alarm you, we personally felt you should know. That's on us. So forgive us if you would've rather been kept in the dark.'

I peer out and see Jarwar almost at the door.

'No,' she says. 'We appreciate being told. No one has told us a thing. Not really.'

'Well, may I ask that you don't mention this to the inspector, as and when she arrives? This might seem irregular, but we trod on a few toes to bring you that information. In fact, it's probably best you don't mention that we were here at all. Can I trust you to do that?'

I home in on Mr Bridges. I fix him like a fly on a drawing pin. He pauses, lost in this revelation and I sympathise. I guess things just got a little more serious in his world, maybe more serious than they've ever been and I of all people understand that feeling.

By the way, after the lighter in the car and letting me speak during assembly time, this was Bartu's third mistake. Not that I'm keeping count.

'Yes, you can trust us,' Mrs Bridges says.

'Good. Now can we trouble you to use your back door?'

We hurry through the garden, out of a bare wooden gate next to their shed and fall out into a back street. Mr Bridges, looking on as if we are a clump of hair being expelled from his U-bend, turns and moves into his living room and I imagine it's the doorbell that takes him there.

On a red brick wall facing us, I notice a small light blue symbol, delicately spray painted. As my eyes run along the wall, I see others subtly placed directly outside neighbouring gates. Some symbols repeat themselves as I analyse them in a small second. But no symbol is the same as the Bridges'. A circle (0) with two diagonal lines (//) through it. They could have been put there by workmen. Something to do with pipes that lie under the pavement. That's what people would think, most people, who tend to explain away anomalies. And they could be right. Could be that. Could be nothing.

Bartu breathes in hard as the gate slams behind us.

And when I unfold the childish drawing of a house next to a playground, on cream A5 paper, which I found in the drawer under the bed, he breathes out hard, too.

13

' Tell me little one,
Tell me you're the one for me, Shoo, sha boo, my coochie coo,
Come and set me free.'

We need to hurry. School lets out at 3.15; I'd almost forgot that was how it worked. Feels like these kids are missing another third of the day in which they could be getting things done; learning, figuring out who they are and what they're good at. The same things I'm trying to do.

The sound of my left foot dragging along the ground sprays the street. Emre Bartu struggles to keep up, scanning the picture as he goes, then rolling it up like a teenage poster and putting an elastic band around it as I turn to scc why hc's lagging behind. He places it carefully into his standard issue document holder. He doesn't want it creased.

'It's identical. Right?' I say, when he appears beside me.

'Not quite. It's the same scene, but the colours are different.'

'Yes, but forget the colours! Other than the colours, it's identical?' I say, eyes to the distance.

'Well… also the whole thing seems shifted to the right a little.'

We're mute for a second, except for the scrape-scrape of my foot on tarmac, as I consider this.

'By how much?'

'A metre maybe,' he says, making a scrunch-faced estimate.

'Good. So they're drawing something specific.'

'Yeah. And they're looking at it from slightly different angles. Do you think they're being made to draw it?'

'I don't know. I don't care really,' I murmur.

'Right. Why's that?'

'Because I'm more interested in the colours.'

He stops. I'd been leading him a merry dance, he only realises it now. Verbally and physically. We're halfway there already without him asking a single question. His hand goes to his radio.

'So... where we going now?' says Emre Bartu.

'Are you going to check in?' I say.

'Yeah. What's wrong with that?'

I pause while my brain clicks into gear. It can be a long process. Sometimes it's like you have to turn the thing off and on again and wait for all the programs to start, like a PC circa 1995. I hear my heartbeat in my ears, my middle finger tapping against my leg.

'I don't think you should,' I say.

'Why?'

'Why this new eagerness to conform?'

'Best to be honest when we can.'

I scan his face. I wish I could read it. But I'm not there yet. Perhaps he's going soft, perhaps he's scared, or perhaps he's been feeding back to them all this time. Yes, that's what I think. I've essentially been assigned to his care, after all.

'Look, as well as the smell thing, and my trouble with faces, I can only focus on the small things. I can see the whole but it takes effort, conscious refocusing, like I'm looking at a Magic Eye picture. It means I can tell you something interesting about the drawing you wouldn't have seen though. But if I tell you, you can't check in.'

He wavers, gripping the radio tight then putting his head against it.

'It's always easier to tell the truth,' he says.

'That's a fallacy. And an overrated one at that,' say I.

Maybe this is all a difference in approach, in philosophy, but I'm suspicious about his motives now.

'Okay. What's interesting about the picture?'

'First, promise not to call it in, promise never to do that unless I say so.'

'Okay, fine.'

'Let me hear it.'

'Oh come on.'

He rubs his hands together, more a shadow move than a gesture in respect of the cold. Shadow moves are meaningless physical gestures that serve to display inner conflict, discomfort or the possibility of untruths. Always look out for shadow moves.

'Put your hand on your heart and swear on your girlfriend's life.'

'You realise we're adults. And police officers.'

'Everyone needs to keep their promises. Especially police officers. Anyway, we're civilian support staff. We improvise. So, double swear promise, with no going backsies.'

He mouths an expletive, unzips his standard issue vest and awkwardly lifts up his operational shirt. I can see his stomach. He's in decent shape to be fair. He puts two fingers to his chest and shouts.

'I double swear promise. On my girlfriend's life!'

'With?'

'With no going backsies!' he rasps.

'Cool. Let's go.'

I turn to see a kid on a skateboard has been watching us. I nod. We walk on, Bartu slightly behind, the shame not even starting to wear off.

'So what's the interesting thing you found, with your mind?'

'Tell you later.'

'But you said you'd tell me. I promised!'

'I didn't make any promises. You did. And even if I did, the truth is an overrated fallacy.'

He must know where we're going. The path leads all the way there. He's just reticent to accept the inevitable.

'You're an arsehole mate,' he mutters, uncharacteristically.

'Maybe. But don't get uptight. I'll tell you soon enough.'

'When?'

'When we've consulted the expert. After we've spoken to the kid.'

'What kid?'

'Asif Akhtar.'

'Fucking hell, Tom. Over my dead body. We don't have the right,' he shouts as we walk along. A couple of old folks raise their eyebrows as they see uniformed men locked in heated sweary debate. Bartu clocks this and his shame swells some more.

'We're not going back to the school!' he whispers.

'Oh come on. We both know that's not true,' I say with a smile.

He falls into a hush as we go, staying half a step behind me, my leg dragging on the ground, making the sound of a 'shh' as it goes.

*

I sign us both in at front desk and smile at the gentleman receptionist behind the glass. Bartu stands upright, avoiding eye contact with everyone. Luckily, we're seen as fairly odd anyway. But we also have high-vis body armour, utility belts and airwave terminal radios, epaulettes and matching hats, which seem to keep the questions to a minimum.

I hand Emre Bartu a visitor's badge and he grabs it without bothering to look, as if even the plastic and the safety pin has betrayed him and must actively be sulked at. It's always unedifying to see an adult in a 'moody'. I take no notice and power on. Otherwise he'd be starting to get me down.

'Could you tell me what class Asif Akhtar is in again? I think it was err... ' I say. As if this was a scheduled meeting. An after dinner date.

'Yep,' the man says, scanning down a computer screen. He is thirty, balding, black NHS specs but in a hip, ironic way. He seems only half here, too, a husk waiting for three-fifteen so he can kick off home and work on his Electro-Folk album. Not for the first time since 'the incident' I feel like I'm the only one in the vicinity who's really alive.

We should be escorted by a member of staff, but as I'm guessing this guy is new and doesn't listen to instructions, I decide to plough through and see if I can dodge the attentions of an escort.

'Maths. So that would be in... M420. Maths block is that way.'

He points a lazy finger in the direction of the doors through which we came, waggling it vaguely to the left, evidently keen to expend as little energy as possible on our directions, like Edmund Hillary conserving his strength for the way down. Then his eyes flick back to his computer, clicking the mouse officiously to signal he must return to important educational business. I catch the reflection of his screen in the glass behind him and see he's on some website trying to buy a hat stand.

My eyes only glimpsed his screen for the merest moment but the image seemed to lodge in my head like a jpeg. It's a feeling I've never quite experienced before, photographic recall. Like one side of my brain was taking a polaroid and the other side was shaking it around until the picture became clear. It's a thrill when it pulls tricks of its own accord. My palm pushes the metal panel on the lime green door and we vacate the reception hall just before a crowd of assorted brown suits and grey uniforms, all armed with their own prying eyes, hustles around a corner.

'Have you got a hunch about this kid or are you just checking in?' says Bartu.

'A bit of both,' I say, cold wind ruffling my hair.

He snorts and looks the other way. I'm punishing him. We're two lovers torturing each other for not showing enough affection exactly when and how we want it. As we head into the worn, maroon-carpeted interior of the maths block, I unbutton his document holder. It's attached to his belt and he finds that a bit too intimate.

'I'm not going to touch your penis.'

'Yeah, I'd hope not,' he responds immediately.

His frown lingers on as we reach M420.

At the wire netted glass of the classroom door we stop, wondering how to interrupt, our heads poking into view like a pair of meerkats.

The teacher's attention is drawn to us when he notices not a single one of his pupils has their eyes on the board anymore. They stare at us like soulless clones. A solid ripple of intrigue settles on them, not gossip, nothing salacious. These are maths kids. They try to work out the problem of us.

Bartu pokes his head in the door as inoffensively as a man in uniform can.

'Little word with Asif please,' he whispers, a tortoise with the rest of the world as his shell. The teacher holds out a hand that says 'be my guest' and 'if you must' all at once. A gangly kid stands and the room hums with silent assumptions.

'When was the last time you saw Tanya Fraser?' I say, cutting to the chase in the sterile hallway.

'Err. Like. *Saw her* saw her?' he says.

'Just saw her. With your eyes.' It sounds more condescending than I mean it to.

'Err. Reckon I saw her in the dinner hall. Day before she went missing,' Asif says.

'How do you know which day she went missing?' I say.

'Err. You told us. You told her whole year, they told everyone else. "Limping police guy". That's you, right?'

Bartu withholds a laugh but I don't think it's funny. I think it's commendably accurate. I focus on clear visual stimuli, too.

'Yes. Exactly. How did you decide that's when she went missing? I didn't give anyone that.'

'Two days before you came in, that's when her class said she'd been away from, so that's what we all reckoned. That was the word.'

Crowd sourced intelligence. Very good. Kids are smart. Occasionally they're smart, I mean; let's not go overboard. But they're smart occasionally because they talk. They can arrive at some useful things using social cross-referencing, but it means their stories are all similar. They know what 'the word' on the whatever is, then they draw their opinions using that as their pool.

'Okay. And are you still... close?' Bartu says. Intrigued enough to throw his oar in.

'Nah. Say hello and stuff. But that's about it. She's nice, but I don't know her anymore, not really.'

He's an interesting kid. And he's good with adults. I hope he hasn't done anything stupid.

'You knew her a year ago,' Bartu says, beating me to the punch.

'Yeah. Funny, innit? Things change fast around here,' he says.

'Great. That's all we need. Thanks,' I turn to leave.

Bartu, leaning against the wall, throws out a stunned 'Err... '

'You sure that's all?' Asif says, amiable, accommodating.

I look to Bartu. He shrugs.

We could ask about their relationship.

We could ask about residual anger on both sides.

We could ask if she got in with the wrong crowd.

If there was anyone in school that seemed to have a thing for her.

Or anyone that didn't like her or seemed just a little offbeat. But...

These questions will have been asked before, recorded by officers with more qualifications and on a better hourly rate. We don't do the obvious stuff. That's not our niche. And you've got to have a niche. I make to go again and so does Bartu, then I grab at his document holder and turn back to the kid suddenly.

'Have you seen this before?' I say.

I hold the picture out for him. Bartu pulls my hand back so the picture is a more acceptable distance from his face, and turns it around. I had it upside down.

'Nah. No, I ain't. Sorry.'

'Where would you say it came from?' I say.

Bartu raises his eyebrows internally but this is crowd-sourced intelligence. There's nothing wrong with that. It's just an opinion from someone far more up on school matters than I.

'Err. Art class. Year 7?'

'Year 7, huh? Good. That's good,' I say.

'Why d'ya say that Asif?' Bartu says.

'Colours are kinda stupid. Purple grass. Yellow sky.'

'Are they? Oh right,' I say.

I saw the colours were wild but I didn't exactly know what they depicted. Purple grass. Yellow sky. Hmm...

He's an accidental Georges Braque, the experimental Frenchman with a will to make his world look a lot more Technicolor. Colours express emotions. Fauvism it's called. But for the Fauvists it was a style; for our artist, it could be the only way they can see the world.

I turn and leave. Asif says a 'Bye' somewhere behind us.

'You don't think we should ask him anything else?' Bartu says as we leave the building.

'Why? He either did it or he didn't. Right?' I say.

'Yes. That's the point, isn't it?'

'I suppose. You think he did it?'

'No idea. We didn't ask. You?'

'Me, personally?'

'Yes, you personally. We risk wandering around here without a chaperone and you barely asked him anything!'

'I didn't need to ask him anything. I needed to smell him.'

His hand goes to his face and I can tell this bit is going to feature pretty heavily in his evening account of the day to his girlfriend.

'Of course, you needed to smell him. Any conclusions?'

'Yes.'

'Care to enlighten me?'

'No. Not yet.'

He smiles. He likes me. He's back. I can tell. I just know.

'Can you at least tell me the other thing now? What the picture told you earlier? Since I made my promise.'

'Yes. Okay,' I say, drawing breath.

It's only fair I suppose, but I let it hang in the air just for a few moments longer because I enjoy these bits. Me knowing, others not knowing. They're a pleasure not often explored.

'Come on,' he says, as I notice the vein in his forehead.

'It wasn't done by a classically functioning brain. Whoever did these pictures, both of them, doesn't think like us. Doesn't think like you, I mean.'

'Okay. Okay, that's good. And where are we going now, may I ask?'

'We're going to see our expert.'

14

'Can't. Get that dah dee dah, dah dah, dee dah…'

Miss Heywood didn't look too disappointed to be called out of class. Her denim dungarees, flecked with paint, seemed to indicate that she's a working artist and will soon be back in the studio. But her world-weary nature tells me she's been stuck here for far too long and her chances of release are slim to hopeless. The tightness with which her hair is held back etches a portrait of personal strain. And a subtle emerald aroma tells me she'd be a more than adequate drinking partner. Whiskey perhaps. And smoke scent that I think is Gauloises, the cigarette of choice for the avant-garde romantic. Her class, well accustomed to fending for themselves I'd say, drew and sculpted beyond the classroom door.

'Does this… in your professional opinion… look like a drawing that could have been done under duress?' I say.

And the penny drops for Bartu. This was another finding. I can picture how they were performed, with a man at their side, watching on, maybe holding them by the back of the neck. Cutting them a bit perhaps. Their hands tense, their pencils shooting across the page, almost digging in and ripping at the paper. These children chosen because they are different, they are special. They think differently, like me. This is the picture I see. Of them, in there, with him.

'Duress? Hmm. In what sense? If we're talking about year seven, most of their drawing is done under duress,' she says, resting her elbow on the flat of her other hand and gently stroking the space between neck and chin with the back of her fingers.

'Why do you say year seven?' Bartu says.

'That's as young as we go.'

'Could this have been done by someone younger?' I say.

'Certainly. If you want my opinion... '

'I do,' I say, butting in.

'... Yes, then let me finish. If we were talking about the age of the kid that did this... '

'We are.' Maybe I did that one just to annoy her, maybe I'm excited that we're onto something, maybe I'm flirting, I don't know.

'... I'd say younger even in terms of ability, but then some of these kids here are well below where you'd expect them to be.'

She turns and regards her students hacking away at their paper and clay. She bites her knuckle then continues. It's not a shadow move, it has a purpose. She's biting down to hurt herself just a bit. Then she says:

'We're not high on artistic ability. But even we're a bit above this. I'd guess it was done by an enthusiastic late first-schooler, or a very bad year seven or eight, in terms of ability.'

'Any idea if that sounds like Jade Bridges?'

'None. Don't have much contact with her. She doesn't take art.'

'So that's maybe a maybe?' I say.

'Perhaps,' she says

Bartu, over my shoulder, feels we're close to something.

'And the question of duress?' he says, searchingly.

123

'I wouldn't say so. Long lines, hard on the paper... '

'The colours clashing as they meet.' My special area of interest, how ferociously they hit each other, how little they blend.

'Exactly. It's like they enjoy the work even if they have no talent for it.' She hits my rhythm.

'And the eccentric choice of colour scheme?'

'Not a choice at all I'd say. They're just doing it.'

'Their bodies, tense,' I say, leading the witness.

'No, more in freedom than in pain, it's a release.'

The picture changes in my mind. They don't do it during, only after it's all happened. Whatever 'it' is. They draw with relief, in the aftermath.

It's just what I see. It's just a picture. It's just a hunch.

Miss Heywood is roused. This is as much excitement as she's had all term, but Bartu destroys the mood with necessary reality.

'And what about Tanya Fraser? Could she have done this?'

The logical next question.

'Absolutely not,' she says as she presses her back into the classroom door, closing it fully before continuing in hushed tones.

'I know she's missing. Is this her picture?' she mutters.

'We can't say,' Bartu says.

'But perhaps I can help,' she says.

'You already have,' I say.

'Did you find this? Is it related to her?' she says, coming away from the door.

'We really can't say,' Bartu says.

'Yes,' I say.

'Tom... ' he says.

'She's an artist, one of the only good ones here. She's interested. Not the best eye but a good hand, the opposite of this,' she says, staring at the scar on my head. In her mind she lifts a hand to touch it.

'I didn't notice the strange colours. At first,' I say.

'Well. They say a lot,' she says, enjoying the drama currently filling up her world, but mixing it with a decent dose of concern.

Bartu rubs his face. He's a third wheel at this point.

'Is there any possibility that whoever drew this... is colour blind?' I say.

'Every possibility.'

'Good. Interesting. I'm not so good with pictures, by the way.'

'What? The colours?'

'Not so much colours, shapes.'

'Then maybe you should see Miss Shelley.'

'And who's that?'

'Special needs.'

Bartu sniggers. I'm not sure if she meant that to be funny or not.

'If that's what you think, then I will.'

I hand her my card and she points us in the right direction.

'Did you have any student contact with Jade Bridges at all?'

We're in Miss Shelley's domain. Her classroom, her rules, but a kingdom she rules with a feather touch. The kids are all here, five or six of them sat attentively around a table. They barely look up. Miss Shelley doesn't mind speaking in front of them.

'No. We're a small department, underfunded, so we'd know.'

She holds one of the students by their shoulder as we talk. She's a half friend, half authority figure. She's warm, copper-haired and bright.

'Would you know if a student in school was colour blind?'

'If they knew I'd know,' she responds breezily.

I review this statement.

'Was that light humour or a real answer? I'm not good with humour, light or heavy.'

She stands and walks over to grab some printed sheets, then

disperses them to the students as we talk. She smiles. She's comfortable. She makes me feel comfortable.

'No. No joke. People don't always know they're colour-blind. It's difficult to ascertain what you should be seeing, when you've only got one pair of eyes, one brain, to last you a lifetime.'

Well, yes and no, I think. But she's right in the main. I let it go.

Bartu puts the picture on the table. The students lean in and stare. A need to know has taken over, our confidentiality is either waning or completely suspended, we rely on the fact that no one knows what they're looking at, if we're relying on anything at all.

'I don't think the colours are a choice. Not only would I call that severe, but I'll tell you something else, if you don't mind speculation.'

'Not at all, it's virtually all we have,' I say.

Emre takes a seat on a desk. We're much too big for this classroom, but here we are, back to school. He takes out his notebook and grabs one of those large green easy-grip pencils from the pot next to him – I'm always stealing his pen – and now he really does look like a kid.

'Please. Indulge us,' he says.

'My guess is this person. The girl? Not only does she not know she's colour blind, but she wasn't always colour blind. Something may have occurred recently to make her that way. I mean, this is so oblique you can barely tell what it is.'

'So. You're saying... they're utterly, obtrusively colour blind... without even knowing it?' I say, noticing that Bartu's brow is as firmly furrowed as mine is.

'I taught a kid at a previous school who'd got hit by a bus while out on his bike. He got a hell of a hit on the head but he survived. His only lasting problem was that the world looked different to him afterwards.'

'So... ' Bartu says. Starting to write and then stopping.

'So, he drew like this girl seems to. The colours of the world got so drained that trying to replicate them was guess work for him, but even he wasn't as bad as this. I started reading up, talking to other teachers and a couple of them said some fascinating things. One of them being... there is a way that the brain stops seeing colour without even telling you it's happening. You think you understand colour but actually you don't. You think you're picking up the same old blue pencil to draw the sky, but in fact you're not. '

We pause to take this in.

'That's my assumption. I'd say that's what whoever created this picture has. The brain can be a strange thing.'

'I know,' I say.

'I know,' says Bartu, more than glancing in my direction.

'I even heard about a man that thought he could see but was actually blind. It's all about what your brain is telling you is happening. And it can be a false friend.'

I'd like to disagree with this but it would be churlish. She holds up the picture and stands. I think this is our cue to leave. We find ourselves taking it back and walking towards the door without even knowing we're doing it. Miss Shelley has a strange power over us.

At the door to the special needs and music block she says one more thing.

'Again, this is just a theory; your guess is as good as mine.'

'My guess is probably even better to be honest,' I say.

They stare at me and I laugh but neither joins in and I infer that the nuances of humour are still eluding me. I opt to let my laugh change to a sober nod and act like it never happened.

'Thank you, Miss Shelley, you are a very engaging woman and I'd like you to have my phone number,' I say.

*

We mull it over in our heads on the way back to the station, possibly because we don't want to affect each other's assumptions yet. We want to find our own conclusions and come together when we've got something. But it's also possible we're already a bit sick of each other at this point.

'If Jade did both those drawings, did she give one to Tanya?' Emre says.

'We don't know if they were even friends.'

'We could ask around. Maybe call in on Ms Fraser?'

He's pushing it on. I like that, it's good to know he's as determined as I am again. It's sweet. But he needn't bother.

'Emre, it really doesn't matter,' I say.

'And why's that?'

The snow starts to come down. It drifts onto us heavy and fast. By the time I finish telling him what I have to say next it will be crunching under our feet.

'I think you're nearly there,' I say.

'I'm not so sure,' he says.

'Come on. It's good for your cognitive reasoning. Guesses? Then I'll tell you.'

'Because... we can't go back to the Fraser house anyway?'

'No, I wouldn't say that.'

'Because Jarwar should be close to cracking it by now?'

'I certainly wouldn't say that.'

Some would say the sky is black at this point, but I wouldn't. I'd say it's blue, a very dark blue, but blue all the same. Specifics are important. The moon and streetlights light our way to the station, which is only twenty or so metres away.

'Come on then.'

'Don't worry. I told you I'd tell you.'

'Well, come on.'

Tick tick tick. Feel it. Anticipation. Power.

We're nearly at the entrance. I take a few more steps. Then place my hand on the door.

'Do you know why Buddhist Monks chant "Om"?'

'Err… I think it's –'

'Because they believe that was the sound of the beginning of creation. By keeping that vibration going they are strengthening the walls of reality. I've been thinking that the picture is a kind of mantra, that helps their captor establish a new reality through repetition, brainwashing them.'

'Okay, that's interesting—'

'But forget that. Because now I'm not thinking that. Because I've realised they didn't draw them, he did.'

I go inside. I hear him. His last attempt at a question gets stuck in his mouth, just the sound of air with a vibration somewhere secret within it. 'Who?' It sounded like. But I couldn't be sure. Too late, he didn't spit it out in time. He'll have to wait because we must be quiet here.

'Who? Who?' say his thoughts. As we walk through the Control Room.

We nod to the passing faces and stride toward the locker room.

'Well. Exactly,' say my own.

15

'Horror in the Walker house
Screaming, moaning in the hall
The girl in the polka blouse
Is bleeding through the wall'

She's there. Doing lines on a black board. Grey skirt. White shirt. Black tights. Yellow and black tie. It is 4.30pm. I see it on the big white clock through the glass into her classroom.

I stare at her from a distance. I've been at after school football practice. I try the handle. It's locked. She keeps writing. I am naked. I turn back to see a trail of water across the long hallway along which I've walked. I'm still dripping. I hear it pitter-patter on the cream green plastic floor. Chunks of it are ripped off, craters of black show underneath. There's someone behind me.

I spin back to her. The handle doesn't turn. I bang on the window. I need to warn her. But she doesn't hear. I bang harder. I try to turn the handle. It won't move. She writes and writes. I turn around. He runs. In slow motion. The blonde man. His tie flies about his neck. I hit the glass harder. It breaks. Behind it, more glass, another layer. I bang and yell and punch the door. My hand is bleeding. I stare down at it and watch it drip onto the floor with a pitter-patter.

The second wall of glass breaks and I push the bulbous flesh of my hand through it and the nerves beneath feel the air of her classroom. I see her blonde hair hanging over her eyes. I shout. She hears nothing. I gush with blood. It pools like a little ocean at my feet. I make a fist and see to the white of the bone. I kick the handle. The door falls open. As she looks up.

I glance over my shoulder. Behind me. And he's right there. I don't see her face.

*

I've got to stop telling you these, other people's dreams are a bore and I'm not trying to bore you. That's the last thing I'm trying to do.

When I wake, I instinctively reach for my pad and without thinking I write: S A R A H.

*

It's an evening shift so we have to catch them before they close up for the night. The surgery shuts at 5.30pm. We meet at four. Locker room. Then debrief room. We disperse our daily lies, the beats we walked, the minor queries, the people we saw. It's not immoral; if anyone needs us they can get us on our radio. For now, we're needed here.

We get there by 5pm and greet the receptionist with little ado.

'Hi there, how are you?' Bartu says.

'Yes all good. Are you –' she says.

'Great. We're going to need a list of everyone in the local area who has been the recipient of a head trauma in the last two years. Anything from a stroke to a car crash, an industrial accident to a minor sports injury please,' I say, firing it at her all at once.

She takes a look at both of us, sees she needn't ask any more questions. We wear our authority. These aren't fancy dress costumes, no matter what Mr Bridges might tell you.

She takes a pen out of her shirt pocket and clicks it while she waits for her computer to load the correct page. Then she fiddles with the fields, presumably, seemingly struggling to bring up the information. I look to Bartu and he does the same to me, casually, like there's nothing riding on this. I don't know how long this list will be but it's a start. All this assumes our man is a local, of course, but the fact that we've lost more than one girl tells me this guy wasn't just passing through.

'Right. Here we are. Should I print it out or... '

'A printout is fine,' I say.

This is working out better than I thought. Another receptionist appears. Older. Similarly dressed but glasses half an inch thicker and on a chain. She pulls the younger receptionist aside and has a word, looks swiftly through us and then exits out the back again.

'Okay. We actually need to see some paperwork before we action that printout,' she says, her enthusiasm to help the nice men clearly amended by her superior.

'Absolutely. That's fine, we can do that, we can definitely do that,' I say, looking to Bartu, who nods unconvincingly.

Then nothing. She waits.

'Perhaps you want to give them a call? Get some paperwork sent over?' she says.

'Yes. We could definitely do that,' I say.

Another silence.

We definitely can't. We're not even supposed to be here.

'Yes, of course, yeah, I'll radio it right in,' I say.

I turn while Emre smiles and makes bad small talk. I walk away from them until I'm facing the door through which we came. I pretend to say a few things into the radio.

'Oh hi. Control? We're going to need that paperwork sent over. Over.'

Emre does a review of the weather. Asks if they've been 'busy recently.'

'Great. That's good. Then send that over. Have a good day. Over.'

I turn back to Emre as he brings up the prevalence of heavy falls by old people during wintery conditions.

'Yeah. Paperwork. On its way,' I say.

She smiles, turns and taps away at the screen. Then looks up again.

'I can wait,' she says.

We do for all of five seconds before I agitatedly tap my fist on the counter a couple of times to suggest some unsaid time constraint.

'I wondered whether you could do me a favour actually,' I mutter, leaning in.

Then she leans in, too, and talks in whispers.

'Yes? What would that be?' she says.

I look just past her, to the glass behind her. The layout of the reception is similar to the one in the school.

'We're going to get called away now. Just got a message about... an old lady... who's fallen down,' I whisper back.

I look past her. I look to the glass.

'Okay? Have they called an ambulance?' she says, keeping her voice down still.

'No, no. She'll be fine. But she's... a fragile character. We'd like to... check in on her. She relies on us... you know?'

I turn to Emre, bringing him into this. He leans in. He smiles a Good Samaritan smile.

'I wondered whether we could get the printout now? And bring over the letter after? Can we do that... maybe... Tracey?' I say. Looking at her name badge.

She hesitates. I look past her still, unable to lock eyes while I do this.

'No, I'm sorry, we'll have to see the paperwork first. And my name's Stacey,' she whispers.

'Okay, that's fine. We'll be in touch,' I say, striding swiftly out of the building.

Emre catches me up as we get around the corner.

'Well, that went well,' he says.

'Give me a pen,' I say.

'You're always stealing my pens,' he says.

'Then give me a pencil,' I say.

'You nick mine, then put it down somewhere, forget where, and then you take another one of mine. This is my last pencil.'

I grab it off him, noticing it's the green pencil he clearly pocketed at the school, accidentally or otherwise. I give him a smile. Stealing school supplies, real smooth, Bartu. Then I close my eyes, open my pocket notebook and put pencil to paper.

'Line, line, line, up. And across and down,' I murmur to myself.

He folds his arms and stares at me. Waiting patiently.

'Just a second. And... here.'

Bartu looks at it. He squints.

'Yeah, that's too clever for me, mate,' he says.

'What do you mean?'

'I mean I have absolutely no idea what those squiggles you've just drawn are supposed to signify.'

'Ah. Sorry,' I say. 'Follow me.'

We head into a new, fashionable, industrially-styled coffee shop, the kind that never could've existed around here when I was younger. I order two Americanos and lead a confused Emre to the disabled toilet.

I lock us both inside and beckon him over, as I push my notes towards the mirror.

'Holy shit. How did you do that?' he says.

'I caught the reflection in the glass behind her.'

'And you just remembered it perfectly?'

'My mind is full of surprises. What we got?'

16

Paul Johnson 84 Ruskin Road
Roy Bruce 28 Renton Gardens
Jonathan Savage 144 Northumberland Park
Veronica Hedges 8 Parkhurst Road
Charles Seymour 11b Poynton Road

At the station I tap up Mona in the office. Blank faces turn. They try to pretend they're not looking but they are. I just walk on. Stealth-like, I am not, but people are pretty pliable in their pseudo-admiration.

'Hey, just need to check a few addresses and date of births if I could?' I say.

'Oh, what for?' she says, not looking up.

'Nothing big. Can I read them out to you?'

She pauses. People peer out from behind their desks in the open plan room.

'Well, is it parking stuff or...' she says.

'No, no. It'd just...'

She's proving tougher than I thought. The room seems to lean in.

'What? Unpaid fines or... ' she says.

I could tell her that was it, but her computer would soon tell her that wasn't it. The white walls and strip lights of the office seem to close in, too. I need Emre, he levels me out, but he wandered off as we entered. The halogen lights buzz. I'm not sure if she's mothering me or being suspicious. I fight for composure as I place my hands on her desk and whisper.

'Listen, Mona. Emre asked me to look these up so I'm doing that. He calls the shots and that's fine, certainly until I get used to everything. But that might take a while and I don't want people to know I forget things. So what I'm really saying is... I don't really know what they're for. But can you help me with this? I'm doing so well, but it's going to take time, you know. Do you understand?'

She looks to the side. She melts.

'Of course. I'm so sorry, didn't mean to put you on the spot,' she whispers.

The room hears nothing as she turns from foe to friend in one easy move. I'm good casting for the helpless one, I play it well, but I'm not planning to practise it much. It's not really me at all. She starts to read them out. Age. Occupation. Previous convictions. I attempt to write them down as I go, but struggle with the pace required.

'Tell you what, it'd make it a lot quicker if you just wrote them down for me. Could you do that?' I say.

'Of course,' she says.

It will be quicker, but also I don't want the room hearing about my leads. Just in case. Maybe this is the paraneea talking, but I'm not sure who I can trust here yet.

Emre arrives at the door, Levine patting him on the back and saying a few things like 'Good stuff' and 'Hang in there, that's what we need.' Then Jarwar arrives and they all whisper conspiratorially to each other. They stand with their backs to me, Levine giving me the odd glance that I'm clearly not supposed to see.

It's then that I notice how comfortable they all look in their uniforms, like the clothes are an extension of their bodies. I glance down at myself and see I have a shoelace undone and my vest zip is jammed half way up. They assure each other of something in the eggshell hallway. It looks like they all know each other more intimately than I imagined.

I grab my list. Thank Mona. And we head outside.

'What was that all about?' I say.

'What?' Emre says.

'You. Jarwar. Levine. The chummy buddies.'

'They're just checking in, mate. I told them all's good. You're good. We're good.'

'Good. Well, that all sounds... good,' I say.

Something doesn't feel right about it. This is exactly why I can't tell Emre everything yet. The things I see that he can't. If I tell him everything it might jeopardise the plan.

'What she give us then?' he says, as we stop by the traffic lights.

'You tell me,' I say, handing him her notes. He's on reading duties indefinitely.

'Right. So... Paul Johnson... is a foreman. Good chance he incurred the injury on site. Fifty-two-year-old male. Moved out of the borough about a year ago.'

'Which is not ideal,' I say.

'Nope. Roy Bruce. Coming up to his eighty-ninth birthday.'

'Happy early birthday, Roy. You are eliminated from our enquiries. Kidnapping's a young man's game.'

'Veronica Hedges? Is a twenty-eight-year-old nurse,' he says.

'Move on. It's never a young woman. I'm sorry, it just never is. And these girls wanted a boyfriend, not a sister. They were being groomed by a male, aged between seventeen and thirty-five.'

It's a wide span. But we're narrowing it down.

'Charles Seymour... is deceased. Sorry about that, Charles.'

'Sounds like a pretty firm hit in the head.'

'And Jonathan Savage... '

He stops in the street and looks up at me. For once he's a step ahead. He grins and withholds. He knows how much that pisses me off. I just about resist the urge to punch him in the throat as he lets the moment linger. Then says... 'Is a forty-two-year-old school caretaker. He lives next door to a school. And I think you know which one.'

Before he finishes I change direction and head back up the hill. The words were barely out of his mouth.

'School's out, Tom. Let's wait till tomorrow,' he says.

'School never lets out for the caretaker. Come on. You know what happens next,' I say.

And he isn't putting up a fight.

*

The cleaners are there so the doors are open, but the reception-ist is nowhere to be seen. He seems to nip in and out of his own accord. The school smells especially sickly sweet, turning the air a thick mauve that's almost difficult for me to see through, as I watch them cover the floor liberally with that cleaning fluid I know and despise. We hustle in and ask the first guy we see.

'Hey, do you know where Mr Savage is?'

I get the blankest of looks from the man. Vacant, barren, spotless. He is the cleaner, I guess. He lives the job.

He has eyes that dart around a little. He has pitch black

hair. He has a touch of heterochromia: different coloured irises. One is brown. The other is dark green. The human eye doesn't move smoothly it flits around in tiny 'saccades'. His do this more erratically than most.

'The caretaker? The err… site manager?' Bartu says.

His eyes roll to take us in at chest level, barely lifting his head as he addresses us, standing as stagnant as the lilac fluid below him.

'You can't be here. School's closed and he's busy,' he says, soft and low, his deep rasping tones barely reaching us, as if he hasn't spoken for a week and is just getting used to his voice again.

'I'm sure he'll make an exception for us,' I say, tapping the symbol on my hat. But as his eyes saccade upwards, I'm not sure he's as overawed by this show of authority as I'd hoped.

'I don't even know where he is,' he says.

It's difficult to determine his age; he's got the posture and personality of a curled piece of pocket paper, which makes him a limp conversation partner and a lacklustre bodyguard.

'It's all good, mate. Whatever the consequences are, we'll be the ones wearing them,' I say. Which Bartu affirms with an intake of breath and a rueful nod. 'Just point us in the right direction and…'

But I trail off, because then I see it.

'Never mind,' I say, as the smoke rises in the quad past the grey-green doors, with the trademark wire-gauged glass, which makes him look like he's behind bars already. He's a few weeks late for bonfire night. But caretakers love a bonfire. And if I know my caretaker chic, the man in the utility jacket and matching neck beard is our man.

'Mr Savage?' Bartu says outside, the fire blazing away.

'Yeah. What do you want?' he says. A touch confrontational. I guess he isn't paid for his bedside manner.

'We just had a couple of quick questions about Tanya Fraser.'

He stops. Wipes some ash off his trousers. Scrapes his boots across the grass. Shadow moves.

'Do you know her at all?' Bartu says, picking the conversation up off the dirt and dusting it down.

'Nope. No, no,' he says.

He almost shoves us out of the way as he throws some pieces of wood onto the fire and stares into it as if there are answers there. Some might assume that Mr Savage may have learning difficulties. Not that there's anything wrong with that, it's just another view on things.

'Ever seen this before?' I say.

I pull the picture out from Emre's document holder. He stops in his tracks. He looks right into it, entranced. He drinks it in, it's more than a passing sip, it's a long slow gulp.

'Nope.' He continues on with his work.

'Sorry. We just had one more question. We wondered what colour you'd say this was?' I say, thrusting the picture into view.

He looks up again. Unlike many others, he sees nothing odd in the question. He gives me a nod that says 'Try me'. I point to the clouds.

'Err... oxblood?' he says.

'Good call.' I point to the sky.

'Uh... indigo?' he says.

My eyes meet his. Only the noise of that Atlantic weather and the manmade fire crackles between us.

'Yeah. Yeah that's what we thought,' I say.

Another dead-end. I suppose I shouldn't be willing anyone on to be a sadistic child kidnapper. I hand him a card.

'Well, if you think of anything. Anything at all?'

He nods and we go. But before we get out of the heat he's created there, he stops us with a shout.

'Saw a man. Hipster-looking bloke. All in black. Leather

jacket. Waiting, sometimes after hockey practice, in his car. Always flustered, like he'd hotfooted it to get there, from somewhere else. He was older.'

Emre and I share a glance. We didn't expect anything from this guy, let alone such an eager response.

'Older than who?'

'The girls he was waiting for.'

'How much older?'

He draws breath and I see the buttons strain on his lumberjack shirt. He's shrouded in the wild green overgrowth of the school quad. It's greener than I remember, pretty verdant for London.

I remember those fields. They remind me of endless summers. A time when playing fields stretched out like summer holidays and my youth seemed like it would drag on forever. As Mr Savage reaches for his forehead in thought and leaves a sooty mark there, I feel like I do remember him. I think he once chased me across the field just behind where we are now, in his car, for taking a short cut over it at the weekend. He swerved in front of me and asked for my name and I wanted to give him a false one but could only think of my own, so spent the rest of term in fear of being called into Headmaster's office, but I never was. I feel an unexpected tinge of shame at my minor infraction, and hope he doesn't remember it. I remember those fields.

That childhood kiss drifts into my mind, then blows away, escaping through my ear. And a taste comes into my mouth. Like metal.

'I'd say he was... thirty-three, lads. That's what I'd say.'

Emre and I silently nod to each other.

'No!' he says. I take a step in.

'Thirty-two.'

I respect a man who values the specifics.

My radio kicks into gear. But I don't want to answer it. I don't want to snap him out of it.

'Remember the car at all? Colour? Make?' I say.

'Nope. Sorry.'

'Where do you reckon he'd hotfooted it from to get here?'

'No idea. But, oh, there was another thing. One time... I thought I saw him taking pictures of the girls, as they came past. All discreet like, camera held low. But I saw him,' he says.

Chh. 'Tom. Where are you? It's Mona. Over.'

'Thanks Jon. If you remember anything else... ' says Bartu.

'I'll give you a call,' says Savage, holding up my card. Then he goes back to fanning the flames, the embers drifting all around then into the greying sky.

We turn and go, the picture becoming clearer. The man outside the gates, a man with a car, a man that draws for them. But why does he draw that particular scene? This is what intoxicates me as the smoke rises behind us.

We pass the cleaner, trying to avoid the sections he's already mopped, and I decide to interrupt him and give him a card, too, for good measure.

'Wondered if you ever saw a guy in black, hanging outside school with a camera, probably about the time you leave?'

He's startled to see the card at first, then his eyes struggle to focus on it. I start to wonder whether, without a mask to protect him, working with those chemicals might make him a little high.

'No, I ain't seen nothing,' he says, offering it back to me.

'Keep hold of it, I've got a job lot. And if anything comes up...'

IIe takes a careful look around him as if there's some rule about accepting self-made vanity cards from strangers on school time. Then he pockets it and nods with a new sense of compliance, before crouching down to get back to his work, as we push through the school doors and my radio sounds.

Cch. 'Tom. We need you back here. We need everyone who can get here. I... I think another girl has gone missing. Over.' *Cch.*

Three's a crowd.

For the first time, I feel overwhelmed by the scale of what appears to be happening at the place where I spent the majority of my childhood hours. To the innocent girls who wanted nothing more this term than to pass some exams, maybe have some alone time with a boy, and get a little older.

I pick up the radio and speak.

Documented Telephone Conversation #2

It rings. The number is withheld. It rings again and I'm going to have to answer it or lose it. So I pick up and hold the handset tight.

'I've called before but you didn't pick up,' the voice says.

'Yes,' I say. 'I was afraid to. You withheld your number.'

'Are you afraid of me?'

'No. Not exactly,' I lie, because I'm afraid of how she makes me feel. Brittle when I want to be anything but. I need to snuff her out.

'I'm worried about you. I don't think you're safe,' she says.

'Worry about yourself. Worry about your boyfriend's blog,' I say, which I immediately regret as it doesn't mean anything except *'I am in pain'*. And I wasn't intending to show her that much.

'Tom. Please consider stopping whatever it is you're doing.'

At first I'm too busy bathing in the fact that I have the power to concern her. I stroke Mark and tut down the line as I review her request, before the obvious thought drops.

'How do you know what I'm doing?'

Her lips are dry so she wets them and gulps. She's tense.

'You told me. Remember? I think you're putting yourself in danger and I think you need to... '

'No, there's something else. You been reading up on me?' I say.

It's an observation she doesn't expect from me. It disturbs her.

'Yes,' she says. 'And... I... I got a call about you. I got a call.'

'From who? Who called?'

'Your doctor. Doctor... Ryans? He wanted me to check in on you. Just to help. To make sure you know what you're... '

I hold the phone away from me and scream into my hand.

'He had no right to do that. I don't even know how he–'

'Tom, this isn't good. Please, I just want you to be safe,' she says, with emotion in her breath that I've never heard before.

'Do you remember when we first met? Do you?' I say.

'Of course... at the party. And we –'

'And we shared a cigarette. And the rain came down and we hid under that tree, and I thought this is the person I'll be with forever.'

'Was there a tree? Rain? I don't... remember it like that.'

'What? Yes, you do. I was choking on a cigarette in the rain, you came up to me, and we decided that since we both hated smoking–'

'I don't remember it like that. Were we... outside?'

'Yes. We were! That's... how I remember it. I'm sure... '

'Tom. You need more rest. You're not ready for any of this.'

17

'I like to flirt,
I'll do it till I'm sick and hurt,
I'll hold your hand to my chest, to feel my breath
I like to flirt, with death.'

When we get to the station we find we're close to full force. Faces litter the room, some with moustaches, some with greying hair. Constables, sergeants, inspectors, some CID.

A face comes to address us all. The room turns. The face, far too blank and far away for me to even guess its owner, speaks. Bartu's eyes scour the room like he's searching for lost property.

'I'm sure you're all aware that a third girl has now been reported missing. Her parents described having had no contact with Nina Da Silva for twenty-four hours. She's fifteen. Her phone, as with the others, is not responding.'

The voice speaks evenly, more of a stating of the facts than the rallying cry I had expected. As the blurred edges of the speaker's face come into view, jigsaw pieces fall into their allotted slots in my mind and the clues point to one man. I was expecting CID to have taken over by this point, I wanted some specialist with experience of this kind of case. But it seems they're still not fully accepting what this is. The topography of his face is the embodiment of an anti-climax.

Nervy Superintendent Matthews drones on. Like Levine, he's new in the role. I watch the pinkish flesh around his cheeks move under the office lighting, and his right leg quiver with the lack of conviction I always note when in his underwhelming company. The possibility of such a big case, one that may garner national attention, falling into his tentative lap was the cause of the shadow moves, which he hid very well from everyone else but me. Don't get me wrong, this city is full of good police, we're up there with the best in the world, but he isn't one of them.

'I have absolute faith in all of you. The spotlight may be drifting our way but that's nothing we can't handle if we stay vigilant and do all we can. I'm confident the perpetrator... if indeed there is one... can be brought to justice, and these girls brought home safely from... wherever they may be. Thank you. I'd just like a word with our safer neighbourhood's team. Yep. Thank you.'

Matthews may be bent on following his rulebook until this guy falls into our lap, but that's not how I see it. It's like he's already preparing his statements on how, despite his best efforts, bla bla na na. This possibility is not in my mind. There will be no excuses.

i)   There will be no lost bodies and empty coffin farewells.
ii)   I will continue to act fast and without hesitation.
iii)   I will keep walking forward, until I walk into him.
iv)   And when I do, only one of us will walk away.
v)   I will put him down or put him away.
vi)   And I will bring those girls home, alive or otherwise.

This is my manifesto. I came up with it as I walked the roads early this morning as the sun rose. When I returned home, as the rest of the city began to wake, I said it out loud to Mark against the solace of my bedroom.

As we walk in hushed convoy over to the debrief room, and Emre glances around like it's hunting season and he's just realised he has a tail, I realise that I've called Levine and Matthews each other's names on various occasions. I'm not regretful, far from it. The faces of these police Caucasians with their short back and sides give me nothing but plain A4. Levine, Matthews, even myself, we're just a shirt with an interchangeable Swiss-army face. It was Matthews that started speaking before the door had even closed. I'm pretty sure it was him anyway.

'Right… there are… a few things to discuss. I think some of you will have already realised what they are.'

Bartu grips his knee hard.

'There has been a breach of procedure, possibly more than one. And it's something we need to clear up, particularly in and around a case like this.'

The room is intrigued, and Bartu's concern whispers to me across it. He wonders why we went so far, why he didn't put a stop to it before it even began. But he only feels this because it's all about to come out. Bartu shakes. I am unshakeable. Levine's arms are folded tight. Matthews looks at me and takes no pleasure in what he says next.

'We have reports that officers have been visiting the school, and roaming around, without our knowledge. They did, however, sign in at front desk, so we have a record of it. And I think it'll be obvious at this point… '

Bartu pictures disgrace. A suspension, then a series of discoveries, a slow unravelling of the stories he's sold to his colleagues. Questions of what he had to gain. Salacious rumours abound. Then the real backlash begins.

'… Anderson and Stevens have temporarily been removed

from association with this investigation. They're on unofficial probation.'

It's funny. Bartu is usually such a thorough man. But he didn't even check the name badge I gave him. That'll teach him to switch off and sulk. It was only a precaution; I didn't foresee it coming to this. He looks at me. He pictures the moment he stood back, while I signed our names. I say *our* names.

'I've questioned them myself and they're sticking to their story. Anyway, taking them out of the firing line on this for a while should remove any complications for them. And cause any imposters some serious problems, should that by any chance be the case. The school, for one, has been informed... '

My eyes flick to Bartu as I drift off during all this. My face is a picture of serenity. I fall into gentle reverie as Matthews goes on and on. I bathe in the glory of my tactical superiority. Stevens is an older gent with no ambition, I'm of far more use to this case and profession than he is. And Anderson is a woman well-beloved of the community, but she's more comfortable handing out on-the-spot fines than anything like this. In a few months this'll be a distant detail. I am resolved. I'd do the same again in a second.

'So, Jarwar, I want you to focus every effort on this,' Levine says, taking over. 'While you hand over any other work, we'll need Bartu and Mondrian to check in with the Da Silva parents. We need them to know we're on this with everything we have. We need everyone to know that.'

I nod sagely. Things seem to be falling into place for us. I *am* on this with everything I have. It's not a pose. This day just keeps getting better. I wonder where Turan is for a second. He seems to keep his own timetable.

'Tom. You might never have spoken to people when they're in this kind of state before but... you know... delicacy is the watchword. Listen to them. Be there for anything they need...

and… that's it. I'm sure you'll be fine,' Levine says, tossing out his coddling as casually as he can.

I nod again as if buoyed by a thumbs up from the captain of the school football team.

'Thanks. Thanks very much,' I say, almost wiping away a tear of gratitude for the advice. We zip up our jackets as we get out of there, before we waste any more time, before my barely concealed joy riles Bartu any more than it already has.

*

On the journey over to the house I fend off any attempts to address what just happened. I'm pretty sure he's planned a lecture in his head about how we should 'dial things back'. If things had gotten really tasty, he might even have told me I'm 'out of control'. But I've got no time for any of that.

However, when I catch the familiar insignia on the kerb outside the house, a light blue circle with two diagonal lines through it, just insignificant enough to ignore, I make a mental note to make time to address the shivers it gives me.

The family are more of a mess than any of the others. The patriarch tries to hold it together for his wife. News about disappearing girls had probably just reached them in time to start worrying. Then, just as their fears slowly started to fall away and they allowed themselves to entertain the possible reality that they were working themselves up over nothing, that statistics would say it was unlikely to hit them, of all people, it happened.

'She was good girl. No drinking. No boys. No skiving off. She wouldn't go nowhere without telling us.'

His father's slightly broken English shouldn't be confused with a lack of intellect. He used to own a company that sold computer accessories in the late nineties, mouse mats, adapted keyboards, that kind of thing. He sold the business long ago to focus on his property portfolio. They are the picture of a modern kind of affluence. I'll bet that London, particularly this borough, wasn't always the easiest place to be. But from the look of their home, sitting proudly on the corner as the biggest in the neighbourhood, they've come through, and good on them.

The mother leads us up to the bedroom. They always do. It's a déjà vu. I run my hand along the polished tobacco-coloured oak handrail as we rise. Bartu takes a quick look to the door. We should get back down before Jarwar arrives.

We don't have to look far for the picture. She didn't even try and conceal it. It sits on her bedside table. It's the same scene. Bartu would later tell me it was from the same perspective as the first, precisely the same dimensions. Each picture almost a perfect replica of the last. Other than the colours. When Bartu clocks it, he nods to me and tactfully turns to lead us all out, giving the appearance of only needing a cursory look at the bedroom, allowing me to place the picture in my document holder behind their backs.

In a smooth movement I also grab for something, that seems to have fallen behind the bed. I only had the briefest moment to take in the room, but it immediately caught my eye. It didn't fit the pattern.

It's a compact black and red item, the sort I haven't seen for a long while. The one enviable present I'd received in my long childhood was a crap camcorder when they first became cheapish. I greet its cool tape like an old friend and push it into my pocket.

I search for that smell but no colours readily offer themselves. The generic scent of diffusers is all I take in as I head downstairs behind them.

'Please forgive me if these questions seem simplistic. I'm sure you've been asked all these before...' I say in the living room.

I'm trying to get a gauge on how far along Jarwar is, which requires a level of tact that doesn't come naturally. We don't want to tread on her toes but we also don't want to get left behind. So if there's anything Jarwar knows then I want to know it, too. Conversely, if we're ahead, I want to know exactly how far.

'Fine,' she says, giving nothing away. I have to keep my intentions close so she can't sense I'm an outsider looking in, nose pressed up against the glass.

'I know you said she wasn't seeing any boys but... has she ever been dropped off by a friend, boy or girl, young or old?'

'Never. I've told the woman. Many questions, very thorough!' Her voice cracks, her breath leaves her and she buries her face in her husband's chest. As I stand frozen under the terrible soundtrack of her panic tears, I see that hardly a wall stands in the house without her daughter's eyes looking in at us from behind an ornate frame. She was their joy, their only child, another only child.

'Forgive us. We don't mean to pry. We're just getting things straight,' says Bartu, but in truth we do mean to pry. It's good to know Jarwar seems to be doggedly pursuing the lines of investigation that suit the seriousness of all this, I had begun to have my doubts.

The doorbell goes and we know what that means, so I reel back towards the kitchen. And as the front door opens, Bartu pops his head in to see me push the picture into a miscellaneous drawer. We have one of them already, which is maybe one too many. We don't want to get caught tampering with evidence, nor do we want to muddy the issue for Jarwar. I'm not trying to put her off; if she solves the thing, so much the better. But as we emerge muttering to each other from the kitchen, no one the wiser, I keep the mini-DV tape safe in my jacket pocket, my digits fingering its dimensions and pushing into its tactile edges with nostalgia as I meet the whites of Jarwar's eyes.

'Emre. Tom. Thanks for everything,' she says, a bit curtly for my taste, as she enters.

We are automatically belittled by her presence. Before she arrived we were the authority figures, as soon as she entered the room, we became just two guys. Local well-wishers but without the warm soup and good tidings. It's the same way your relationship to whatever girl you were talking to changed whenever Paul Lawrence entered the Roller Disco. Before he walked in you were at least there, now they only have eyes for him. That reference might be pretty niche, but it's the one that springs to mind.

Jarwar stares at us as if we've missed our cue. The Da Silvas glance to her. We haven't moved a muscle. It's like a scene from the theatre of the absurd. A strange inertia has come over us. We're trying to go with a little dignity, without seeming like the spare bolts left once you've assembled your flat-pack wardrobe.

'Great. I'll take it from here,' she says again. Bartu even gets a hand on the shoulder, which you can tell he wants to wriggle away from, but he manages to behave like an adult as we're pushed discreetly towards the door.

'Anything else you nudge?' I say, near the door, in a last gasp attempt to gain back some masculinity, slightly undercut by my aphasia offering me the word 'nudge' instead of 'need'. I wince and stand by it anyway.

Any odd jobs you need doing? Any plugs you need rewiring? Any flat-pack furniture you need assembling? I may as well have said.

'No. Thanks though, Tom,' she says, giving me the shoulder-hand, with the matching stare.

Emre is halfway out the door but I have something to say, my brain just won't tell me what it is yet. I work it through:

She didn't even ask if anything important had been said while we were here, just on the off chance, or if we had any read on the situation, even out of politeness. It dawns on me; we were only here to babysit. Nothing more. Warm bodies in the room.

I stand open mouthed, grasping for the words.

'Er... yes, Tom?' Jarwar says.

Bartu is used to this and Jarwar knows about my problem but the Da Silvas are suitably disturbed.

They wait.

I have the urge to ask if anyone knows exactly what those blue symbols on the kerb mean.

The impulse to probe why exactly Nina had an old camcorder. The father dealt in nineties electronics, I suppose, but it's another element that stuck out as not belonging in these girls' worlds.

And I want to talk photographs. Maybe there's a way of tactfully mentioning them, not just to find out if Jarwar found the set at the first house, but also to show our initiative. I'm a child who wants to show his big sister he can ride his bike one-handed.

Jarwar? Have You Found Any Photos? At All?

Say it. Maybe she has. Maybe she hasn't. Or I might be able to tell she's concealing knowledge of them and then we'll know she doesn't trust us. Alternatively, it could just give her more than I really want to give. She looks at me patiently. I know I shouldn't. But I want to say it anyway. Just so I've said it.

'Thanks then,' I say.

The word photo wasn't even presenting itself, my aphasia making something of a comeback, exacerbated by the heightened nature of the situation.

I leave with Emre not far behind. The room shrugs, acknowledging with relief that the strange man is gone.

18

'Can't. Get that dah dee dah, out of, my head…'

'I've been thinking we should make a copy of the picture,' Emre says.

He's trying to lift me as we walk, low and utterly undermined, to get my mind back on paramount things, and I appreciate it. At least I didn't reveal what hand I was holding to Jarwar. Sometimes it's worth everyone thinking you're nothing if what you've got will really blow them away in the end.

'Yes, good, make a copy. Why's that again?' I say.

'Cos we have to get the original back to the Bridges' house soon. If they figure out we've removed evidence from a victim's house, then we're screwed.'

I squeeze the mini-DV tight in my hand, as his thought hits. We could put that back, too, if needs be, but I'd like to think it might be small enough for no one to know it even exists. Either way, I decide to delay the good news of its discovery until a more apt time.

'Jarwar doesn't seem to be our biggest fan. And Turan may be many things, but nothing we can count on,' Bartu says. 'Hey, and later, if you're a good boy, I'll show you something *I* figured out,' Bartu says.

I grunt-scoff in return.

It's unlikely that he could come up with anything I haven't already, so it's probably just a bargaining chip to find out what else I've got up my utility jacket.

'Sure. By the way, did you notice those blue markings outside on the curb, Emre? Blue circle? Two diagonal lines?' I say.

'Err, maybe. Always assumed they were to do with gas pipes.'

'Yeah, that's what I thought you'd say,' I say. Because that's what I thought he'd say. And I stay quiet about my assumption until I've got a compelling picture of exactly how wrong he is on that.

Speak of the devil; not long after we utter his name, he appears before us. We don't usually come so near to Turan's beat but Levine had radioed us to make a request as we left the Da Silva house. There had been some petty vandalism on Green Lanes, which everyone else was too busy or important to take a look at. As we had reached the phone box and stared at the last bits of jagged glass that clung to it, Bartu had decided it was time for some fried chicken.

We had a thought that maybe we weren't supposed to approach him when in the field. When I hear the name Turan I always get images of this slick, cocktail stick in mouth, leather jacketed man moving silently through crowds like a shark navigating bare ankles close to the bay. But for whatever reason, he seems never to have pursued the role of detective and the mufti that goes with it. As he waited for his chicken dinner at Perfect Chicken, in his white shirt and black tie, clip-on for easy removal, it seemed safe to assume anyone watching was well aware of the role for which he was being remunerated.

After we'd spotted him it would've been almost impossible not to say hi. It's a bit like going to a costume party dressed as a bear and seeing another guy there also dressed as a bear. Sooner or later you're going to have to at least give him a nod, and the longer you wait to do it, the weirder it gets. So with immediate thought of getting on the front foot, I chime in as soon as I open the clammy chicken shop door.

'Hey, how you doing?'

The look I get back tells me everything isn't quite right. No recognition drifts across his face, only a flick of his eyes to our uniform. It's only when Bartu taps me on the shoulder that I realise Turan is at the other end of the counter and the man who I've tapped on the back is merely some other tanned man in an unpressed shirt. Bartu gently places a hand on my back and turns me towards Turan who looks up from the other end of the counter and gives us a look that could never be described as respectful. I turn back to the man that doesn't own an iron as Turan's food arrives and Bartu goes to sit down.

'Sorry mate. Just checking in.'

The thick smell of batter and oil fills my senses and makes everything cider coloured. I feel the texture of gravel against my skin and the gentle of hum of an A flat. It overpowers, the room taking on a murky quality, like it's covered in dark orange smoke, but I try to push it away as I head over to my new friends.

At the ripped red leather booth, Bartu and Turan are already into smoother conversation than I was expecting, probably largely due to my late entry into the fray.

'So what you doing this end?' Turan says, chicken bones between his fingers.

'Kids smashing shit up again, we were sent down to check it out. Your PCSO is on other duty, and it's not in your job description, I reckon,' says Bartu.

'Ha, yeah, could say that. These kids around here, I gotta tell ya, they're a different breed. It's not like nicking a bag of sweets or even sawing the lock off a bike with a hacksaw from DT. That's nineties stuff. That stuff... you could understand it.

They wanted something, they didn't have the money, they nicked it. I get it. It's raw economics.'

'Different now round here, uh?' Bartu says.

His voice changes, lowering a semitone. They both seem to have dropped into a new groove I feel excluded from. I'm a local boy, but I'm not from right here, not exactly. Travel a mile down the road in any London borough and you'll find a different culture, not just in terms of race. They speak in inferences and with an easy cool that's lost on me and that I'd be foolish to try and replicate.

'These fucking kids, destruction for its own sake. It's next level,' Turan says.

'I'm sure you're right. We just collect the information and hand it on, mate. Ours is not to reason why,' says Bartu.

'That's right. It's not. You stick to your fucking remit, boys.'

He nods as he chews, agreeing with himself as he brings a fistful of serviettes to meet his mouth, before breaking into a smile to show he's not entirely serious.

'Whatever you say, Inspector,' Bartu says, giving him a mock salute. Turan's smile disappears as his teeth plunge into more chicken. Then he smirks again, keeping the mood as light as he can in the silences between the words, while revelling in his implied authority.

Then his head turns towards a man who has just entered wearing a bomber jacket, shades and a baseball cap. He's not over-layered for the time of year but it's getting later on one of those murky days when the sun has hardly risen, so the sunglasses seem a bit droll.

The cider colour fades as another scent enters the mix. But the smell of oil fights back and covers it over, the orange mist thickening over whatever this man has brought with him.

He has a bolt-upright posture like he's a straight, clean line, but when he sees Turan looking up at him he instantly turns away and his shoulders drop a touch, I notice. Then he takes in the faded pictures of chicken behind the counter with an excessive level of interest.

'All right, fella?' Turan says.

The man turns and gives him a stiff nod, when a 'Hi there' might've been warmer.

Turan frowns in our direction, hinting that either he isn't keen on this stranger's etiquette, or conversely that this is a man he knows, and he isn't taking too kindly to being snubbed by.

The door slams, the man has left without ordering. As Bartu's chicken strips arrive, I see Turan's look linger almost imperceptibly longer than is necessary, as he goes, suggesting he's keeping him under close watch, another tiny moment you might miss if you weren't as keen on the little things as I.

He's plugged into the community all right, he seems to know all the local characters.

'Anyway, you don't need to worry. You'll be running this place in no time. Keep your head down here, get bust up to constable, then on and on in a place like this. They need guys like you, no doubt. Know what I mean?' Turan says, glancing at both of us.

I know what he means. A local Turk and a man of questionable mental ability. We're good for the statistics. Hell, we'd even look good on a poster together advertising diversity, doing some sort of high five to show how 'down' we are with our differences. We both know our USPs and we'll stay in control of them, thanks. He doesn't need to say it.

'Okay, boys, that's me done, better get out of here,' Turan says.

He wipes his mouth and stands and so do we.

We turn left, back towards the phone box and shattered glass. As Turan crosses the road. The same direction the man in the baseball cap was headed, I notice.

*

We get a call about something that's been found in Tottenham Cemetery. A man apparently stumbled across it while walking his dog. That's why I'm jogging my version of a jog.

Despite the fact I don't like to have work dictated to me these days, and today has already seen us suffer one unwanted detail, we have a feeling this might be important. And Bartu was not unreasonable in stating that if we were going to go, we should get there before anyone else does.

The dog, named Treacle, was apparently being characteristically wayward and bounded deep into some nettles, not far from the cemetery's mini-waterfall. Ordinarily we'd be having a chat about keeping canines firmly on leads when in the graveyard. Out of respect for the dead and all. But this time Treacle stumbled on something that looked from a distance like a large dead animal. His owner pulled him away and called us instantly, not wanting to brave the nettles or the possible gore himself.

'Give me a... I can't... catch my catch... ' I say, my aphasia dropping half the words I'm looking for in any given sentence as we run.

'No. No! We always go at your speed. If we keep being pushed away from everything we won't have anything to work with.'

'… Agreed,' I say, as we reach the entrance and break into a more respectful walk. I know this place pretty well. But I haven't been in a long time. Not since well before the incident.

'And you're going to stop holding out on me,' he says, as we walk past assorted grave stones of concrete, sandstone and granite, some better kept than others, and I struggle to catch my breath.

'Okay. Tell me your thing first,' I say.

'No, yours first!' he shouts, disturbing the peace and a line of rooks on top of a family tomb that's evidently seen more moss than upkeep of late. I'm not going to disagree with him in this mood. He's newly charged with a determination, injected by the possibilities of what we're about to see.

'I know you see more than you tell me. No more secrets. Give me everything as you see it, now!'

I was going to say 'not here'. But as we head towards the slightly more unkempt end of this burial ground, it seems as appropriate a place as any.

'Three girls. Our man was seeing them all,' I say, my voice rasping as my breath crawls back to normality. 'Showing them they were all special in a way they'd never had before. A fifteen-year-old, a sixteen-year-old, a seventeen-year-old. He's methodical, he likes the game of it, but he also can't help his little patterns. Since the injury, his brain just works like that. He gives them tiny keepsakes. He knows he can't get into their houses, but he can put a piece of himself in there. That's part of the game.'

I feel a sickness somewhere in the back of my head. I've put this all together internally. Speaking it out loud hits me in the gut and spreads out to every other part from there. I wipe the sweat from my brow as we see our dog walker, pointing fearfully into the weeds and overgrowth.

'He gains their trust, gives them things their parents wouldn't, like a puppy or a fireworks party, so they gradually learn to put him first. He knows he wants all of them, wherever he has them, at once. He wants them to go missing day by day, that's part of the game, the pattern. And he wants people to see that he's left next to nothing behind. Just a few photos that are nothing but a boast.'

We wave back to the dog walker as we approach. Treacle straining to get at whatever he sees, breaking up the otherwise restful place with his stark, wild barks.

'So they exchange gifts and gestures. These men tend to like trophies. They'd even trade something as substantial as the puppy in the car for a piece of clothing,' Emre says.

'Exactly, it served its purpose as soon as it allowed him access to her car,' I say, whispering to almost inaudibility as we nod to the man and survey the scene from his vantage point.

'Hello, mate. Have you got any closer than this at any point?' Bartu says, as I approach the edge of the heavy morass of untended green.

'No bloody way,' he says, somewhere behind me.

'What did you think it was when you first saw it?' Bartu says.

'Pff. A big dog? All cut open. But there was no hair. So then I thought, maybe a pig?'

I stand on tip toes and see the size of it, laid bare. The surface layer of blood on top, and the flesh below.

'What about a teenage girl?' I say.

'Oh God. I...' he says. 'No, God, I didn't think that.'

Bartu says nothing. I kick down the nettles, getting closer. My hands getting stung as I stamp through the stingers and thistles. Then I see it, lying there in front of me. A long, messy lump.

'It's not,' I call back. 'It's not a girl.'

There aren't any bite marks on it. If he got close, then Treacle was kind. It stares up at me. Dumped. Abstract.

'It's not big enough,' I say, failing to hide the darkness in my tone.

'Then what the hell is it?' The man says, as Bartu wades in to join me.

'It's part of one,' I say.

'Oh no. Oh fuck,' Bartu says as soon as he sees it. Detached from its owner. Lying there. Its top part broken open to the bone.

Chh... 'Jarwar...we're first on the scene at the cemetery. I think you'd better come and look at this. Over.'

163

Chh… 'Tom. I'm already on my way. What is it? Over.'

Bartu has distanced himself from it as I analyse exactly where it has been cut. That's the part of the picture that stands out to me above anything else.

Chh… 'It's a …it's a girl's leg…it's still in its sock… Over.'

Chh… 'Okay, Tom. Err… Okay. I'm coming. Over.'

The man has staggered away next to a tree, stroking his dog, who now appears to be whimpering, high and pained.

'It was sawn through, at the very top,' I tell Bartu. 'I can see the femoral artery.' If it comes out a little cold, it's because I'm in a partial trance. He shakes his head, then punches his thigh a few times in anger.

'How does this fit with anything?' he says.

'Oh. I don't know,' I say, my hand over my mouth.

'Do you think a kid like Asif is capable of something like this?'

'I can't count him out. He's old enough to drive. He could've made the girls keep a secret. Secrets are sexy in an age when everyone's constantly sharing their souls with each other from behind a screen. What's left of their souls, anyhow.'

He wipes his face. Our breath is high in our chests now and the emotion touches us. That was somebody's child once. Another layer of all of this has been stripped, and beneath it the puzzle drops away, and only the horror of flesh and bone lies in front of us.

I don't know whether to get angry, or be sick, or cry hot tears. Neither does Bartu, but he's keen enough to take the reins.

'Stay there please, sir. An officer will be with you very shortly,' he says as he walks and I follow. Jarwar will be here any second and we'd both rather avoid that tête-à-tête again. It would be more of a tête-à-tête-à-tête-à-jambe to be exact. A head to head, plus another head, and a leg. My mind plays games to stave off the darkness.

'Where are we going now?' I say.

'We're going for a drive,' he says, taking out his keys.

'And why's that, Emre Bartu?' I say, as he pulls the picture from his document holder.

'Because I think I know where this is.'

Documented Memory Project #1

At Christmas I received between five and ten books. Which I soon realised had stamps in them, that told me when they should be returned. It gave me a time limit and a challenge, to know that I must consume Roald Dahl and books about astronomy, within a certain date, or receive a hefty library fine. With the fear of not getting a proper Christmas if I didn't enjoy them all, and without the knowledge that you could renew, I would start reading right away.

After my parents stopped this practice I read much less, so I suppose I have to thank them for this. They would at least get me one action figure of my choice every year, too, which didn't look quite right and I reckoned was a knock off from the market. But then, they got each other little, if anything, seeing Christmas as a materialist event they wanted no part of.

By the time we started delving inside the body in biology, I already had a pretty good grasp on things, owing to various colourful books on anatomy mum had loaned for me. I remember sticking my hand up and answering every question before the teacher even got there. The pretty blonde girl next to me, hair dangling in her eyes, scowled continuously, but I think somewhere in there she was impressed. I wish I could remember her name. It escapes me.

Kids are always afraid of falling down and cutting their wrist, once they hear that it holds the key to so much blood. But you'd get more rich, oxygenated blood out of your femoral artery. It's very close to the surface, around the groin area. If you put your hand on it now you should be able to feel a pulse. It's where you'd insert a cardiac catheter. It's where a mortician would pump embalming fluid to preserve the body after death. People think the source of life, your centre, is your heart. But I think of it as that fat, elastic femoral artery. After that lesson, our whole class became morbidly obsessed with it.

About a month later on a school trip I was taken to the first aid point in the visitor centre of a castle. I'd been running around and smacked the bridge of my nose into a bar of scaffolding. It hurt like hell and the blood came thick and fast. It only didn't break because the contact was so high up. But I was surprised to be eclipsed in the drama stakes by another girl from school already in the medical room. They were taking whatever was wrong with her very seriously. As she was engulfed by teachers and staff from the castle, she looked at me through the crowd. It was that same blonde girl from biology class. Sarah, I think her name was. Yes, Sarah. She had sliced her femoral artery. Some say she did it herself, out of curiosity or a dare, but we never found out for sure.

Later that summer, I ended up in full-blown hospital. I had to have my appendix out and after the operation my parents arrived to see a made–up bed. Dad instantly began to fear the worst and cry, yet mum, cooler of head, asked around and soon found that there were no complications. I was around the corner in the next ward. A nurse had taken a particular liking to me and found a small black and white TV with built-in video that could play Top Cat, and had set it up for me. I can still remember the doctor counting down as I succumbed to the ether. I coughed hard and then the next thing I knew was the crackling TV screen.

It was Ryans who advised that I should write descriptions of the first memories that came into my mind when I closed my eyes. This was the first piece that made any sense, which I began shortly after my encounter with my own reflection.

It was only later that I found out that, as I wrote, somewhere in a not too distant room, Ryans was describing me as having only a one in fifty chance of returning to a normal job. Six months after an injury like mine, you'll get some idea of where the patient is heading. After two years the brain's recovery process slows and wherever you are at that point is likely to be all you get. Three months after the bullet, and after warnings about forcing recovery too soon, I was back at work. I'm told that at twenty-nine I was just young enough for the brain to still benefit from a certain youthfulness that makes recovery by natural plasticity and self-healing more possible. So you could say it all happened in the nick of time.

I had recently wound up short of gaining a next of kin. I managed to hold out and not give Anita's name, thereby successfully avoiding a bedside reunion that was the last thing I wanted. When my pen hit the paper, I'd just been informed that I'd reached recovery level six. So I think under the circumstances this was a good day. That's how I'll remember it.

19

'She's so pretty
She's so wonderful
She's irreplaceable
And she's gone.'

At the other end of the borough our doors slam in unison. It's good we drove. It would've taken twenty minutes or more to walk and Bartu needed to drive to get the shakes out of him after seeing the leg. The leg that told us we better start breaking down some doors.

Our boots hit the tarmac that leads to the playground.

A slide.

A horse on a spring. To the back and to the right.

A roundabout to the left and forward.

A scattering of oak trees behind them. Four to be exact.

A metal fence running around it. The tops of which form into loops.

We enter a small gate and step inside.

'What's this remind you of?' Bartu says.

'A standard inner city playground,' I say.

'Okay, look at this.' He holds the picture out and turns us around to the angle he has asserted the picture is from, the two views merging and becoming one in all but colour. It's as if we're seeing the world through his eyes. There is a kind of magic to seeing the thing static but colourful on paper, then stripped to blandness in the dull reality behind it, but quivering with small signs of life in the wind, in the navy light of early evening.

'How did you know?' I say.

'I took a long drive last night,' he says. 'There are six of these playgrounds with this kind of equipment within a five-mile radius. This was the first one I came to. I remembered I'd been here before. With my girl.'

I feel that Atlantic wind move harshly past my ears. I blow into my hands.

'Your girlfriend?' I say.

'No, Tom. Not my girlfriend. My little girl.'

I take a walk over to the swing and sit down into it. Its dissonant squeak as I rock back on it, telling tales of frequent use and negligence and rust.

'I didn't know you had a little girl.'

'I don't,' he says.

'Oh,' I say.

I'm not used to this kind of thing. I'm not trained for it. I get out of the swing seat and put my hands in my pockets.

'Was… Was it? Was… '

'Meningitis,' he says, mercifully helping me out. He knows this isn't my forte.

We listen to the air in the trees. He takes in the scene. Somewhere lost in memory.

'And are… are you…?'

'I'm still with her mother, yes.'

I blink. He runs his hand across his face. Shadow moves.

'I'm sorry to hear that. The first part I mean. I'm very pleased to hear the second. That sort of thing can break people apart, I hear.'

He agrees, in deep contemplation. Partly in some other place. Partly, thoroughly here.

'But there's nothing you can do. Nothing. About that... kind of thing. The only thing you can do is carry on.'

He nods, feeling my effort.

'From the beginning of it to her going was three weeks. One minute she was a beautiful, healthy thing. Starting to run around. Next she could barely breathe. Then we found out what it was and she was mostly in hospital from then on. No promises were made. After that, every noise... she made... sounded different to us. Each one was a tiny struggle for a life. All children cry, but not like this. Noises it's difficult to hear. To forget. Like she knew it was serious. Like she knew the crying would never stop. Until it did.'

I nod. He breathes.

'I still hear it sometimes, the crying. She passed away a year and a half ago. Last month I woke in the middle of the night to check on her. I thought I heard her fighting to breathe. I guess I was half awake, half sleepwalking. When I got to her room, of course, there was nothing there. When Aisha woke she found me on the floor in the baby's room. She helped me up then held me close, then we went back to bed and said nothing more about it. We've already cried about it a hundred times, now comes everything after.'

I nod.

'I don't want to think this guy. Him. I don't want to think he was watching us, from that window up there, or that one there, watching me and my little girl.'

His features tense. He holds the picture and matches it to the view from the first floor of the surrounding houses. But before he goes too far I stop him.

'He wasn't. I can promise you that,' I say.

'How can you?' he says, his face reddened.

'Because this isn't the playground,' I say.

He pushes out smoking breaths. His fists ball and punch into his pockets. The snow around us has turned to sludge.

'And how the fuck did you come to that?' he says.

'Because it's not right. The trees aren't exact. The distances between them.'

'Don't do this. Come on. You can see. You can see it's the same,' he says, animated, pushing it into my face.

'Not exactly, I'm sorry. This man draws out of compulsion. Every single one is correct to the absolute minutiae, not in colour but in perspective, this is his skill. He cares about the specifics. It's important they're all in separate years so they don't know each other. It's important they don't have siblings that they might open up to. He's watched and taken photos of them at the school gates, looked them up on various websites and social media to corroborate their backgrounds and find out things that they like, so he can appeal to them on their level. He's picked them especially for this before making contact. He sees patterns, like I do. He is struck by the image and he has to draw it perfectly. I've read about this feeling, I've *felt* it, I know. He wouldn't make a mistake like this.'

His feet kick gravel into a pool of half-frozen water.

'I think you're guessing. I think you're trusting your instinct too much. We can't hang everything on your brain.'

I'm reminded of what Dr Ryans said. He shared the same concern.

'And I think you're adding importance to this place that isn't there. It's a memory, Emre. It's not anything calling to you. Don't confuse the mystical with the practical because of personal bias. People do that all the time. It's not good instinct.'

He charges towards me and punches me on the arm. I can tell he wanted to go for my face, but thought better of it. I hold onto it and then hold onto him, too. Two strangers pass and watch the community police officers holding each other to stay upright.

'Even if the trees were right, Emre. Look...'

I hold the picture up again.

'There are bars missing from the gate all along the left side in this picture. There are too many differences. This isn't it.'

He steps away. He looks to me. His face rich with creases and colour.

'It was close. You're going to be a great police officer.'

He stares at the icy puddle in front of him, reflecting the shivering sky at us.

He sighs and lightens the smallest amount.

'I'm sorry, Emre. I'm sorry for everything.'

'Just tell me we're going to catch him.' His voice comes back, changed. Like it's coming from another part of him.

'Yes. Yes, of course. Yes, we are,' I say, taking a step towards him and then stopping.

I can tell he wants me to keep my distance for a moment. He's so still. It lasts for a while. We stand stiff, held up only by the cold.

20

'I always prefer to be a driven around.
I see their faces, but hear no sound.'

The trip is pretty pin-drop other than the occasional grunt. I imagine it's good to talk about these things, but less good to be stuck in a car with a man you didn't intend on sharing your soul with when you pulled on your boots that morning. He wanted to show me the place without giving it all away, and he couldn't, but there's no shame in that. His feelings are closer to the surface than I realised, closer than most, certainly closer than mine.

Our tour continues in East Tottenham but a quick look shows no line of oak trees. We don't even get out.

We drive and drive. Four more council-built playgrounds to go. The streets that pass form the centre stage of the Tottenham riots. I still remember the broken glass on the high street like it was this morning. I was working in a call centre in Dalston at the time, my life drifting away before my very eyes. When I arrived home there was a 'before the storm' feeling. At least there was something going on, I thought. You could feel it. An energy, an excitement. I assumed that a particularly lairy footy match had just finished at White Hart Lane or some sort of carnival was about to start. That was before it all really kicked off.

TVs were dragged through broken windows. I saw a Chinese kid punched in the face and his bag nicked from off his back, so I picked him up and took him home, while around us a brother and sister sprung out from a trainer shop with cuts on their elbows and glass on their backs, carrying an armful of white socks each.

We get out at another playground and give it the once over. Same roundabout, same swing, same horse on a spring, surrounding houses and some oak trees. But the layout isn't right, it's more spread out and the swing and the horse are at a diagonal to each other rather than adjacent. Without saying a word, we get back in the car.

Three to go.

After I'd dropped the Chinese kid off at his flat, I went back into the chaos. It was palpably dangerous and I liked that. It felt like everyone was waking up. A guy in riot gear, caught on the wrong side of the line, flew past me and I hid in a doorway as teenagers hurling bricks, bits of scaffolding, bottles and anything else they could find, charged past. I turned a corner and saw embers rising into the sky and flickering away like fireflies. Beneath it the shell of a car lay burning. I walked towards it a few steps to feel the heat more keenly. On closer inspection it was clear that it was a police car. The windows were smashed and in the passenger seat sat a bin that'd been wrenched from the street where it once stood. And a few yards away, shimmering like a pond, two sets of shutters were sunbathing in the glinting trickle of the nearby firelight.

Then I heard the cries. 'Missile up! Get some missiles. Anything.' They were coming back.

Bartu scans the next playground while I stay in the car. The roundabout is too far away from the swings. The angle isn't right. Snow starts to fall again. He gets back inside. And drives.

Two more left.

Later I'd find out I'd missed the worst of it. It had been ramping up throughout the day. Our area was cleared when Turkish shop owners with blades chased the looters away. As I pulled back from the burnt-out car, I heard the heavy footsteps of a running crowd. I took a look inside a local pharmacy, torn open. I thought about quickly stepping foot inside and grabbing something as a keepsake. Something practical like headache tablets, condoms or that cream I use for my hair.

A *whoomph* from what sounded like a petrol bomb, woke me from my haze. Then the sound of distant cheers. I got out of there. As I ran hard for home I saw a young police officer running for his life in the gaps between the buildings. Away from the rest of his group, he sprinted into the distance, pursued by a twenty-strong mob, armed with chair legs and rocks.

I've never met a member of the armed response unit who carried out the hard stop on Mark Duggan, which resulted in an officer, only known publicaly as V53, firing the deadly shots that kicked off the riots. But that's what Tottenham is remembered for, to the ends of this island and in the footnotes of international newspapers. Duggan's name will forever be inextricably linked to our force, his death tarnishes us, and we accept it; his body around our necks, deepening chasms of mistrust, that we must sweat to close.

I thought about turning up the day after it all happened to tidy up the streets, like many others did. But I didn't. I watched from my bedroom window and didn't do a thing. I just waited, powerless. I waited for them to reach the top of every tower, kick down the doors of the penthouses and remind the owners how stupid they all were to think that they could get away with their charmed fucking lives.

I feel differently now.

It's my time to jump out and I grab the picture. It's getting dark. Headlights pass. A car in the distance stops and then keeps going, a silver one. I feel like I've seen it before.

No oak trees. The central swing seat almost completely torn off. I sit back in the passenger seat and keep the car sighting to myself.

One more to go.

21

'She.
She, she she.'

By the time we get to the last patch of playground we need our flashlights to poke into the dark and illuminate the subject. We started as night was falling and it had come in thick as tar.

The first hopeful thing we saw were the bars missing in the fence. We couldn't tell if they were at the exact point we needed them to be, but the similarity was enough to beckon us to peruse the rest with forensic conviction. We pick out the slide with a light. The roundabout is in the right position and the trees are good enough. Bartu steps back while I try and cast a beam over the whole thing as best I can, pushing my hand into the middle of the light source to spray it out onto the vista of the scene. He turns, trying to draw an imaginary line from the windows behind him to the playground. He folds up the picture and puts it away. I don't know why he does that at first.

Tottenham's association with outrage began in 1909, during an event which has come to be aptly known as the Tottenham Outrage.

Two men named Helfeld and Lepidus hatched a plan to rob

their place of work. Having established which day wages were collected from the bank in South Hackney and brought over to the rubber factory, they decided to strike without delay.

Armed with semi-automatic pistols, they shot the driver of the car that carried the money. Two Tottenham police constables, Tyler and Newman, hearing shots, gave chase and finally found George Smith, a local gas stoker, beating Lepidus on the ground with his fists. This work of civic duty backfired a touch when Smith was shot twice by Helfeld and the two assailants made off. But miraculously, Smith did not die, despite being shot in the collarbone and head, which sounds fairly hard to believe, but then who am I to talk?

Then a fracas ensued, with the two men firing at a crowd who had started to give chase. During the rampage through Tottenham a stray bullet hit a ten-year-old boy, who died in another by-stander's arms. Constable Tyler, who had initiated the chase, also caught one in the head and officer Newman stayed with him until the ambulance arrived, but the bullet did what it was born for and Tyler wouldn't kiss his children goodnight that evening, or any other.

Meanwhile the criminals escaped into the marshes and headed for the River Lea, managing to hijack a tram. Officers commandeered one too and started a genuine full-blown tram chase, during which another constable, Hawkins, arrived heroically on horseback, but he was dispatched when Helfeld shot his horse.

However, when they opted to continue the escape on foot, the police soon caught up with Helfeld, who had failed to climb a six-foot fence and, not loving his options, pressed the gun to his right eye and fired.

Lepidus managed to find his way into a cottage away from the river, and when police stormed the building he holed up in one of the bedrooms. After a volley of fire, they finally opened the door to see Lepidus was dead. An autopsy would later show he had ended the episode with a single bullet to his own head.

In the upshot, Helfeld was not so fortunate, surviving for a good while before passing away from the smoking hole his bullet had made in his tired face. All of which served as a kind of justice to some, but was of no comfort to the mother of the ten-year-old boy who lay, five miles away, killed by Helfeld's earlier stray discharge. She requested to keep his shoes, and was buried with them fifty years later.

Both men were Latvian Jews, and their act of terror helped ignite a new wave of xenophobia and fear of immigrants in Britain.

'It's not right,' he says.

'Why not. Looks pretty good,' I say, flailing my flash light around.

'Let me help you out,' he says, running the beam along the entire area.

Trees.

The fence with missing parts.

Roundabout.

No horse. No horse.

'See?' he says, as the snow turns to rain, brown mud and ice gathering around our feet.

'Shit,' I say.

He searches again, in some distress at our disappointment, his feet sloshing around like his boat's capsizing. The beam continues its search, unbroken by my hand, insisting on some kind of revelation.

'Not there. Not there. Not here. Definitely not there. Not... shit!'

A figure emerges into the light.

'Christ!' I shout, dropping my torch.

Bartu reaches for something instinctively but has no apparatus to defend himself with.

The rain comes down.

The silhouette gets closer. I stand frozen in fear as Bartu fumbles in a pool of water and ice below.

The figure steps in. Then Bartu, having located the torch, points it onto some legs, then a body, then a face.

'What are you guys doing out here?' Jarwar says. Her cold stare looking back at us in the pounding rain.

Bartu breathes sighs of relief but I don't quite feel the same. I scan behind us to see what must be her car, parked up with the driver's door open, rogue splashes leaping inside. It was her car we saw earlier. I'm almost certain she's been following us, but I keep this to myself for now.

'Ah, hi. We... had reports of some kids hanging around this place. Some undesirables. Graffiti or whatever. Ripping a swing off its hinges. All that,' I say, my voice struggling to stay steady, post the shock, in the freezing rain.

'You're due back,' she says.

'Yeah. I know,' I say.

Patter patter. Pitter patter.

'You remember me, right?' she says.

'Of course,' I say.

'You see me. Right?' she says.

'Of course,' I say. The odd question lingers.

Still Bartu says nothing. And neither does anyone else for a few seconds.

'It doesn't belong to any of the girls, by the way,' she says.

'Sorry? What?' I say, looking her up and down.

'The leg. It belonged to a woman at least five years older,' she says.

Her voice dying away under the sound of the rain.

'So don't say I don't keep you in the loop,' she says.

'Thanks. We're coming now,' I shout through the squall.

And still Bartu says nothing.

'Great. Can I give you a lift?'

Pitter. Patter. We stand stock still.

'We're in Bartu's car. It would've taken us a while otherwise. What with me holding him up and all.'

'Right.'

She still doesn't move.

'Why don't we catch you back at the ranch? You knocking off now?' I say, my voice straining with phoney pleasantries.

'Sure,' she says. 'Sounds good, I'll follow.'

The noise of compliance carries away on the wind as she turns, resolutely. When her chokehold gaze relinquishes, I look to Bartu and get nothing from him either but the signal to move towards his car, which we do, as my hand touches the crackling rust on the green wrought iron gates of our last exhausted playground.

And our feet slap the mud and grass on the other side. And I wonder where else I've seen her car. And who exactly that leg belongs to. As the rain comes down so hard against the dark.

22

'Dee. Dah dah dah dee dah, dah dah, dee head...'

'You *remember me, right? You see me. Right?'*

That's what she said. And it's funny she said that.

When we got back it was all good feelings and checking in. They shot the breeze about anything but what everyone was thinking about. The girls. I thought about bringing them up myself but I didn't feel so much like talking.

The silver car. Not just any car. A police car. As clear as daylight to most people. Unmistakeable. What's the use of noticing the strange things, if I can't spot the obvious ones? I start to think that if I can stare that in the face and not recognise it, then what else have I missed?

Maybe I'm not ready for this. This is a borough of riots, of bloody chases and innocent kids taken. Second thoughts, maybe I'll never be ready for this.

'You guys need a lift?' she says outside, in our civvies.

The tone implicitly changes again out of uniform. We're just people, off the clock. Three people doing a day job that don't know each other so well.

'I've got the car,' Bartu says.

'I'm going to walk,' I say.

'You sure?' he says. 'I can drop you back.'

'I need the exercise.'

They turn towards the weather. There is an unsaid question about 'letting' me do that, but I'm not staying around for that.

'Yeah, I'll get off. See you for another round tomorrow,' I say, as I turn. Before spinning around again as a sudden question occurs. 'Hey, Jarwar, you ever seen a light blue circle with two diagonal lines through it? Just a little marking, in paint, outside a house?'

She's still. Giving the impression of sustained and deep thought.

'Yeah,' she says. 'They're for utility companies. So the water guys can signal to the electricity guys where pipes are and that.'

My neck quakes under the rain. 'Ever heard them used for… anything else?'

'What else?' she says, meeting my blank face. 'They're so companies can communicate, not step on toes, help each other out. Why you ask?'

I shrug. 'I love to learn, Jarwar. Guess I'm just a curious guy.'

They shout as I make off as fast as I can, resolute against the elements.

'Hey, remember tomorrow is Friday, yeah?' she says.

'That Friday feeling, Tom. Nice long day off after that to forget all your troubles,' he shouts.

Without turning around, I put a thumb in the air above my head as I walk. I don't know what he's talking about. He of all people should know it doesn't stop for me. He could be playing along for her benefit, but there's something different about him whenever anyone else is around.

As I go, I hold up my phone and pretend to check it but actually I'm watching them in the dark reflection of my screen. Their bodies change. They seem to know each other better than I thought they did. They're deep in conversation. I see it all as I walk away, and then I see it disappear into the distance.

I put my hood up to shield me from the falling rain, the outside world and everything else. The image of that leg burnt into my mind.

'You remember me, right? You see me. Right?' That's what she said. And it's funny, you see, that she said that. Because if she was talking about my prosopagnosia, I've only told Bartu about that.

I wonder what else has been going from my mouth to her ears. And anyone else's, for that matter. This might be the paraneea talking of course. But I do start to wonder.

*

The next day I'm frustrated to find that Levine has charged us with another gift we certainly can't return. You can elaborate and exaggerate things from your shift when you've done very little, but there's no lying when it comes to things you have to do.

However, I was just considering that perhaps it'd be good to have some time away from thoughts of the girls, to let my mind decompress, when I felt a hand on my back.

'Oi! What you two doing around my neck again?'

It was Turan, and maybe he was joking, maybe he wasn't. He seemed to be protective of his little fiefdom.

'Kids smashed up a shop this time. Pissed in the till. All sorts. Another blessing from Levine,' Bartu said.

'Fuckers. Told you. As you were,' Turan says, and he would've ended the conversation right there if I hadn't had other ideas.

'Hey, Turan. Who's that guy, err...' I say, clicking my fingers, '...came into the chicken shop? We see him about a lot.'

'With that conclusive description? No idea, mate,' he says. He does have a lot of faces in his life, I guess.

'Yeah, but... skinny guy? In sunglasses? Maybe I'll ask a –'

'Oh yeah, I know the one. Poor bastard. His dad went down for fiddling with him. Jarwar put the fucker away. He had to tell her some gruesome shit,' he says with some steel. 'Few years ago, I think she said. Can't remember his name. Why d'you ask?'

'Absolutely no reason,' I say.

'All right then. Best of British,' he shouts, as he crosses the road. 'You get home all right last night, Tom?'

While I'm slightly surprised and maybe even flattered to hear him use my name with a warm inflection, that's more than balanced out by the negative of how aware everyone seems to be of my movements. I shut this down, though. Keep some authority in my stoicism and save some suspicion for later.

'It's only rain,' I say.

Turan merely nods and waves from over the road, unsure how amusing to find this plain speaking. Then he heads down a side road as we make towards the latest landmark that's taken a beating from the local residents.

I want to ask Bartu how Turan had been told about the less-than-scintillating story of me walking home in the rain. But instead I focus on thinking about why I can't exactly see anyone charging around pouring all their effort into bringing these girls home.

'Is this it down here?' I say.

'Yeah, this is it here,' he says, our tired mouths chuntering out adequate conversation.

We find the place has been more ravaged and fucked up than anything I've seen before. After struggling with the till, they decided to repurpose it as a Portaloo, then set about smashing out all the lights, with a baseball bat, presumably. What seems to place an age on the culprits is the amount of gelatine-based sweets and crisps that have been taken, and the feeling that anyone over the age of sixteen who might have done this seriously needs some better friends.

What's more worrying is that at the back of the store, near the toilet rolls and cardboard boxes, is a bullet hole.

Need for stimulation, impulsivity, poor behaviour controls. Vandals have similar profiles to shoplifters. And psychopaths. Strange how one thing can bleed into the other, once you've crossed that line. Criminal versatility, that's another thing that scores highly on the psychopath checklist. Not that I'm calling these kids psychopaths. Or anyone else for that matter. Not yet.

'Emre, you wanna come and take a look at this?'

'Jesus. They're not just angry,' he says.

'They're armed,' I say.

A chill has followed us into the store. Organised crime is one thing. The kind Turan seems to be trying to solve at basement level. The drugs trade, at its leaden heart, is still just an industry. There are paper trails to hang on to and bad reviews from unhappy customers. But this seems like mindless crime and I don't know how you reason with that. Turan was right, they are a different breed.

Then a sensation comes over me that I haven't felt for a while, and I think Emre Bartu feels it, too. The unwanted creep of apathy, brought on by the meaninglessness of the crime and how small I feel under its suffocating weight.

We are Sisyphus. And that boulder only gets heavier.

When we review the tapes with the red-eyed shopkeeper, my spirits fall further. In the blaze of bats and glass fractures, a young boy with a distinctive scarlet birthmark rears his head. The sort of face that even I can place, so clear are its markings, no cheat sheet needed.

I think you could definitely call this a violation of the terms of his ASBO. I picture his scared look as he peered around a corner in his brother's house, before I decided to shop him.

As the security video is rewound and replayed, and I see Eli's body hungrily lay into the corner store again, I wonder if all I've ever done since the beginning is make things worse. If kids can ever be straightened out by intervention. If whoever has taken these girls will ever be found, unless they want to be.

I feel relieved it will be someone else that picks him up. Not that I'm scared of the kid or anything. But he already thinks I'm victimising him. And I've got enough trouble following me around as it is.

The dead eye of the security tape runs on, as my insides turn. And I feel a sense of overwhelming futility, and melancholy for the future. Like there's a hole in my chest, as well as in my head.

Documented Memory
Project #2: Tape

Still reeling from what I've just seen, on the tape I found at the Da Silva house, I push my camcorder to the back of my wardrobe where it's lived for many years alone.

As it makes its way past miscellaneous boxes of school ephemera, my hand brushes against the smoothed down end of another tape I'd forgotten existed. I hold it up and force my memory to surrender the details; the plain white sticker on its face remains blank and stiff-lipped. I shake the tape as if this will better confirm its reality.

When I slot it into the camera deck and the image fuzzes into being, I recall smuggling my new toy into school. I was the January kid with the covetable gift to show off that he really should have left at home. The shot glides past the oak trees of the school field. The auteur adopting the style of a hidden camera exposé, zooming in on various faces. Only tracings to me. Plump freckly wads, like pug dogs, melded into one single zip file in my mind entitled 'what children look like'.

The shaky cam starts to make the viewer feel seasick, as it struggles to focus, particularly in zoom. Mercifully, the director pulls back, a moment of wonder happening as we are greeted with nothing but autumn term leaves being blown from heaps at the edge of screen, which the camera with cinematic instinct follows, soon hitting an open mouthed face that dominates the screen. The architecture of which I feel like I almost recognise. I tingle from my shoulders, to my spine, all the way up the vines of nerves to my brain stem.

'What are you doing?' she says.

'Filming a documentary,' says the film-maker. It's disturbing to hear your voice as a child, a different voice box in your throat. My London accent, far spikier then, must've become dulled by university and adulthood's journey towards neutrality. I was a different collection of cells then. Strange how we change, someone pulling the sheet out from inside you, as you hardly notice nature's ultimate magic trick.

'Do you want to film me?' she says, stepping back to centre herself in the frame. Her face. Those eyes. I feel something.

She does some handstands that aren't befitting for her age. This girl, I remember, she remained childish, babyish, the word we used, until quite late I think. She rushes the camera and soon it's swivelling around. We glimpse the milky white sky and worms in the dirt, before it settles on the close up of her bloody knee.

The cameraman has little choice, confronted with the sight, it's pink wrinkles stained in excessive levels of black blood. She pushes into the abrasion for the viewer's sake. Children love picking at scabs. They can't help themselves. Her fingernails burrow into the wound as fresh blood bubbles up like lava to the summit, this display finally causing audible sounds of distaste from young Tom.

'Eugh,' he says. Which peculiarly makes her stop. As if she was unaware that her actions would be anything but adorable. She turns around and lifts her skirt up to flash the viewer and then spins back to judge the effect. But young Tom has already averted the camera's eye, to a tree, almost avoiding the sight of her white knickers altogether.

When he pans back she has closed down the distance.

'I want it,' she says. I feel like I can touch her. Smell her.

And soon he has given her the camera and they are lower, partially hidden, the oak tree dirty in the blurred foreground. The camera zooms *in on younger girls, cross-legged and playing pat-a-cake some distance away. Her Attenborough-like voiceover draws a laugh from old and young Tom alike. Could this be Sarah? I can't tell.*

'And now. In their... natural habitat. We find here... A rare sighting... Of these horrific creatures. In their checked summer dresses their mummies make. These... little squirts. These bitch geeks.'

The camera swivels onto young Tom's face. He's no more familiar to me in close up than any of the other malnourished children.

'And now an even more hideous beast.' At which Tom frowns his disapproval, causing her to laugh wildly, the camera spinning around to catch her falling out of shot. Then she reappears, newly angelic. The mood changing as the viewers, Tom then and now, say nothing.

She's colouring herself in. In my mind. But I can't quite connect the dots. I start to remember things about this girl, but is she Sarah? Perhaps the shot is too close and blurred even for someone more blessed in the area of facial recogntion than I. I don't know.

As the shot holds, to the soundtrack of the wind in the trees, I look into her green eyes. And think about the other tape, the one I found at the Da Silva house. The one I watched before this, containing the shadow of a woman in the background, who swiftly disappeared from shot.

The image of this little blonde girl on screen now will soon be erased from my memory, too. Unless I can hold on to her. Track her down. There's something about her. A feeling I can't put my finger on. The fractured pieces are slowly forming a whole person. What I remember about the girl in the video is this: she will move to Battersea and out of the boy's life in a few short weeks. I feel like I have stumbled on a minor miracle. We didn't have many of these encounters, she and I. She was, more often, a distant shining figure. I watch the wind blow her blonde hair, so softly, as the brown leaves shoot away, in the distance.

23

'It's just you and me baby, on the edge of the park,
Can't see anyone else lady, in the pool, in the dark.'

'I'm going to be alone tomorrow,' I say, as we drag our bones back to the station to deliver the security tapes. It falls from my mouth without me thinking about it. One second it's rolling around in there, the next it's on the pavement.

'Well, I'll see you Sunday,' says Bartu, clearly not picking up on my physical, emotional and verbal cues.

It's been a long week. I know I have to go home and think, talk it through with Mark and review our dead ends. Ponder what our next move might be by looking at the strands from further back. But the long stretch of the weekend lays out before me like a spectre, casting a shadow over my brain and every single thought.

I'm afraid of the passages of unchartered nothing. I'm afraid of black holes in my diary. It's a modern complaint, but I'm sure you understand.

'Hey Emre, what you eating for lunch tomorrow?' I say.

'Well, we're staying in. Aisha is cooking.'

'That sounds good. I could do that,' I say.

He stares at me, the guy with the limp and nobody to go home to but a judgmental cat. But still somehow he hesitates.

'It's kind of particular cooking. You know, she's trying this Turkish dish... '

'That sounds perfect. Thanks.'

'You might not like it.'

'Come on, man. You can't scare me. What kind of thing are we talking about?'

'Goat's head soup.'

I breathe in through my nose and nod sagely. Pushing down the image that is forcing my face to fold inwards. Trying to generate an expression somewhere between 'Oh man, I thought it was going to be something unusual' and 'Hmm. A Goat's Head? I've always wanted to eat one of those, ideally in the form of a soup.'

'That's great. Looking forward to checking out your place.'

'You really... okay, if we're doing this, then great. Fine,' he says, through sighs. It's hardly the most enthusiastic dinner invitation but I'm looking forward to it all the same.

'Okay, pick me up at twelve thirty,' I say, reasonably.

'But, I... Okay, fine. See you then.'

If Emre was caught off guard then, the feeling is far from diminished when he picks me up at my flat the next day, Miss Heywood smiling at him as she sits in my kitchen in an old shirt. I can tell he's judging me, the way Mark did, muted but none too discreetly, but I'm not entirely sure what their problem is. We are two relatively young, free and unencumbered people, one with a taste for wire sculptures of livestock, the other with problems of his own.

She has a birthmark in the shape of Brazil and, when she's not 'vaping', she smokes far more than is acceptable. She had called apropos of nothing, just after I'd watched the two mini-DV tapes. I'd hoped it was about the case in some way or other. But the long talk had turned into something else and before I knew it there was a warm body on my second pillow, a heartbeat from a sleeping partner in the stillness, to provide the company I've come to crave, and I wasn't about to complain.

You can actually make three meals from one goat's head. As well as the soup, you can eat the tongue by slicing it into sections of about one inch then cooking it with chicken stock and adding salt and pepper. Finally, you roast the brain and then mix it with rice and onions and whatever else you feel like, perhaps ginger and a little cilantro, depending on how you like your brain. I researched all this before arriving at Bartu's flat, in an attempt to make myself more comfortable with what I was about to indulge in. However, efforts to do so have only resulted in further apprehension thus far. If Aisha is doing it the proper way she'll start by smashing the head with a mallet or small axe, depending on what she has handy. Typically, in Turkish cuisine, the eyes are left in and offered to the guest of honour as a delicacy. The best method is to stick a fork into the eye, twist it and remove. A website told me 'there is little resistance when consuming it and they are considered to be delicious'. They're eaten first, along with the ears, because it's best to get both while they're hot. If I am considered the 'guest of honour' then this is not an honour I'm whole-heartedly looking forward to having bestowed upon me.

Before the bullet I was a fussy eater. Not a conscientious vegan, or raw food caveman purist. I was one of those fussy eaters who ate reasonably badly and was suspicious of the lesser-known vegetables. I've branched out in my tastes but this is taking things much further than I ever intended.

The goat is popular in many countries, including Nigeria and the West Indies, and as I meet Aisha and find she hails from the latter, I become somewhat more confident given that she may have some prior experience of the dish, meaning that the meal will be executed correctly even if I fear the finer details of eating it. She kisses my cheek warmly and pours me a glass of water. Then goes back to poking around at the pot in the kitchen next door. The sound of which calls to mind the noise of feet outside a cell door in the morning light as I'm about to be led to the gallows.

I think I'm sweating.

'Are your family from around here, Emre?' I say.

'Not far from here,' he says, sitting opposite me at the Ikea dining table, sipping supermarket cola from a tall glass. They take turns to go and poke at the dish, but at the moment she's in the driving seat. They have one of those hatches, which allows me to rubberneck at what she's doing in there while we talk.

'They mostly live in Edmonton. There's a big community there. I was there at first but when I got the job around here I thought I'd move closer to my beat. It's home from home. I've got an uncle around the corner.'

I find myself locking hollow eyes with him, unable to concentrate on anything he said past the word 'They'. My mind is on what we're about to consume. I am open to new experiences, it's what my life recently has been all about, but I can't help seeing that goat's head peeking out at me from behind a wooden fence. I picture grabbing its head and giving it a lick. I taste his forehead on my tongue.

'But, what about you... you – what are you doing, man?' Bartu says.

I pull my tongue back into my mouth, a good deal too late for him to avoid catching me in an unhealthy daydream with a live billy goat.

'Nothing, man,' I say, still tasting him on my tongue.

As Aisha arrives beside him with a steaming pot, she can sense Bartu's concern but chooses to ignore it. She's heard stories of me, I can tell by the way she stares. I smile at both of them, surreptitiously bringing the back of my hand up to my mouth. I lick it gently to take the imaginary taste I've conjured away, as her ladle delves into the pot and brings out lashings of hot goat juice.

The smell is chestnut coloured. It fills my field of vision like I'm wearing brown tinted shades. I hear a G sharp lightly ringing. And I feel the texture of khaki trousers on my fingertips.

'Here you go. So are you from London originally, Tom?'

I try to answer but I don't want to breathe through my nose. I know it's all in my head, I know it's only food, but not for the first time, my head is getting the better of me.

'Yes, yes. Hmm. Not too far from here, actually,' I mumble.

Bartu can see what's going on and I think he's enjoying it. But I'm doing a passable effort at being comfortable for Aisha's sake. She smiles indulgently and gives me some 'Mm-hm's, the sounds of which possess a West Indian tone, light and sweet.

'And do the family still live nearby, Tom?' she says. I close one eye and gaze down at the soup, poking at it with my eating implement and watching it ripple. I look up and catch Bartu's eye, which says, *'It's perfectly good food, mate. You asked to come here. Don't put on a performance,'* he telepaths.

'It's not a performance,' my mind tries to telepath back.

'Well, my family... they were actually driving over... err... ' I mumble. Glancing up at them, then down at the spoon paddling below.

I pause. The room clicks with only the sound of delicate and considerate eating.

'They were driving over... to pick me up from university... a few years ago now. Mum and Dad. They used to be pretty wild but became very careful people. You know? Ha. Those kind of parents. My dad wouldn't go on the motorway. Only ever used A-roads. Don't ask me why...'

Mm. Hm. Ha. Dampened laughs as they eat.

'And there was some sort of... I remember it because I was waiting... It was my first term, I had all my stuff piled in the corner in the hallway. The warden stayed with me... because when everyone's gone the cleaners come in straight away... to clean up the intense levels of mess the students have made in their first term away from home... I remember one guy had three piles of pizza boxes in his room that went from floor to ceiling, and one day he just threw them out of the window... no consequences... and I... they died, they were killed, on the road, on the way. So they're... they're dead. Yep.'

My spoon dives deep into soup. I hear the plink of hers being left to gently lie against the bowl and in my periphery I see Emre holds a piece of bread that he is yet to tear.

'I'm... I'm really sorry to hear that,' he says.

'Yes,' she says. 'So, so sorry, Tom.'

The spoon reaches my mouth and the liquid travels over my tongue and to the back of my throat. My tongue searches around my teeth in its wake. It tastes fine. It's better than fine, in fact. It's good. The G sharp rings out warmly and the room glows in a shade of chestnut.

'Well, it was a long time ago now,' I say. It's surprising how few times I've actually had to tell people this story. You can certainly cut down on reliving things if you're willing to have few close friends.

'I still live in the same room I did when they passed away. Passed away... ' I say, picturing the crash I saw in my first week of being a PCSO. The first dead bodies I ever saw couldn't help but remind me of mum and dad.

'... But, you know, now the place is mine. I can stay up as late as I like. Eat what I want. I've turned their room into my workout space. That sort of thing.'

Aisha makes a different kind of 'Mm-hm'. The stuttering

sound of eating commences again. I haven't stopped for a moment since the first spoonful.

'This is good,' I say. 'Mmm. This is really good.'

And I mean it.

'Right. I'm sorry, Emre Bartu, I've been thinking I don't like days off. I want to run a few things by Aisha.'

24

'Put away your pencil cases,
It's the end of another long day,
Boys and girls, all their pretty faces,
Are coming out to play.'

'I wanna know who that leg belongs to,' she says, shaking her head gravely.

'Well, that's a good question, Aisha,' I say.

'And what about the lipstick on that car window?' she says.

'We shouldn't even be talking about this,' says Emre, sitting back in his chair.

Everyone likes to play the amateur sleuth these days, everyone has a thirst for true crime, it's a zeitgeist I'm all too aware of. It's something real. Blood and bone. In a world of fake news, politics and corporate interest, it's difficult to know who to trust; what's real, what's advertising and who's kidding who. But here are real life mysteries, and even if their absolute truths are buried, there is an undeniable reality somewhere to be found. And right now we have an unquenchable thirst for that. And yes, that includes me.

'What would you say the lipstick means?' I say, one hand gently on my stomach, sated.

'I don't know. Is it a sign from the kidnapper? A cry for help from the victim?' Aisha says.

'Both good options. And the one thing about kids is there are always a hundred examples of their handwriting around.'

'But that means going back to the school,' Emre says, putting his drink down, calmly enough.

'Or going back to the second house. The Bridges' house,' I say.

'Can you do that? Are you allowed to do that?' Aisha says, another hint that Emre has already told her how far I push things. That he's told her that he doesn't want me to drag him into any kind of trouble if he can help it.

'No, we're not doing that,' Bartu says, fixing me with a stare.

'But if it's important. If it's going to bring these girls home?' she says.

'The lipstick handwriting thing? That's going to crack it?' Bartu says.

'Could be nothing. Could be everything,' I say.

'You're not more interested in that leg?' he says.

'Forget the leg, we can't get anywhere near the leg. Having said that, what're your guesses on the leg, Aisha?'

I haven't forgotten my suspicions about Emre. I want to bring her in close and get her on my side, just in case he's planning to do the dirty on me in some way I haven't quite figured out yet.

'I don't know, but it's horrible. That poor, poor girl. Whoever she is. Someone's got to do something. Are they doing all they can?' she says, with a fresh sense of purpose. She glances at me supportively.

'Of course they are,' Bartu says.

'Well... ' I say.

'Hey, Jarwar is leading a "stop and speak" around Tottenham, which'll have covered around three hundred people yesterday alone,' Bartu says. 'Showing them pictures of the girls, and they'll do the same today and –'

'No, no. There's no point, the girls will be locked away somewhere already. Unless they have a picture of him, then it's pot luck.'

'Right, and how do you plan on getting one of those?' he says.

'Now that's the kind of question we should be asking,' I say.

'Photo-fit? Or –' she says, but Bartu cuts her off, much to the detriment of the mood.

'I've told you, they're doing all they can.'

I'm not using her. I really do want an outsider's view on things. I'm so close to it all, I have to make sure my next move is a good one. Minimum risk and maximum result.

'Of course. I'm just saying it's not a bad thing for us to gently follow up our leads. The picture was a dead end, but the caretaker did place someone suspicious outside the school; someone must've got a better look at him, we just need to speak to the right student. Stop in at the Da Silvas' home as well, and I know there's something going on at that Fraser house –'

'We shouldn't even be talking about this!' he says, bringing his glass down hard on the table. The air in the room gets less healthy. Aisha goes to clear up, tactfully deciding that Emre and I might have things to discuss that he isn't comfortable with her hearing. But she's still just beyond the white hatch doors.

'I get one day off. That's all. Just... please. Tomorrow. We'll talk about it tomorrow. I like to keep the work where it is, all right?'

'These girls don't get a day off, Emre. They don't get a day off. And they're scared. And God knows what's happening to them! Listen, there's something I found, something I've seen and I should've told you.'

'Oh man. No, I don't think I want to hear this. You've

actually reached the point where I don't want to… Fuck it. What is it?'

I glance up to where Aisha is then lower my voice further.

'I found a mini-DV tape. At the Da Silva house. And I dug out my old camcorder last night and put it inside.'

'Was it Nina's? What was on it?' he whispers, with penetrating hush.

'Just girls playing. At first. She must've got it as a gift, but I'm guessing not from her folks. It's retro, like the polaroid. The video starts with her doing silly voices. Then she's presenting her own TV show. Then it cuts and she's in her gym skirt and top, talking to the camera again, but this time it's different. She introduces who she is. Kind of dead-voiced like she's done it before. She takes off her top. Shows her bra. And you can tell there's someone else there.'

'Who? Do they speak? We need to turn this in.'

'We don't hear their voice. And they certainly don't step in front of the camera. But in the room, which isn't her room, there's a TV. And in the reflection of its screen I could make out the silhouette of the other figure.'

'What did he look like?'

'Not he, Emre. She. Long hair. I think – I think it was a woman.'

His eyes flicker up to Aisha.

'The image wasn't clear enough for more than that. But we're no longer merely looking for a him. Maybe it's a him that looks like a her. Or vice-versa. Or maybe it's a couple, I don't know, but I can't sleep well until they're found.'

'So what's our next step? What are you saying?' he says.

'We'll hand the tape in on Monday. Come clean. It's too big not to. But right now, I'm saying… with no other options available to us, we need to take another gamble–'

He leans in and talks animatedly in violent whispers.

'You're going to go over to that school? Say you're right, say someone has seen something, it's a fair assumption, but we don't know who! You want to question them one by one? Maybe they don't even know the significance of what they saw and even if they do... they sure as fuck don't want to come forward about it. The school isn't even open today. Go home! Watch a movie. Better still, join a club, get a hobby.'

I stand to leave. It's a good thought and it sticks in my head.

'You're right. A hobby, that's a good thought. I'm going now.'

Emre pulls on his jacket hurriedly and calls to Aisha. 'Just going to be a minute!'

I want to thank her again for her hospitality and it bothers me not to, but he's hustling me out of the door already.

'Okay, where are we going?' he says.

'You're going to drive me home, right?' I say.

'No, no. You're not that good a liar. Your eyes are lit up like fairy lights. Wherever you're going, I'm coming, too.'

How transparent I must've become. I'm going to have to get a better poker face.

'I can do it on my own,' I say.

'No you can't, Tom. I'm not going to let you go. Not because I'm worried about you, not because it might be dangerous, but because everything you do is now linked to me.'

It's a fair point, but he's the one who's been dropping the ball; information, his lighter. So I find that speech a little rich, but I decide to let it go because I don't want to walk.

'So, what are you thinking?' he says

'Hobbies,' I say, biting my bottom lip. 'I'm thinking about clubs and hobbies.'

*

We'd already rung the bell twice. I was considering a third

but didn't want to seem pushy. If the Da Silvas reported us for intruding on their time, that really would leave us firmly stranded up the proverbial creek.

Mr Da Silva opened the door and wordlessly stood back to let us in.

'My wife is sleeping,' he says.

He takes a long look at the two plain-clothed men standing before him.

'We... thought it was best to come without the full costume,' Bartu says.

'Thought it might soften the blow, given how much you've seen of us lot recently,' I add.

Mr Da Silva scratches his head and examines his kitchen tiles before looking up at both of us again. It's the subtlest acknowledgement that someone has just spoken you could imagine, but then Mr Da Silva's mind is understandably on places far away from our feelings.

'One thing I'm not sure anyone asked... that we really need to know... ' I say.

I lose my train of thought as I notice his sensible shoes are just slightly muddy. It's not uncommon for loved ones of missing people to spend most of their days walking around the local area, in the hope that at some point they might see their face around a corner, in the back of a car. Every minute that ticks on is like another ton weight around their necks. I don't know how much it ever helps, but it feels better than standing still.

'Mr Da Silva. It sounds silly. And again I'm sorry if you've been asked this before... Was she part of any after school clubs?'

He breathes out hard and places his right hand on the small of his back.

'No,' he sighs.

Bartu is already looking for the exit.

'No. No one ask this before. She did go to them. Lots. She

go to computer class, Monday. Extra maths study group on Wednesday. Tennis Club, Thursday,' he says.

'Good. That's good,' I say, standing and resisting punching the air.

Bartu is already at the door, as a defeated and heavy Mr Da Silva follows us out and my mind is working overtime.

It's important he can meet them following after school clubs so he can avoid the visibility of 3.15 home time. And it's important their clubs are all on different days so they don't realise they're not the only ones getting this special attention. I've already found out from Miss Heywood that Jade Bridges did art club with her on Tuesdays, and had no interest whatsoever in sport or anything else. However, Ms Fraser told us Tanya played on three different sport teams. If we can figure out which day he met each girl, then we can narrow it down to the fifteen or so others who were in that group and jog their memories about anyone hanging around outside the school gates on those days. There'll still be work to do but god knows it's better than interviewing the whole school, and better than just asking the handful of kids in Heywood's art class alone. With around forty or so pupils, I like the odds of one of our little information processors remembering a guy hanging around with a camera. Then throw a photo-fit of a guy like that to a community like this? Someone will know him. No one's that good at hide and seek.

I make a mental note to have a second shot at leaning on the shoe-gazing cleaner with the different coloured irises at some point, too. Going by the fact that he was almost finishing up around the time we met him at the school, I'd say he leaves around the time that the school clubs finish, and I think he knows more than just how to make people uncomfortable.

'You should be looking into the paedophile ring. You done this? This Tottenham paedophile ring?' says Da Silva, voice low. He has been looking up local rumours, spending his time wandering through internet threads, as well as outdoors.

'We're not counting anything out,' says Bartu.

But in this case, we are. It's a myth perpetuated by a buzz word. By the time 'Paedophile Ring' entered the lexicon, every local area had one. The news makes monsters and keeps people scared. Rumours make the monsters real. We can't stick around for this, it's too 'tin foil hat' even for my taste.

'We really shouldn't take up any more of your valuable time. Thank you,' I say, smoothly reaching for the door handle and letting us out with a deal of acumen I often struggle to muster. It's smooth tact that Bartu appreciates as he strides purposefully out of there. But it can't save either of us from what happens next.

We see a uniformed figure appear at the end of the drive.

Radio in hand.

Wearing a look that only a smarter man than me could decipher.

25

'Danger...
Real danger, troubling danger. Danger!'

'You know... Jarwar... I've been so worried about those girls, about the families. I can't sleep.' I say.

She walks us around the corner and out of sight of the Da Silvas and their neighbours. Then pushes Emre against her car and frisks him, taking a look for any stray eyes as she does. I'd say it was a bit uncalled for if I didn't know it was fairly called for.

'Yeah I get it, but you're in a position of authority and there is protocol. You can't go off doing whatever you like. I'm serious! I need to call this in,' she says, a tad rougher as she gives me my going over. And I'd be nervous about that mini-DV in my pocket. Had I not palmed it to Emre behind my back in between his pat down and mine.

'I know. I know, I'm just... I'm so afraid. For them. My nerves got the better of me. Don't blame Bartu, I m-made him come with me. He just didn't want me to be alone. I can't be alone. At the moment.'

I pantomime it out accompanied by a fixed stare to the horizon. I opt for the 'storm-inside-that-I-can't-express' angle.

I bring my hand to my face, cover my eyes and hang my

head to increase the dose. Bartu looks on, his mouth shut fast around his heart.

'You know what... I...' she says, turning away.

She's trying to keep her composure, but she really does have a storm inside. She turns back to us.

'I'm gonna... look, consider this a warning, okay? They want blokes like you, your age, your... profile.'

There we go again. I read the subtext. There's the inflection.

'But... they don't *need* you. Not that badly. There are blokes with far less going for them than you two, but, If you cause top brass any trouble they'll switch you out in a second. Believe me. So consider yourselves... warned.'

I nod, as if struggling to take it all in.

I could give her a heartfelt thanks. Yet, tactically it's always better to make people intuit that their words have had such a great effect that you feel winded rather than relieved. That can only play better for you later on.

My brain struggles to get myself out of the zone. Smile, and you feel great. When you frown, you feel bad. The body is a simple thing. It can be led by any sector and they're all tied together with strings of emotional information. My breathing falters and I find that my eyes are indeed full of tears.

Jarwar clocks this. She doesn't want to reference it full on, it's the kind of thing that's awkward for an adult. It's hard to look at, like the sun, so she makes a snap decision.

'Look, if it makes you guys feel any better we have a firm lead.'

We barely blink. The joy of revelation is not meant for us. We push it down and hide it away.

'That's good. That does make me feel... a bit... better, certainly,' says Bartu.

I just wipe my eyes and start to walk back to Bartu's car. They follow.

Buoyed by Bartu's response, but prompted for more elaboration by mine, she decides to go on.

'Someone had been sending Tanya Fraser messages about meeting times using Facebook. And other stuff, flirtatious stuff.'

'Grooming,' Bartu says.

'Well, maybe,' she says, as we near our vehicles.

I start to wonder whether Jarwar was planning to visit the Da Silvas at all.

Perhaps our meeting was just a case of bad luck.

Or something else entirely.

'No photo on the profile page. False name. We're tracing the account now and should get news on it soon.'

The air between us tells a story of disappointment. If it leads back to a home internet source they'll have an address. It's good they're close, but I wanted to be the one to find her. Not least because I trust myself more than I trust them. Call it instinct.

'Any news on the leg?' I say, eyes adorned with hope and tears.

'None yet,' she says. 'We've got people out looking through the cemetery and other open spaces. For… you know, the rest of her.'

'That it, is it?' I say.

'No. No, that's not it!' she says, my baiting effecting a shift in her. 'We're checking other recent corpses that missing a limb. We're sampling it against some other body parts that were found inside a sofa dumped on the side of the Parkland nature trail. And we discovered signs of a partially erased tattoo on the back of her calf showing the initials KG! That okay with you?'

'Yeah. All right,' I say, shrugging. 'Good. And how does KG, whoever she is, fit into the disappearance of our girls?'

'She doesn't, Tom. She has nothing to do with it. At all,' she says.

That's not what I think. But I stifle anymore petty disagreement, as even I can see I'm wearing away her good will.

'Look. Seriously. No poking around in other people's cases, lads. If you get further up the ranks, you'll find people don't like that. People like to finish what they start, it's bad form to muscle in.'

This is the toughest she's been during the whole encounter. The steeliness inside is back, the sort of thing that makes her good police I suppose. But that steel is also what made me think something was off the night before last, in that playground as the rain fell.

'Stick to what you do best, boys, and you'll be fine.'

Her door slams and she pulls away, eyeing us as she speeds off, while I reach for Bartu's passenger door.

'Right, I need to make a call,' I say, dropping my 'touched by emotion' vibe. Emre clocks this, grimacing with disbelief as he backs the car out. Maybe it already feels like strike three for him. Maybe that nudge is enough to scare him off.

'Make the call on the way. Better still, do it at home. I don't want anything to do with it. I'll drop you back,' he says.

'No, not a phone call. A house call,' I say.

'Miss Heywood? That's fine. You do what you want, you're an adult. I'll drop you there,' he says.

'No, not there. We need to go to see the Bridges.'

The car stops. Emre punches the steering wheel.

'No fucking way! Do you understand what just happened there?' he shouts.

'Yes, I do, all the more reason to cover our tracks. We need to get rid of that picture before they start looking back over everything.'

'No, not that. Not now,' he fires back.

'Yes now! She thinks we've just taken it hard and are backing off, this is the one chance we've got.'

'Okay, just so I'm clear, to cover up the shit we've done, you want to do more of this shit? And to go and see *them*? Of all people? Furious Bridges who fucking hates PCSOs?'

'I don't see that we have another choice.'

He starts the car again.

'Not today, man, not again. Not on my day off, please.'

'Okay,' I say, putting my hands in my lap.

Silence. I watch the world pass. It doesn't quite feel real, like we're in a car from a fifties movie. The backgrounds are pre-recorded. I half expect them to come around again on a loop.

'That's it? Okay?' Bartu says.

'You said you didn't want to. So we won't. Drop me home,' I say, staring out the window.

I can sense he thinks I'm moving towards a sulk, but I'm not. I'm being pragmatic. He's a horse with a sore hoof, he can't go any further today. Time to bed down in the campfire light until morning.

The pre-recorded background goes on. It's a game you can play next time you're in a car, look at it and imagine you're on a set. It's easy. This is how it is when the world loses its previous resonances.

When we arrive, it takes me a while to get from seated to standing, Bartu turning away as it makes him uncomfortable to see me struggle. He only turns back when the car door slams.

He calls out the window and throws something to me. That I actually catch. Which surprises no one more than me.

'There's your tape. Get some rest,' he shouts.

I hold onto it as I see a man wearing a black baseball cap on the other side of the road. I start to wonder if it's the same guy that left so abruptly from the chicken shop. Ever think you keep seeing the same stranger everywhere? Ever feel like people are watching you? This is known as 'The Spotlight Effect'. I suppose I'm just another person who thinks the world revolves around them. As I watch him walk away, I realise he seems completely oblivious to my presence. But I still wait for him to disappear before I speak again. Just in case.

'Nah, better if you keep it till tomorrow,' I say, flinging the tape back to him. It makes sense, as eyes are always on me, while he'll soon be safe at home.

'Enjoy the rest of your Saturday,' I shout holding up a hand that I only realise I've kept raised far too long when I check to look at it as I get out my front door key. It's been up the whole time, as I turned and walked. Bartu probably shook his head as he drove off. I release my arm and let it drop to my side.

I need to change my shoes. I went with sensible black for lunch, but the Bridges' house is a bit of a walk away and these are starting to rub. I don't know if I feel safer without Bartu or with him, but it was clear this was the end of the road for him, for today.

I'd already smuggled the picture out of his glove compartment as I excited the car, taking advantage of the fact that my fumbling made him uncomfortable, affording me a window in which to spirit it away. Funny that no one sees how fast your disabilities become opportunities.

I know I have to put things back as they were, if I get to ask the Bridges' a couple of questions while I'm there, then so much the better.

*

'Come in then,' Mrs Bridges says.

'Thanks,' I say. 'This is PCSO Heywood, by the way.'

The two women nod, Miss Heywood taking the ruse in her stride. When I returned home earlier than expected she was still there and was pretty sheepish about the matter. She'd stuck around to sketch out an idea she'd had in charcoals in my kitchen, time had run away from her and it seemed rude not to ask if she would like to tag along for support. I didn't expect her to say yes. Maybe I'm too amenable.

Mrs Bridges leads us into their pockmarked living room, past her half-dressed husband. He's naked to the waist but not in the direction you'd expect. He wears a red T-shirt that barely covers his potbelly and some Y-fronts to protect his modesty. It hasn't worked.

'What the fuck's he doing here?' he says, which is a kinder greeting than I got last time.

'I wanted to keep you in the loop about everything. I know how these things work, families get shut out, I just wanted to say... if I hear anything... you'll be the first to know.'

Mr Bridges shifts back into his arse groove in front of the TV and says nothing. We seem to have drawn some truce. However hostile it may look to Heywood it feels relatively permissive to me.

'And I just wanted to check one more thing, up in the bedroom.'

'Fine,' Mrs Bridges says after a second's thought. Heywood gives Mrs Bridges an assuring nod as we head upstairs.

I stand perusing the posters on her wall.

Occasionally I eye the drawer beneath her bed where I found the picture originally. Then I glance up to see Mrs Bridges there. Not watching me with any particular eagle eye, but there all the same. A presence. One that will not let me do what I need to do.

I wonder whether Jarwar followed me here. I don't know what I was thinking bringing Heywood. I always push things just a little bit further than is necessary. It's a filthy habit. The colour grey drips from the walls; her childish perfume scattered around the room. I try to take her in, I feel the imperative here more than ever.

I see the younger version of Jade staring at me from the corkboard photo collage above her headboard. The shot she looks happiest in catches my eye. A bouncy castle party on the front lawn of this house, only a couple of years ago, I'd imagine. Peeping out, blurred in the bottom of the shot, is the blue circle symbol. But without its diagonal lines. And a copper coin drops, somewhere in the back of my mind.

I swallow it down, blink away my concern and save that black theory for later, as a poster next to it intrigues and disturbs me, too.

'Bieber,' I say. Pronouncing it Biber.

'Beeber,' says Mrs Bridges. I raise my eyebrows and nod, scanning the room. I'm waiting for my chance. I can't be here long. They could burst in any minute.

Jarwar. Levine. Bartu. Our nervy chief. A litany of other faceless faces, all of whom I've grown to mistrust.

I need Mrs Bridges to go, even if it's just for a second. Her face has formed itself into sternness, and all this after my opening gambit was about openness, honesty and keeping her 'in the loop'. Whatever that means. I'm well outside the loop, the loop doesn't want me in it. I couldn't find the loop if I tried.

She stares at me. Then at Heywood. Heywood stares at me. Two strikes in a day would be more than a warning. There will be consequences and endings. That much I know. I could slip it back in there without even opening the drawer.

I walk around to assess the gap. The picture sits patiently in my document holder. She watches.

My prints will be all over it. And Bartu's. But it's too late to worry about that, I can't imagine they'll be looking for our fingerprints, but still, what amateurs we are.

Heywood turns to the window.

I sneeze.

'Bless you,' Mrs Bridges says, no feeling behind her words.

'Thank you.' I cover my nose. Give her an embarrassed look. 'Could I trouble you for a tissue?'

A micro-nod, her head hardly moving, she turns towards the

bathroom, which is only about five paces to her right, keeping her arms folded the whole time. I burst into action.

It was a good sneeze, I consider, my best bit of make-believe yet. I kneel down and feed the picture into the drawer below the bed. But it won't go in. I pull at the drawer. Heywood comes around to help, too. It's stuck. We pull at it. It comes loose. I drop the only slightly creased picture back and close the thing softly with my right hand, Heywood replacing the light blue valance in one swift move.

Then, standing there, holding a wad of rolled up toilet paper, with a face like a question mark, we see the lady of the house.

'What the hell is going on?' she says, uncharacteristically raising her voice.

'I needed to put something back. I took it the first time. I shouldn't have,' I say.

She's got me. I'm a shucked oyster.

'What are you really doing here?' she says with understandable force, but coming down to a whisper now, creating a pact between us. Just us three. No Mr Bridges. No angry white man flying off the handle. Just us. It's a good tactic. I walk right into it, hoping it's not a snare or a deadfall trap. I think about traps a lot recently. I run the scenarios to see how to escape them. And how I'd trap others.

'We found a picture at each of the missing girl's houses.'

'Right, well, she likes to draw. Look, I'm calling the police, the real police,' she says, turning towards the door.

'Not like this, we think these were given to her by a man. We think this man has your daughter,' Heywood says, putting it all out there before I can stop her.

Mrs Bridges draws breath. It's no wonder this offers her no comfort. This theory isn't pretty, even in its optimism. She looks at Heywood in her black trench coat, wondering what story

215

it tells. She looks at my trainers. Casual Sundays. I'm the still image of an interloper. Maybe her husband was right.

'This is fucking ridiculous,' she says, tucking her black hair behind her ebony ear, shaking with exasperation. 'This is my daughter's life. Do you understand that?'

She's right to be angry. Of course. A shudder runs through me.

'I'm so sorry. I care so much about this case, about these girls. I promise you. I can't let it go. And I won't, until they're found.'

It's the whole truth and nothing but. But she's not convinced. She shakes her head firmly, biting down hard on her bottom lip.

'So... I don't know you're here then? Is that the plan?' she mutters, stepping further in to the room.

'That's right,' I say hopefully, laying some of my cards on the table, but eminently aware of my shitty hand. We have to get out of here.

'Sorry. I don't see why I shouldn't shop you in?' she says, taking her phone out of her pocket.

'Because we're giving you everything,' Heywood says, which is true. But Mrs Bridges, in the half-light of the room, doesn't look convinced. She knits her carefully plucked eyebrows and then turns away again with intent, but I move in and grab her arm.

She looks at my hand and I let go.

'And there's something else. They got into Tanya Fraser's Facebook account and they found someone... no picture, no name, trying to contact her. If they can link it back to the computer it came from, then it could all be over very soon.'

She lifts the back of her hand to her mouth and her eyes moisten. There's a certain energy between us.

'That's all I've got. I promise. On my parents' lives.'

A hint of warmth. She grabs my arm and squeezes it. I give her the slightest smile back. Heywood glances out the window.

'I don't care who brings her home. But if this all goes to shit and I find that's anything to do with you then I won't hesitate to speak up. Get out,' she says.

We don't need a second invitation, but I stop with a hand on the door frame and whisper once more.

'What... does she like? I mean, what are girls her age... into? I don't know a thing about them.'

She bites the right side of her lip.

'I don't know. Snapchat. Kanye West. Horror movies. Shopkins. Constantly checking their gmail.'

Then we're gone without another word. We bluster past Mr Bridges, only the breeze of our bodies causing any ripple in his world. He doesn't stir, like we're friendly ghosts he's learned to put up with. There doesn't seem to be anyone around outside but I put up my hood anyway, and we hurry for home, my leg dragging just a little less than usual.

And as we walk the streets and Heywood buzzes with the fever of it all, I think: I'm going to have to get into these girls' heads.

26

'And in spite of the weather
I feel closer than ever.'

The first thing that strikes me is that any attempt to understand these girls may be fruitless given what Shopkins are. These small plastic characters are mostly sold in American grocery stores and have names like 'Aspara-Gus' and 'Noni-Notepad'. Children of all ages are known to buy maybe fifty at a time and then video themselves opening them so they can display their reactions for others to watch. If this seems odd in theory, the practice of viewing half an hour of these on YouTube almost sent me into a parallel dimension.

The second thing that strikes me is that Jade Bridges is either kind of naive for her age or has some level of irony, as most of the girls in these videos are far younger than her. If her interests turn out to be far removed from Tanya Fraser's, this presents a significant problem with my plan. Not all girls are the same, by any means. This much, even I already know. But these kids are marketed to in the same way, live in the same area and go to the same school. My theory is that if they've been grown in the same petri-dish, they should share some of the same cultures. I have to try this.

We get some tips about hacking Facebook accounts from a corner of the internet we shouldn't be on. It's clear that with the situation not applicable to the usual methods of hacking: Phishing scam (getting her to respond to an email), or setting up a Keylogger (installing software on her computer that will capture every piece of information she types on her keyboard), we need to guess her email address and password.

I'm prepared to hazard that Tanya is on gmail; it seems to be the one girls her age are most into, which was borne out by Mrs Bridges namechecking it. Our first task is to construct a set of words that would be big in her world. While I don't know Tanya, I do have key details such as her address, date of birth, her school and her full name, and a site told me I'd be unlucky if her gmail account wasn't some kind of mixture of these. I also have Miss Heywood to throw some words into the mix, who wants to see this train of thought through to its natural end, and is far closer to ground level with these kids than I.

Tanyaf1999 is her relatively simple email, which we manage to crack in about half an hour. In truth, we get lucky, as Heywood manages to source it using Twitter; finding that it appears in the contact info of an old account she seems to have set up years ago and forgotten about. It's amazing how transparent our lives can be from a distance.

This carelessness from Tanya is a boon for us, as it means we don't have to try multiple address and password combinations. Despite the belief that people can't read our minds, even a hacker who doesn't know his victim has a better than twenty percent chance of guessing a password within a hundred tries. And as we've downloaded some software from a Russian website that gives you multiple attempts at guessing Facebook passwords without locking you out, these statistics look good for two people with time on their hands.

However, this doesn't mean the process isn't painful. We're

forced into a seemingly endless litany of word and number variations like:

Shopkins99

ShopkinsTanya

Kanye1999

Kw01kardashian

Yeezus1999

Horrorfan99

Halloweenbabe

And

Bieber001

Gradually, as we begin to tire, we start to lose track of which ones we have and haven't tried. But just as we start to consider giving up, as the glow of intrigue is leaving Heywood, Mark jumps onto my lap and sparks a useful remembrance. I recall the encounter with the Siberian at the Fraser house. And 'Monkey1999' runs out our winner.

And so, three hours deep, we are in.

The site appears like a blur of text and fury to me, so it's just another reason to feel blessed by Heywood's presence. Though I quickly remind myself not to get too attached. After my last relationship disaster, I'm going to try to play this as close as I can to cool.

'Type carefully, we can't afford any slips.'

'Don't worry. I'm a safe pair of hands,' she says as she types.

I make a pact with myself not to touch the keyboard, no matter how hard the urge. Of all the footprints I've made over this case, a new Facebook update from a girl who's been missing four days is not one I want to make.

The curser gravitates towards the envelope symbol. He isn't hard to find. 103 messages from an account with no photo attached, just as Jarwar had said. The man calls himself Mr White. This is where Heywood feels a little squeamish, and says she has to run to a meeting with 'her group'. What the 'group' does she doesn't divulge, as she grabs her leather rucksack and stands.

'This is all between... '

'You and me? Yes. I know,' she says.

'Of course. Call me?' I say.

'Yes. Yeah,' she says, and I hold out hope that it might actually happen, as she takes her grace and easy-going charm with her, breezing out like this was the most ordinary first date in history.

I don't delve into the messages too deeply. It would be a night's work to sift through them all, even for someone with a decent reading age; for me it would take a lifetime. But what I do find is one sentence, the shape of which is repeated throughout. 'Don't tell anyone at school.' Again and again and again.

Mr White's need for secrecy is understandably paramount. The words 'after school' are also present. As well as 'need to see you.' I even grimace over the words 'car', 'hard' and 'get me off'.

I sign out, carefully. But they can possibly link this sign-in activity back to me no matter what I do from here, I had earlier learnt. I feel sick to my gut. Not just because of seeing his words, tapped out presumably in some gloomy residence, where they are now being kept, I imagine, but because I used to be worried the police were a step behind me; now I'm worried they're not. And if I'm the front runner and their computer lead goes nowhere then it really is up to me to make the next move.

My phone rings again. It lights up and rumbles with urgency. I'm getting better at the shapes of short names, so I take a look, but all I see is numbers. I get that rotten feeling in my stomach again.

I pick up.

'Yes?'

*

A bang on the door and for once I'm not ready. I don't usually sleep so much as wait for morning light. But last night brought more surprises and disruption to my daily routine.

The bang comes again, ominous in its haste. I throw on my clothes. I've already showered but then I went back to bed. It seemed rude not to.

Bang. Bang. Bang.

'Coming!' I shout, picturing Jarwar, Levine and the others at my door.

We know, we know. You did, you did.

I prepare a few get outs in my mind. Not good ones. But ones all the same. But all I find is Bartu there, beaming out at me with his car framed behind him like it's the front page of a blog post entitled 'me and my motor.'

'Thought I'd give you a lift. Now I know where you are.'

'It's out of your way,' I say, eyeing him.

'That never bothered you before. Some thanks for a lift!' he says.

He's full of beans this morning. Perhaps it feels good to get caught. To be exposed and find the punishment isn't as severe as feared. But I have a feeling he shouldn't breathe so easy so soon.

He knows I'm hiding something. He peers in as if expecting Miss Heywood around some corner. But if he's looking for her he'll be disappointed. I shrug and grab my bag, just as Miss Shelley's head appears at the top of my stairs as she goes to the bathroom.

'Food and coffee in the fridge!' I shout up.

He gives me a 'Jesus Christ' look and we get on our way.

In the car, after a couple of minutes, he finally asks the question.

'You do know those are two different women, right?'

I leave it a few seconds before answering.

'Who?' I say.

'The two teachers you appear to be… sleeping with?' he says.

I love toying with him, I think I'll do it more often.

'What the hell are you talking about, Levine?' I say.

Then we fall into silence. That was a joke about me not recognising faces. I'm pretty sure he gets it, but a laugh would've been nice.

'I've got something bad to tell you,' he says, but I hardly hear it at first.

'Women are different these days. Sometimes they just call. Apparently. Why they're calling me? I have no idea. Maybe I'm an easy target.'

We pull in. Bartu parks, badly.

'Listen…' he says. But still I don't hear him.

'Maybe I'm giving off some sort of vibe,' I say, sticking out my bottom lip, unable to explain this current phenomenon.

'You're definitely giving out lots of vibes, mate,' Bartu says.

'Oh, thank you very much,' I say. Sadly, I'm confident that my level of conversation, plus embarrassment about my body and my handling of theirs, will mean I never get to see either woman again.

He tries to speak once more but I shush him as we enter the station and heads rise to look at us. Maybe it's just 'The Spotlight Effect', but I'm sure Bartu also feels it.

I needn't have worried about them moving slowly or having limited ideas, technology, or the ability to make fast decisions. When we get there it's clear they're gearing up for an arrest. Jarwar speaks animatedly to Levine and there's a certain feeling in the air somewhere between anticipation and success. As if it's already a done deal.

'Jarwar, I had an insignificant question. There's this skinny guy I've seen around, stiff posture, always wearing shades. Apparently you helped put his dad away, for molestation…'

'Sorry. Don't remember,' she says, after a diminutive pause.

'Ah, okay. Few years ago... the abuse was when he was a kid –'

'Not now, Tom,' she says, silencing me with a raised hand and sending me sloping back to the margins without a turn of her head.

Anderson and Stevens mill around, Bartu stepping into a corridor as he sees them, worried about repercussions from that direction. I stand tall and play innocent. Police get enough things levelled at them by the public, there's no need to consider a work colleague would be messing them around or setting them up. The only thing that might make them suspicious is seeing a guy acting strange and suspicious. I casually communicate this to Bartu. A 'be cool' look at last makes him take a breath and come out from behind the wall.

He gives Anderson a pat on the back as Jarwar leaves, flanked by a couple of faceless constables. We four are left to watch on limply.

'Good to have you back. What a load of rubbish that was,' says Bartu.

'Tell me about it,' says Anderson.

I give them both a smile which echoes Bartu's sentiment, and then lean down to tie a lace. Silence has its own power. Especially when everyone's aware of the question on your lips.

'Looks like that's that then,' says Stevens, hands firmly in his pockets, while Anderson fiddles with her zip.

'That's what?' says Bartu, playing it casual.

'Come on,' says Stevens. 'The link's a bit too close to ignore isn't it?'

'What link?' I say, rising. Seems like we're always the last to know, unless we make it our business to be first.

'Dirty messages. Sexy stuff. As you'd expect,' says Anderson.

'And with his son's ex-girlfriend, imagine that. That Akhtar fella. Horrible. He... I... doesn't bare thinking about,' says Stevens.

But I am thinking about it. Because someone has to engage with this taboo, rather than gaffer tape their mouth shut, as the words 'adult', 'child' and 'sex' are simply too distressing to be spoken in a sentence together. You need a sterner constitution than that. We're the police after all. We do the moralising so the rest of society doesn't have to.

The conversation collapses into the nods of professionals. I recalibrate. Bartu pats them on the back as they head into the daylight.

'Do you mean the Akhtar's that live on... ' I say, following after them, clicking my fingers twice.

'Myddleton Road. That's right,' Anderson says.

'That's right,' I say, turning to Bartu brightly. But his face is a brick wall. For once, I read it easily.

'Oh, by the way, you hear about Katherine Grady?' Stevens says, stopping just beyond the entrance and pulling on his gloves.

'Who's Katherine Grady?' I say.

'Exactly,' he says, adjusting his hat and striding away.

My eyes roll around. My brain unsure what just happened.

'Sorry, what?' I yell.

But Stevens is too far away to hear or to care.

'Who's Katherine Grady!?'

27

'I wish I'd stayed in with you in bed
Ducked under covers together instead.'

I've got a tune stuck in my head again today. It's not always the same one, it shifts periodically, but I always wake up with something. It's usually one of those lullabies I made up to keep myself thinking and developing. I even bought a little Casio keyboard so I could flesh out the melodies and play them to myself. I'm not very good, but it's another little challenge that helps.

Today it's this one. I tap out the tune with a single finger and sing it to myself, but I can't get past these first two lines, to the next ones, where something lies. I run them over and over, in my mind. Each time expecting the proceeding line to come naturally, to fall down like those copper coins from the coin pusher ledge at the arcade.

'…under covers with you instead… This time, this time, it will come, the next line, here it comes… Can't get that, da da da…

But it never does. Maybe it never will and I'll move on to the next tune where mental constipation will strike again. Perpetually waiting for the meaning to drop, as I continue to not glean these whispers in my ear.

'Give me the tape,' I say, in the locker room, with its beige-tinged look, to my eyes, from the overuse of anti-perspirant.

'That's what I've been trying to tell you. I don't have it,' he says.

'What? Go and get it. I'm going to cut out Jarwar and hand it straight to Levine, along with an innocent mistake story. It'll be fine.'

'No. No, it won't be fine. Because last night my car was broken into, and now the fucking tape isn't fucking there.'

I size him up. He's aware of what this looks like. Police don't look kindly on concealed evidence. But tribunals are even more suspicious of police that mysteriously lose things altogether. So am I, and I'm making sure he knows it.

'I know. I know I shouldn't have left it there. Fuck!' he says.

'Well, at least we've got rid of it. And no one knows we had it,' I say. A touch coldly, more theoretical than actual commiserations. 'Unless they did know, and that's why they broke into the car…'

'Yeah, I get it. But we can't report stolen evidence that we stole in the first place, so I say we let it…' he mumbles, as his phone rings.

I give him the 'take it' face and overhear that Aisha seems to have been liaising with the insurance company. I start to mouth to him but he pushes me away; he knows better than to tell anyone what was stolen. I curse my naïve self for tossing something into his hands that could be so important.

While Emre takes the call, I dismiss coincidences and wonder who could possibly know we had that tape. The walls appear to close in and lights flicker as I see conspirators around every corner and find myself walking uneasy.

I hurry past the interview rooms, and see a boy sat alone in the second. He looks to the floor, biting down on his hand, everything and nothing on his mind. He's like one of those hologram stickers that changes as you walk around it. Look at him from one angle and he's a lost little thing, stranded and scared. He would be angelic if he could find reason to smile.

When I'm not dreaming about the blonde girl in the classroom, or daydreaming with endless hollow lyrics in my head, it's this kind of child that fills my mind. The ones that distant generations and apathy and the internet built. In my mind they are angry and festering and hold broken bricks and they are hopeless and hopeful and there are swarms of them. An Atlantic Ocean squall of them. And what happens next could go either way.

He looks up and I recognise him as I see his scarlet birthmark, but I duck from view before he sees me. I'm not scared of him. I wouldn't say I'm scared of him.

But just to test myself I lift my head back into view and stare in at Eli. And leave my gaze there as he rolls his neck around and looks back at me.

We stay there for a few seconds. Him carrying his grudge, me trying to hold onto what authority I have. But I'm not making any apologies. I put my hand on the handle, turn it and step inside.

He sits next to the tape recorder, ready to give his statement. I shouldn't be here, but he greets my presence with an odd inevitability.

'PCSO Mondrian,' he says, flatly, like he's been drained of something.

'Eli. You've got to stop…'

My thought drifts away. But I don't need to finish it. It looks like he might nod in agreement for a second, but then he decides not to give me that much.

He looks down to his hands. Clenching them together and wincing.

'I never meant – ' he says before stopping himself.

'Never meant… what?' I say.

He looks up.

'Shit, I never meant –' But he stalls again, his mood changing as he stirs and tenses. It's just me and him in here. He shouldn't have anything on him, anything sharp, he really shouldn't have anything like that, I remind myself. But I still shouldn't be here.

'You've got to keep your head down. Stay out of trouble,' I say, slowly. 'CCTV places you at an incident where shots were fired. So play ball. If one of your lot has a gun, tell the officer where they got it.'

He looks to me. Surprised somehow at the sentiment and sense of care. He clenches his fists, harder this time.

Then, as if from nowhere, he cries. It's absurd, like seeing a statue weep. He doesn't soften, but the tears come sure enough.

'I'm sorry,' he says.

'For what?' I say.

'Everything.'

His body crumpling now. I hear footsteps down the hall.

'Hey. I don't know who would want to do that to you. But I'll find out. Okay? I know people. I could find out,' he whispers.

'It was an accident. A stray bullet,' I say.

More footsteps. He shifts in his seat before continuing.

'Yeah, I reckon you're right. Still… I could find out whose bullet. I could get them back for you.'

I notice his eyes are dry now. I don't know what to make of this kid. And what he's trying to make me swallow.

'Eli. Don't be fucking stupid.'

'But, I could…'

But I can't stay to hear the rest. Seems like Eli wants to make a bargain. The kids a mess, but he's someone else's mess. As I slam the door, I get a firm tap on the shoulder and turn sharply to find Bartu standing behind me.

'Let's go,' he says, without looking or considering the boy behind the door at all.

*

Emre Bartu insists we don't break our shift. Not today, not after the warning, but he does say we can drive, and if we go past Myddleton Road then so much the better. He says it with an air of finality, as if it's early January and he's taking me to see the last of the neighbourhood's Christmas illuminations before they all come down. But I don't see it quite like that.

'Slow, slow,' I say as we go past. Keen to catch the smallest glimpse of him, even if we are merely passing on a parallel road and he is twenty or so metres way.

'All right,' he says, slowing, but not so much as to be conspicuous.

He doesn't want to even breathe next to this case today. We're detailed to go and check on a lady that's had a fall, and Bartu is more than happy with that.

As we glide past, I only have a second to take him in, Jarwar pushing his head down as he is carefully placed into the back seat of her car. I don't have long to make a profile. His hair is flecked black and grey, as if the colours were flung from an art room paintbrush onto his canvas. He's tall and thin. He wears black, round spectacles and is fifty I would guess. But this is all I get and I'm lucky to get that.

'You think that's our man?' I say, with only a hint of provocation, as we get up to speed again.

He responds with a look that says 'It doesn't matter what I think' and 'Let's not talk about this' and 'You know what

I think'. But I'm not sure I do know what he thinks, not anymore.

'That deaf bastard didn't even tell us who Katherine Grady is,' I say, as we speed away.

'Steady, mate. You need to manage your mood,' he says.

'All right. He's not a bastard. But we still don't know who she is. And Stevens is partially deaf. Those are just facts,' I say, as he falls quiet.

When we arrive at number 42, Evelyn, a lady that Emre has looked in on a few times before, flings open the door. And, after a second of wondering who the hell we are, throws her arms skywards and bellows.

'Darling boys! Come on, come in!'

He's referred to her as the Grand Dame of Tottenham and I can see why. He thinks she used to be an actress, or photographer's muse, or a dancer of some repute, but he can't remember which. Either way, it's nice to be where you're wanted for once. Her face shows a fierce purple bruise but she wears so few signs of anxiety about it that it could be stage make up. She seems more concerned about what tea we'd like than her own problems. Her mind isn't what it used to be, Bartu has told me, and her falls are becoming a frequent occurrence, but I see no sign of weakness from her here, as she flirts and flits around like she's still backstage at Drury Lane, or in the photographic studio, or wherever her natural habitat used to be.

Her home smells of the colour peach. Of exotic hot drinks and lavender. I dream of this kind of grace in age for a moment. Her home is small and might offensively be described as humble, but it's also full of knick-knacks; a pink chaise longue, an antique Victorian card table, a fulsome collection of Chinese fans, lanterns and parasols.

But if Bartu hoped for a respite from the case, it isn't entirely forthcoming.

'Have they found those girls yet? Probably on holiday together, I reckon,' she says.

'I wouldn't know,' says Bartu. 'Not our area.'

'And anyway they didn't know each other,' I say.

'Oh yes. No, I did hear that,' she says.

I start to play with my phone distractedly and then remind myself that's rude.

'Sorry. How did you hear that?'

'It was in the paper, love. Here we are,' she says, holding out today's front cover of the *Tottenham Advertiser*, emblazoned with a picture of the three girls in school uniform.

'I keep them all. I've got the ones with you in them here,' she says, presenting a pair of front page stories with lines reading 'PCSO shot by stray bullet' and 'Back on the beat' respectively. The second showing a picture of me in uniform for an unwanted photo opportunity the Friday before I started back.

'I know rumour travels fast but I didn't think it was in print. Does everyone know about this?' I say to her, glancing to Bartu.

'I'd say so darling,' she says, as Bartu lazily scratches his chin. I have a natural mistrust of the press getting into things. I'm also uncomfortable with how much the image in the article about me shows my scar and I can't remember agreeing to that photo. But maybe I did; the mind plays tricks.

I scan the room and see the multitude of newspapers stacked into corners, locals mostly and not just her own. I'm not sure whether you'd call her a hoarder or if she just likes to stay informed. It looks like she gets the free ones from anywhere within a ten-mile radius. They somehow fit the decor and go back quite a way, judging by the number of them. Bartu comes over and joins me, calling out the names as he sifts through. He takes them from piles respectively at knee, hip and chest level.

'*Stratford and Newham Express... Hackney Citizen... Haringey Advertiser... London Turkish Gazette?*'

'It's not all in Turkish! You should know that, right Em? Can I call you Em?'

Emre shrug-nods, resolving that the words 'Err, I'd rather you didn't' weren't on the drop-down list. That's how nick-names work; it's very rarely your decision and if you insist on one you've come up with yourself you get pegged as 'a-bit-of-a-knob-end', and usually are one.

'I like to stay up on the Turks. Like to stay up on everything.'

'I can tell,' says Bartu, scanning the room. The stacks of papers, only registering as soft furnishing on first entering, now seem to pen us in. I pick out their particular smell. Cream and chalk. Yellowing paper, print ink and dust.

'Aren't you lot interested in local news?'

'Not as interested as you, obviously,' Bartu says.

'And I don't read,' I say.

'Well, you should. Your generation, I worry about you lot. With your computers and what not,' she says.

'It's not so much "don't" actually. As "can't". Yet. But I'll get there,' I say, tapping my scar.

'Oh, love. Well you will do, and when you do, you keep reading, 'cos it's what separates us from the fucking morons.'

It's supposed to be heartening, I think, but makes me feel slightly belittled.

'Do you actually... read all these... Evelyn?' Emre says.

'Yeah, course,' she says, sitting back in her chair.

Even if it's a half-truth it's impressive. We look around at the pages and paragraphs, arms folded, prodding me like bigger boys.

'Matter of fact, wondering what you thought about something.' She sniffs and takes in the room with a sideways glance.

I'm all ears. Emre Bartu is slightly less composed of ears, but he's still interested.

'All this? Bit similar to those girls that went missing down in Battersea. Ten years ago it musta been. You remember the ones?'

A few beats, we turn to face her, her bruised visage pinning us with keen eyes.

'Yeah, they weren't from around here. But I think one of them was Turkish, which accounts for the interest from the *Turk Times*. Three girls… from the same school… I think.'

I scratch my head, just next to the scar. It itched when she said the words 'three' and 'girls', so I put it out of its misery.

'What happened to them? Were they found? D'you remember?' she says.

Her grandfather clock ticks as she looks at us.

'I steered clear of serious news up until I started this job. And no one's mentioned… any case like that. So, no, I don't know what happened to them,' I says.

She snorts and flicks her nose with the back of her knuckles.

'No, neither do I. I remember it happening though. Sure of it. Turk Times. Two thousand and four.'

I blink at the reams of paper. When I look to Bartu it's clear that he's already twigged that I won't be the one doing the reading.

'Go on. Turk Times are in those five piles there, and there's one more in the utility room. And three by the stairs.'

*

Evelyn wasn't messing around, she'd kept them all. Her system means that Bartu can find the year easily enough, but as she has no handle on the month that still means fifty-two papers. He starts with front pages, a suggestion I had made, which I thought might just reduce the arduousness of the task at hand. However, if it didn't make the front-page we'll have to dig a little deeper, which is certainly possible, as Emre mentions that natural curiosity found him searching through similar cases on the internet a few days ago, to no avail. If this is real and not an older lady's fantasy, it's either buried deep in the search results or not on the net at all. We put our faith in the web as if all of history naturally resides there, but you still need someone to put it there. Sometimes our faith is better placed in black and white.

When the front pages return nothing, I signal to Evelyn to put on another brew.

'Now try pages two and three,' I say, sitting back in Evelyn's chair, settling into the warm groove she's left behind as Bartu struggles with unwieldy papers on his knees. I'm the strategist, he's my eyes; that's just how it works out.

When it comes, Bartu yells in relief as much as in excitement. It was early in the year, January to be exact – just as it is now. Not ten years ago to the day, but not far off.

Three girls had been taken from their school on consecutive days; the similarities had been greater than Evelyn had even remembered. Bartu read it all to us, failing to play down his unease.

He was still manfully trying to show only passing interest, stuck in the mode of not giving too much a way, while I had begun to ill-advisedly invite lady friends to tag along whenever it seemed apt.

'... the girls were not said to be friends... They haven't been heard from for three, four and five days respectively... Police are appealing for any information anyone may have at this time.'

'Fucking hell,' Evelyn says.

'We think Mr Akhtar did that one, as well, do we?' I say.

I don't know much about the Akhtar family. Nothing at all, in fact. Maybe they move around. Maybe he has a pattern, a way of doing things. He could've done it in other boroughs or cities and then he gets out just in time without leaving a trace behind him, only this time, when the internet made it that much easier for him to find and groom the kind of girls he was looking for, he naively didn't count on his Mr White creation leaving an electronic trail. It's a theory.

Occam's Razor is the law that states that the simplest solution is usually the correct one:

Mr Akhtar + the previous crimes = a dangerous man with a very perverse obsession.

That's the conclusion that Bartu must be lost in, too, and if the police know about the other crimes, if they've looked that far back, then they'll be checking Akhtar's previous addresses against any similar unsolved acts. The only problem is I'm betting Occam's Razor doesn't work every time.

'Damn it,' says Bartu, pinching the top of his nasal bone with his thumb and index finger, like a migraine just came on fast. This thing just keeps on getting bigger, and falling back into his lap. Meanwhile I look at the paper and just for practice try to read the names.

'We get back on this. Tomorrow. And we do it right,' he says.

'You boys be careful,' Evelyn says. 'Best to think before you bluster.'

'Don't worry, Evelyn. Thinking's all I ever do,' I say. As I put my hand against hers for a moment I think about my Grandma, my family, and things I haven't thought about for a very long time.

'Hey, you don't know who Katherine Grady is, do you?' I say, hopefully.

'Err… no,' she says.

'Worth a shot,' I say, casting my gaze back to the papers. I give up trying to read the names and focus on the pictures. Then when I look into the eyes of one of the girls, I see her staring back at me.

And I feel something I haven't felt for a long time with regard to a face.

Any face at all.

Bang.
True recognition.

*

At home, halfway between waking and sleep, I picture the back of a blonde head. A girl, or a young woman. She's writing on the blackboard, but this time it's not in chalk. What is it? I can't see. She writes in red. Something stops me from getting close to her, to seeing her face, but I can see her writing, in lipstick, red lipstick. No, not writing. Drawing. A symbol, the same one that was on the car window, and now I see it, it's less clear cut. And now I know I made a mistake.

It wasn't a heart. It was something stranger. Something else.

*

Buzz. Buzz. I'm awoken by my phone vibrating next to me. My left hand reaches for it and the screen glares. Unknown numbers, again. Maybe I've been giving my card out too liberally.

Mark appears around a corner and skulks over to roll in the single shaft of light that shoots through the curtains from the streetlights outside. Then, seeing the phone ring, he jumps up, looks at it and then at me, beckoning me to put it out of its misery. He falls into the crook of my arm and gives me a knowing look that I can only interpret as rousing encouragement.

Buzz. Buzz.

He certainly seems to have more faith in me than he used to.

Buzz. Buzz.

I open my eyes wide and put the phone to my ear.

'Hello?' I say.

No answer comes back. Just a sound like a wave, or a shirt against the speaker, or a long 'shh'.

'Hello?' I say again.

Then nothing. Then...

'I'm... I...' comes the voice.

'Hello? Who is it?' I say, despite knowing already. I am a directory of voices.

'I... I'm... I...' it comes again.

'Who is this?' I say. Quieter now. Patiently willing them on, but giving them room. I think I already know what they want to say.

I wait in the silence of my room. In the silence between us.

Just the distant movement of ripples across the wires.

Then a shh.

Or a wave.

Or the rustle of a shirt.

And then he says it.

'I'm Mr White.'

I punch myself hard in the arm to check I'm not dreaming. Yet, I already know I'm wide awake.

Now the silence is from my end.

Then a thought takes shape and crystalizes.

And it starts to make sense.

28

'So close I can feel it,
Your face, your feet, your hands,
Your body.'

'I saw a face yesterday,' I say, as Ryans sits me down.

He scratches the back of his neck and puts his feet up on a footstool. His office is far more welcoming than the room full of machines we were in last time. Talk is all we can really do now that the bullet shards have put the proverbial spanner in the works regarding any further scans. We're left with pen and paper, sometimes pictures, sometimes shapes to rearrange.

'Good. That's interesting,' he says.

'Is that normal? To suddenly see one?'

'Look, I remember years ago, when scientists were experimenting with using LSD, some test subjects started forgetting faces. They thought their recognition would never recover, then slowly it did.'

'What's your point? Other than that the sixties was weird.'

'People have been trying to understand and affect that part of the brain for years. Scientists, governments, cults. So my point is, everything is a voyage into the unknown, for both of us.'

'Okay. So it is possible?' I say.

'Anything is *possible*,' he says, after which I look up expecting to see a smirk, but it's clear he is deadly serious. 'Except for people who claim that after a stroke they can suddenly play the piano or talk Japanese; unfortunately, that sort of thing is what we call in the medical profession "utter bollocks". I mean the realities of the brain are far more amazing than any of that kind of fiction. But, I digress. You were saying... you saw a face?'

'It was in the paper. The face. I won't bore you with details...' I say.

'No, please do, this is all very exciting... well, interesting. I really think you look better. You seem like something's happening, a development. So please, tell me. Tell me everything.'

For now, I'm going to hold it over him. The fact he somehow sourced Anita's number and called her against my wishes. I'd given him her name in confidence, early on, as I drifted in and out of consciousness. A thought hits me about Ryans that hasn't before. I am a big story, in some circles. Local news. Neurology. Niche markets, perhaps, but however much I try to ignore it, people are aware of me. And Ryans has always had an insatiable appetite for my stories.

'Well, obviously I can't talk too extensively about my work. Certain things are secrets... ' I say. Ha. That's a laugh.

'... but I was looking at a picture, from ten years ago, and I saw a face. One that's been on the tip of my mind for a while now. I found the picture, almost by chance, and then there she was in front of me.'

'What sort of face? Male, female?' he says, crossing his legs.

'It was a girl. I went to school with. I sat next to her in biology and she left when I was fifteen, I think. Strangely, I'd stumbled on a tape in my wardrobe from my old camcorder recently, and she... she was on it. And I could almost recognise her. I felt I remembered something about her moving schools, which, it turns out, she did. And then a year later I now find that... she went missing.'

'Incredible. And did you know? Is it possible you knew this before and it had been hidden in the recesses... do you think? A stowaway thought. That she went missing?' he says, talking a mile a minute now.

'No. I... I'm sure I didn't know. I don't remember attaching too much significance to her. She was a pretty girl. A crush for a while. I kissed her once. But I couldn't really tell you much about her. Even if I have suffered some memory loss, I'm sure I never knew she went missing.'

My chest is pounding, Ryans seems to notice and softens his manner slightly. He analyses my face. I put my hand to it, I'm flushed.

'Go on. I don't want to push you, but go on. If you can, Tom. It really is very... err... '

He leans down and pushes a Dictaphone forward. I didn't notice him turn it on. It almost puts me off but I do want to go on nevertheless, so I can get to the next thought.

'And the prevailing feeling is... more than confusion... more than... trying to work anything out... it's guilt, because I don't remember my parents' faces, or my grandparents', and they're all gone. You know, they say – people say – of old people, things like... "oh, left alone in that big house with just their memories..." that sort of thing, they say. But memories can do a lot for you. You can live a whole other lifetime with memories. It's time travelling for the heart. But mine don't have faces attached. It's only struck me now that if they're gone in my head, then it's like they never even... existed.'

Without looking I find a tissue on my right and give my face a single dab. He's visibly touched, but that doesn't stop him pushing the Dictaphone just a little closer.

'And you got that from the picture of her?'

I blow out hard to gather myself. My emotions seem relevant and yet still incongruously sudden and overwhelming.

'Yes, because I never gave that girl a second thought, not for a long time anyway, but she's the only one I see. That face. Sarah Walker. And what's more, I've been dreaming of her.'

'Since when?'

'Since the accident. I know it sounds mad. I'm not mad.'

'I know you're not. Tom, look at me, I know you're not.'

'Good,' I say, my tissue now damp with tears.

'And did they ever find her? This Walker girl.'

'You know, it's stupid I... I had a brief look, on the web, to see what I... and then I gave up. I had a lot on my mind, last night.'

Amongst other things, I was thinking how I'd broach his betrayal. My eyes zero in on his pad. He writes greedily in purple ink. I don't know whether I'm to be the subject of an article or a case study. Perhaps he wants to bring me to a convention and parade me around. Perhaps there is some award or money at stake, I don't know. Some value in me that I heretofore have not quite grasped.

'Any other news?' he says.

'Yes. I got a call just before I got here. They found a girl's leg a while ago. We thought it might be one of our girls, but it wasn't.'

'Yes, I read about that. How awful, how macabre.'

'Well, now they've found the rest of her.'

The moment takes me over and now I'm telling him everything. I'm only reliable in my unreliability. I can see him trying to stay calm; you can't be squeamish in his line of work, but then not many patients bring so much blood in with them.

'And...' he says. Almost afraid to hear what comes next.

'Katherine Grady, she was called. They don't think it had anything to do with our missing girls. She had been cut around the top of the thigh. The rest of her was intact. They don't know why they cut the leg off. They went through bone. Went through the femoral artery.'

'Is that what killed her?' he says, his hand to his mouth.

'No. She was shot in the back of the head, then they took the leg off. And what's stranger? There's already a man in prison for her murder. Been there for four years. He'd confessed to killing the five men, but not the three women he was done for, of which Katherine was one. A man named Edward Rampling. So that's another conundrum. So there we are.'

I leave that in the middle of the room for us to struggle with, before Ryans tries vainly to lift proceedings.

'But is there any news on the shooting? Tom?' he says.

'Which shooting?' I say.

'Your shooting,' he says.

My fingers drum out a rhythm on my knee. I'm looking at him and don't like what I see. I'm not sure what he's getting at, what he wants; he's not a therapist is he? I don't know why he seems to want to make me feel vulnerable.

'No. It was a stray bullet, that's still their belief. Some kid called Eli has thrown a few names our way but nothing turned up. Looks like he was just trying to get a shorter sentence on gun possession or... I don't know what. But they do think it was a gang. Perhaps shooting at someone on the bus. A lot of people scattered after it happened; it was mayhem, apparently. They infiltrate these gangs and find out where the firearms and drugs are coming from. The sort of operation they're working on, they don't want to jeopardise for anything, not even an officer down. So they have their suspicions but they wait, they play the long game and when they've got everything they need they'll move for whoever's near the top. I can already see you're making a face, but don't...'

Ryans shakes his head innocently and adjusts his position.

'... because the police do a bloody good job around here,

mostly. And if this does in some way help them close down a gang, who are at the core of the North London smack trade, or... then I'll be happy to have been a small part of that. And that's what they say, so good on them, I say, and what do I need closure for anyway? I've moved on.'

'Already?'

'Already? Yes, already. Can I go now?'

'This sudden swing...' he's thinking. 'Is the brain producing too much of *this* or *that*. He's a slave to his mind...' But I *am* my mind, I'm not ashamed of that, and my mind is on to him.

'I want you to consider something...' he says.

I feel like he's trying to cover me with a glass tumbler.

'...which might be irregular. But it's merely a suggestion.'

I'm not sure I like where this is going, but I stick around to find out. I raise my eyebrows and wait for the rest.

'I know that you've done incredibly well. I know that your job can be dangerous. And I know that, at times, someone to talk to is the best thing one can have. And a human is even better than a cat... '

I don't know where he's going with this but I hope it's not what I think. I've already had two women keen to share my bed, I don't want an aging neurologist to be next.

'My wife and I are fortunate enough to have a big space near Clissold park, too big for us really. You could have a floor. A study, a bedroom, a bathroom. And you could stay there until you felt absolutely on top of your game.'

I see. He wants to keep the project close, just in case anyone breaks it.

'No thanks,' I say, standing.

'It's just a suggestion,' he says, staying still in his chair.

'I am on top of my game. Thanks,' I say, turning to leave.

'That's it then?' he says.

I stop. A white feeling shakes me from the inside out.

'That's it,' I say, as I grab a glass paperweight of his from his side table and slam it into the wall. It shatters and he flinches as the shards settle like falling snow.

'And if you call Anita again, I'll...' I say, unable to think of anything. So I just slam the bloody door.

*

My phone goes as I head to the station. It's an afternoon to evening shift and they will have their hands full with whatever they think they've found.

My phone vibrates: Mr White. I'm pretty sure that's what the shape says. I hit the 'accept' button.

'I don't know what to do, I'm so... I'm so... scared, I... I just need you to tell me what to do. Can you do that? Please, Mr Mondrian... ' he says.

'I shouldn't even be talking to you. Okay? But I thought about all the scenarios objectively and you've only one option. You have to tell the police everything.'

The line goes quiet. The sound of waves.

'I know, I know. I'm kind of scared.'

I hold the phone away from my face for a second before continuing.

'Asif. If you used the computer, then I would come out and say that. I don't know if they have anything else on him or not, but if those messages came from you then you should speak up, because it couldn't get much more serious than this,' I say, and I don't wait for a reply as I reach the station.

Inside, Levine seems light and relieved and wants to talk to us about 'how well we've been doing'. I keep playing with my phone a second longer than I should because I don't really respect him.

He brings us into the debrief room and talks casually, with

the air of a man off the hook. It looks as though they like what they've found with Mr Akhtar. They think those girls could be coming home soon and the arrest looks good for their statistics.

My phone rings. I make an apologetic face to both of them and step outside to take it. I'd been dropping in comments intermittently throughout the week to Levine about having had trouble making my next appointment with Ryans, so I'm hoping that's what he thinks it'll be about.

I answer it and stand with my back to them, but within glancing distance. The untended grass under my feet has hardened due to the frost and taken on the look of an aging officer's short back and sides, salt sprinkled and world-weary. The edges are so unkempt they bubble ice cold mud onto the pavement. After muttering into the phone for a while I hang up. There was no one on the other end of the line, to be honest with you. I'd used an app I downloaded last night. I set the timer for four minutes, just as we reached the station. I have things to do right away and I don't want my time wasted with friendly chit-chat.

Useful, these apps. This one's a clever little thing. It calls you. Even mutters to you on the other end of the line when you pick up. I see Levine's eyes are not on me, and I push the speed dial for the number I need.

I get the automated message and choose option one. It rings.

'He-hello.' He offers no other introduction. He's probably still trying to buy that hat stand. I'm not good with faces but I'm a killer reader of a voice. When you lose one sense the others get stronger, they say.

I was hoping I'd get him. I know he's not a bastion of school rules and procedure.

'Hello, Jim Thompson here. Physics,' I say.

'Hi Jim. How are you?' says the receptionist, as if he speaks to

Jim every day. I suppose it's better to fake it rather than admit you haven't a clue who anyone is.

'Yep, fine. Listen... I've had people drifting off in the last five minutes at the end of last lesson on a Tuesday and Thursday, claiming they have to get ready for their after school clubs.'

'Okay, Jim,' he says.

'So I'd like the names of the teachers that run Computing on Tuesdays and Running Club on Thursdays. And all the students in those two groups, for good measure,' I say, biting my lip. I've already got Miss Heywood's Wednesday Art Class list. I obtained it on my own personal time.

'Err... I don't know if we have those kind of lists,' he says.

I pinch my thigh inside my pocket. I see Levine laugh about something through the window.

'You don't have them? Or you don't know if you have them?'

I hear muttering in the background.

'Yeah. Err... hang on a sec,' he says.

I think on this occasion I might be disappointed. Bartu looks to me and I wink. He just goes back to Levine and his chat.

'Hi, Jim?'

'Yep?'

'Mandy's found the lists actually.'

'Oh good,' I say.

'Shall I zip it over to the physics inbox?'

'No! No, then I have to pick it up and sometimes someone else picks it up and then it's not down as a new message and I can't – I've got my pen and paper out now, so why don't you go ahead.'

'Okay, Jim,' he says, through partially gritted teeth.

'Mr Hargreaves takes Tuesdays and he's got Charlene...'

And two minutes later I have my names and the muttering in the background starts again.

'Sorry, what's your last name again, Jim?' he says.

'Sorry... *chh*... bad line... physics.'

I hang up, tuck the pad away and head inside with a pocket full of pupils and a new purpose. One of those names, I recognise.

'Let's walk,' I say, as Bartu comes out to meet me. I offer a salute to Levine, who is framed perfectly by his office window, incarcerated within it. A house husband to the force. I keep my eye on him as we walk away, and he gets smaller and smaller.

'What was the call about?' Bartu says.

'First, what did you get from Levine?' I say.

'No, you first!' he says, pleasingly irate. I've got enough stuffed into my head already and feel like releasing the pressure.

'Okay, first thing is, you should tell anyone who thinks the Katherine Grady murder has nothing to do with our lost girls that they're an idiot.'

'I'll put it on my to-do list. How did you come to that then?'

'Because of that severed leg. I'm still grappling with it, but I'll give you the whole picture when I've looked into the Ed Rampling trial. The second thing you should know is that I hacked into Tanya Fraser's Facebook account.'

'That's not... You shouldn't do that. That's some serious shit. How did you do that?'

'Oh come on, Bartu, that's not the most interesting bit of the story.'

'Then what the hell did you find?' he says in a choked gasp, almost forgetting to breathe.

'Mr White's messages. Words that confirmed that he'd been in contact for a while. But, again, that's not the most interesting bit of the story. Anyone could have got to that bit and I know anyone could get there, because they got there too, but what they didn't get... is a call from Mr White.'

'You got a call from –'

'Try not to repeat everything I say, it'll take at least twice as long if you do that. The next thing you say is "so how did he have your number?" then I say "obviously I must've given it to him" then you say... '

'So you're saying, it isn't Akhtar?'

'To which I say, no; I'm saying it is Akhtar. Akhtar Junior. He used his dad's laptop because he doesn't have one, or a smartphone, or any of those things kids from richer, less strict families would have. The upshot is, Asif says he didn't do it.'

'Didn't write the messages?'

'No, of course he wrote the messages. But what Jarwar and the rest think is grooming from an older man, with words like "don't tell anyone at school about us", could simply be a kid trying to have an affair with his ex-girlfriend without anyone at school knowing about it.'

'And he doesn't know where the girls are?' Visible air rises between us. I rub my hands together and look around; mindful of our lost tape, aware of listening ears and passers-by, in this frozen world.

'He says he doesn't. He wanted advice on what to do; I said tell them everything you know and leave nothing out and that's what I want you to do to right now.'

'Okay... ' Bartu says, glancing around as we continue walking. Walking to just to keep moving, to stay warm. We don't know where we're heading yet.

'They think they've got their man. They've already got neighbours willing to say they never trusted Akhtar Senior. A couple of parents, white parents, who say they refused to let him give their daughter lifts home because there was something odd about him. He also has previous for GBH. The strategy is to lean on him with all this so he'll give up where he's hiding them. Oh, and they're not looking at it in conjunction with any other crimes, and certainly not one in a different borough ten years ago. Levine nearly pissed himself laughing when I asked that.'

'You've got to admit that yours sounded a little less good than mine. Just saying,' I announce.

'Okay. So what now?' he says, as we walk up the hill, the ground crystallising beneath our feet.

'You haven't even heard the best bit yet. That last call wasn't Asif. I phoned reception and found out exactly which students and teachers were present at the school clubs the girls were snatched after. Don't ask how I did that.'

'I won't.'

'So now we have thirty-eight people who realistically may have been the last ones to see those girls. Thirty-eight people who might have seen this guy at any time in the last few months. Thirty-eight chances to jog some memories. The only thing that sticks in my craw, is that one of those thirty-eight, in a school of over a thousand, is Asif.'

'Shit,' Bartu says, as we pass the empty library. 'So... where are we going now?'

'Either way, we are so close, I can feel it!'

'Yes, but which way now?' he says.

'Well, we could go to the school... '

'Which is stupid and dangerous for us... '

'Or we could go to Tanya Fraser's house.'

'What's at Tanya Fraser's house?'

'There we go, good on you; now that is a good question,' I say. Then the radio crackles and the voice comes through.

'Mondrian. Bartu. This is Jarwar. Over.'

'Go ahead. Affirmative. Over,' I say, quickest on the draw.

'Thanks for everything on this case. I know you've been close to it. Over.'

'What is it? Over,' I say.

'I just wanted you to know before you hear it second hand. We're near Tottenham Marshes. I think we're about to find the bodies. Over and out.'

And I drop to a crouch, get low and breathe.

Documented Memory Project #3

When I saw my old playing fields I was reminded of days lying on the yellowing grass. By turns idyllic and mundane, depending on which day the images come to me, they form a dream room landscape I return to, like my mind is a lo-fi TV show, with only the means for a few sets, constantly recycled due to budget restrictions.

But this image is specific and has only just come back to me. I don't think it's a false assumption. I don't think it's been deformed by current events. I gaze at the maroon canvas of the back of my eyelids.

A friend of a friend had passed the message on to me in woodwork. I crumpled up the lined paper and didn't show a soul before it made its way deep into my grey trouser pocket, never to be seen by other eyes.

It was the Monday of the last week of term and I was headed to the kissing tree. True to its name, it was picked out as it was big enough for two young bodies to hide behind, out of view of the mass of kids scrambling around for the football on the concrete schoolyard with its porridge-like consistency from a distance. I had never been invited to the tree before and never would be again.

Sarah Walker leaned against the other side as I made my way around it and stood limply observing the single curl that fell from her otherwise tightly-wound blonde hair. It lay just below her chin like a hook and as I reached to touch it she took my hand and pulled me in, causing me to fall and slam both hands against the tree, either side of her head. I narrowly avoided head-butting her and was still recovering from this as *her green eyes met mine and I noted the constellation of freckles, which I had seen recede and fade over the years but not disappear completely, clustered lightly around her mouth as if she had been freshly dusted with tiny biscuit crumbs.*

She wore her tie the other way around, small bit at the front, large bit tucked into her shirt, in a way that I never dared to, and her skirt wasn't from the usual suppliers. As such she was often questioned about it by teachers, who always let it slide. She pushed her tongue out so I could see it. I just stared at it. So she grabbed the back of my neck, pulling my face closer, then forcing my lips onto hers, my tongue eventually poking into her mouth and staying rigid as she did all the work and I hesitantly closed my eyes. She tasted of cigarettes and an orange alcopop procured from cooler kids. When it finished I realised I had rather rudely kept my hands in my pockets throughout. And as she left I lifted my middle finger to my bottom lip and tasted fresh metallic blood on my tongue.

29

'The girl next door is playing on my mind
Digging in my garden to see what she can find'

When we get there, there are no bodies. But there are clothes. And blood, a lot of blood.

'Not sure you should be out here, lads,' the gent says, but everyone else is. There's police tape, vans, detectives who I don't think I've ever seen before, people in white jump suits taking samples. It's certainly a scene. We stand tantalisingly far back, unable to go further for fear of being caught in the midst of it all. Particularly by Jarwar, who did us the courtesy of letting us know it was happening, so we could forget about it, not stand next to her while she stands next to bigger boys who administer the last rites on this thing. Fortunately for her, we couldn't get close enough to cramp her style even if we wanted to, and she has her hands too full to notice us in the distance.

She buzzes around trying to conduct the orchestra as another car arrives and Turan steps out. Jarwar immediately sees him and her body language says she didn't expect to. There are enough cooks putting their feet in the broth as it is. Metres and metres away on the other side of this, a gentleman special constable stands guard at the front of it all, in our way, warning us off in the kindest possible terms. He's a volunteer; expenses only. But even he has more status than us: the power of arrest and other privileges we can only gaze at from afar.

'We'll get off then,' I say, and none of us moves a muscle.

Stonebridge Wood offers decent cover, particularly by night, but also there's an area at its centre you would only venture into to take a piss, or to help a kid build a covert tree-house. The likelihood is that this was done last night, but it's possible they've been in there for longer than that. Time is one of the first things they'll be trying to ascertain.

We see the clothes. Three sets. Laid out in perfect order. Coat over jumper over shirt, all carefully together as if worn comfortably by the girls who no longer lie within them. Conspicuous by their absence. And below them school skirts. And below them ripped black tights. And below them patent leather shoes. All in a neat line next to each other. The shirts are red, thick with blood, the rest of the clothes may be, too, but the blood shows up strong against the white of the shirts at this distance, like it's been poured over fresh snow.

Spotlights have been erected by men and women in luminous jackets to point into the darkness of the woodland.

To say look here, look here, see this, see this.

Miscellaneous material hangs from the trees. It could be items from their rucksacks, which lie below, next to their clothes. Could be underwear. Could be pieces of torn shirt. The spotlight reveals them to be reddened too. Real blood is a lighter shade than you would imagine.

Steam rises to them from the breath of the men beneath, in the wood. People tread carefully, in the wood. It's like a silent movie. As, for all the jostling and heat of bodies, there is a library hush, only usually replicated in Catholic Mass or a cemetery or in the presence of the bodies themselves. But there are no bodies here, in the wood.

The Special starts to look, too, too uncomfortable to force us away physically or ask us to leave again. He turns in time to see a suited woman, presumably a detective, walk over to the edge of the water that runs nearby. She leans in and with a pencil, pokes at something and then lifts it. She brings it over and holds it up near one of the spotlights. She doesn't seem to recognise it. But I do. I know exactly what it is. It's a Tottenham School prefect's tie. The normal tie was black with yellow stripes, but if you were given a special award or were a prefect you got the inverse pattern, a yellow tie with black stripes. It's supposed to separate the good kids from the bad kids. I never had one.

'Anyway. All the best,' Bartu says, nodding to the Special.

'Thanks, lads,' he says.

We amble back to Bartu's car. I feel nauseous.

'What stings more, seeing the clothes and the blood? Or the feeling we were so close?' I say, as he pulls out and we head back to the beat. I like to break things down into their smallest parts. Even the tiniest atoms of thoughts. Even the quarks.

'How close did we really get? In the end?' he says.

'I could feel something. I've got this thought in my head, like I've forgotten to do something.'

'I get that all the time.'

'Yeah, well yeah, it's like that. Only I've had it for a long, long time and it almost hurts me. It pings around my head, it makes me uncomfortable, it's like a Post-it has fallen down from my brain stem. Something I made a note to do, and now it's rumbling around in there, in my skull, getting all mushed up. And every so often it turns over and I see a piece of it. A word arrives to me like a tune or a lyric in my head sometimes, when I wake up, after my thoughts have had a chance to reorder themselves in the night. But, I can't, for the life of me, remember what is on that Post-it. And it makes me so uneasy it makes me feel... sick.'

'It's probably seeing the blood. Their blood.'

I gaze at the faces going past as we drive. I recognise nothing. The world moves past on a carousel for me and everything either really does mean everything or absolutely nothing. Emotion sickness. I picture their terrified faces, stricken with the fear of what might come next, before next came and eclipsed even their very worst nightmares.

'If it is their blood.'

'What?' he says.

The white lines in the road pass on and on.

'We're assuming it is their blood,' I say.

'It was their uniforms.'

'Maybe. But they'll have to test the blood.'

We stop at a red light.

'Who else's blood could it be?'

'You can get blood,' I say, with unintended foreboding.

'Okay, mate,' he says, shutting down the conversation.

I gawp aimlessly out the window as we get going, but the light-bulb is still flickering away inside of me.

'I was starting to think,' I mutter to myself. 'If they are still alive, they're going to start running out of room down there.'

'What?' Bartu says.

'I said, if those girls are all still alive, wherever they are, one day they're going to run out of room.'

'Tom. I think you have to accept that this is –'

'Stop the car.'

'No, Tom, you need –'

'Stop the fucking car!' I shout, and for the second time in our short friendship I go to grab the wheel, but this time Emre Bartu knows to brake before I do this.

The door opens and I'm running, my version of a run anyway, but it's a damn sight better than it was a few weeks ago. After a woman with blonde hair. I hear Emre's door slam but I don't feel his presence behind me, I feel like I'm on my own. I push past the crowds and then slip on ice, but I'm back on track quickly as I head down the main road.

She's got a head start but I'm gaining on her.

I turn the corner and run into some young parents holding hands with their cute-looking kids, dressed as bears and angels, and I barge through them.

'Sorry. I'm sorry,' I shout back as I turn the corner and then see her turn right. This isn't like before. Last time it only seemed like she was trying to steer clear of me, there was a possibility she didn't know I was there. This time she runs full pelt, as if she's running for her life. We head down a side-road and I could shout 'Stop, police!' but I'd rather gain ground without her knowing precisely where I am. She's gained some leverage because of my pace, but isn't looking back and that could give me an advantage. Plus, these streets are coming back to me strongly. We turn again. This is a cul-de-sac.

Our bodies cut through the air. I hear only the sound of my own breathing. It's surreal to find yourself calm at moments of such high tension. Running is only running after all. We do it for the bus. Sometimes we do it because it matters, but it all looks the same. My own body doesn't even fully grasp the importance.

At the end of the road, she turns. I don't think she has any-where to go but she doesn't falter, she runs in between two houses and keeps going. There's a path. I haven't been around here since I was young, so maybe it's new. She darts down it and turns her head as she does and I see her.

I recognise her.

That face.

It's so clear to me, unlike all the others.

She slips on the ice. She falls hard and grabs her leg. She lets out a yell and I want to help her. She gets up gingerly. She's right there.

The girl of my dreams.

She hobbles for a moment. A spot of blood drips from somewhere, her hand I think. She's flagging. She moans in pain. I remember her hand touched mine when we wrote in biology class from time to time.

She was left-handed. I am right.

I remember seeing long cuts above her knees when my eyes wandered in summer term. I'd keep watch on their progress. After a few days they'd fade to almost nothing. Then the next day they'd open up again, even deeper than before. I wondered what her home was like, after that rumour, about her angry father catching her playing rough with another girl. She always seemed tough, but I had a feeling there was a world of niceness inside if you could only get to it. If you could only touch it.

'It's done. It's over!' I shout as I reach out and touch her back, feel her hair.

But then I lose my grip on her as we turn onto a new road. Then something hits me hard.

I hit the ground. My ribs ache. I'm not sure what's happened. The pain isn't here yet, it all happened so fast. My hand is numb, perhaps I hit my head, it's too early to say.

I see her feet disappear in the distance. Her feet. Sarah Walker. If she's really been missing for ten years, then I've found her.

Hide and seek.

Then a car speeds away and I realise that's the cause of the unusual sensation in my ribs. I'd try and catch the number plate if I was in any state to do that. I feel like I'm back where I started. I know a hell of a lot more than I did, but not what any of it means. I'm in no position to take it any further. I'm not even in any position to get up.

Another car pulls up with a screech, heavy footsteps, a door slam. They stand over me. I hide my face, instinctively. I am vulnerable now. One hand goes to my side, my other towards my scar and I brace myself for the worst.

'What are you doing?' Bartu says, pretty commanding from this angle.

'Being hit by a car, I think,' I say.

'Ah,' he says as he picks me up, very carefully. I can't be that hurt or he'd have called me an ambulance and not moved me until they got here. I have to take it from him, because my adrenalin's up too high to assess if I've broken a bone or cut myself open.

'Evelyn's,' I force the words out. 'We've got to go back to Evelyn's.'

30

*'Out for a walk by the waterside
the girl sat smoking, she choked, she lied.'*

'Hi, we need to use your collection,' I say, holding my ribs on the right side, a bruise fattening under my eye. Along with Mrs Bridges and Miss Heywood, she's part of a very exclusive inner circle of confidantes I've built.

'Great, come in!' Evelyn says without a beat.

Five minutes later we're flicking through the 2004 copies of *The Turkish Chronicle* all over again. We only have half a story so far; there must've been some kind of resolution.

We don't go too fast just in case we miss any little update that might be hiding in the corners. It's an irksome task, but this time I know there's a face capable of catching my eye, which swells my fervour as I search for my kissing tree friend. My first crush, in truth, the one whose face I looked for in the barrage of faces that spilt onto the playground every break or lunchtime. In that sea of freckles below undercuts and ponytails, she shone out formidable. It's coming back to me, bit by bit.

I remember the day she left. I looked for her all day, expecting her alabaster complexion around every corner. And I'm still looking.

As we move onto pages seven and eight, the bag of frozen peas I've been given for my face starts to drip down onto the paper below, the contents becoming rather less frozen and more garden fresh. Our encouraging words to each other soon drop away to the odd mumble and, more painfully, the occasional noise of excitement that quickly fades to a disappointed nothing.

Then Bartu stirs with a slow epiphany. Evelyn rushes in to take a seat as he reads aloud. The date was just two weeks after the original January story, and was lodged in the corner of page nine.

'Police feel they have a strong lead on the disappearance of three girls from Battersea. Their clothes and rucksacks were found in the wooded area of a nearby park... '

'Bloody hell,' Evelyn says. We'd told her what we'd seen today.

'The families of Sarah Walker, Natalie O'Hara and Aliya Akkas have identified the clothes as their daughters'. Traces of blood were also found at the scene and have been sent for tests. Police are still appealing for witnesses.'

We all sit, dug down into the enormity of it, deep in the trenches of things that we know and that others apparently don't. I feel closer to them both. A sort of foxhole brotherhood took over; a closeness I haven't felt in a long while, since I sat listening to Elvis in the back of the car on a long drive with mum and dad.

'We need to tell people about this. Now,' says Emre Bartu.

'Maybe they already know,' I say, clicking at my phone. Lazily seeking comfort in a warm white screen. Even I do it. The sort of person who would take a full five minutes to type out 'funny cat pics' or 'three girls go missing.'

'We have to make sure,' Bartu says, insistently. Annoyed that I seem to have checked out of the conversation and straight into modern distractions.

'Or...' I say.

'Or what?' he says.

'Or we follow our last hunches, see where they take us, then come back to Levine and the rest when we have something concrete.'

'What if we never get something concrete?'

'I'm not stopping until a man's in prison, or I see a body, because until then I think they're out there.'

'That's what you think, is it?' he says.

'Yes. You want to know what else I think?' I say.

'I'm going to hear it anyway, so...'

'It's definitely not their blood. They leave the scene looking like a ritualistic serial killer thing, throw some blood on the clothes, offer the police a mystery. The police do what they tend to do, they Occam's Razor themselves up the most likely suspect. They make it stick. Then the real kidnappers get to do whatever they want with those girls on their own time.'

'And this is based on... ?'

'The bits of the puzzle the way I see them.'

'Well, forgive me if I don't think that's fool-proof logic!'

Evelyn rises and turns. Too embarrassed to do anything about the raised voices in her house, but too uncomfortable to stay still.

'Sarah Walker is alive! We know that!' I shout, thunderously.

'No, you *think* that. You *think* you saw her. I didn't!'

'Please...' Evelyn says.

'Do you know what these people do? They capture them. They brainwash them. That's what's happened to them. You don't have to be clever to do this. You just manipulate people, dominate them. Err... my doctor mentioned this only the other day. Cults, rings, they...'

'Oh, come on!' he shouts, standing now and pushing me. The childishness of which startles me and hurts my ribs, too, but I don't want to show it.

'No, you come on,' I say, pushing him back, misjudging the level of force needed and sending him reeling back against the wall. I decide not to apologise, instead I advance on him as I speak.

'There are news stories, people who've been kept inside houses for years. Then in the end you can train them to go out and they'll come back of their own accord. You learn to love your captor. Call it Stockholm Syndrome. Call it reprogramming. Whatever. They'll come back because you've starved them of every piece of reality –'

'Oh, look at yourself! Even if you're right, don't you think someone else would be better placed to do this, than a... than...'

'Than what?' I say, close to his face. I'm smaller than him but not by much. My heartbeat throbs in my head as I yell. 'Come on then!'

'Boys. Just hold on a moment, for fuck's sake,' Evelyn says, lighting up a cigarette, which she has placed in a holder. She takes a long drag.

'If there's any chance, any chance at all of finding them, alive, then you have to be sensible about it,' she says.

Emre agrees, sagely nodding as he eyeballs me. There's a petty air of 'You see?' about it.

'I'm talking to you, Emre. Be sensible. What did you get into this for? Have you lost your bollocks or something? Look, make a compromise, but then go. If you wanted to follow regulations you would've been an accountant or something – not that there's anything wrong with that – but you mugs chose this. So go and do it!'

They glance at me. I've been on my phone during most of her speech. I look up, wide-eyed, innocent, passion quelled.

'What? No, I'm listening, but... '

Headshakes from both and she takes another long draw on her cigarette.

'Emre? What does this say?'

He grabs my phone and reads aloud.

'Three girls go missing from Woolwich school... girls are... unconnected... they were in different years... one girl was said to have been initially contacted on social media... It's dated January 2009. The girls are... Rita Singh... Sophie Chang... Katherine Grady...'

Bartu slumps down into his chair, still looking at the white screen. It was buried on page 5 of a Google search. I wouldn't call Grady unrelated. I'd call her part of the jigsaw.

'I told you in the car. If they're still alive, wherever they are, they may be running out of room.'

This, I glean from their faces, after a revelation of this magnitude, is not what they expected me to say next.

'I'm saying, I think that when our lost girls joined Sarah Walker and Grady and whoever else, wherever they are, Grady saw new flesh and thought her time may be up. She saw an opportunity to run and she took it. But he chased her out into the woods, and stopped her in her tracks,' I say, tapping Bartu in the back of the head.

'All I keep hearing is missing girls, blood, a lot of appeals and not many witnesses. This exact thing seems to have happened twice before, and it doesn't look like the police solved this thing back then. Our ideas have to be worth a shot.'

Three's a pattern. Three's a charm. Maybe we're the only ones far back enough to see the whole picture.

*

We strike a deal on the way. We will lie through our teeth to whoever we have to, to get wherever we need to be, until this thing is solved. We will go where I want to go next, to the Fraser house, back to that scent of light blue.

But first we've arranged to speak to Turan, privately. We're going to give him everything we have. We'd feel like shit if we didn't and it could have led them somewhere. I have thirty-eight names and a lot more that I think he might be interested in, and I have to concede he's better placed than us to follow it up.

He leans back in a plastic chair with his chicken sandwich.

'I'd have taken you to the snooker club but there are too many people there who can't see me consorting with uniforms.'

Levine laid out Turan's work during a rare candid chat. Sure, everyone knows he's police, but talk to him long enough and you might start to believe he's police that's on your side. Look up and he's telling you to come to him with any information. Look again and maybe he's asking around for good coke and saying he'll look the other way if he gets a taste himself. He's half well-connected man of the community, half law enforcer. The trick is not to let the community know that his loyalties will always lie with the police. Although, Bartu, for one, seems far less certain than Levine about where exactly Turan's loyalties lie.

'We wanted you to know a few things,' I say. Bartu stays quiet on the subject but his presence should show he's complicit.

'That's good. What have you got?' he says. A man very used to this kind of relationship.

'First. Don't share this with Jarwar. If you can, keep it as close to your chest as possible.'

'Okay,' he says. I expected him to stifle a grin and humour us but his ears seem to prick up.

'We've been chasing a few things maybe we shouldn't have, recently, and Jarwar didn't take too kindly to it. If I'm honest, I think she confiscated a mini-DV tape from Emre.'

Bartu widens his eyes at me, slightly castrated by this notion.

I hadn't worded this theory out loud, but then communication isn't our strongest relationship attribute.

'I think she saw me palm it to him, then, for whatever reason, nicked it from his car.'

Turan takes a bite of his sandwich before speaking.

'I won't ask, sounds like naughty stuff, but you're safe with me. Trust me, she's all right, but it's not like we meet up for a beer and a chat about our sex lives.'

Something catches Turan's eye outside, as I look to Bartu, before spilling it all on the table.

'We got some information from an old lady who lives locally, about three girls going missing ten years ago.'

'Yep. Girls go missing. Sometimes they come back, sometimes they don't,' Turan says. He's going for professionalism and experience but he can't spin it without it seeming a little numb. He's more interested in his burger than me. I look on as he lays down three lines across his fries, one of mustard, one of ketchup, one of mayo. It has a certain ceremony about it.

'Anyway, we looked into it and it was all dead on. Down in Battersea, three girls go missing in one week, not friends, in different years. Then their clothes turned up, in a wood, covered in blood.'

'Oh yeah, that is interesting. Rings a bell. Reminds me of... I think I know this old bird, she that Miss Marples?'

He's looking for a snigger but it's not forthcoming from either of us. It's usually my levity that clashes with the mood.

'And when we looked further, we found that the exact same thing happened five years later over in Woolwich. What's more than that, one of those Woolwich girls is Katherine Grady, and there's already a guy called Ed Rampling in prison for her murder,' Bartu says.

I turn for a second and see the guy walk past casually on the other side of the road. Dark glasses on a gloomy day. The same guy we saw last time we were here, for certain. The one no one seems keen to talk about. Turan also spots him but isn't giving anything away. The abused kid that grew up. He could be an informer or a dealer. He could be anything. Turan is into a lot of stuff we don't know about. That's part of his job.

'Seriously, that's good work boys. London's a big city, lots of crime, lots of shit to sift through. I don't think anyone's looked into this Woolwich or Battersea stuff yet. I'll make sure they do.'

'Thanks,' Bartu says. But I don't want to thank him for doing his job.

'I have been trying to keep in touch with it, but now the bodies are in the detectives are out. Pretty soon I'll get shut out too. I can, however, follow up a few things if they're important. And this seems important, so thanks.'

'Hey, Turan, did you ever follow up that car?' I say, casually gazing out of the window.

'What car?' Turan says, before sinking his teeth wet and deep into his burger for one last firm bite.

'The err... there was a blacked out car we found just after the first girl went missing, smashed up and left at the side of the road. We found it. Just being amateur sleuths again, I guess. Levine was talking about looking into it. Did anyone do that?' I say.

He looks out the window, too, and seems hurried.

'Yeah. Oh yeah, course. Followed it up myself. It was burnt inside. Plates off. Couldn't find which dealership it might have come from, nothing. Dead end.'

'Who is that guy? What's his name?' Bartu says, as the man in the shades heads away. I want to follow and have a word, but with Turan here our hands are plasti-cuffed. It wouldn't exactly suit our 'staying out of it and handing everything to you' theme.

'Which guy?' Turan says, nonplussed.

'Yeah. That's *the* guy. You remember?' I say. 'I tried talking to Jarwar about him but –'

'Oh. That fella? Yeah, he keeps me in touch with a few things. I got plenty of his kind about,' Turan says.

'I get it,' I say, but I don't entirely. Is he forgetting we've spoken about him before?

'Think maybe I talked to him once. His name's... err... ' I click my fingers a couple of times.

'Rabbit?' Turan says.

More people enter the restaurant that Turan seems to know, and he nods sagely at them. This really is his part of town. Maybe it's difficult to keep track of everyone.

He pops the last of his burger into his mouth and stands.

'Yeah, that's him. Rabbit,' I say.

'Yeah, listen, thanks for the heads up, I'll get on it,' Turan says.

I can't go without giving him everything. I'd feel bad if I didn't, now we're here.

'Hey, and take this,' I say, palming him a slip of paper. 'It's a list of kids that might have seen the girls with someone. Don't ask how I got it, but someone should check it out. And talk to the cleaner too. Youngish guy, seems like he knows more than he's letting on.'

'Cleaner?' he says, as if he's never heard the word.

'Yeah, you'll know the one, possible curvature of the spine, averse to eye contact, really knows how to make you feel welcome.'

He looks at it me for a second, blinks, then folds the note.

'You given this to anyone else?'

'No, we haven't,' Bartu says.

'Okay, I'll go by the school and handle it later today.'

I lift my hand to my bruise. It throbs for a second.

'Between you and me, boys, there's good police and bad police. It's mostly hierarchy stuff and I don't want to go too deep into it, but you might be right not to trust some people. Anyway thanks for this, this is good.'

He pockets the paper and goes.

We watch him turn right.

As 'Rabbit' drifts down a side-street, far away in the other direction.

31

'Can't. get that girl dah dah, out of, my head...'

'Sorry, Ms Fraser, it's us again,' Bartu says.

She thankfully greets us warmly, but also with the threat of hot drinks and small talk to slow us down. I observe a mania in her behaviour which I can't place. Perhaps whatever hadn't sunk in last time has had ample time to drop. She insists on us making ourselves comfortable, when comfort is the last thing on our minds. She doesn't make reference to my bruised and bulbous face at all, but then Turan didn't either. I guess they assume people like me tend to fall down a lot, and it's rude to ask the cause.

I don't mention to either of them that I found the small blue circle with two diagonal lines on the kerb, as we stepped onto her drive, because that's what I expected to find. It's not on all streets. Just certain ones.

Our small-talk descends into so many little fragments of nothing, broken sound bites and pleasantries: 'You do a top job, you guys... ' 'I suppose you don't feel the weather after... '

I begin to think her disposition is not in fact an effort to stay positive and busy, but is instead an indicator that she's hiding something.

'I'm afraid we don't have anything for you at present. But as soon as we do, you'll be the first one to know,' Bartu says.

It's true in a way. In other ways, it's utter hypocrisy. Hearing this affects her more than I thought it would. I don't know why this surprises me. I curse myself inside for this disassociation. I have an instinct to dig my fingers into my eye for forgetting that the bloody core of these people's lives is entirely bound to the gruesome scene I witnessed in the woods.

The truth is, the elements of 'solve riddle' and 'soothe victims', have a metamorphic relationship.

I breathe in through my nose and smell the blue. I can feel the mahogany that goes with it, and the hear the note 'F' playing lightly. It's so strong to me it distracts me as I struggle with the problem of whether to tell her what we now know. I've been happy enough to tell before, to break the rules, why not now?

- I can't stand to see her cry, here, in front of me.
- I am a coward.
- I should tell her the flat reality and let her decide how far she indulges in it.

'No news, at all?' she says, tears forming in her eyes like the threat of some far-off hurricane that hasn't hit yet but surely will.

She repeats, 'Nothing?', attempting to elicit a different response. Bartu can't help me. She's asking *me*. Pleading with me.

I start to question what I see before me. A performance. A construction, designed to misdirect?

I bolt before I have to make a decision about her question. Resolving that I have more important queries of my own. I dart upstairs. Leaving her standing, stunned in her living room.

'Where are you going? This is my house!'

'Tom?' Bartu is not far behind, but I'm at the top of the stairs and heading into the bedroom. Hers. Tanya's. I open the cupboard. I see nothing but the bear that falls out once more.

'Wanna play? Wanna play?' it says, shrilly.

The cat scarpers from somewhere under my feet and I want to kick out at the bastard, only just managing to keep my grip and remember my new found love for the animal kingdom.

I turn and bang my fist on the wall just next to her wardrobe.

I can smell blue. I knock methodically, testing for a difference in sound. Then turn and I bang my fist on her chest of drawers, the one that held the photos the first time we were here. Ms Fraser and Bartu arrive in the doorway just as I burst out and head into Ms Fraser's bedroom.

I throw open her wardrobe. Nothing. I go to the wall that separates her room and her daughter's. I rap on it with my knuckles.

Knock. Knock.

I explore its expanse.

Knock. Knock. Knock. Knock. Knock. Knock. Knock. Knock. Knock. Knock. Knock. Knock. Knock.

'You can come out now,' I say.

They stand in the doorway watching.

A silence. Nothing.

I knock again: *Knock…Knock.*

Bartu takes a step towards me. Carefully, like he doesn't want to spook the inmate who has sharpened the end of his spoon to a point.

I knock, feebly: *Knock, knock.*

I look to her. She seems terrified. Not guilty, nothing like that at all. As Bartu runs in to smother me, I escape his grasp and go back into Tanya's room. I take a deep breath through my nose.

'Oh,' I mutter.

At full flight I lunge towards the chest of drawers and reach for the exact spot where the photos were. They're not there, but it's not the photos I'm after. I reach into my jacket pocket for my gloves. And only after I've put them on do I lift a blue scarf from the wardrobe and put my nose to it and breathe deep.

'I'm – I'm so sorry. I've been so stupid.'

Ms Fraser looks on, calmer now, but justifiably wary of me. 'What is it?' she says, desperately.

'I've been so... I've missed something.'

Bartu holds both palms to me, showing me he is going to approach with caution. She stiffens up and her wide eyes seem to feel for me across the room. I look at her and speak before I tap Bartu on the back calmly and head downstairs.

'I'm sorry,' I say. 'I need this.'

'Please find my baby,' she says, barely holding it together as I nod to her, offering all the assurance a man such as I can.

And then I'm gone, out the door, and we rush towards the car and the station and I curse my lack of care and inability to master my own senses the last time I was here.

*

The forensic specialist isn't hard to find. When we see him, he recognises Bartu and comes out from behind his window.

'Hi, we need something testing,' I say, steamrollering their greeting.

'Oh, hi. Tom, isn't it? Good to see you,' he says taking a plastic glove off awkwardly, before offering his hand for a shake. It still unnerves me how many people know my name.

'We need you to run some tests on this, mate,' Bartu says, as I push the clear plastic bag containing the scarf at the guy.

'Tests for what?' he says, innocently.

Emre looks to me.

'Dammit,' I think. 'What am I asking for?' My actions are

running ahead of my thoughts. I'm certain it's one of those keepsakes they exchanged, so there should be traces of him all over it. Him and her.

'A man has held this in his hands. I need to know who he is.'

I watch the lab guy's thoughts swim around his head and harden into barriers. The logical questions come next.

'Err... sure, but what tests do you need, specifically? They all take time and we're kind of busy, Tom.'

'The tests. You know... .' I say, as Bartu's body language changes, separating himself from this fumbling man in the technical area.

'You know, DNA?'

'Right. Are we talking tests for blood, hair and skin? 'Cos a conclusive serology test will take some time. And you should know that if this man doesn't have a criminal record, then he won't be one of the lucky six million people in our DNA database. So, unless you've got some of the guy's blood, skin or hair handy to test it against...'

I give him a blank face. Then devote a couple of seconds to wondering how on earth I would have that to hand. It's only later, when replaying this conversation, that I realise this was the frank yet belittling humour of the expert.

'No, I don't have any of his blood, hair or skin with me.'

'Right. Your quickest bet is a preliminary test for saliva and semen with a UV light. And if there's something of that nature there then it's not too hard to draw the DNA and try the database,' he says. My heart pumps fast and my tongue rolls around, exploring my mouth with excitement.

'But, we're a pretty busy right now,' he says, with an apologetic wince. 'I don't know whether you know but some blood was found –'

'Yeah, we know. Is it possible to check for fingerprints too?' Bartu says.

'In theory, yes. I mean, I'd prefer glass for a good print. Paper, a dashboard, not bad either. Fabric is... formidable, but possible. It'd take weeks to get a beautiful, full print, but I could tell you fairly quickly whether there's anything vaguely usable on it.'

'Okay, deal, we'll go for saliva, semen and prints,' I say, dropping one of my cards on the cold metal table between us.

'Right, well, I'll try to do it by end of day, but no promises. Who's this for by the way?'

'Call me when it's done,' batting away the question. 'And thank you... err... err... ' his name is written on his badge, and I'd been eyeing it distractedly throughout our conversation.

'Thanks Aar...'

Bartu is at the door. Lab guy smiles at me encouragingly.

'Alan!'

'Yes. That's... no worries,' says Alan who, I would later find out, is named Aaron, and is far too polite for his own good.

'Oh guys?' says Aaron. 'I'm going to need a name?'

I look to the floor and say it.

'Turan,' I sigh, out of moves. 'Inspector Turan. But... he'll be tied up all evening and I'm your best first port of call.'

I'm pleased with the dexterity with which I end the conversation, but not delighted with having to throw the name.

'Well, that went well,' Bartu says, as we go. And if I didn't know better, I'd say he's being sarcastic.

32

*'The boy next door likes a shake and fries
He'd like to take you home and try you on for size.'*

Bartu had pointed out the snooker hall our man tends to frequent in the evenings, so I knew I had a decent chance, but it was by no means a sure thing.

For a hundred reasons I've decided to go this one alone and leave Bartu and Aisha to a meal for two. The fissure of mistrust in our relationship has by turns narrowed and gaped of late. That's why I didn't even tell him I was coming here, instead concocting a high concept story about an early night, which he believed, as it suited him to do so.

However, arriving at 9.45pm, paying my two-pound entrance fee, and getting ogled by every punter in the place, makes me wish I had company on my side, or, failing that, had at least informed someone of my whereabouts. I clutch my facial recognition sheet as a mascot, my eyes scouring the room in search of Turan. I have a request to make. And a quiz question to ask too.

I'm pleased to see that not everyone is engaged in a game of snooker, or some other table sport. Some chat, some see it as a quiet, out of the way place to start the business of drinking long into the small hours. All of this helps me feel a little less like a lost tourist in a shark tank. But, as I clutch my lemonade, plenty of sharks seem to be probing me with wandering eyes. Sticking out like a sore thumb is something I'm used to, but people seem to stare in this sleazy place more than anywhere else. A sea of faces, colours and races. My presence seems to offend them all. Some looks linger on me longer than others, probably recognising me from the paper. I'd naively tried to cover my appearance with shades, but that doesn't seem to have worked. As I look across the room I'm pleased to see I'm not alone. Another guy sits drinking and talking, shades on, in a low-lit room.

I almost smile at him as he turns around and glances my way. He's helping me to blend me in. But he doesn't smile back, instead he looks away faster than most, carrying on his chat as if slightly disturbed. I tend to have that effect on people. Just as I start to take a closer look at him, I get a firm tap on the shoulder.

'Hey. What you doing here, man?' Turan says, out of the corner of his mouth, as if caught talking to the least cool kid in school at lunch.

'Looking for you,' I say.

He nods and takes a look around again. Above all, I don't want to get on his bad side. He's not Jarwar. He's the outsider. The guy on the force who isn't so caught up in procedure and the whispers that go on behind my back.

'That's cool. What's up?' he says, sitting down next to me, keeping his eyes on the room.

'I know this seems unusual…' I say.

'It always does with you mate,' he says.

'I dropped something in at the lab today. Got backed into a corner. Said it was courtesy of you. If they ask, can you back me up?'

The thought seems to take a while to hit. His brow furrows.

'You're going to have to tell me what it is my friend. I should at least ask that, shouldn't I?'

He has a point.

'Something I found at one of the girls' houses. A scarf.'

He nods tentatively, troubled by this, I sense.

'You think you might get what? A trace of someone on it?'

'It's a shot in the dark. One of the last we have.'

He knew I was following my own lines of investigation, but I guess he didn't know I was in it this deep.

'Okay, whatever. Whatever I can do to help. I'll vouch.'

'Thank you,' I say. 'Thanks a lot.'

And I almost start to rise. Then decide to stay right where I am. I'm finally putting something together.

'Hey, Turan, who's that guy?' I say, nodding towards the man in the shades, who's looking over to us again.

'What guy?' he says.

'The guy over there? All in black. Shades. I think we saw him before. Don't you remember?'

'Did we?' he says, nonplussed again.

'Look, I didn't tell you something else and maybe I should've.'

'What? About this guy?' he says.

'Maybe. The caretaker at the school said he kept seeing a guy hanging around school. His kind of age and look. Maybe I'm being paranoid. He just seems to be around an awful lot.'

Turan stays still, thinking. Then I go to speak again, but before I can he rises and goes over to the guy, and starts talking at him intensely. I amble over too. Possibly he's someone Turan knows well. Someone he keeps close but doesn't exactly trust. The scene in the chicken shop certainly suggested that. By the time I get to them things have become physical. I notice an old cut on the guy's forehead.

'Take a walk with me,' Turan says to the guy.

But the guy doesn't want to budge, so Turan grabs him by

his shirt collar and throws him into a dim backroom. The pool hall doesn't even flinch. As if this is an ordinary occurrence.

Lit only by neon pints of lager, Turan has the guy up against the wall. He's no procedure man; this is his world.

'Tell me about your side-line taking pictures of little girls.'

'I don't know what the fuck you're talking about,' the guy says.

'Well, my mate here says you do. My mate here has got another mate, who caught you at it. So you fill in the rest, okay?'

It was still a hunch. I'm nervous for the guy. I start to worry about where this goes next.

'No, I… got a sister that goes there, so sometimes I'm around…'

The guy tries to spit it out but is stopped in his tracks by a firm blow to the face. He took the hit like he didn't see it coming. Which interests me. He didn't seem to sense the fist until it was right under his nose. He didn't even flinch.

His glasses fall and I glimpse his full face, but it's too fast and half-lit for a man like me to glean anything useful from it before he replaces them. Fortunately for him the force of the hit wasn't enough to break them. But two more vicious kicks to the groin and stomach aren't helping his wellbeing.

I notice the shape of the cut on his forehead again. It's like a small red frown.

'Okay, fuck!' he groans. 'Someone asked me to. Wanted pictures of the girls. I didn't know what it was for. I don't ask questions. It was just a fucking job!'

I take off my shades, slip them into my pocket.

'Who? Who asked you to?' Turan shouts.

I get the impression that this guy is a kind of mercurial, fair-weather friend of the law. He helps them out a little from time to time. Certainly does a few other shadier things that they know less about. Turan raises his fists again.

'A name! Who asked you to take the pictures?!' he says, eyes wild and wide, just before he gets a rising kick to the balls and Rabbit breaks for the exit.

I try and make a grab for him, but he barges me to the ground. I labour to get up and by the time I open the door to the main hall, he's heading down the stairs and out of the exit at a pace that's far too much for me.

'I'll find him, don't worry,' Turan says as he rises.

We assess our various damage for a second, my bruise and scar throbbing again. Then I go for it.

'Hey Turan?' I say, my adrenalin up. 'Did you ever hear anything about a paedophile ring? One involving police officers? I was reading that this murderer, Ed Rampling, said in court that –'

'Yeah, those kinds of people are always bargaining. Or trying to throw blame elsewhere with some bullshit. Everyone's got a story.'

'Sure. Only thing is, I've been thinking… Rampling's other five victims were white collar white males; the girls don't make sense, in terms of the pattern. Evidence wasn't so concrete either, but the police seemed to want it to stick. So I'm just saying it's possible.'

He cracks his neck while taking it in. This is what I like about the man. Anyone else on the force would give me a straight no. He's a maybe man.

When I looked at the two women that etched themselves onto my screen the night I watched those two tapes, I couldn't help but place the silhouette from the first video, and Sarah in the second, side by side. I think they're inextricably linked. I believe this other woman is responsible for Sarah's disappearance. I also want to believe Sarah is alive. Her old cells, now made entirely new. Her life, irrevocably shifted on its axis. But her heart, beneath her callow skin, still beating somewhere.

'…on that tape, that got stolen, was the silhouette of a woman.

And when I asked Jarwar about Rabbit, she was evasive. So, I just –'

'Does anyone else know about the tape? That it ever existed?'

'No one. We didn't tell, 'cos we weren't supposed to have it.'

'Okay, look, I'm not saying some shit doesn't go down here. But I can't see that. Not a copper. But do one thing for me? Keep all this close to your chest, for now. For both our safeties.'

'What are we going to do?' I say, looking him up and down.

'Leave it to me. I haven't had a chance to look into those thrity-eight names yet, but I will. Tomorrow. Till then, just to be safe, don't go anywhere with any officer if you can help it. Don't get drawn into anything. Not for a few days.'

'Not even Bartu?'

'Not even Bartu. Not if you can help it. I'll let you know when our photographer pops his head up again. When he does, I'll grab it.'

'Ha. They call him Rabbit, right?'

Even lit only by the neon glow, I can see Turan's white T-Shirt is now damp with sweat. He makes a face like a zero, giving nothing to the positive or negative. Then sniggers.

'That's right. I'll grab our Rabbit. You're right, he does always seem to be hanging around. Leave it with me, okay?'

I bow my head, my hand on the door of this dark room, thoughts rumbling through my synapses. I don't know what I've got myself mixed up in, maybe I shouldn't have come here at all. Maybe Anita and Ryans are right, maybe I do need to take better care of myself.

I hustle to leave but before I do he squeezes my shoulder tight, like a big brother, not letting me go.

'Trust me. We're gonna sort this out,' he says.

But I'm not sure who I trust less at this point.

Him. Them. Or myself.

Documented Telephone Conversation #3

'Yes?' he says. A dog barks in the background.
'Hi. Hello there. Can I speak to Mrs Castle please?'
'Who is this?' the man says. Deep and weary of voice.
'I'm a friend of her daughter.'
'Who is this? How did you get this number?' he says.
'Well, I'm a member of the police force, you see –'
'You were a friend of hers? Or you're a member of the police force? Which is it?'
'Both. Sir, my name is Tom Mondrian and I'd really like to –'
'She won't want to speak to you.'

I'd checked in with Amit at the The Corner Shop. Unlike me, he's got an excellent memory of everyone we went to school with. He remembered Sarah just fine. Said she'd kept her father's name when her mother remarried. He said her stepdad's name was Castle. Once I'd found this out, it made their number a whole lot easier to find.

'I really need to talk to her, sir. It's about girls that have recently gone missing,' I say.
He says nothing. The dog's barks become more insistent.

'You can talk to me. I was here when it all happened. I don't want you upsetting her all over again. You can talk to me.'

'Okay. I know this may seem a strange question. I… err… listen…'

'Go on then. Spit it out,' he sneers across the line.

'Have you seen Sarah recently?' I say. And the seconds tick by.

'I'm hanging up the phone now.'

'Listen to me! Please, I think – I feel… like I've seen her recently.'

'She's dead. They found her clothes and her blood. It's been ten years. I'm glad I didn't put you on to her mother, filling her head with this shit all over again. Now leave us in peace.'

'Wait!' I say. 'Does she… has she ever mentioned seeing her? Ever? Since she went missing?'

The dog is quiet now. There's nothing but silence across the line.

'Tom. Tom is it?' he says. His voice stiller now. A calm pond. 'That's the sort of thing that grief does, Tom. If she ever has, seen her, if she thinks that she has, then that's what grief does. It's a trick of the mind. Or perhaps a message from the Lord, in whom we trust. Who sends such things to comfort sufferers. But it's not reality. You say you were a friend of hers?'

'Yes, I was. I am,' I say, though it stretches the truth.

'Then I would suggest to you that you are merely grieving for your friend. I'll tell you what I tell her. Get over it. Just, get over it.'

He crunches down on the words. And he's not done.

'Sarah was killed by Edward Rampling. Along with the other girls, and many other people too. And he will burn in hell for it.'

'But Rampling wasn't convicted of killing Sarah or any of the girls in Battersea. Just the ones in Woolwich. And that was years later. When Sarah went missing it's doubtful Rampling was even active –'

'I'm sorry! Tom? That's what we choose to believe. You have to find closure in this. That is ours. We've looked into this from every angle, trust me on that. That's what we believe!'

'But Rampling never even admitted to those Woolwich murders, did he? He admitted to killing five people, but not Katherine Grady or any *of the other Woolwich girls. And, I'm sorry, certainly not Sarah. There was only circumstantial rumour linking him to her –'*

'I know what was said, Tom! I was there. I was in that fucking court room. So don't tell me what was and wasn't said!'

We both breathe again.

'Then what was said?'

He breathes in wearily. I feel like I hear weakness in his breath. This god-fearing man is quieter now. Wary of waking his wife upstairs.

'Nonsense, some bloody nonsense about a paedophile ring, one involving police officers. He was trying to shift the blame somewhere else with some cock and bull story. He got away with a lot more than he was done for. He was done for Katherine Grady and should've –'

'I'm sorry. I'm sorry to disabuse you. Katherine's body turned up a week ago. Time of death was around thirty-six hours before she was found. Rampling, meanwhile, has been in prison for four years.'

'Tom,' he says. His voice is wet and gravelled. Suddenly vulnerable. 'Either way. Sarah is gone and she's not coming back. Of that we are in no doubt. As her... friend... I'd ask you to respect that.'

He's not moving. We're going in circles. I go to hang up.

'Not that I believe you were her friend. She didn't have any friends. That's what a normal girl would have, and she wasn't normal.'

'Sorry?' I say, off guard. 'What do you mean?'

He takes a deep breath. His voice concrete again.

'She'd get into trouble. She met up with the wrong sorts. Men. Girls. Messing about. She was always doing that. One of those girls, making mistakes, pushing her luck. Caused us no end of grief. She had to be... carefully handled. Disciplined. She was a bad girl. A bad girl.'

And the line goes dead.

33

'She dah dah at half past nine
Dirty shoes, every time.'

When the next phone call comes it wakes me. Which is unusual. I don't need much sleep and I almost never drift off before 1am.

When I got home after everything that happened today, though, I lay on my bed on top of the cold duvet cover and Mark came and rested against my head as my eyelids closed and I drifted off and away. It wasn't Heywood or Miss Shelley. They'd both gone pretty quiet on me and I was left cursing my social skills and levels of physical attractiveness again, for leaving me divorced of good intelligent company.

'I should tell you before anyone else does,' says the voice without a hello. In my waking slumber, I don't recognise it.

'What is it?' I say. As ever, my sleep had been far from restful, and filled with fractured images, just as my waking hours have been ever since I saw the stacked clothes and blood.

'I've been suspended with immediate effect,' it says.

'Bartu. Is that you?'

'Yes, Tom. Yes, it's me, for fuck's sake.'

'How? Did one of the parents call? I bet it was Mr Bridges or... '

'It doesn't matter, it could've been anything, anything we've done – you've made me do... it doesn't matter! What matters is that I can't go anywhere near this case or even the station for one week, and when I get back I'm not coming anywhere near you either, otherwise I won't have a job or a future anymore. Is that clear enough for you to understand?'

'Yes,' I say, guiltily.

'Is that the whole picture? I know you only usually notice the corners. I know it's easier if I spell things out for you.'

'Don't get mean, Emre Bartu. It doesn't suit you.'

I think I hear a noise outside. Then I realise it's the wind. A wild storm that's whipping up the trees and casting everything below into a freeze.

'I'm getting the feeling you haven't heard anything about your position. Have you?'

'No,' I say, feeling very alone, looking for Mark, who must have wandered downstairs.

'So I'm wearing this one, it seems. Ha.' He laughs down the line. It's a bitter, dry laugh and I want to laugh, too, but I don't see what's funny. I don't think this is funny at all. I feel isolated.

'Which is weird. Don't you think?' I say.

'Oh come on, it's not that weird. They can't suspend you, it'd be like shooting a puppy. 'Scuse the phrase.'

'Not to worry,' I mutter.

'No. They need you around. You know what for.'

'No. What do they need me for?'

Silence on the line.

Then nothing. He hangs up and I don't think we parted on good terms. I understand the inference. I'm part of some quota, I can do what I want, I am... bulletproof. 'Scuse the phrase.

I hear a smash outside my bedroom door.

My hand goes to my chest and I stifle a shout. Then Mark walks in sheepishly and offers himself for a stroke. I look at the broken pieces of a mirror that used to hang in my parents' bedroom. I'd taken it down and leant it precariously against a wall, so I suppose it's my fault as much as Mark's. I look around and realise how many other little ghosts there are. Of my parents, of the stuttered attempts to make the place my own I've made over the years. The false starts, the lamps without bulbs. The pictures not framed. I sweep the broken pieces up and take them to chuck into my bathroom bin. I remember broken mirrors are supposed to signify something, but I can't remember what. Good luck maybe, but I'm not so sure. There are thoughts that still lie out of my reach. Maybe I'm not getting better. Maybe I'm not progressing anywhere, in my rehabilitation, or with this case, or my life. Maybe I've been careless about too many things.

The phone rings. I feel uncomfortable in my own skin and afraid of it. I want what appears on the screen to be a name, the shape of which I may recognise, perhaps one of the strong women in my life who might be able to come over and keep me warm for a while. But it's numbers, ones I couldn't attribute even if I could read them, each stabs like a compass, each one a possibility, each one a threat. I should've known. I was always destined to be alone.

'Hello?' I say.

'Tom, it's Aaron. Couple of things.'

'Aaron, did you call Turan?'

The sound of an uncomfortable sniff. I picture him as an illustrated figure, pacing from one foot to the other.

'Right, well. Let's tackle that first. I checked in with Turan –'

'And?'

'And he said yes, yeah, of course. Wanted to know what I had exactly and what the results were. He was trying to cover your back, that's for sure.'

288

Good old Turan, friend to the outsider.

'Then when the detective called to ask about the blood results, I asked if he wanted details of the scarf, too, just in case he –'

'Fucking hell, Aaron!'

'Right, maybe that was... but look... ' He whispers now, conspiratorial. 'If I'd known it was all your little side project then I wouldn't have... look, they weren't happy. I'm sorry if you got a slap on the wrist, but you shouldn't have –'

'Bartu was suspended.'

The wind whips up again and the windows in the house begin to shake.

'I'm really sorry, Tom. But how was I to know?'

'Can you at least tell me the results?' I say, cutting in.

'Yes. We got virtually nothing. It looks like there may be three different sets of fingerprints on the scarf. But they're so faint it would take a month to get them to a standard good enough to test against our records. I'm sorry.'

I pull the phone away from my head and punch the bed. Then I think...

'But we did find traces of iodine on it.'

'Great. I have no idea what that means,' I say.

'Well, it's often used as a strong disinfectant or –'

'What about the blood results. Are they the girl's?'

'Oh, come on. I can't tell you that. Not until the parents are informed.'

'Aaron, I like you. I think we're going to get on very well. But I think we can both agree you owe me this.'

'Right. Yes, they're consistent with their blood types, but don't say you heard it from me.'

I hang up and slam the phone down onto the carpet. I hear nearby thunder and picture the calls the parents may be about to get.

A) Mrs Da Silva on her mobile, arm in arm with her husband, conjuring theories as they walk Tottenham's streets.

B) The Bridges answering after the twelfth ring and listening before the phone drops to the ground and their lives finally do collapse under the weight of it all.

C) Ms Fraser, alone, despite my foolish suspicions.

I do need to trust myself less.

My head hits the pillow and it feels like it's a sleep in my clothes evening. The rain lashes against my window. I hear a branch break outside. I hear the squeaks of what could be the long chains of neighbouring hanging baskets, or nearby swings, or my back door opening.

The night moves on. I sweat in the small hours. Taking a piece of clothing off hour by hour as my broken sleep is anything but restful. I picture them opening my back door, picking the lock, then stepping onto the cold kitchen tiles.

I feel like I hear a door close, but it could be a noise caused by the winds outside. It could be.

I dream of the shape she draws in lipstick on the board. The one I saw on the windscreen of that car. It changes in my mind. I haven't seen it in so long. I didn't make a copy of it, but my brain has been smoothing out its edges since I first saw it. I know now, it's not about what it looks like, exactly. Jade loved to draw, but lipstick was a new tool. The question is: *what was it meant to look like?*

It's not so much a symbol, as a picture, of a creature.

It was a childish off-the-cuff gesture that was shooting for romance. It's meaning lies hidden and she didn't get a second draft. As soon as he saw it and her, a thought took him over and he acted.

A new picture perfectly forms. I grab it and wrestle it down, dragging the colours and the shape in different directions. I manipulate its aspect until it becomes familiar. And I finally see it…

Then I wake. I think. I wake but I don't open my eyes. I have the awful sensation of something being in my room with me. Another human. I feel and hear their gentle footsteps like a father as Santa Claus in a childhood bedroom. The door falls closed, that familiar creak, pushed by this being I cannot bear to open my eyes to see.

I could be asleep, I could be, I suppose.

Now I hear its breath. It. He or she. Calm and steady and definite, like they do this all the time. I keep my eyes closed because I can't bear to look and it's my best chance of not riling it. He or she. Just let them get what they came for and they'll leave.

Its feet slide across the floor. Like an ocean. Or a pillow against the ear. Or a slow 'shh'.

I picture its silhouette but I daren't look. Not now. I know I am awake and my ears and skin sense the presence of another being. It's an animal instinct and one I've always keenly had. Those people that turn around and shout, startled because someone has arrived in a room without being seen by them; I've never had that.

I think of the lipstick shape, distracting myself until it's over, even if the 'it' is 'my life'. I'm not in one of my gung-ho moods. If this is 'it' then I am going down without a fight. I will come quietly. I cannot locate the guts to fight it head on.

It seems to pause. Right over me. I feel the faintest hint of its breath as the wind rages on outside. The dark behind my eyelids seems to drop a shade further. It bears down on me heavily. Examining me, like the CT scanner did. I breathe deep and play act that I'm sleeping sound. The rustle of its clothes. The creak of the floorboards below me as it rouses itself so close to my face, just above me. The smell of it. I'd call it an aroma, but it's really a smell, coloured blue, as it takes a long good look at me.

Emre Bartu lies at home next to Aisha.

I am here.

They have finally got me alone.

I hear a sharp intake of breath in preparation.

I remember, a note, she passed…
Documented Memory Project #4

Yes!

To me. Biology.

'You're so cool,' it said.

Unusual. She didn't always feel that way. She scrawled it, handwriting like ink on spider's legs.

But hey, that day she wanted to talk and I fizzed like pop.

Then. Under the table indented with tracks made

by fountain pens, I wrote [*concealed from Mr Sugar's eyes*] something like…

'Biology sux' but I didn't feel that way. Really.

'You sux,' she wrote. With a frowny face next to it.

She watched my eyes as I looked at it and I smiled (because what else could I do?)

Changing to my red pen I wrote…

'Why the blood?'

Her eyes were mischievous bored, as she scribbled. And I watched the ragged wet knuckles of her fist again.

'It's not mine,' it read.

Mr Sugar's eyes drifted over us as he turned on the overhead projector and the organs of a body appeared behind him, as the lights were flicked off by Kelly at the back after his nod.

'Whose then?' My next said (something like that.)

'Kelly's.'

Looking back. Through the light rays of the projector, I saw Kelly had a cut lip, (*all fat and bust*) and a bruised cheek.

'Why?' I write. (Feeling a bit sad for both)

'Like fighting + she's a bitch.' *The 'i' ripping paper.*

(She was often fighting. I heard. She never got caught.)

She passed me another note: 'my mum keeps having miscarriages.'

(I'll never forget that. Cos it was *weird*. She snatched it - wrote again.)

'My stepdad slaps her around.' *Her face, so blank.*

Then the lights came on. It got like the sort of thing an adult should know. But then. *She was known for some tall tales and games, you see.*

She was resilient. That girl.

Fuck knows. What Kelly did.

If Sarah was taken, she wouldn't have gone without a fight.

I remember thinking... I wonder why she wrote me notes that day.

Maybe, she was just bored.

34

'She never knew that kooky wooky love,
That hokey-cokey chokey love.'

Ring, Ring.

For a second, I don't know where I am. A long second, in which my head cracks in its tiny places.

Night Reality is pulled together from dreams, waiting, and bits somewhere in between, elongated and amalgamated into each other. But the phone has the unerring ability to drag you back.

Ring, ring. To whatever you call *Day Reality*. Which, for me, isn't much less psychedelic. The corners of my room soon blur into view. I wonder if I can move my arm.

Ring, ring. I can. And the diagnostics seem good for the rest of my body too. I turn and seize it. No name or number on its face. But its rumble stops, dead in my hand. Looks like I missed that one. I feel sorrow for my phone like it's a dead canary. Its screen fades to black. The dark reflection splayed across its heart, mine I assume, looks awful.

The morning comes with little evidence of a presence in my room. Yet downstairs in the kitchen, my window bobs in the wind, ajar. Its jaws big enough for a body to sneak through. Below it, a knife and fork, which I left last night on the drying rack, lie kissing on a tile next to my bare feet. I could have left the window open, of course, it wouldn't be the first time. The wind, or Mark, could have knocked the cutlery off the drying rack. But I'm sure I remember closing that window.

I could ask my neighbour if they saw or heard anything last night, I think. Neighbours are good for that sort of thing.

Then a memory comes back to me that has lain dormant for a while. Something from my first week, before Christmas, before any of this happened and my brain was a mundane place and so was the world outside it.

I examine the memory. I pick it up.

Then I put it down,

shake it off,

and leave.

*

Levine gives me a knowing smile when I come in. He doesn't treat me like a thug or a terrorist. We aren't that kind of threat. He sits me down and talks carefully about Bartu leading me astray. About a short, sharp slap on the wrists, 'which he'll learn from'. He talks about it being time for me to 'go it alone'. It's an opinion I don't share.

'You're right. I've been so confused this last week or so. I'm sorry if I got in the way,' I bumble out.

'No, no,' he says. 'No, no. I'd call it encouraging exuberance. Nothing wrong with that. As such.'

He talks with kid gloves gaffer-taped to his thin wrists. I wonder why.

'By the way, Tom. There's a man coming in to speak to you tomorrow morning. From the press, a local, but a lovely big piece. About you and us. Wondered if you could share a few good experiences. Obviously, be candid. Camaraderie of the team...

the pleasure of serving the community... err... I don't want to put words in your mouth.'

Well, you do, you want to force them in, one hand squeezing my nose, the other penetrating between my lips and teeth. I'm good for Tottenham. I'm a gateway to good press and changing attitudes. Levine is not a bad man for craving any of this, like our nervy chief he's just a little timid and benign and I have trouble respecting that.

'Forgive me, sir... ' Levine sits up in his chair when I use the word 'sir'. It's not a method of address I usually bother with. '... but I just wanted to check something, sir.'

'Of course.'

'Do you remember that car? The one that blew up?'

'Yep, haven't forgotten. We've had a hell of a couple of weeks,' he says, wincing in mild pain.

I picture the colour chartreuse, the taste of ink, the E flat sound.

'We ever find out whose car that was? Where it came from?'

'Ah yes. Well, we tried, but the plates were gone and it was burnt out. Turan escorted it over to the garage on Hale Road himself but they couldn't enlighten us at all. So they'll hold it for a while, then strip it and scrap it from there, in time.'

It strikes me that he doesn't mind me asking any of this. I'm not even a hassle anymore. Despite everything, maybe they don't think I'm as much of a situation as I thought I was. Just an eccentric worth bearing for the positive benefits. No real possibility of infamy. Especially now I'm isolated.

'Sure. Thanks, Levine. Thanks,' I say.

It was worth a shot. Just in case Turan's story didn't match. Or something had come back from the garage to Levine without Turan knowing. Or just in case the car hadn't burnt out the glove, the glove that I now realise matched the scarf, the scarf that is sitting in the lab right now with three unidentified prints on it.

It was his car, our man's, I'm sure now. I remember seeing the matching glove before the car went up. Even though it was dark in there I saw the outline, then the pattern, and managed to store it somewhere in the back of my mind. It was only when I smelt the scarf at the Frasers, the one he must've given Tanya, that smelled of men's aftershave when it's true that they 'haven't had a man in the house for years', that it all came back and the dislocated bone of thought popped into its socket.

As the car went up and the pattern incinerated, it must've been hiding tiny pieces of secrets that could've helped. But it's on the scrap heap now, or in as many fragments as the mirror I smashed last night.

My shoulders dropped as I wandered into the debrief room and took a look at my pocket notebook entries for my first week. The uneventful one before Christmas, as I wondered where my life was headed and the snow fell for the first time. The week that only started bugging me this morning, as the vapour trail of a memory stormed across my brain and started to spark other neighbouring spectres.

I pick up key words as my eyes scour the pages that fill my senses with days and the minutes within them...

'Traffic'. I see my log of when I redirected cars along the main road.

'ABC'. I picture giving Eli Minton the Acceptable Behaviour Contract.

'Accident.' I breathe in the outline of the day I saw dead bodies for the first time, in a smashed up car that brought back traces of a familial horror I'd tried to bury. The memory colours itself in rapidly with sharp and useful emotion. It's not an exact science, the memory. It's easily corruptible.

While relied on in court as facts, memories are known to be more like negatives that get altered by your fingerprints every time you touch them. Their perfect sheen spoilt with new ideas and prejudices every time they are reflected upon. But while short term memory does work like this, like a tracing a sparkler might make against the night sky, scientists have recently found there is also a master copy stored in your long term memory bank. The true memory, indented onto your brain, never to be erased.

I search my mind for the master copy, the one uncorrupted by the trails of things that have happened since, that jostle to blur the image.

Then I read 'Neighbour.' And I recall the hint of the memory I'd been searching for all morning. Letters from a past version of me who didn't know what he was looking for. I don't so much read them as inhale them and relive the thoughts, my fingers pushing into the ink on the paper of my notebook…

'…as I approached the house in question, the neighbour on the left side came out…when she saw me she hustled back inside quickly. She had a look of supreme fear about her… She didn't want any trouble…and to her maybe I meant trouble…She gave me a funny feeling, her presence sparked a strange sensation close to déjà vu.'

I hold this woman and her significance like a plastic figurine. I pick her up and place her against the façade of my skin-blanketed skull, pushing her to my mind:

Her scent, leather, with taste notes of tangerine. Her touch, like an arch-backed Persian blue. I shake her at my ear, for whispers to fall out. She is marble coloured and a harbinger on a model plastic street. I hover over it like a flawed god. I will turn her sideways. And use her as a key. To the house she sits next door to.

Where two other action figures, adorned like man and wife, sit.

I feel the thoughts hit, one by one.

I count them through.

This is a thought.

This is a thought.

This is a thought.

I feel them hit the bottom of the well, like copper coins thrown long ago, that only now strike against the depth and echo up to the listener.

The woman figure in the house I had stood in during my first week, had been conditioned to stay deafeningly quiet. These figures are not bride and groom, plucked from an icing cake, but abuser and captive.

Sarah Walker perhaps, not saying a word, as I, an emissary from her previous life, limply stood on her kitchen tiles, as she sat too scared to make say a word. Her brain's creases washed out, the very thing that had allowed her to graduate to above ground. Taught that even if she was chased, or saw a member of the police, and particularly if a uniformed man happened to see a hint of recognition in her face, that she must be faithful to her keeper.

After she had avoided my last attempt to get to her, and I was laid low by an oncoming vehicle, she may have collected herself and headed for the house. This plastic bride might have opened the door of her own accord, sat with her groom and not said word. While the girls kept below hid their heads and prayed like they never had outside of the confines of their school hall.

I push the neighbour figure aside. Because my thoughts tell me she is merely a trigger. And if that's true, then the chamber lies in the house next door.

*

My whole body is poised as I knock at the address from my notebook and the déjà vu hits hard as I wait for a response.

Then a form, blurred by the effect of the front door glass, gets bigger and bigger until I hear the top bolt go, and then the bottom, and then the lock turns.

My palms open instinctively. If this is her I will make a grab for her, one hand to her wrist and another to my radio to help me spirit her to safety. I mentally practise the move and motion. I prepare.

The body in front of me fills the doorway too well. He is olive-skinned, stout, bald to the bone and has a full beard. I peruse my mental checklist and judge him to be the same man as before. I take in the size of him as I struggle for the right approach.

I see the relevant thoughts shoot through him. His head moves from side to side a fraction, as if to say 'Yes, what? Go on then!' but he doesn't say that. He doesn't say a word. Obstinate in his belief that it's not up to him to start the conversation. I'm the one that knocked.

If I was to break this down to a micro level, I'd say it goes like this:

3 eye saccades. The slightest move back. His lips quiver.

5 more that size me up.

4 saccades as his hand comes to hold the door handle on his side to assert his position. I'd call it a shadow move.

2 saccades signal recognition of me, and his body primes itself.

The stillness speaks and says 'What's this for?' but my silence doesn't offer him anything. It's a sales technique I was taught and retaught in a series of dead end jobs. State your offer. Then silence. Every second they wait puts you in a more powerful position, but this time my only offer is me. Here I am. And he falters.

4 saccades and a tightening of the jaw, a couple of muscles that lie on top of his cheekbones twitch.

He's threatened. He's under attack. He starts to ready himself.

Before he can, I push myself at him with all my weight, both hands at his chest, and knock him off balance.

He's a big man and it seems to take a while for him to reach the laminate floor below. This is because at this point my brain is in a heightened state, working hard to make more memories, which, in effect, makes time appear to slow down.

It's doing this because when your adrenaline is as high as mine is now your brain wants to remember exactly what you did that either saved you from, or caused the pain resulting from, the impending threat you're headed towards.

This makes each step towards her seem to take an age.

They say people remember moments before and after serious injury as if the episode lasted a day rather than a matter of seconds. Maybe falling to your death would take a whole lifetime.

She sits up in her chair, her back to me in the kitchen. I can't see her face. She starts to turn, glacially, probably slow at normal speed, but at the pace I'm currently seeing things it's like her reactions have been dulled to almost nothing.

I hear him shout behind me. One step more. Then another.

I dislodge a mirror from the hallway and it falls down fast behind me.

Before it hits, I take another step closer, I see she wears a head shawl or veil. My mental encyclopaedia reminding me of a case in South London where a woman held captive for years was made to wear such a thing to hide her face, lest she was recognised when out on the street. I try to remember whether Sarah Walker had something like a veil at a resting position around her neck when I saw her.

The mirror hits. I think she did, I think so, but some memories are negatives of negatives. I get another step closer, then another. I reach out my hand, I'm that close, but he's behind me.

I want to call out, like in my dream, to the girl in the forest or at the blackboard, but there's no need. I'm right here now, I've come to save her. Her face was stuck somewhere inside my head, since before the bullet and everything else, and then it finally came loose.

I picture the girls below the floorboards, hearing the moan of her captor and the smashing of the mirror that followed.

Her hands come up. But why? To protect herself or show contrition?

I hear his foot crunch on the mirror pieces behind me. I see the side of her face and my fingers touch her blonde hair.

I see him in my peripheral vision. And all my muscles ready themselves. Instinctively. For what must come next. As her head turns. And her eyes saccade. To meet mine.

I see no recognition in them. And I know there's none in mine. My eyes flit around desperately as he enters the room. Looking for a clue to who this woman is, of a trace of Sarah Walker, or of anything. But nothing comes.

I see a purple bruise around her right eye. I see her offer no expression and notice a cut on her lip, the space around which bloats and distorts her face a touch, like mine. But, I know deep within that this woman is not Sarah, nor is she connected to her, and this man pushing my left shoulder and asking me 'What's your game?' has no connection to any of this either.

It should be like turning on the lights to find yourself dancing alone in an empty basement room. My head pounds like a drum, or an alarm that I should interpret as a reprimand, from within and without, but I don't quite feel like that. Because judging from her face and what brought me here the first time around, he is not a good man.

I grab him by the flesh between his right shoulder and neck and raise my right fist. He ducks and cowers. Holds both hands in front of him and lets out a small noise. He's afraid to be hit.

I'm not afraid to be hit. And if she was the first time, then she's come to understand the blows and pain. Their shape and reality. But her punisher's neck sweats beneath my grip, his every cell screaming mercy.

So I drop my hand and his head drops too. I wonder if she might leave after this. Or whether she'll wait.

'Just get out,' he mutters.

She transmits a thought to me which is difficult to express in words. Then I send my fist plunging hard into his stomach with as much force and effort as I have ever put into anything.

He splutters, gasps, that desperate winded sound that you only really get from the bottom of the lungs. But he'll live.

I turn and make for the door. The shattered mirror pieces cracking and inserting themselves into my soles, as I drag my feet through the hallway.

35

'But, oh me, dang, me oh my,
the way she took to it, brought water to my eye.'

The first thought I have as I leave is 'Maybe I shouldn't have done that.' I decide I'll report it when I get back to the station. I won't tell them about the punch, I'll say I made a point of following up a previous domestic violence query, and that my second visit made me extremely suspicious, and furthermore I'd advise that this should be followed up by uniformed officers at their earliest convenience.

If he hasn't already made the call, this would be when the man of the house would mention my minor infraction. I resolve that what will be, will be. Best-case scenario, I think, could be joining Bartu for a firm wrist slapping on the naughty bench. It's possible that's what I wanted when I decided to punch him. A way off this escalator my brain has put my body on. I don't know.

The second thought I have is 'What next?' This is less easily resolved. Deprived of a clear head, a fully functional body and a method of transport, Bartu's loss is big. It leaves me stranded in more ways than one. I arch my back, somewhat feline, against the cold.

I observe my skin turn bone white at the wrist as I walk,

but it isn't just the elements that leave me vulnerable. My eyes tell me that around every corner, Jarwar could be waiting. My ears seem to crackle with white noise yearning for the shipping forecast. Every window I pass holds the distinct possibility of malignant strangers. And, far worse, with every second that ticks I feel the inevitability blossom, that soon a silhouette will loom then ripen as it draws closer. Maybe it'll be the car that ran me down. Or the hooded figure, who'll get another chance to plunge a knife towards my chest. Or perhaps it'll be a bullet travelling towards my skull at a rate of knots, which, this time, will make no mistake.

At the height of these suffocation thoughts, my feet strengthen and I discover they are walking me towards the garage on Hale Road. Some say that the body makes most of the decisions for us anyway. That we give too much credence to so-called 'consciousness'. You don't think about the act of moving your legs one by one when you run. You just... run. Taking this to its extreme, you'd save yourself a lot of bother if you stopped believing in the myth of choices. Sure, there's white or brown bread. Poached, fried, hard-boiled or scrambled. But other than that, don't stress yourself out too much about choices. They find you.

Garrett's Motors do the lot. If you need a certain make or model they'll find a way to get it to you for a certain price. They lose vehicles that need to be got rid of, too, possibly for good people and bad alike. Either way, they operate a pretty strict 'don't ask, don't tell' policy. They are also the best mechanics around and mostly make their money from repeat custom, rather than stiffing people on their MOT. It's their mixture of knowledge and ingenuity that grant them the questionable privilege of being called on by the police with decent frequency.

I'm sure I know the old shrink-wrapped, grey haired gent that comes to greet me in blue overalls, but luckily I think he sees as many faces as I do on any given day, and he isn't too much better than me at recognising the old ones. But we've probably conversed a number of times that's well into the double figures over the years. He probably sold me my first car.

'What can I do you for?' he says.

'One of our boys brought a car in that'd been burnt on the inside. Wondered whether you'd sent it to scrap or if it was still here?'

'Oh... yeah... yep. Come with me, you may be in luck,' he shouts over his shoulder, leading the way.

It seems stupid to tell him exactly what I'm after. I could say 'I want to see whether there was anything left of a cotton glove, in a car I accidentally blew up, because its owner kidnapped three local girls and if I can get any physical evidence off it then it would probably still be hopeless but better than nothing, and I haven't got anything else to go on, so here we are.' Yep. Could say all that. Don't.

And I could say my hopes are hanging on a thread, but I won't, because even I realise that's a very poor excuse for humour at this late stage in the game. There goes my frontal lobe, failing to edit me again. My ability to supress my urge to say everything that comes to me is getting better, but I'm nowhere near fixed yet. Maybe never will be. So... sorry if those last few sentences were difficult for you.

'Somewhere... along... here,' he mutters to himself as we pass endless vehicles to our right.

Skeletons of cars with smashed out windows, heavily rusted exterior bodywork and semi-crushed shells. I wonder if any of them could still drive. I picture myself trying to take one out of there, all beaten up, but still somehow running. Kick in your TV or smash your car against a wall hard enough and there isn't an engineer in the world that can fix it without new parts. But brain plasticity is a great thing. You can take out significant portions of the machine and it finds a way to keep you going.

My brain is a banger, all busted up, patched together enough to get me from A to B. There are moments when I curse myself for not being able walk straight. And others when I recognise that the level of comprehension required to get me this far in this case is a minor miracle. Then it strikes me that the miracle really is that we're all built this way.

'Ah. No,' he says, starting a chin scratch that soon takes over the whole left side of his face.

'No?' I say. Picturing the glove. Time seemed to slow before the explosion, as it had done in the domestic abuse house. I replay the scene in my mind. The memory snaps it took. To be rerun later, to reassess the danger.

There it is: blue. Like the colour of which it smelt. She left it in the car. *I see it. It can't be gone. I can touch it.*

'No, mate. I remember now. Usually we keep them until a few of you have given them the once over.'

He places his scratch-hand on his hip and the other in his pocket.

'Why not this one?' I say.

'The fella told us not to. One of your lot. The Turk. Big, sporty type. Said to scrap it right away.'

My breathing changes, long breaths now, like when I was pretending to sleep last night.

'The inspector? Or... the PCSO?' I say.

'I... err... ' He looks to the sky for inspiration. Night is falling. Mechanics pass. The chill is deepening. 'I... dunno, mate. Sorry.'

'Okay,' I say. And what I do know and what I don't converge again. And I want my body to start dragging itself somewhere, but it doesn't know where to yet.

'I told him where it came from though,' he says.

'I'm sorry,' I say, my mouth falling open. 'Where did it come from?'

'Here. It came from here. I told him. I remembered it. Not

good with faces but I never forget a motor. I told him, some bloke bought it off us with cash. The Turk never passed that on?'

'No,' I say. 'He never passed it on.'

'All right then. That good? That helpful?'

I am lost in thought and he is forced to ask once more. It's a peculiar form of time travel that occurs when I'm off in the back room of my mind. Fumbling around in the store cupboard, working it out. It's odd to be reminded that while I'm back there, life continues unabated right in front of me.

'... Mate? That helpful?'

'Yes. Yes, I reckon so.'

'Then I can do better than that, mate. Fella that bought it... err... lived down on Tollington Road. I remember seeing it parked on the street when I drove past. Sure of it. I never forget a motor.'

As I start to walk away, I remember things too. Mirror pieces roll around and form themselves back into place. Thoughts I'd lost return to me as the snow starts to fall again.

And so my day circles on itself and I end up back where I started. On Tollington Road. Where I'd seen that déjà vu neighbour all those weeks ago. Where I taught a gentleman a thing or two about chivalry this morning.

When I look around at the back of the houses I notice something else. Something I should've seen the first time around. The view. The view is astounding. The view is of a playground. A playground myself and Bartu had stood in just a few days earlier.

Ring, ring.

Ring, ring.

My phone chirps in my pocket. So I pick up and put it to my ear. Noticing the (*number withheld*) as I do.

'PCSO Mondrian?' comes the voice. And I'm a directory of voices.

'Err... yes?' I say. Turning in instinct, just in case they're near. Ice under my feet.

'We need to meet,' he says, as if trying to hold his nerve.

'Did you call this morning?'

'Yes. Yes, I did.'

'Rabbit?' I say.

'How did you know?' he says. Not an expression, but a genuine question.

'How did you get this number?' I say.

But the silence that follows informs both of us that we shouldn't expect a satisfactory answer to our respective questions.

'We met… at the snooker hall… do you remember?' he says.

'I remember,' I say.

'We need to meet, but alone, not with him… not with… err…'

'Turan?' I say.

I start to pace away from the street, my thighs stiffening to counter the effect of the frozen ground. His urgency increasing.

'Yes. I don't want him there. Or anyone else. Just us.'

'What about tomorrow?' I say.

'What about now?' he says.

I lift my pace, noticing the ripples of cold air pushing out and expanding into the world, the particles breaking off and going their own way until I can no longer see them. I notice sides of occasional faces moving past top floor windows.

'I have something planned for now. But I'd love to meet tomorrow,' I say.

'We don't have long, I'm afraid. I'm afraid we don't have long. You. Me. Them. All of us,' he says. And I picture him in some dank bunker.

'I know. Tomorrow will do. Early afternoon,' I say.

'There's… something I need to show you,' he whispers.

'What is it?' I say, chancing my arm.

And some seconds tick on.

'Tomorrow, early afternoon. Watch your phone. I'll call.'

And with that, in the same manner that he tended to arrive, he was gone.

*

Dr Ryans' estate car smells the same colour as his office. *Playing Field Green*. I'm not entirely sure how his wife puts up with it. By the time we get to his house I'm sure I'm slightly stoned but it seems rude to complain given his levels of hospitality.

The last thing he helped me put in the back was my computer. Then I slammed the boot closed and looked at my little life in there. It was surprising how many things I felt I didn't need from the house. All I saw was books that were now only for decorative purposes. Clothes. Some family pictures just for recognition practice. A drawer full of too many chargers, miscellaneous grooming items, a picture book about spiders, a subscription's worth of a magazine I mean to read one day, my good lamp, a 1991 book of magic eye pictures, my filter coffee maker with a cracked handle, and an automatic umbrella my nan gave me. This is how much my life weighs. With comics, an artificial Christmas tree, my childhood and a whole world left behind and put on ice for later.

It was all done in one relatively painless trip. But I can honestly say, getting Mark into his cat carrier was one of the hardest things I've had to do in the last four months.

Ryans' wife Marie is French, and speaks four languages by the way, and I have no idea what she sees in him. She makes food for us for when we arrive. It's a soup from scratch and the obvious care it was made with makes me emotional. The taste sticks with me as I tell her that she's very kind but 'not to worry about food in future as I won't often be eating with you as I keep my own rather eccentric hours.'

The taste sticks as I tell her that despite these hours I will 'always keep the noise down and I insist on cleaning the whole house every morning because it will clear my mind and make me feel far less indebted to you.'

The taste even sticks as he later tells me it's 'his recipe', which I doubt, despite her affirmations. But maybe I'm just defensive about how much I owe him, for his encouragements and his warnings, and for offering me a sanctuary where people don't know where I am, at the zenith of my paraneea.

He apologised for contacting Anita. And I conceded that although it was 'an idiotic idea' that his 'heart may have been roughly in the right place.' For my part I was never good at climb-downs. Or apologies. This is why I ended my phone call to Ryans by saying:

'This is not to do with your kindness or my weakness, by the way. It's about your proximity to the park.'

But in some unknown language, in between the words, I think he heard a thank you. Because he responded with 'Great!'

Before he arrived I'd set everything up for the next day. It involved some research into the seamier sides of the internet, places I don't usually go, links to links to links. To the corners where you can get things you really shouldn't.

It's partly research. But I also need something for tomorrow. And fast.

Just as I thought I was about to get it, I realised I'was talking to someone from something called The Live Action Role Play Society, and they'd got the wrong end of the stick. Surprisingly, there is a LARP Society in most big towns. Plenty in London. They enact everything from famous battles to alien invasions in the parks of the suburbs at 6 a.m. Get up early and you might see them. But they only deal in pretend; I needed a real thing.

So that's when I called Bartu and told him everything. About where I am, what I've found and where we go next. I told him I'd long thought that there was too much inconsistency for this to be about one person; it's about more than that, a group. Up until that exact moment I had been too cautious to tell even Bartu that, but then my need became clear and I had to call and lay it all out for him.

After some resistance he said, 'Yes, okay.'

And then I said something he didn't expect or want to hear.

'One more thing. Where can I get hold of a gun?'

When he said he wanted no part of that, I only had ninety minutes until Ryans came.

I left the house. In search of what I needed. Ninety minutes came and went. And I was back just in time for Ryans' arrival.

*

When everything is in my new space, I take a long look at it all. Then I set up my computer and find a picture of a girl they found. Rita Singh. A long search through pages and pages brings me that.

She was the only other one to turn up out of the nine that went missing over the years. And when she did turn up, she wasn't alive either. And she had deep cuts on the top of her thighs, which didn't surprise me one bit.

The mental image takes me a while to shake off, but then I finally manage it. Then I sleep and dream of the lyrics that were trying to tell me something all along. The thing stuck in the folds of my cerebellum, fighting to get out.

The subconscious was biting at the edges of my mystery to get my attention. And show me what I should have already known. Known for some time.

36

'I don't know what you're waiting for.
If you can't see it anymore
I'm thinking 'bout the girl next door.
Can't...'

There's one detour I have to make as I head from Ryans' place towards work. I cut through the park then take the bus on the other side.

There's no one around when I get to the playground behind Tollington Road. So I approach the bin. Remove the top layer of waste products. And push the gun discreetly inside.

I gaffer tape it to the side about halfway down then replace the rubbish I'd removed, to mask its presence, just below the surface.

Once I'm confident no one followed me here, or any other stray eyes caught the act, I continue on foot towards the station.

I enter gingerly. I called in my possible domestic violence issue before I left last night, and half expect Levine to call me over for 'a bit of a talk.' But all I see is nervy chief Matthews beckoning me to the precipice of his office and saying things like 'it's all set up' for me 'to use'. And 'He's already in there.' They're sentences that mean precisely nothing to me.

He holds me by both shoulders and looks into my eyes with what I'm sure he thinks is a reassuring smile. Then he summons all his brittle energy to tap me on the bicep with a force that makes me flinch. He seems to be prepping me for something, like a doctor preps a patient before amputation. Then he steps out of the way and gestures for me to enter and greet whatever it is that lies in wait.

But instead I grab the handle and push the door closed. Then stand with my back to it as I beckon Matthews closer. I've spent so long keeping everyone else in the dark. But that had to end sometime. When he finally steps towards me, I take a look over his shoulder to make sure no one is watching us, then speak quietly.

'I have to tell you… I figured out something that's important to the case of the girls, and to the wider community.'

He also takes a discreet look around, as I draw breath and find my thought. I take a piece of paper out of my pocket to show him. If I don't tell him this now I fear I might not get another chance.

'Sir, there are these markings near certain streets and homes. Usually chosen because they're low income housing and easy to make an exit from onto a main road. I discovered through certain online forums that a blue circle seems to mean that there is a child in the house. Put two dots next to it, like this… ' I say, pointing out the relevant symbols on my piece of paper, '…and that seems to mean the child is sometimes left alone. A square in the middle of it suggests they are left with a vulnerable parent. A cross next to it is a "no go", for whatever reason. Lastly, two diagonal lines through it means the child has already been taken. I think there is a paedophile ring at work in London. And members signals to aid each other. No smaller cell, of say three to ten people, within that larger ring, wants another to get caught and give information that may lead back to them. So they're bound together. By necessity.'

I finish, my breath heavy in my throat.

'Good work. We'll look into that,' he says.

I'm not sure he's entirely taken on the seriousness of the revelation. The fact that this may well be the work of a small group, who are almost certainly linked to a larger network.

He grabs my right shoulder once more and speaks in a hushed and ill-fitting alpha tone, using a mode of being I haven't seen in him before, which is presumably the one that convinced someone that he might be good for a managerial position.

'By the way, Tom, we sent officers around to speak to the couple on Tollington Road early this morning. He was physical, highly aggressive. We think we're going to get a conviction on that one, one way or another. So good work again,' he says.

I'm half expecting 'but', but it never comes. Seems as though the husband kept his mouth shut or his complaints fell on deaf ears. They tend to look after their own. They're a little cabal aren't they, I suppose. And now I'm in it. I've never been comfortable with anything like that. I never wanted to be a freemason, or a member of a 'Role Play Society', nothing like that.

I wouldn't want to be part of a club that would have anyone else as a member. Only problem is, maybe I'm already benefiting from a club I didn't think I'd fully signed up to yet.

Matthews opens the door again and gestures for me to go inside. A scruffy man with glasses sits leaning over a notepad.

I walk in, placing my piece of paper back into my pocket, not sure that I've been adequately heard. I look back as Matthews simply smiles, closes the door and walks away.

I cautiously sit and wait for the scruffy man to finish writing.

'Hello, Tom, I'm Mike,' he says with a weak smile and a weaker handshake.

'Hi Mike,' I say, still with no idea what this is.

'So, how are you enjoying being back on the force?'

I hear the tick of the chief's carriage clock, which sits staring at me on his desk. This wasn't part of my plan for today.

'Fine. Fine,' I say.

He goes to write something down, then stops.

'Riiight. Hmm. Okay,' he says, shifting in his seat. 'Any high-lights?'

I find myself holding on to my right knee tightly. Whatever's going on, it doesn't seem to be going well for either of us.

'I... keep in touch with the local community... '

I picture my fist landing in the husband's stomach.

'... There are ups and downs. Good days and bad... '

I picture being attacked in The Corner Shop and smashing a man's head into a glass door.

'... I've made friends... for life, perhaps... '

I picture driving in silence with Emre Bartu.

'... In the end it's about the community. People I grew up with... '

I picture Sarah. I picture giving Eli Minton his Acceptable Behaviour Contract.

'... Good guys and bad guys... '

I draw a blank. An empty space in my mind. Except for the tiny flicker of a silhouette. And one or two faces.

'... And you've just got to do your best and see what happens.'

Mike writes it down in a tired fashion and then looks up at me, nodding guilelessly.

'Yep. Cool. That sort of thing... is... great.'

I turn and see them all gearing up for something. Levine and a detective coming from the debrief room, flanked by a constable and a couple of others, leaving in a hurry.

'I'm sorry, who are you?' I say.

'Mike? From the Advertiser... ' he says as I stand.

'... Are you doing it now? You having a... vision or whatever? You're a... savant, right? Is that the word?'

'Just a second,' I say, without turning my head his way, as I walk out the door and up to a woman I think is Anderson.

'Hi, Tom, how are you getting on without –'

'Fine. Anderson?'

'Yes?'

'What's going on?'

She looks on as they jump into their vehicles outside.

'Well... it's all done isn't it? That's what it looks like,' she says, taking a sip of her tea.

My eyes saccade to the door, then back her. So many fast little movements and comprehensions.

'In what way?' I say.

'They found his tie. The kid. Guess what? It even had his name stitched into it.'

'Asif?'

'Yeah, yeah. Results came back. The tie had the girl's blood on it. He must've tried to chuck it in the river, but one of our guys found it on the bank. They're off to arrest him now. They've got enough. So by the looks of it... that's gonna be that.'

'Okay. They find any iodine on the bodies? Heard iodine mentioned in any way at all? Cleaning fluid?'

'No, why? They don't tell us that much, you know how it...'

And now her voice fades away and she can only watch on as I walk. I turn back as I go to see Mike through Matthews' office window, still there, waiting for me to return. He scratches his head and drums on his knees. He's going to be waiting for some time. I see the police cars driving away in the distance and I pick up my pace, dragging my body in another direction.

Not far now. Just a ten-minute walk, I'd say. I look up at the faceless bodies that drive the cars. I've probably been passing them all my whole life. The difference is this walk through

318

Tottenham might be my most important ever. The snow crunches beneath my feet.

Ring, ring.

My phone announces itself in my pocket, desperate to get out.

My bare icy hand, shivering, plucks it into the cold. *Number Withheld.*

Ring, ring. But I've no time for Rabbit, not now.

Ring, ring. It rings, back in my pocket, until it rings out.

Cars pass to and fro.

Then I hear one screech to a halt, skidding a little. I see the door open and a body get out. His steaming breath covers his face in the cold wind, not that it would help me if I could see it.

'Get in!' he shouts.

And I know that voice.

'That you?' I shout back.

He stays there, his hand on the car door. Not venturing out into the icy metres between us.

'Yeah, come on. Get in!' he shouts again. And I walk towards him.

Take away the context of the uniform and I'm pretty lost. I see him take shape as he taps me on the arm. Brown face, black hair, well built. Then he opens the passenger door for me, uncharacteristically graciously, and we head away far faster than I was going on my own.

'How'd you find me?' I say.

'You tend to stick out.'

This must be Aisha's car. The seat feels different under me. He must not want to be seen in his.

'They picked him up, you know,' I say, as old red brick houses pass.

'Who? Asif?' he says.

'Yeah. Who else?' I say.

'No, no. I don't know, ' he says, keeping his eyes on the road.

'So they're going for it, Emre,' I say.

'Oh,' he says, as we bounce a bit too fast over a speed bump and I feel the road underneath us.

'That it? "Oh"?' I say.

'I mean, we'll see. That's bad luck for Asif.'

'Yeah. Bad... bad luck... Emre Bartu,' I say, looking in the rear view mirror. No one else on the roads for miles around it seems. He clocks me looking.

'You think he did it?' he says.

I silently realise something.

'I know he didn't do it, and you do too, right?'

I see the road. The houses. The abusive husband's. And, more importantly, the one next door.

'Yeah. I don't know,' says Bartu.

We come to a standstill and he puts the handbrake on.

'I went to see Turan. We met that guy, Rabbit, who said he'd been given the job of taking photos of the girls as they came out of school. Turan said he'd look into it all, but then I didn't hear anything. I should've told you earlier. I think you're right not to trust him.'

'Is that right?' he says.

I close my eyes and take a deep breath in through my nose. I smell the musky scent, orange to me, of an aftershave Emre Bartu doesn't normally wear.

'Come in a second, will you. I've got something I need to tell you.'

I breathe in through my nose again and review my options.

'Okay, Emre. Sounds good.'

'Yeah. It will be. It will be good,' his hushed voice comes back.

'How long will it take? Got some house calls to make,' I say.

We're still sitting there. In the parked car. Neither us have moved yet.

'Oh, don't worry about that.'

My hand, already in my pocket, begins to twitch. I grab for something in there. Hold it tight. Press it into my palm for comfort. It feels good.

'You mean... it won't take long?' I say.

'Yeah,' he says. 'You don't need to worry about any of that.'

He gets out of his side of the car and I pull subtly at the handle from the inside but nothing gives. He walks around the front of the vehicle. Then opens the door for me. I stand and he stays just behind me. As if he's my protector.

Similar skin.

Similar build.

Similar voice.

Now I'm not good with faces. As I've been at pains to illustrate. But by the time he escorts me from the car to the house, even I know for sure that this man is not Emre Bartu.

37

'Can't, get that girl next door, out of, my head.'

It came to me in a rush in the end. What my subconscious had been trying to tell me. Those lyrics that my mind was playing around with, as if my body knew but my consciousness hadn't quite twigged; that when I saw Sarah Walker, in the paper, it wasn't for the first time for ten years. I'd seen her more recently than that.

I'd looked the girl next door in the face the week before the bullet, when I first responded to the domestic abuse call. That déjà vu neighbour. And though a spark of recognition formed across my face, one she must've clocked, my brain hadn't made the link to who she was at all. I hadn't thought about her in years at that point, you see. I certainly didn't know she had been missing. But she assumed I did know her, which must've made her tell the people who were keeping her in that house that she'd seen a familiar face. And that that face had stared back, fixing her with prying eyes. That face from a half remembered childhood flirtation that clung to the back of her mind.

Which could be why I've been so closely watched recently. They've been attempting to get rid of me before I piece together what I may or may not know.

The final shards fell into place and played like a picture show last night. Perhaps just a little too late. As I tapped out a song I wrote on the Casio, called *'Girl'*. An earworm that wouldn't stop playing until it was satisfied.

Turan takes a subtle glance around as he takes out his key. A gesture he's clearly well versed in, whether he's checking out who's around on a crowded street or in a local bar when he's doing whatever he does there, or when he steps inside this house, as he has done many times, despite the fact that this is not his house.

The key turns and we go inside.

As soon as I'm in and the door is closed he pushes me up against the wall. He grabs the hand that's holding something for comfort inside my pocket.

'Slow!' he says. Pulling it up, bit by bit, but all I have is my phone.

He checks my pockets, a real thorough professional pat down. Searching every bit of me, as intimate as he could get without taking my clothes off, but all he finds is my wallet and keys, because that's all I have. Nothing concealed against my ankle, or on my inner thigh, or anywhere like that, because he would've found it if I'd put it there.

Then he holds my shoulders and pushes me into the wall.

'Emre? You... okay?' I say, as his left hand rummages around, doing his final checks.

'I didn't believe it at first. But it's true, innit?'

'What? Emre, what are you talking about?'

'You're not fucking around. You really dunno who's who? Do you?'

I let the silence run for a second. I smell the place, trying to sense some sign of feminine life. Trying to figure if they're just below my feet, in the basement. *It smells blue.*

'You really are a fucking retard,' he says, gripping my neck with one hand and using the other to force my arm behind my back. It reminds me of school. It's not violent as such, not excessively so anyway.

'Retard means slow. I'm not so slow. Not anymore,' I say, as he leads me into the living room. I'm staying permissive, but being no push over. Not giving him anything to go on either way. He kicks open the door. I think he thinks this is going to be very easy for him. There, in the dim light of the room, curtains closed to bar eyes from what comes next, stands a man in sunglasses.

'Who... who are you? What's... going on?' I say.

I had planned to act like this. The shock and the fear. I'd planned to do so because I'm not surprised to see this man. Turan couldn't do it on his own.

You see. The shape, on the car. The lipstick. Wasn't a kiss. But an attempted bit of art. A creature. A rabbit. Rabbit, who was always around when Turan was, who was the sort of age I was expecting. Who always wears those glasses, which serve two purposes:

One, to mask his face somewhat.

And two, because they make it easier to come to terms with his new world.

You see, if Rabbit has what we think he has, Miss Shelley and I – an acquired colour-blindness derived from the fact that he has had carbon monoxide leaking into his car for the last few months – then the world will have started to look like a very strange place for him too. Poor Rabbit. He could have got it fixed if he'd only taken the car in to Garrett's Motors. They're good like that. But then, carbon monoxide is so difficult to sense, for most people.

I don't need to act the fear now because when I see the ropes and the chair it strikes me that I might not get out of this. Rabbit has been waiting for me, and holds a Japanese blade they call a *Sai*. A dream weapon, owned by fantasists, but it's sharp as hell. It's not the sort of thing you'd find on the high street. The violence is not pretend. It's a fantasy that they've made real. Together.

He talks as they push me down and tie my legs to the chair. I'm not entirely sure how they're planning to do it. But they'll need me pacified for it.

'I think those photos were so you could work out who you wanted to take. Weren't they, Rabbit?' I say.

'You're a nosey fuck, aren't you? And persistent,' Turan says.

'Ahh,' I let out a wail as Rabbit pulls the ropes tight around my ankles. He hasn't said a thing yet.

'Shh,' says Turan, like he's lulling a baby to sleep.

All my theorising drifts away. All the humour. All the games. And only this dark room and the possible horrors that lie in store remain.

'I'm sorry. I'm sorry. I'm sorry,' I say, hearing my voice rather than speaking. I am out of control for the first time in a long time. They'll get rid of me, like they got rid of Katherine Grady, I think. Then I stop that thought and stay in the here and now as my hands get yanked behind me, the strain of which burns my wrists and breaks the skin. My left arm, halfway between the base of my hand and the elbow, feels wet. It trickles. A wet pat sounding beneath me as they pull the knots tighter.

'Ahh! I don't know what you think I've seen. But I promise you, I don't know a thing –'

'I saw you. At the garage, I fucking saw you, I was watching, so don't fuck around,' he shouts, managing to control himself before he flies off the handle and lands a blow.

'I... I... I... ' My voice strains, I'm so scared. They pull off my tie and open my shirt. Rabbit withdraws, so I only see his back. He removes his sunglasses but I still don't see his face, not full on. He rubs his eyes and then replaces his eyewear, keeping his back to me. He jogs up and down for a second. Geeing himself up, the *Sai* in his hand the whole time. His fingers flex and roll around it, adjusting his grip on the handle.

'I... I... shut up,' Turan says, and this time he blows his top, punching me hard in the stomach.

'I tried to work it out, I tried, you're right, but you got me, you got me. I didn't... I couldn't... '

Turan rolls out some plastic sheeting. Soon it smears the whole living room. They're very particular about mess it seems. They like to get away with things. That's the thrill.

'Listen to yourself. You know what you sound like?' says Rabbit. He lifts the blade and kneels down. 'You sound like a baby. Are you a fucking baby?'

I analyse what a high and distinctive tone he has. One I knew straight away on the phone. He'd have to conceal that if he wanted to go unnoticed, to fool people he was someone else.

He clutches my knee. I'm aware of my phone in my pocket. He didn't take it.

'Please... ' I say.

Rabbit drags the blade along my trouser leg and cuts away, exposing my right thigh. I see the bruise on his cheekbone that Turan gave him during their little improvised show, to put me off the scent, in the snooker hall backroom. I see the old cut on his forehead I gave him when I smashed his head into the glass door of Amit's shop.

'No, no "please". Nothing more from you, ever. That's it,' Turan says. 'Are we going to do this then, Rabb, or what?'

My breathing shudders as Turan lays some white powder out onto a sideboard and they both take a short hit. Rabbit rises, his tongue searching his mouth. He bends over to get a good look at me.

I feel his cigarette breath on my mouth. *I see the blue scent, rising from him like steam.*

He taps the blade on the ground. He opens his mouth to say something. Then doesn't say a word. It's all part of it, for him. He wets his lips.

'Do it then,' says Turan, keener on cutting to the chase and starting the bloodletting.

Rabbit is less practical. He cares more about indulging his urges than covering tracks. I wonder where Turan is planning to lay my body to rest.

I hear the pat-pat of the wetness from my hand below me.

'By the way. What was it you wanted to show me?' I say to Rabbit.

Turan sniggers, as Rabbit lowers his head, then shakes it. The constructed shadow of the quaking snooker hall man drifts away. Only these darker manoeuvres remain.

'This,' he says, gently pressing the blade into my scar tissue.

'I don't know anything,' I whisper.

'I think you do. But, then... ' Rabbit says, biting hard on his bottom lip. 'None of that really matters. What matters is that I like to do this. I really... like... to do this,' he says.

My phone is in my pocket. As he brings the Sai down towards my leg with his left hand, he places his right hand on Turan's shoulder, their pleasure has a mutual masturbatory element. Then I feel the pain, hot and raw as he digs the blade into my thigh and drags it across, making clean red inroads into my skin. I don't look down.

I steel myself and bite hard on my lip, drawing blood there too. The taste, metallic, reminds of my first kiss with the girl that brought me here.

'Natalie O'Hara... Rita Singh... Sarah Walker... Aliya Akkas... Katherine Grady... Sophie Chang... Tanya Fraser... Jade Bridges... Nina Da Silva!' I shout.

They stop for a second. Rabbit lets out a giggle.

I hear my heartbeat in my ears.

'I knew it. Every time I turned around I saw you somewhere. It's a good job we kept an eye on you, too, right?' Turan says.

Boom, boom. A wave of blood oceans inside my head, but will soon depart for where it's needed more and leave me cold.

'Those names are your suicide note. Goodnight.'

He nods to Rabbit and he lifts the blade as my pocket gives way and something falls out.

'What's this?' he shouts, picking my phone up and pushing it into my face. My leg is bleeding hard onto the plastic below. Not pitter-patters but long drips, like from a drainpipe onto the tarmac after heavy rain.

'Calm it down man. Just do it. Do him! Do it!' Turan shouts.

'He's got some fucking app running, some fucking... look!' Rabbit shouts.

And then the front door goes. Not the bell, but the breaking of the glass.

*

Commotion beneath me. Women's voices I'm sure. It's not my imagination, I don't think it's that, it's screams and then the slapping of skin on skin. Then the rumble of stamping of feet. Then they fall silent again.

Rabbit and Turan hold still, like their feet are in cement, staying quiet so maybe it'll just go away. But then there's another smash and this time I call out. Rabbit rushes over to put his hand over my mouth and the blade to my throat. I don't think Rabbit's blade quite found my femoral artery, but I'm bleeding hard, I feel my eyes droop.

Bang. Bang. The door is being kicked now, you can hear the strain of the wood, but it sounds like the bolts hold strong. Turan reaches for something stuffed down the back of his trousers and goes out to address it.

I hear Turan's shouts and the strained voice of another.

'Shh,' Rabbit whispers in my ear, and for a second there's nothing to be heard. Then the sound of the bolts. And the front door opening. And the steps that follow.

There is an app for everything these days, it turns out. You can set the one I'm using now to make your call at a certain time, without the phone making a sound, or appearing to have a call running at all. All I needed was something to relay what was happening in here to Bartu. My phone made the call halfway through the drive over here. Once he'd heard enough to convince him it was necessary, he made his way over to the address I gave him last night.

Rabbit's hand tenses and the blade breaks the skin around my throat just a touch. He doesn't need any chemical assistance to stay jumpy, it was what first drew my eyes towards him, but unfortunately he's pumped full of assistance now. The door flings open.

Two hands. Turan's. Open palmed and in submission.

He walks in slowly, his eyes castigating me and attempting in vain to calm Rabbit, as behind him appears Bartu, pressing a gun firmly to his neck. I didn't want to take a gun in with me. I wasn't braced for a shoot-out and they'd only take it off me. That's why this morning I taped it inside the bin, just inside the playground, for Emre Bartu. Just in case he felt that what he heard justified a need for it.

Admittance. Guilt. Violence. For my part, I'd planned to elicit this by wandering moth-like into the flame, knocking on the door, maybe asking some dumb questions and seeing how much trouble I could get into.

I hadn't bargained on Turan picking me up before I got here. But then, he hadn't bargained on Bartu.

'Put the blade down!' Bartu says to Rabbit.

Rabbit holds his gaze behind his glasses in the dim room.

Bartu's eyes saccade to the blood on the plastic sheeting below. Then to my leg. I'd like to say 'The jig is up, they just don't know it yet.' That's what flashes into my head as my eyelids droop.

But in reality, I'm not so sure.

Rabbit removes the blade and steps back, keeping his arms low. Turan glances at Rabbit out of the corner of his eye, conveying wordless thoughts we need to cut off. It's their subtle coercion that helped them evade me and everyone else for some time. Their only misstep was Rabbit appearing unsure how to play it when he accidentally walked in on us and Turan at the chicken shop. He got jumpy and Turan had to think on his feet every time I mentioned or got close to Rabbit from then on.

Bartu, unsure quite how to play this, thinks about turning the gun on Rabbit but wisely keeps the theoretical advantage of the easy kill shot to Turan's head.

We have the added bonus that a bullet or two in the house would surely be like a distress flair around the neighbourhood and blow their cover. Maybe things have stacked up pretty well for us.

'Now untie him,' Bartu says.

After a few seconds stand-off, Rabbit complies. He is, as you might imagine, a deeply unsettling and unsettled man. At one glance the beaten skin around his face could make him look sixty years old, but he's also got a youth about him that could make you mistake him for sixteen at a distance. I wince as the last knot comes loose and drags across the brutal rope burn on my wrist.

Bartu takes a step towards me. Then a noise from below. A whimper, a cry and another slap of skin on skin. Bartu turns his head to look at the door where the sound appears to come from.

I'd tell him not to if I had enough energy left. But I don't. And he can't help himself. And seeing the tiny window of opportunity, Turan acts: he elbows Bartu in the stomach, but as he goes to grab a gun of his own, stuffed down the back of his trousers, he only gets his hand on it before Bartu hits him firmly between the nose and the cheekbone with the butt of his weapon.

Turan's legs give out from underneath him and he hits the ground, out cold.

In the melee, Rabbit rushes at Bartu and when Turan's gun goes loose he makes a dive for it.

I sensed Rabbit was ready to go before he made his first move, yet weak as I am all I can do is stick out a leg that sends him into a fall. But it doesn't stop him from reaching the ground below Bartu.

Compounding this, the force Bartu used to put Turan down caused his own gun to slip from his hand and fall, allowing Rabbit to drop his blade and grab that one too.

We're two nil down on the gun front. Rabbit lies on his back below us, both barrels pointed up at Emre.

Now it's Bartu's turn to show his palms in submission.

But mine stay by my sides. I'm not sure I have the energy to do anything else with them. But I keep thinking.

38

'The girl next door, well, well, well,
the girl next door's living in a little hell.'

Rabbit gets up carefully and leans his back into the door that must lead down to the basement. He points one gun at each of us. I'm not sure if he's handled one before. My guess is he has, but more as a frightener; he's never fired. That's a duck it's good to break before you enter the big time, I'd imagine.

'I found your pictures,' I say, still sitting. 'For the girls. They're good.'

'Shut up,' he says, tightening his grip, focusing his eyes on me. 'They're not for you.'

Bartu adjusts and Rabbit turns his attentions back to him, keeping the other gun pointed in my direction poised. Sooner or later, Rabbit has a choice to make.

'I know. It just makes me wonder why you keep coming back to a scene like that. And I've been reading a lot about acquired savantism lately.'

'What the fuck is that?' he says, flinching as we hear more noise from beneath. I see his jittery outline quaking in shadow, and I realise I saw Rabbit the day I was shot. His car stopped right in front of me. As I held traffic. They'd started watching straight away.

'It's kind of what we have. You and me, Rabbit. I got a hole in the head. You? You need to get your car fixed more often. I suppose it's difficult to find time for that sort of thing, with all you've got on, I get it. You've been gassing yourself. It's what makes colours difficult for you to see. It's what made you crash your car –'

'Who the fuck are you!?' he rasps.

'I'll bet it was hard taking her the rest of the way on foot. And a risk. It put a stop to the fireworks night you had planned. You're such a sweetheart, planning these little date nights.'

'This is it. I'm the last face you'll see, so... '

Bartu steps in a touch. Rabbit's eyes saccade with nerves. I start talking a mile a minute.

'You know, Rabbit, I've been wondering why you chose to draw the playground so often. And why it's different in each picture. And I realised that if you're anything like me, and I know you're at least a bit like me, you're obsessed. That's what people like us often are. Some paint, I write songs, you draw. And your brain is telling you to draw something you couldn't work out. Your brain is trying to resolve things, you know? Like therapy!'

'I'm gonna fucking tear you apart!' he shouts. And now that trigger finger could go at any time.

'You're drawing the playground you saw out of your old bedroom window, not this one. You have an obsession with that moment! Just after they'd done what they did to you. In that room. You're still trying to work it out! If you deserved it. We're so nostalgic, not just you and me, all of us. Cycles of abuse. In a way, none of this is your fault. It's always patterns. In a way, you're the victim. Bartu, you remember that Taser?'

'I couldn't get a Taser,' Bartu says.

'Shit,' I say.

'Fuck you!' Rabbit screams and as he fires I dive from my chair and keep moving. He has the other gun trained on Bartu who doesn't flinch.

Rabbit shouts for me to 'Stay still!' He can't seem to find me.

'What are you doing?' Bartu shouts.

'Stay fucking still. Both of you!' Rabbit screams.

I keep moving. Shadow moves, big and small.

'The sort of disorder he's got. He can't see movement that well. Shades help him judge depth better, breaking things down into clearer blocks, but not movement. I noticed it, Rabbit, when you took that punch from Turan. Didn't see it coming, did you?' I shout.

'Stay still!' he screams.

And this time I move towards him and when he fires he misses by a long way. And when I slam him hard against the door, Bartu picks up the gun he came in with and slams it into Rabbit's head. Two or three times. Until he stops moving.

'Careful, he can't take many blows to the head. And if those girls aren't down there we need him alive,' I say.

As his glasses fall from his face, one feature of him is distinct enough even for me. He has one dark green eye and one brown. They may have been that way since birth, but it's also possible the pigment in his one eye was degraded by the carbon monoxide poisoning.

Rabbit must've constructed a different version of himself for whenever he was working at the school. It helped that without glasses the world scared him, introverted him, which changed the way he held himself and interacted. Then add a different voice, and the whole act gave him a decent chance that, if anyone did see him with any of the girls, they wouldn't recognise him as one of the school cleaners.

I guess those industrial iodine-based fluids he worked with

meant he often felt pretty light headed, which he thought was the cause of those headaches he had whenever he drove his car. But, luckily for him, they also masked his aftershave on the day we met at the school, otherwise I would've matched him to that blue smell at the Fraser house right then and there.

'He picked those girls from ones that were around after school. Then some days he got changed quickly, so quickly that when he arrived outside school he was slightly breathless, like he was late for something, just as the caretaker said. Then he took photos for Turan, so they could choose which ones they wanted,' I say.

Bartu nods through heavy breaths as he drags Rabbit away from the door and kicks it in. It comes open with one big blow and we see concrete steps leading into the darkness. But there's no noise. Not a sound.

He passes me the other gun and I fiddle with it discreetly as we head down. Doing something with it that I know I have to.

It's so dark down here but we see a shaft of light at the bottom of the stairs. We hear breathing. Bartu grips his gun tighter and so do I. For me it's a threat more than anything. A chess move. My leg bleeds heavily. I can hardly hold myself up. It's an effort to keep my eyes open. I hear the breathing. Bartu finds a cord above his head and pulls it.

In the blinking light I see them arrive in my field of vision one by one. Tied tightly with various ropes and telephone wires. It's damp down here but there are beds forged from mattresses, old blankets and plastic sheeting. It smells grey. Sweat and dust that hangs in the air above our heads like cobwebs and dances in the yellow light.

There is a bucket to catch the drips from the damp in the ceiling. And a couple of tables with leather straps that allow you to hold someone down firmly if you need to. And there are our girls. Their mouths stuffed with rags. And now I see their tears and hear them cry through the material.

Tanya Fraser

Jade Bridges

Nina Da Silva

And Sarah Walker.

The girl next door. My first crush.

Bartu names them for me in a whisper one by one. But he doesn't need to name check Sarah. Hers is the only face I can see. The one blown up and shot onto the canvas in the back of my mind. Bartu moves towards them and then pauses for a second. He looks back to me and smiles. He can't believe this is it. That everything we've done has come through. I agree, it doesn't quite seem real.

I wonder how Sarah stayed alive all this time when the others are nowhere to be seen. I wonder what she had to do. To survive. What her story is.

Bartu lingers over Sarah. She looks at Bartu, pleading with him with her eyes. Her hands seem to be tied to a metal pipe with cord.

'You got the blade?' he says.

'Yes,' I say. I picked up the *Sai* on the way down while messing with my gun.

'Then let's get them out of here.'

But I waver for some reason. Now the other girls are crying. I look into their eyes, they're different to Sarah's. They wail through the rags.

'Come on, man. Let's go,' Bartu says, grabbing the blade and starting to cut away at Sarah's shackles. The girls scream. And I put out a hand, but I'm too late to stop him.

As her left hand comes free her face changes, and I see her right was already loose. She holds a *Sai* that matches the one Bartu holds, which she plunges into his stomach.

The girls scream and try to dive for Bartu's blade as it drops from his hand. But they are still trussed up and Sarah Walker now has her weapon and Bartu's gun too.

She kicks the other *Sai* away to the corner of the room and points the gun at me, as I lift mine wearily to her.

'Oh, there you are,' she says. 'Been waiting for you.'

'Here I am,' I say. 'It's been a long time.'

Bartu writhes and bleeds onto a mattress between us.

'Yes, you found me,' she mutters, blinking wildly. She holds my gaze and I see right into her. That face I know so well. That girl I hardly know at all.

'I was wondering how you survived so long. When the others didn't,' I say. It's hard work to hold myself up, let alone push words from mind to mouth.

'Tom... ' she says, in a feral growl. 'I didn't survive. It's just that they didn't survive me.'

Bartu breathes deep, desperate breaths.

'You cut their thighs to let enough blood to leave at a scene. Then when everyone thinks they're dead you can do exactly what you want with them,' I say.

'Your friend is going to die even faster than you. Those little bitches got what was coming to them. Every one. Give me the gun and I'll tell you about it,' she says.

'Why would I do that?' I say.

The girls writhe and scream. Sarah kicks out at one of them and they whimper and fall back to their places against the damp wall.

'Because you need to know, and because you're both hurt and time is not on your side, and because you want me to put you out of your misery,' she says, my dream girl.

'You started this off the cuff. You decided to take a few girls on a trip. Girls you didn't know well, who you'd selected. Then, almost on a whim, having got hopped up together on illicit

337

ideas and other substances, you ambushed them with your boyfriend. Cut them. Did what you wanted to them. You laid low and thought for a while. Then you played dead and got a new life,' I say.

'Give me the gun, Tom,' she says.

Bartu is bleeding out between us. I notice the scars around her lips.

I place the gun on the ground. Slowly. I slide it to her as the girl's wails rise. She places the blade down carefully and now she has two guns. Just like Rabbit did.

'Your friend is in some real pain. I should put him out of his misery.' She points at Bartu and her trigger fingers twitches.

'Okay, I'll bite. Why keep re-enacting it? For the thrill?'

'Enough questions. You're bleeding hard, too. I don't mind the sight of blood but you're making the place look ugly.' She raises both guns, one at each of us. Bartu rouses himself into a kneeling position. He holds up his hands, palms in submission.

'Do you just love the repetitions too? The patterns?' I say.

'Goodbye, Tom. This is where the bullet does its job.'

She points at my head.

'I didn't recognise you. The time I saw you outside the house. Not really. Maybe if you hadn't come after me, I never would've ended up here,' I say.

'It don't fucking matter, Tom. I like you here,' she spits, as she holds the gun nice and still. Then pulls the trigger.

Click. I never did like guns. That's why I emptied that one on the stairs as soon as I got a chance. I reach into my pocket and show her the bullets.

'Sorry,' I say.

She grimaces only for a second. Then her eyes run to Bartu and the other gun she holds. And this time she looks into my eyes as she pulls the trigger of the barrel aimed at him with relish.

Click.

'Now, that one, Sarah. That's not even a real gun. It's from something called a Live Action Role Play Society. I was worried you might know the difference actually. It's tough to get hold of a real gun these days.'

Her face becomes a dark cloud.

'You didn't give me a real fucking gun,' Bartu shouts.

'And it saved your life,' I shout.

And Sarah screams, digging her nails into her palms, rousing herself.

'Do something then!' Bartu shouts.

'I can't. I could never hit a woman. Certainly not while I'm on duty... '

Nina twitches. Tanya keeps her eyes on Sarah. Jade points to the *Sai* at their feet.

'You really are fucking strange, you know that? You always were,' Sarah says, as her eyes flick to the blade below.

'... But Emre... ' I say. '... Emre? You're currently off duty. Aren't you?'

She crouches for the weapon. Bartu lifts himself into a punch, the force of which sends Sarah's head smacking into the wall behind her. Her body slackening before she hits the ground.

As my blinks get longer and the light flickers above me, I look up at Bartu and I give him the thumbs up. His face has questions that I'm in no state to answer. I'm not sure if he thinks either of us are going to make it. We've lost a lot of blood.

Then the footsteps come. Four sets, five sets, six. Shouts of 'Police!' and gasps at the scene from above us.

Then my eyes close. And as they do I hear my name called and the voice is Jarwar. And her call comes out for an ambulance. The last thing I see is feet, and ankles. Girls untied and rags falling from mouths.

The rest really is like a dream. But for once, Sarah doesn't feature.

Or threatening faceless figures.

Or lipstick shapes.

Or lullabies.

I think of shots being fired. And the neighbours on the phone that saved our lives. The men in uniform above us who do the rest.

'Thank heavens for neighbours. Thank heavens for... ' I think. As I drift away.

Thank heavens.

Whether you believe in heaven.

Or hell.

Afters

'Can't forget. Can't forget yet.
About that night. Never will, I'll bet.'

I set off early as it's a long walk to Holloway Prison and I'm doing it on my own. Bartu declined an invitation, he's still a bit sore with her about a couple of things, and it was really only me she asked for.

She sent in a letter to the station and they said I should throw it away and forget about it, but I read it and decided to grant her this little request. I feel like I owe it to her, which is a strange sensation, but then she is a very old friend. We go back as far as anyone I know.

I've been trying to keep my head down recently. In fact, Levine and the nervy chief pretty much insisted on that. In their ideal world, they would have washed their hands of me and Bartu as soon as the blood had been washed away at the house on Tollington Road.

The fluids and carnage we left in our wake, the litany of complaints that followed us around, and the general ball ache we caused everyone involved when they had to unpick it all, left them red-faced and palpitating. Jarwar and the rest looked at us with new eyes but it understandably irked those further up the chain. Grudging respect is an understatement. Especially when they still haven't got a good interview from me saying what an inclusive multi-racial non-disablist group hug the police force is.

Fortunately, when the press came in and looked at the whole thing from a distance they could only see it one way. We brought those girls home. That act was the sin-eater that saved our skins. It even made the national press. As soon as that happened those cold looks turned to morning winks and conversations about career advancement.

That's right. After a twenty-three-week course, I will emerge from the chrysalis as PC Mondrian. I said, 'Twenty-three weeks is too long, I'll fast-track it, please.' They said, 'That isn't a thing that exists', and that I should 'count myself lucky'. Which, in many ways, I do. At least Bartu will be coming along for the ride too.

'Hello there,' I say.

'Hi, Tom,' says the guard. I'm known by the unknowns even better these days.

There are more enthusiastic 'Hi Tom's as I walk through the corridor and greet the other uniformed guards. My stomach tightens as I realise the next greeting I'll get will be from her. Bartu did ask me to say hello from him. Maybe this was humour, I don't know. But I took it at face value and earnestly said I would.

He was pretty cross with me for not telling him about the hunch I had about Sarah. But I tell him the same thing every time he brings it up. 'I was still piecing it together right up until the end. And I had lost a pint and half of blood by the time you turned up.'

It was that deep cut they favoured, the one to the femoral artery that should ensure a lot of blood but not necessarily fatality, which gave me the last hint I needed, that those girls might still be alive. Memories of other curious cuts on Sarah's exposed childhood flesh came drifting back to me. Sometimes it was wrist, sometimes calf, sometimes thigh. Practice makes perfect.

They had left a similar tell-tale scar behind some years earlier, on Rita Singh's body, the one who was found from the second wave of missing girls. She wasn't supposed to die. But they dumped her in a shallow grave when she accidentally bled out and was of no use to them.

After they shot Katherine in the head for finally making an escape after all these years, they didn't want to leave the thigh scar as any kind of clue that might link back to Singh's death. Which is why they cut the leg off to muddy the issue.

Singh's death happened, you see, because Rabbit was new to this. Sarah had to show him how to do it and his first go didn't go so well. She'd started out using another guy. His name was Shane and he disappeared one day, quite a few years after Sarah and he had 'disappeared' the first group of girls. No one in 'the ring' could locate him. We haven't been able to either. He could be anywhere.

But that meant Sarah needed to move on and when she found Rabbit she had the perfect ally to start the thing up again. To take it further, to push her fetishes and obscure tastes. Turan was part of the ring, too. They all found each other online. Along with two other officers operating in other boroughs, one who had helped pin the Katherine Grady disappearance on Ed Rampling. She found these men in the recesses, the places normal people don't go.

Sarah named names in the end. This is how we eventually went even further with our investigation, how we discovered and broke 'the ring'. She gloried in telling it all to us. Like a mother driving her kids around to show them her old neighbourhood. Knowing where it all started, pointing out those blue signs on various kerbs, and the nostalgia of living it all over again, seemed to be part of the thrill.

So I followed her to the basement. And then we followed the wire further down into the depths of the web. Yes. It all started with the girl sitting in front of me now, fingering the scars on her lips.

'Don't play with those, you'll give yourself an infection,' I say as I sit.

'I am an infection,' she says, looking deep into me as she continues to play with the abrasions.

'What makes you say that? Bartu says hi, by the way,' I say.

'I *know*. I know I scare you,' she says. And of course she's right, but I don't want to give her that, so I find another emotion from somewhere and play that.

'Is this why you asked me here? So you could say that? It's pretty brief. You could've tweeted me that.'

There's no wall of glass in between us. Her head rolls to the side.

'I make you nervous,' she whispers.

'You make me something,' I say.

'What is it about me that makes you nervous?' she says in an intimate bedtime whisper.

The guard, overhearing this, frowns. Everyone knows about how I caught Sarah by now. There have been pictures of her in the paper, photos of her with knives, of picture messages she's sent to 'friends' over the years, images that wanted an audience. That required a reaction of titillation or distaste. It hurts me that she's getting exactly what she always wanted.

'Maybe it's because... I understand Rabbit. He was an abused kid. It's a story that seems sadly recognisable, and it's one I understand. Rabbit –'

'Rabbit's dead,' she says.

'Yes. Rabbit's dead,' I affirm.

He hung himself the morning after he was refused bail. She makes a mock-upset face.

'How does that make you feel?' I say.

'I don't *feel*... anything,' she says.

'See, I think you do. The feeling of crossing that line, then going further into the gore of it. Turan is an addict with a fetish and a means of abusing power to get it. But you're not that, you're different. I'm not religious. But you're what hell is. For me.'

She taps on the table and looks up at me.

'What are they saying out there? That I'm crazy?'

I draw breath and then swallow. My eyes turn back to her. The horny-prudish media have obsessed over her 'feminine perversions'.

'No. They say you're evil. But I don't believe in evil.'

She just smiles and keeps her eyes on me as I continue.

'That's what they say every time we find another one. Another man you sold a girl to for their pleasure, in basements and airless rooms.'

'Yes, that's it,' she says. 'Tell me what I am.'

It's like the moment in a wrestling hold when the guy underneath gets his leg free. Everyone else sees it but the one who thinks they're on top.

'Oh. The fact is, now that we have them all, no one is interested in you.'

She stops picking at her skin.

'I don't know what you mean,' she says. 'You don't know me.'

Her breathing changes.

'Oh, Sarah. It's a feeling, isn't it? And you can't do anything about it. Can you?'

'Yes. Yes,' she says.

'And that's why I could never be afraid of you.'

345

We go quiet. All is quiet. Except for the faint murmuring from other tables. She snorts, she looks away.

'And I can't hate you because you're in service to your mind. I'm a slave to mine too. The only difference between us is that what makes me get up is stopping people like you. And what sates you means you end up here. You have an obsessive psychotic imbalance. Plus, your step-dad doesn't seem like the easiest man to get on with.'

'Don't talk about him. You don't know him.'

'I do. We spoke,' I say. 'On the phone.'

Her fingers drum on the table. 'He didn't like me,' she says.

'He didn't like you… kissing other girls. That sort of thing?'

'He…' she runs her finger from cheek to chest '…caught me. Told me it was wrong and when I wouldn't listen he beat it into me. And when –'

'And when you do that to someone with a psychotic…'

'Fuck off.'

'…imbalance, then you can forge a real hatred for… other girls. Put your pain into them. Right at the top of the psychopath checklist is shallow effect, meaning a narrow field of emotions. You got spite, shame, disgust. Next on the list is… need for stimulation, then lack of remorse, criminal versatility, insatiable sexual urges, lack of empathy, impulsivity, poor behaviour controls, lack of realistic long term goals. I did the test for you and, well done, you scored very highly. Welcome to your mind. It did all this to you, to a certain extent. So, you see, the last thing I could do is hate you. I feel sorry for you. Truly,' I say.

I idly lay my hand flat on the table. I feel it in my heart. How lucky I am that nature has given me my mind. Her eyes wash themselves. She claws the table, her fingers digging into it like they're plunging into grave dirt. She snatches at breaths through her nose to exert control but her lungs betray her and give her only panic gasps, like her diving tanks are running dry still fifty feet under, she shakes like a blacked-out car about to stall.

I lean in and put my hand near hers.

She screws up her face and makes indiscriminate sounds. They're almost inhuman. But she is as human as anyone else, as fallible, as capable of love. Just wired differently, as it happens. How fortunate many of us are to be so well wired.

'Did it feel like... life?' I say.

I am still so curious.

Her impassioned glare turns into a dead glaze and then a strain. Her momentary vulnerability disappearing. The mask rises again, like she's trying to summon some unknown power.

'Sarah?' I say, softly. 'What are you trying to do?'

Her face is flushed. Her breathing has changed. A guard stirs and takes half a step towards us. I hold up my hand.

'I'm picturing what I'd like to do to you. For doing this to me.'

And I let her. I hold still. I stare back. And I am not afraid of it. I'm not afraid of the things that hide in the corners of rooms and cities in the stale 4 a.m. air. I stare into her for as long as it pleases me to do so. Then my hand plunges down and I pull something from my pocket and stand.

'It didn't have to be this way. You were so close. You were just missing one of these,' I say, placing my gift for her on the table. I probably shouldn't have brought it in, but I didn't think they'd search an officer. Certainly not a universally adored head case like me.

She looks down at it. I watch her face fall as I turn and leave.

Behind me I hear her obscenities and hate as she is taken away. There's a struggle but I don't have to turn. I hear it all. I sense it.

In front of her, on the table that lay between us, sits a single bullet.

As I head back to my new home I consider how close they really were: they must've thought they'd struck gold when they realised that the yellow school prefect's tie Tanya had given Rabbit had originally been Asif's, and even had his name stitched into it. A piece of material they could sew into the jigsaw to give the police what they needed.

When I get back to the Ryans' house I head up to my room and lie down looking at the plain brilliant white ceiling above my bed. I grab a white tennis ball and start throwing it against the ceiling as I check my voicemail.

Bang. I catch the ball.

Bang. There are three messages.

The first is from another journalist. This one is particularly persistent.

He got me on the phone once and said he loved 'my story'. Said he could scarcely believe it. I said 'Me neither.' He said he thinks it should be a book. I asked him to give me a few weeks to think it over. In this message he's talking me through how the book would go. His angle. He said he wants to understand what goes on inside my head. And I want that too.

So today, I will start writing it myself.

Bang.

My eyes wander over to the lacklustre CT scan of my brain Ryans managed to make all those weeks ago. I stuck it next to my bed, and sometimes I watch its colours spill out over the sides, chaotically, like blurred constellations.

When I told Ryans that Sarah was the architect all along, and that his brainwashing theory was 'way off', he claimed it wasn't his theory at all. To which I said 'Well, whatever, you threw it into my head' and took another sip of his best brandy, which is fairly disgusting stuff, but I appreciate our chats and his company all the same.

Mark jumps onto my chest and curves his body downwards until he finds that perfect spot, his limbs elegantly arranged, his chin on the apex of my sternum, giving me 'We need to talk' eyes. My armchair psychiatrist. He spends a lot of time inside with me. I hope I haven't warped him. It's certainly possible, but I need the moral support, particularly whenever I get a call or voicemail these days. Especially today.

The second message is from Miss Heywood. It's been a while and I hadn't expected to hear from either of my lady friends. But after a brief meeting with Anita in that new middle class coffee shop last week, as I tried my best not to feel self-conscious about my scar, she suggested that I should give one of them a call and get on the front foot for once. I'd always taken a backseat on such matters, she'd said. She also said she'd always found me quietly obsessive, and a driven solver of problems. I am, she said, not so different after all, perhaps just a little more me than I ever have been. It was a good coffee. One of the best I've ever had. Heywood wants to meet up after her life drawing class.

The third message is about a sentencing for Eli Minton. When it all came out and the relevant people cracked, I was proven correct that it had been Rabbit that had tried to stab me in The Corner Shop, and had stolen the mini-DV, having been keeping tabs on us for a while. And it was Turan that ran me down. But neither would admit to breaking into my house and standing over me that night.

I assumed they engineered my shooting, too, and that in the end some tests, or one of their cohorts in a sweaty interrogation room late at night, would eventually give them away and put that one to bed too.

Bang.

When I found out Eli had confessed to firing the bullet that hit me I couldn't hide my surprise.

But they didn't believe it was a stray one, an accident, like he said. They thought he'd been given the task as some kind of initiation. Or, worse, that he'd done it under pressure, after being beaten from every side, as excessive revenge for what he saw as my 'victimisation' of him.

Kids are strange these days. Things get stranger every day.

Maybe I just want to believe he wasn't firing at me, or at least that he was the pawn backed into a corner in this whole thing, not the mastermind of anything. It feels better that way.

I catch the ball and feel it in my hand.

Spite and lust for justice meted out aren't going to make anything better. You could read him turning on the waterworks in that room with me in a thousand ways, but I choose to believe in his remorse, because maybe that's how I want to see it. My life is how it is, his can heal with some restraint. So I spoke on his behalf, as a kind of character reference, in search of leniency and hope for the future. He'll get five years and serve around two if he behaves. He told me he will, but it could go either way.

I forgive him. But maybe forgiveness isn't quite the right word. I want to thank him.

For... my miracle mind. I like these words.

I'll use them at the start of my story, I think.

Along with other words I love. Like cerebellum. And gift.

And with the realisation that we are all just unique individual meteors, flying towards each other at incredible speed.

Like fireflies.

Like debris in a hurricane.

Like neurons and synapses, firing off in all directions.

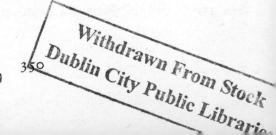

ACKNOWLEDGEMENTS

Thanks to my wonderful editor, Anna, for another great working experience, and a superb job shaping and developing this book into what it is.

Thanks to Catherine, for her wise words and for tacitly and legally agreeing to spend the rest of her life on a laptop next to me.

To Juliet, for her brilliant thoughts, incredible reading speed and other indicators of her genius. Most days I find myself sparing a moment to feel lucky she's my agent.

To Headway, who work tirelessly for those with Acquired and Traumatic Brain Injury and their families, and to Dr Mark Lythgoe for invaluable conversations about their work. Thank you so much for picking up the phone and indulging me. I'm pretty sure you thought they were all prank calls, but thanks for taking time to answer my strange questions anyway.

To Lisa Milton and everyone at HQ for your belief in me and my writing, and for your excellent company. I'm fully aware that no one gets to even consider reading this book without the work of teams like publicity, sales and design. I'm lucky enough to feel a sense of collaboration with everything we do at HQ, and it's a rare and wonderful thing.

Thanks to Mum, Dad, Jim, Al, Carly, Antonia, Evan, Darcy, Margaret and Jeff for your familial support. And to our dog,

Edie, for putting me through a routine, and for her looks of encouragement or scepticism when I needed them.

Thanks to Jamie Groves for a copy edit that handled Tom and I with care, and added excellent thoughts and minor explosions.

To the late Oliver Sacks, whose accounts of his work on the brain have been incredibly informative and inspiring for me. And, for that matter (pun intended) to Daniel Kahneman, David Eagleman and Alain De Botton whose books helped me understand some of my own thoughts and become interested in those of others.

Lastly, it's very difficult to get to the point of having something published without feedback on your writing. People who spared the time to read or come and hear stuff I'd written over the years include: Jonathan Munby, Martin Hutson, James Rigby and more recently Duncan Robertson. If a piece of writing falls in the woods and no friend is there to read it immediately, has it been written at all?